ALSO BY

PHILIPPE GEORGET

*Summertime, All the Cats Are Bored*

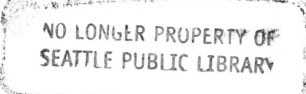
# AUTUMN,
# ALL THE CATS
# RETURN

Philippe Georget

# AUTUMN, ALL THE CATS RETURN

*Translated from the French
by Steven Rendall and Lisa Neal*

Europa
*editions*

Europa Editions
214 West 29th Street
New York, N.Y. 10001
www.europaeditions.com
info@europaeditions.com

Copyright © 2012 by Editions Jigal
Published by arrangement with Agence litteraire Pierre Astier & Associés

Translation by Steven Rendall and Lisa Neal
Original title: *Les violents de l'automne*
Translation copyright © 2014 by Europa Editions

Library of Congress Cataloging in Publication Data is available
ISBN 978-1-60945-226-1

Georget, Philippe
Autumn, All the Cats Return

Book design and cover photo by Emanuele Ragnisco
www.mekkanografici.com
Cover photo © Andrew Penner/iStock

Prepress by Grafica Punto Print – Rome

Printed in the USA

# AUTUMN,
# ALL THE CATS
# RETURN

# CHAPTER 1

His old, knotty thumb, deformed by rheumatism, gave him a violent electric shock when he cocked his gun. With his free hand, he adjusted his glasses on his nose. In front of him, the target was rolling terrified eyes.

His swollen hand closed on the breech.

He'd been right to attack the weak link in the group. Fear made people talk. Now he knew everything. The bastards were going to pay. One after the other.

It hurt when he put his twisted index finger on the trigger.

The target was squirming desperately on his chair, even though his hands were cuffed behind his back. The target would have liked to shout, scream, or weep, but the gag that had been stuffed into his mouth allowed him to emit only rumbling noises.

He didn't understand this pointless agitation. When your time came, you had to be able to resign yourself to it. There were two men in this locked apartment. One of them was tied up, the other was holding a Beretta 34. There would be no escape, no happy ending, no last-minute turnaround. This wasn't the movies, it was life. True, hard, pitiless life.

*El-Mektub* . . . Destiny was going to strike.

He found the old man facing him pathetic and ugly. Fear deformed his features even more than age. He could hardly recognize him.

Memories flooded in like waves. Long ago was yesterday. Years could be bridges, walls, or simply parentheses. He hadn't forgotten anything. Anything at all. The blinding sun burned his skin and dazzled his eyes when he emerged from a shaded alley that was still cool. It was blue everywhere, the sea and the sky. The sound of the waves, the breath of the boats, the aromas mixed of anise, iodine, and spices. Shards of voices, laughter, insouciance, an unparalleled *joie de vivre*.

He had to avoid nostalgia. He knew that. It was stronger than he was. He'd succeeded in forgetting it for several decades before it came back to take possession of his heart and mind. He tried to think about the last months of his youth, the paradise that changed into hell, the sound of the beaten saucepans, the cries, the tears and the blood. And above all a smell of gunpowder, a heady, intoxicating smell, savage and violent.

He winced. His ailing hand gripping the gun was hurting.

The target facing him showed him what he looked like. He himself was old and ugly. All the better if his Gabriella swore to him that it wasn't true.

He was old and he hurt.

Severe polyarthritic rheumatism had led to painful calcium deposits on his joints. First it had deformed his fingers, forcing the extremities of his digits to assume unexpected angles. Then it had gnarled his hands. Bumps had risen up here and there in the course of sleepless nights. He smiled when he thought about Gabriella, who liked to run her fairy hands over his gibbosities.

Gibbosities . . . Where did that obsolete word come from? His French had gotten stuck at the beginning of the 1960s. Since then, he no longer spoke his native tongue.

His prisoner, sitting on the chair, seemed to have calmed down. Was he resigned to his fate? Maybe . . . Or else he'd given him a fleeting smile in the hope of being spared. Hope is an invincible phoenix, it can be reborn from a sigh or a breath. It can also die in a look.

Their eyes met and stared at each other for a few seconds before shifting to the three letters painted in black on the door of the living room.

Three accursed letters.

Three magic letters.

There would be no pardon. That was impossible. He hadn't awakened his sorrows for nothing, he hadn't traveled so far, crossed the sea, to draw back now. He'd go all the way to the end of the mission he'd assigned himself.

The last one.

His tongue clicked in his dry mouth. He was thirsty. Slowly, he got up. His bones cracked. He tried not to sigh. The illness had spread from his hands to his whole body. On some days, living—just living—meant suffering. Then he thought about his grandmother: she, too, had suffered the torments of hell. "The day I don't hurt anymore," she said, "will be the day I die."

He took a clean glass off the drain rack by the sink and ran tap water into it. He drank a few sips and then set it down again. Coming back to the old man tied to the chair, he grabbed the pillow he'd put on the table. A little while ago he'd taken it out of his target's bedroom.

Soon his target would be his victim.

He felt strange and forgotten sensations again. The surprising calm in action, the impression that he was outside his body, the curious feeling of being merely a witness to his acts.

The sound of the neighbors' television came through the wall. He could hear the canned laughter of an American sitcom. He'd wanted to turn on the TV in the living room to mask the sound of the gunshot that was coming, but quickly gave up the idea when he saw how complex the remote control was.

The target opened wide his rheumy eyes. His despair and fear could be read in them as in a book. But the old killer no longer saw anything, he no longer heard the groans, he was elsewhere. Fifty years ago.

"It's time," he said.

Then he went around the chair and put the pillow against the nape of his prisoner's neck. He put the Beretta on the worn fabric. His deformed index finger caressed the trigger. He counted to three before firing. The shockwave transmitted by his tormented bones made him cry out in pain.

# CHAPTER 2

After several blustery days, the cold, dry wind out of the southwest had just died down. It had swept the sky clean of its last clouds and a still-bright autumn sun was drying the puddles on the asphalt and the tears on people's faces.

It was a fine morning to bury a child.

The crowd in mourning clothes gathered around the little church of Passa. About a hundred people hadn't been able to squeeze inside it, and were following the ceremony as they stood on the village square. Gilles Sebag, one of the first to arrive, had insisted on staying outside. Inside the church the despair was too great, the pain too personal.

Leaning against the wall of a house, he hugged his daughter to him. He felt her young body shaking with sobs. He would have liked to be able to help her more, to assume some of her suffering and thus preserve her innocence. But Séverine was thirteen years old, and she had just suddenly understood that death was definitive. Life wasn't like a video game. When the game was over, you couldn't play it again: Mathieu could never start his game over.

Claire's hand was softly caressing Séverine's hair. Gilles turned to his wife and smiled at her. It was good to feel her here at his side, he'd been so afraid of losing her the preceding summer. But he quickly shooed away these bad memories; this was not really the time to think about all that again. Claire responded to his smile. Her shining green eyes were filled with sorrow.

From the densely packed crowd, here and there painful, heartbreaking wails shot up. Tears, cries, and moans fused in a threnody the teenagers sang in canon. Some of these kids had no doubt already encountered death: that of a grandparent, probably. They had suffered, they had sincerely wept, but that death hadn't touched the very depths of their being. On the other hand, the death of their classmate was their own. Their pain was mixed with a mute fear. To avoid being drowned in the children's suffering, Sebag forced himself to examine the buildings around him. Unfortunately, Passa's church had no special charm. Its façade, which was covered with concrete-colored stucco, was decorated only by a marble porch leading to a semicircular flight of stairs. The church was imprisoned in a row of small, unattractive houses. However, on the left his eye was drawn to a post office. Its assemblage of bricks and pebbles was typical of Roussillon but not really interesting. On this Saturday morning, the post office's shutters were closed because of the funeral.

Mathieu had died three days earlier in a scooter accident. On a street in Perpignan, a small van had suddenly swerved toward him and Mathieu, coming in the opposite direction, had not been able to avoid colliding with it. The crash had been violent, but at first the boy got up and seemed unhurt. He'd been able to talk with the driver of the van and together they had decided to call an ambulance anyway. Just in case. However, before the ambulance arrived, Mathieu suddenly collapsed. Internal bleeding. Everything had gone so fast. The doctors couldn't do anything to save him.

Mathieu . . . one of Séverine's friends. A ninth-grade student at the Saint-Estève Secondary School. An athlete, a rugby player. A kid who believed that he had everything going for him.

Goddamn scooter!

The black hearse was slowly making its way, in reverse,

through the crowd. The mass was coming to an end. The employees opened the doors of the hearse and began to arrange the funeral sprays in the back. A long line formed on the square to offer condolences to Mathieu's parents in the church. Sévérine left her parents to join a group of her girl-friends. Sebag started to follow her but Claire stopped him. At the same moment, Sévérine turned around and gave him a look that made it clear that she wanted to go alone. That is . . . with her friends. Without him, in short.

Sebag felt a twinge in his heart and immediately reproached himself for it. He was suffering at seeing his daughter grow up too fast, but this was neither time nor the place to complain about that. Sévérine was alive. Nothing else mattered. Mathieu's parents would never have the good fortune to see their son become an adult.

A bell started to toll. A sad ring followed by a long, plaintive echo. People looked up. The church in Passa had a square tower with two bells in it. The smaller of the two swung slowly. Its peal floated out over the village and carried its lamentations far out toward the hills covered with vineyards.

The church slowly emptied. A shiver ran through the crowd when the parents came out. The father, ramrod-erect, followed his son's casket, involuntarily nodding his head, as unaware of what was around him as a groggy boxer. The mother stumbled along at his side, supported by a young son. Sebag recognized the boy's big sister. He'd seen her two or three times over the past few years when he'd taken his daughter to Mathieu's birthday parties. Sévérine emerged in turn with a bunch of adolescents, boys and girls holding each other up. Her mascara had run and marked a path for the tears on her chubby cheeks.

The casket was put into the hearse and the cortege moved off toward the cemetery. The chorus of sobbing teenagers was like a dirge. Claire took her husband's hand and they walked three rows behind their daughter. Gilles was biting his lip, struggling to control his feelings. He had to keep a grip on himself and look strong. For Séverine, for her friends, and for the others as well.

It was true that in his work, he'd seen lots of terrible things. How often had he had to inform someone of the death of a relative, a wife, a husband . . . a child? He'd long reproached himself for not knowing what words to use to soften the blow. Until he'd realized that he'd never know. Because there simply were no such words.

The hearse stopped at the gate to the cemetery. The funeral home's employees slid out of the casket and then, followed by the mourners, carried it along a row of family vaults. Gilles leaned against the cemetery wall and lit a cigarette. He smoked only rarely. He'd picked up a pack on the way that same morning. Claire grabbed his cigarette, took a puff, and then gave it back to him.

"You okay?" he asked her.

She shrugged.

"You?"

"The same."

He passed her the cigarette again. Across from the cemetery, workers on a construction site were smoking, too. They'd stopped working when the cortege passed and were waiting for the ceremony to end before starting up their bulldozers and backhoes again. The streets they'd already marked out indicated that they were getting ready to build a new residential subdivision. Another one. Every year, five thousand more people moved to the department of Pyrénées-Orientales; they had to live somewhere.

Sebag saw Séverine coming back toward them, accompanied by two of her friends. The girls had their arms around each other's waists and swayed back and forth as they walked. Their black mourning clothes made them look more mature. Real little women, Sebag said to himself. But no! Now that he thought about it, it wasn't the clothes. It was the sorrow itself that had matured them.

When they stood in front of him, his heart ached at the sight of their swollen eyes. They looked as if they had just smoked a whole lid of marijuana. That's a stupid idea, he reflected angrily: you had to be a cop to have such thoughts at a time like this.

"Papa, I have something important to ask you," Séverine said.

Her whole face seemed to be a plea.

"Mathieu's sister says that there's something wrong about her brother's accident, that the driver of the van is not the only one responsible . . . Apparently the police think the case is closed and don't want to investigate it any further."

Sebag waited to see what she would say next, but he'd already guessed it.

"I told her that you could try . . . "

His first response was to blink his eyes. It was Saturday, and he was going back to work two days later after a week on vacation. His partner Molina had told him that everything was quiet at police headquarters. He would probably have time to have a look at the case.

"I'll see what I can do," he promised.

Séverine smiled through her sadness and added in her sweet, fluting voice:

"I told her that if there was anything to find, you'd find it."

Despite his sorrow, Sebag felt a deep happiness. Ultimately, mourning had not completely transformed his daughter: she was still a girl of thirteen, a child who still saw her father as a miracle-worker.

"I also told her that you were the best policeman in Perpignan—that's right, isn't it?"

He nodded, trying to look confident, and then gave his daughter a kiss on her cheek that was still cool and damp.

# CHAPTER 3

H ello, Lieutenant! Did you have a good vacation?"
Gilles Sebag turned around before realizing that the
question was in fact addressed to him. Lieutenant . . .
it had already been more than fifteen years since the government had tried to modernize the police just by renaming its
ranks in accord with American practice, but he was still having
trouble getting used to them. In fact, he was now sure that he'd
never get used to them; for him, the terms "lieutenant" and
"captain" would always have the moronic, exotic aroma of an
American TV series. "Lieutenant Colombo" or "Lieutenant
Horatio Caine" might sound good, but "Lieutenant Sebag"?
What a joke! He found it as ridiculous as combining an Anglo-
Saxon first name with a very French surname. Politicians sometimes proved as stupid as the average man in the street. Some
people found that reassuring. He didn't.

He finally realized that Martine, the young female cop on
the front desk at the Perpignan police headquarters, was
expecting a reply.

"Vacations are always good. It's when they're over that it
gets complicated."

Martine was kind enough to smile.

"Have a good day and good luck, then."

"I'll need it . . . "

"You sound like you're being led to the slaughterhouse!"

Sebag limited himself to giving her a polite little smile. He
passed his badge in front of the electronic reader. The security

door opened and he entered the part of the station inaccessible to the public. There he recognized without pleasure a familiar odor, a mixture of disinfectant and sweat, coffee and raucous laughter. He climbed the stairs two at a time, not out of impatience to get to his office, but because as a good marathon runner, he did not overlook any effort that might be made part of his training.

When he got to the third floor, he delayed his arrival by stopping at the water fountain installed in the middle of the corridor. He served himself a cup and drank it slowly. The last few years, he'd found his work disagreeable. The routine, the violence, the lack of internal recognition, the citizens' scorn. You had to put up with all that, and for what? When he'd enlisted in the police force, he'd imagined he'd be a kind of physician for a sick society. It took him a while to understand that he was no more than a minor nurse doomed to dress suppurating wounds with outdated ointments. Criminality would never stop, it couldn't stop, it was part of human nature. The most you could hope to do was bring down the fever a little. But no one had yet invented a reliable thermometer.

He drank a second cup of water, trying to think about Séverine and Mathieu's parents. He couldn't change the police or society all by himself, but he could at least give a few people some comfort. All he had to do was set modest objectives and get off his duff. He crushed the paper cup and threw it in the trashcan. Then he strode off toward his office.

He opened the door. To his great surprise, his partner, Jacques Molina, was already there.

"Well, you must have fallen out of bed today," Sebag said as he hung his jacket on the back of his chair.

"People say hello when they're polite," Molina replied.

"Hello when they're polite."

"You're not in great shape today. For you, the end of vacation is like a huge hangover . . . "

"A little, yes. I was expecting it to be hard, but I think it's even worse."

"Fortunately, you were gone only a week . . . Would you like some coffee?"

Sebag couldn't repress a shiver of disgust. He loved coffee, real coffee, not the murky stuff you could get for forty centimes from the machine in the police headquarters cafeteria.

"No, thanks. Going back to work is already a torture; I don't want to add a poisoning to it."

"Whatever you say."

Molina rose from his chair.

"I'm going to get some, I need it."

"Do we have a meeting with the chief this morning?"

Every Monday, Superintendent Castello met with the group to review the ongoing cases.

"No, he cancelled it. I think that when things are quiet these Monday meetings bore him as much as they do us."

Molina left the room while Sebag booted his computer. The machine woke up slowly, sounding more like a 1930s locomotive than a third-millennium IT device. From the top drawer of his desk, Sebag took out three photos that brightened his professional universe. He set them down one by one: Claire's sunny face against the blue background of the swimming pool, Séverine smiling as she blew out her thirteen birthday candles, and, finally, his son Léo proudly sitting on his shiny new scooter. Gilles thought of Mathieu's accident and felt a pain in the pit of his stomach. Not Léo, never Léo . . . He was mad at himself for not having been able to resist his wife's and his son's wheedling. He'd ended up giving his consent and Léo had been riding that engine of death for the past year.

The computer had finished booting up. Sebag decided not to look at his e-mail. A week's vacation . . . There would be too many messages, memos, copies of reports, union tracts, ads, and maybe a few personal notes. He knew that if he dove into all that, telling himself "just for five minutes," he wouldn't surface for at least half an hour. So he went directly to the headquarters data bank. A password, a click on the "accidents" button, and he easily found Mathieu's case. He looked for the signature at the bottom of the document. Lieutenant Cardona. The head of the accident section himself. A surly cop who was not always very conscientious. That was both good and bad news. Although he might hope to discover something his colleague had missed, Sebag also knew he was going to get into trouble. Too bad. For Séverine, he was prepared to do anything.

He was beginning to read the report when Molina suddenly burst into the office.

"Stop playing on the computer and put on your jacket," he said breathlessly. "We've got work to do."

Sebag looked up. Molina was heading toward his own desk.

"A body, in an apartment in Moulin-à-Vent, Place de Montbolo. Discovered this morning by a neighbor woman."

He grabbed a bottle of cologne and squirted it under his shirt.

"The guy's been dead for at least three days. He was found because of the smell."

Sebag picked up a package of tissues, took out two or three, and put a few drops of lavender scent on them.

"I'm ready," he said as he started printing Mathieu's file. "A natural death, a suicide, or a homicide, do they have any idea?"

"According to the ambulance crew, there was blood all over the walls and the victim had a very clear wound to the back of the head."

Sebag got up.

"I see. There are, in fact, more natural ways to die. And suicide is unlikely, unless he was a contortionist."

"Especially since the victim, a certain Bernard Martinez, was handcuffed to a chair."

"Okay, that reduces the hypotheses further."

The printer started spitting out the first pages. Sebag put on his jacket, telling himself that today he probably wouldn't have any time to devote to Mathieu's accident, and that he ought to take the file home to mull it over that evening after dinner. A great way to spend his first day back on the job.

"The smell is unbearable."

The face of Thierry Lambert, a young cop with the Perpignan police, was as white as a toilet bowl in a luxury hotel.

"And yet you are bearing it," Molina replied. "That means you're learning the job."

Sebag and Molina had joined Lambert in the apartment on the Place de Montbolo. The three policemen were waiting in the hall, observing from a distance the members of the forensic team, who had put on their coveralls and were working around the body in the living room. Sebag shook his perfumed tissue in front of his face and succeeded in driving away for a few moments the bittersweet aroma of death. Having been the first to get there, Lambert had been able to get a quick view of the scene.

"He's a rather old man, I'd say at least seventy. But part of his face is gone. The bullet did a lot of damage when it came out."

"It was probably about money," Molina suggested. "Burglars who wanted to make the victim tell them where he hid his nest egg."

"But why would they have killed him?" Lambert asked.

"Because he refused to talk, or because he could have identified them."

"You think so?" The young cop was indignant. "The bastards! I hope we can catch them fast."

Sebag was half-listening as he contemplated the dark hallway. Faded wallpaper, black-and-white photos, a worn mauve carpet, and a gilt pedestal table with a telephone on it. In addition to the door open on the living room, the hall led to three others.

"What do you think?" Lambert asked.

"Me? For the moment, nothing. I haven't seen anything, so I don't think anything."

He went up to the photos. They all showed the same white-walled city by the sea.

"Just as prudent as ever," Molina said, disapprovingly. "You don't commit yourself."

Sebag shrugged.

"I avoid forming ideas as soon as I arrive on the scene of a crime. The more ideas you have, the more blinders. A cop should be wary of his imagination."

"Did you write that down, Thierry?" Molina joked. "That was Lieutenant Sebag's lesson number one."

Gilles shook his lavender-perfumed tissue again.

"Lesson number two: a good cop is a sponge. He has to imbue himself with his environment."

He clasped his hands in front of his belly and then raised them to chest level. Then he slowly spread his arms to describe the arc of a circle.

"You keep quiet, you observe, you listen, you look, you sniff. Calmly. And you note down everything. It will be useful later on."

With a gesture, he stopped Lambert, who was already getting ready to follow his recommendations to the letter.

"When I say 'sniff,' that's just a figure of speech. Take it easy today. I don't want to have your breakfast all over my shirt."

While Molina was laughing, Sebag opened the other doors: a bedroom, a toilet, and a washroom. He spotted two tooth-brushes on the shelf over the sink. He turned to Lambert.

"I thought Mr. Martinez lived alone."

"That's what the neighbor lady told me when I got here."

"Don't you want to go back and talk to her again and get her statement, to find out a little more about the victim? And then you could also question the other neighbors. When we got here, there were at least a dozen curious people standing around on the landing, might as well take advantage of that."

"O.K., no problem."

Delighted to escape the olfactory torment, Lambert already had his hand on the handle of the entry door when he froze.

"By the way, I didn't tell you: there was a word on the door."

"Which door?" Sebag asked.

"The living room door."

"This one?" Sebag pointed to the open door.

"Yeah . . . or rather on the other side, otherwise you'd be able to see it."

"And what was the word?"

"I don't know."

"You didn't read it?"

"Well, yeah, I did. There were only three letters. But I didn't understand it. It must not have been French."

Sebag wasn't sure he understood.

"A three-letter word . . . written on a note attached to the door?"

"No, written on the door itself, big letters in black paint."

"Paint? What was the word?"

"I don't know, I tell you, it wasn't French . . . "

"But just three letters—you must be able to remember it!"

"Hey, I didn't pay attention. It ended in 's,' I think."

Sebag heard Molina chuckling behind him.

"Is it serious?" Lambert asked worriedly.

"For the investigation, no, we'll look into it later, but for you, it's serious: not being able to memorize a three-letter word."

"I know a three-letter word you can easily remember,"

Molina broke in. "There are two s's in it but they come at the end."

"O.K., I get it. I'm not an . . . "

Lambert suddenly interrupted himself, stared at his amused colleagues, and went out, slamming the door behind him.

"I think you made him mad," Sebag observed.

"That's also part of learning the job. The problem is that he immediately forgets what he's learned."

Molina looked at his watch and groaned.

"They've been in there for more than an hour. It seems like every time they take longer to do stupid stuff: all that time to put a few pubic hairs in a test tube."

"That's a fine image of our trade: it's always nice to feel appreciated!"

Dressed in his traditional white coveralls, Jean Pagès, the head of the Perpignan forensic police, had suddenly appeared in the hallway. He looked at Molina with unconcealed contempt. Sebag tried to defuse the nascent conflict.

"You know Jacques, he's old-school."

"Yes, I know," Pagès grumbled, "the school of strong-arm interrogations and miscarriages of justice."

"A good whack on the head with a phone book often produces more evidence than your DNA samples," Molina instantly replied. He liked to play the role of the obtuse cop.

Sebag cut him short.

"Have you finished? Can we go in now?"

"Yes, we're done. Now we're going to tackle the other rooms. I hope you haven't messed things up in there."

"I had a look but didn't go in," Sebag answered.

"If that Neanderthal there stayed in the hall, I'm okay."

Sebag pushed Molina into the living room before he could reply. The smell of dead flesh grew stronger. It didn't bother Elsa Moulin, Pagès's assistant; she had put away her instruments and was beginning to take photos.

"You know, you look beautiful dressed like that," Molina said, running his fingers over the cap that covered the young woman's hair. "I find this outfit more and more exciting. You'll have to invite me to dinner at your place some night or lend it to me for one of my girlfriends . . . "

Elsa Moulin pulled her mask down over her chin and stuck her tongue out at him before retorting:

"I'll lend it to you whenever you want!"

The living room was about three hundred square feet in area and was separated from the kitchen by a bar. A French door led to a sunny balcony. In the middle of the room stood a table covered with a red-and-white checkered cloth. There were four chairs; two were still in place at the table, while the corpse was on the third and the fourth faced it. It wasn't hard to guess that the murderer had sat there to look at his victim. Or to talk with him.

"Can you sum up briefly for us?" Sebag asked the young woman. "Molina annoyed your boss."

Elsa Moulin went up to the body. It was attached to the chair by the chain on the handcuffs. What remained of the head leaned toward the right shoulder. She pointed to the wound at the back of the head.

"The bullet went in there and came out in the middle of the face."

She raised the body's head. It no longer had a nose and had lost part of the right cheek.

"A bullet fired at point-blank range?" Molina asked.

"Not entirely."

She indicated a pillow wrapped up in a plastic sack.

"The killer used it to muffle the sound of the shot."

"And that was all it took?" Moulin said, astonished.

"It seems so, since no one reported it to us."

"What was the time of death, in your opinion?" Sebag asked Elsa.

"The putrefaction of the body has already begun. I'd say five, maybe six days ago."

"Do you realize what that means?" Molina said. "Six days without anybody looking in on him, that's really incredible. When I was young, that wouldn't have been possible, but nowadays, damn it, it's all about selfishness and indifference. What a society we live in . . . Shit!"

Sebag let his partner express an anger that seemed to him as pertinent as it was pointless. It was one thing to use angry words and display noble feelings, and another to put them into action. Sebag had never heard Molina talk about his neighbors except to complain about them. He himself had always limited his relations with those around him to a minimum, and if something serious were to happen in one of the two houses next to his, he wasn't sure he'd notice it. So why spill your bile if you aren't capable of changing your own behavior? What shocked Sebag most in today's France was not indifference or selfishness, it was that so many people were more eager to tell others what to do than to set an example.

"Five days, maybe six," he repeated out loud. "It's not going to be easy to get reliable witnesses."

"The medical examiner will be more precise. The temperature in the apartment being more or less constant, he'll be able tell you the time of death within a few hours."

Sebag was delighted to hear that good news.

"How old do you think the victim is?"

"Seventy-eight."

The two inspectors couldn't hide their surprise. Elsa Moulin grinned at them. She nodded toward a chest of drawers.

"In the drawer on the left you'll find all the documents you need. Identity card, driver's license, social security card, tax return, and so on."

Sebag went up to the body. A little old man, apparently

harmless, dressed in a dirty, tattered dressing gown that gaped open to reveal an undershirt from which a few little white hairs emerged.

"According to his papers, the victim's name was Bernard Martinez," Elsa went on. "He was born in Algiers in 1934."

Algiers . . . Of course. The white-walled city in the photos.

"But the most interesting thing is here," she said, walking over to the door to the living room.

She shut the door and Sebag saw the notorious word written in black paint, the three letters that Lambert hadn't been able to remember. "What a fool that guy is!" he said to himself.

Even though they weren't separated by periods, the letters formed not a word but an acronym. And there was nothing foreign about it. Without having any particular knowledge of history, Sebag was very familiar with this acronym. It designated an organization that had shaken the streets of Algiers fifty years earlier and sown terror among the Arab population.

OAS.

OAS, as in *Organisation armée secrète*.[1]

The letters painted on the door were a kind of death sentence. Molina went over and saw them as well. He gave a long whistle before exploding:

"Fuck!"

---

[1] The OAS was a dissident paramilitary organization that sought to prevent Algeria from gaining independence from French rule during the Algerian War (1954–1962).

# CHAPTER 4

Superintendent Castello raised his hand to call for silence. His carefully trimmed salt-and-pepper goatee could not conceal the satisfied smile on his lips. Despite the recent changes imposed on his office by the top brass, the chief of the Perpignan police still cared more about people than about statistics: nothing got him revved up more than gathering his "cops" around him to work on an important case. When he learned about the murder in Moulin-à-Vent, he'd immediately mobilized his whole team. Seven men in all. That same morning Llach and Ménard had had to give up their current cases to help Sebag, Molina, and Lambert. But earlier it had not been possible to contact Raynaud and Moreno, the two inseparable partners, and they had just joined the other members of the team in the meeting room at police headquarters.

It was time to assess the results of the first day of the investigation.

Castello handed out the report that Sebag and Molina had just written, along with Jean Pagès's analysis.

"The victim's name is Bernard Martinez," Castello informed them all. "He's a *Pied-Noir*,[2] born in Algeria in 1934. He came to France in 1962 and settled in Pyrénées-Orientales, where he worked as a winegrower. Since he retired, he's been

---

[2] Lit., "Black-Foot" (pee-yay nwar). A French person born in Algeria before it gained independence.

living in an apartment in the Moulin-à-Vent neighborhood. So far as we know, he's a run-of-the-mill retiree. But first let's look at the facts. Jean, please get straight to the point: give us your conclusions. We can find the details in your analysis."

He tapped the pile of papers on the table.

"And congratulations on your rapidity. As usual, it's perfect!"

The head of the forensic police blushed. Despite his forty years of service and surly air, he still loved compliments. He cleared his throat before beginning.

"The murderer acted alone and took no precautions. We were able to get some excellent sets of fingerprints off the door handles, the chairs, and the handcuffs. Unfortunately, for the moment they are of no use to us because the murderer is in neither our files nor those of the gendarmerie. That's probably one reason why the he didn't bother to take precautions."

"They'll be useful to us later on," Castello replied with a certain optimism. "They'll provide solid proof once we've got our hooks into him. Anything else, Jean?"

"The killer used a handgun, probably a rather old model 9 mm. The bullet was found in a molding. He attached his victim to a chair with handcuffs. But we can't do much with that, either, for the time being. They're a common kind easily found on the internet."

"You can buy handcuffs on the internet?" Lambert was surprised.

"You can buy anything on the internet," Llach told him.

"Yes, but handcuffs . . . to do what?"

Several of the men smiled. Molina put his hand on his young colleague's arm.

"They're also found in sex shops. Some people like them. I'll explain it to you someday, Thierry."

Castello didn't care for this excursus and immediately refocused the discussion.

"How did the killer get into the apartment?"

"There was no trace of a break-in. It looks like the victim let him in."

"So we can conclude that Martinez knew his murderer?" Llach was always good at drawing quick explanations based on simple arguments.

Jean Pagès pulled a face. The wrinkles on his face got even deeper.

"That's one hypothesis, but it wouldn't be the first time that a victim innocently opened the door to his murderer without their ever having met before."

Joan Llach frowned. His thick brown brows formed a stubborn line over his dark eyes. "Nonetheless, with all the increased security these days, old people don't open their doors so easily to people they don't know . . . "

"That's probably true for most of them, but not all," Pagès replied. "Some remain very gullible. All you have to do is give them a calendar from the mailman or the fire brigade and they'll let you come in. They'll even take out their wallets and open them in front of you."

"It's only late October. That's a little too early for calendars," Llach replied, splitting hairs.

"That was just an example. But people open their doors just as easily to electric company workers, census takers, or even someone pretending to be a policeman."

Castello addressed Sebag:

"Gilles, what do you think?"

Sebag hated to be called upon that way. Considering him the de facto head of the team, Castello often asked him to give his opinion when there were arguments among the inspectors. But not only was Gilles not the head of anything or anyone, he had also refused all the promotions that had recently been proposed to him. He eluded the question:

"Both hypotheses are plausible."

Castello, annoyed, turned to Pagès.

"Anything else?"

"There is one thing that might have reassured the victim and led him to open the door to his murderer. For the moment, I'm not sure, but we can't exclude the possibility that the killer is also an elderly person."

"Come, now!" the superintendent said.

"An old gunslinger," Molina joked.

Jean Pagès ignored the remark.

"On the back of the chair facing the victim I found a white hair . . . "

Loud sniggering interrupted him:

"Wow, a white hair found in a retiree's apartment," Molina scoffed, "what a discovery!"

The head of the forensic police did not turn to look at him and continued to address Costello.

"The hair seemed to me to be of a different shade of white and length than that of the victim."

"A retiree who sometimes had other retirees as guests," Molina went on, "another great discovery! I'm willing to concede that your job consists of splitting hairs but here you've really gone too far!"

Jean Pagès bit his lip. He was having trouble controlling himself and now regretted having postponed his retirement for a year. He'd planned to leave at the end of the summer, but couldn't bring himself to do it.

"I'm well aware of who has gone too far," Castello retorted, coming to Pagès's aid. "We won't get anywhere by making those kinds of sarcastic, indeed aggressive, remarks."

The superintendent glared at Molina. Then he brightened and adopted a softer, almost honeyed tone.

"You have to admit, Jean, that basically—and only basically—Molina's remark is not entirely groundless. I trust your intuitions, but they'll have to be confirmed. Did you notice anything else in the apartment?"

"No, nothing else," Pagès grumbled.

Castello turned to Lambert.

"Your turn, Thierry. What did you learn from canvassing the neighbors?"

The young inspector's eyes opened wide in surprise. To be sure, he'd been the one who had begun the canvass of the neighbors, but he'd quickly been joined by Llach, and wasn't expecting to be given the floor at the meeting. The team's most recent recruit, he had come to work at the Perpignan police headquarters one year earlier, after completing his training.

He sat up straight on his chair and this movement alone released into the small meeting room the spicy aroma of cheap deodorant. Molina held his nose and looked at Sebag. Lambert had a phobia about body odor, and his worst fear was that he might smell bad. The time he'd spent around the corpse must have led him to use up a whole bottle of deodorant in one day.

"As you said a little while ago, Superintendent, he was apparently an ordinary retiree. His neighbors had no complaints about him, except that he sometimes turned up the sound on his television a little too much. They said he'd been living in that apartment for some fifteen years. Martinez had been a winegrower, and you said that, too, Chief, a winegrower in Les Aspres, but he'd gone bankrupt and had to sell his land. No family, no children, probably just a girlfriend. Well, I mean, a woman friend. Since he moved to Moulin-à-Vent, Martinez's main occupations seem to have been crossword puzzles and pétanque. He also belonged to an association of *Pieds-Noirs*."

"Hmm . . . " Castello was nodding pensively. "The neighbors didn't notice anything unusual these last few days?"

"Since the murder took place at least five days ago, they couldn't say. They don't remember anything."

"What about the neighbor woman who discovered the body? Did you see her?"

"She was in shock. She was crying and trembling all over. It hit her hard . . . "

"What made her finally look in on her neighbor this morning?"

"At first we thought it was the smell that had tipped her off, but in fact it was Martinez's woman friend, the one I mentioned a little while ago, who asked the neighbor to ring his doorbell. At the moment, she's on vacation at her daughter's home in Barcelona. Martinez hadn't replied to her last telephone messages and she was getting worried."

François Ménard raised his hand to indicate that he wanted to say something.

"Her first name wouldn't be Joséphine, would it?"

"Yes, I think it is," Lambert said, spreading out in front of him his notes rapidly taken on supermarket receipts. "Here it is. Josette Vidal."

"I found a recent postcard signed by that Josette," Ménard explained.

"Since you've taken the floor, François, I'm going to ask you to keep it," the superintendent said. "You were assigned to go through the papers found in the victim's apartment."

In his turn, Ménard spread out his notes, unfolding several sheets covered with dense writing.

"Everything is very run-of-the-mill in fact, the kind of thing everyone keeps in his drawers: bank statements, gas and electricity bills, a family record book, a few photos—not many—a property insurance folder, letters and postcards, mainly from this Josette Vidal. In short, nothing of fundamental importance, but I was able to glean from all these documents a little information that adds some details to what we've just said."

His long face bent over his notes.

"For instance, that Bernard Martinez is the first child of Jean Martinez, who was a shopkeeper in Algiers, and Odette Blanchard, a seamstress. He had a younger brother who was born in 1937 and died the following year. Like most *Pieds-Noirs*, Martinez returned to France in the summer of 1962. He landed with his parents in Sète. They went to live in Marseilles, he went to Perpignan. His parents died in the 1980s."

Ménard took a deep breath. -

"In February 1963, he bought twelve hectares of vineyards in Terrats, near Thuir. He worked them until his business was put into receivership in 1997. The subsidies for pulling out the vines and the sale of the land allowed him to pay off his debts. Since then he's been living on welfare."

Ménard looked over his notes, shuffling his papers.

"So far as we can tell, nothing was stolen from Martinez's apartment. His credit card and cash were still in his wallet."

"Valuable objects, maybe?" the superintendent suggested.

"Impossible to say for the moment," Ménard replied. "We'll have to find the woman friend Thierry mentioned. She'll be able to tell us if there's something missing. But it's not very likely, since he wasn't rich."

"So there's little chance that the motive was money?" Llach asked with concern.

"Very little, in fact," Castello answered.

The superintendent took a few seconds to think before he took up the question that seemed to him the most worrisome.

"For the moment, the letters painted on a door of the apartment seem to be the only lead we have."

At the back of the room, Moreno and Raynaud, who hadn't yet shown any interest in this case, finally stirred. After clearing his throat, Moreno said in his bass voice:

"In other words, it's a political crime!"

"Vengeance taken on the OAS," his partner added.

Castello raised his hands to temper the enthusiasm of these two, the most uncontrollable on the team. Raynaud and Moreno never left each other's side. They spoke to each other only in whispers, looking warily about as if they were exchanging top-secret national security information. They told themselves that they were always on the lookout for the big case that would make their careers, but they hung out in shabby bars and shady milieus in which nothing important would ever happen.

"Easy now, gentlemen, let's not get ahead of ourselves," Castello advised. "It's true that at this stage in the investigation, anything can be imagined. And the press, unfortunately, will do that soon enough. Our job is to proceed step by step. And the first thing to do is to check any connections Martinez might have had with that organization. What do we know at this point about the victim's distant past?"

The question was addressed chiefly to Ménard and Lambert.

"I didn't find any documents in Martinez's apartment that indicated a link to the OAS," Ménard replied. "Except that he subscribed to some pretty immoderate magazines for *Pieds-Noirs*."

The superintendent turned to Lambert.

"What did the neighbors say, Thierry?"

Lambert squirmed on his chair and stammered:

"Uh, I didn't think to ask them. At that point I didn't know he was involved with the OA . . . the OA thing!"

The superintendent sighed and glared at the young cop. Sebag quietly looked at his phone. It was already 7 P.M. Putting his hands under the table, he began composing an SMS to tell Claire that he wouldn't be home in time for dinner.

Castello put his hands flat on the table and took a deep breath.

"I think it would be useful here to remind you of what happened back then. I knew you weren't necessarily experts on the Algerian War, but I thought you would at least have heard of the OAS."

Molina elbowed Lambert.

"The OAS," the superintendent began, "was a clandestine movement created in 1961 in reaction to the FLN's terrorist attacks."

Castello stared at Lambert again and took care to speak very clearly:

"FLN stood for *Front de li-bé-ra-tion na-tion-ale*, an independence movement that had begun armed resistance in 1954."

Then he went on, speaking to the group as a whole:

"So the OAS, in reaction to the FLN's actions and to General de Gaulle's policy of self-determination . . . "

He paused again.

"Self-determination, Lambert, do you have some idea of what that means?"

"Uh . . . Vaguely, yeah," the young inspector mumbled.

"What about General de Gaulle?" Molina asked maliciously.

"Ah, sure . . . the general . . . de Gaulle, yeah, I know about . . . "

"By the way, how is he?"

Jacques's joke made the inspectors laugh and even managed to elicit a faint smile on the superintendent's face, but he continued his account.

"So the French in Algeria who were against independence created the OAS, which in less than two years set off a good ten thousand bombs, not only in Algeria, but also here in France. They are said to have killed more than 1,600 people."

The figure made a cold shiver run down the policemen's backs.

"Yes, I know, that seems incredible today, but I checked the number: 1,600 deaths. The OAS attacked mainly Arabs but it also executed French police officers who were doing their job."

A scandalized murmur rumbled through the room.

"Some of the leaders of the OAS were shot after they were arrested. Many of them did time in prison. But most were granted amnesty in the late 1960s."

Castello waited a few moments to be sure that he had his whole team's attention.

"The letters 'OAS' written near the body thus draw our attention to this troubled period, which is still very sensitive, especially in the community of the former French of Algeria—a community which, I remind you, still includes more than ten thousand people living in the department of Pyrénées-Orientales. And I assume you are aware that here in Perpignan there have recently been tensions between the *Pied-Noir* associations and their opponents regarding several monuments erected in public places. Each time there have been demonstrations for and against the monuments, and conflicts have been narrowly avoided. In short, we are walking on eggshells here, and I can tell you that many people around here will be keeping a close eye on our investigation."

A leaden silence followed. The inspectors remained pensive. Nobody in the police liked to work under the pressure of politics and the media.

"However, we will not exclude any lead," Castello went on. "Including the possibility of a personal settling of accounts disguised as a political matter. Tomorrow Llach and Lambert will meet with Martinez's woman friend. In particular, they will go with her to the apartment to see if she can confirm that nothing has been stolen. Raynaud and Moreno will investigate Martinez's past occupations. We have to find out whether the bankruptcy of his business involved legal disputes."

Sebag took a sideways glance at his two colleagues and noted with pleasure that they were disappointed not to be assigned to the political lead. Then he concentrated again on the superintendent's instructions.

"Sebag and Molina begin by looking into the local *Pied-*

*Noir* community, and question first of all the officials of the association Martinez belonged to. We have to learn very quickly if the victim belonged to the OAS or not. Then they will meet with the people who were opposed to the various *Pied-Noir* monuments. Finally, Ménard will work particularly on the historical aspect. I think you already have an appointment with a professor at the university?"

"Yes, he's a specialist on the Algerian War. More on the FLN than on the OAS, unfortunately, but he will probably be able to direct me to colleagues and people who were there at the time."

Castello looked at his inspectors, one after the other, and then concluded gravely:

"Gentlemen, I'm counting on you to be here first thing tomorrow. We have to move fast because there is one fact that we haven't yet mentioned because it was too soon, and, as I repeated a little while ago, I don't want to cut corners. But I'm sure that some of you have already thought about it."

Again he surveyed his inspectors.

"If we're dealing here with an old desire to take revenge on the OAS, we can't exclude the possibility that this murder is the first of a series. Dismissed."

Molina made a phone call while Sebag collected the papers from the file on Mathieu's accident that a breeze had scattered all over the office.

"That's fine, Mr. Albouker. See you tomorrow."

Molina hung up.

"The president of the *Pied-Noir* Circle can see us tomorrow morning at 10:30. He'd have preferred afternoon because he wants his treasurer to be there, and the treasurer isn't available in the morning. But I told him we had another appointment in the afternoon."

"That was the right thing to do. If we did as people want,

we'd be working day and night. And then I've had enough for my first day back after vacation."

"The treasurer is retired, so he can make an effort. I've had enough for today, too. And I still feel like I'm carrying around with me the smell of that body mixed with Lambert's deodorant—a disgusting mixture that would be enough to drive off the most eager nymphomaniac!"

Molina got up and put on his jacket.

"I have a particularly bad feeling about this case. I'm afraid we're opening an incredible can of worms. And we're going to be under pressure."

"That's for sure. I hope we can move ahead quickly."

"With a little luck, it will be his woman friend who killed him, and she'll cry on Lambert's shoulder and confess it all. It wouldn't be the first crime of passion committed at the age of seventy, right?"

"Yeah, no doubt, but that's not very likely."

"You don't see it that way, huh?"

"No. Like you, I'd put my money on the can of worms."

Sebag had finished picking up all the papers and putting them back in order. He tapped them to make a neat pile and slipped it under his arm. Then he followed Molina out of the office.

When Sebag got home, Claire and Séverine were sitting comfortably on the sofa, watching television. He kissed them and saw them grimace. He hadn't had time to change his clothes since his visit to Martinez's apartment.

"I know, I'm going to take a shower."

Without saying any more, he disappeared into the bathroom adjoining the bedroom. He put his clothes in the laundry basket and stepped under a spray of hot water. He let it run over him for a good five minutes while he cleaned his skin and shampooed his hair.

After he dried off, he put on a bathrobe.

"Is Léo here?" he asked the girls, who hadn't budged.

"In his room," Claire answered.

Gilles crossed the living room and went down the hall that led to the children's rooms. He knocked at his son's door. No response. He went in. Léo was wearing a headset and was totally focused on his computer.

"Hi, there," Sebag said in a loud voice.

Léo hardly moved his head.

"Hi, Dad."

"Did you have a good day?"

"It was O.K."

"Not too much homework?"

"No, it's all right."

For a few seconds, Sebag contemplated the nape of his son's neck. He hesitated. He'd planned to remind Léo one more time to be careful on his scooter, but he was well aware that this "one more time" would be perceived as "one time too many." It was better not to push too hard. His relationship with his son was not conflictual—not yet—but their old closeness had waned over the years and Gilles missed the time when they played games together in the yard or on the computer and had long discussions in the evening before going to bed. But that's life, after all. Léo had grown up. He'd become a teenager of sixteen. A boy of his time. Autistic with respect to his parents, but capable of talking all day long with his buddies on the internet.

Sebag sighed, shut the door, and returned to the living room. It was separated from the kitchen only by a bar. On the counter he found, under a glass cloche, a plate with stuffed zucchini and a little rice. He put it in the microwave to heat. While he waited, he glanced at the television screen. An American series, obviously a cop show. That's all there was on TV now.

The microwave beeped. Sebag took out his food and sat down at the table. Claire soon joined him. Séverine had put on a headset so she could watch the rest of her television program in peace.

"How did your day go?" Claire asked.

"A lot like your TV show."

"A murder?"

He'd just put a big forkful in his mouth and had to limit himself to nodding.

"Was that the smell?"

He explained the main outlines of the case.

"That was a great thing to come back to after vacation," she said.

"You can say that again. But aren't you going to keep watching television?"

"I saw the first episode, and with what you just told me, I no longer want to see the rest."

"As they say, fact is stranger than affliction."

"Haven't you already used that one?"

Gilles loved to give proverbs a new twist, but after twenty years of living with Claire, he no longer had any new ones.

"Probably. How was your day?"

Claire told him about her routine as a French teacher at the middle school in Rivesaltes, the tensions between the faculty and the new principal, and then the difficulty of maintaining order in overenrolled classes, especially 4-C, which included two or three students who were a little more insolent than usual. She also talked about relaxing for a moment at the gym, the pleasure of letting off steam physically and then ending her session with a *hammam* with her girlfriends.

Sebag's mind wandered. He just couldn't focus on what Claire was saying any longer. A word or a gesture was sometimes enough to make a sickening jealousy rise up in him, a wave of malaise, an ache in his stomach and his guts that had

been with him since the preceding summer, when he had discovered by the cruelest and most painful of chances that Claire
had been lying to him. Precisely about a gym class, which he
knew she hadn't attended. He'd had doubts, but had never
said anything about them.

The suspicion that his wife had been unfaithful to him had
grown stronger over the following days, to the point that he
became almost certain it was true.

And he still hadn't said anything.

It would have been easy, however, for Lieutenant Sebag to
use his detective's skill to find out the truth of the matter. He
could also have simply talked about it openly with Claire. He
knew her well; if anything had been going on, she'd have told
him all about it. He was sure of that.

But in the end he'd decided he didn't want to know.

In view of the love and desire that Claire continued to show
him, he'd concluded that the truth was of no interest. The only
thing that counted was their love, their mutual love, always
their love. That was the only sincerity that really mattered. And
this love was so strong that it could easily cope with a little
scratch. Especially since he hadn't noticed anything unusual in
Claire's behavior since school started. If his wife had had an
"adventure," it was over.

Being able to take philosophically such a painful and com-
monplace misfortune that would have broken up many a couple made Sebag feel noble and great. Sublime and generous.
Magnanimous. And this positive image of himself had been a
balm for the wound to his pride.

But now the balm no longer had any effect. And it was himself that he doubted. More and more often he wondered
whether his fine magnanimity was concealing something else.

Fear, pure and simple.

The fear of knowing and not being able to bear the truth.

He'd let the scratch heal over with bits of gravel still under the skin. The wound had put its mark on his soul and from time to time reminded him that it was still there. More and more often. Like a deep-seated infection that was eating away at him.

"I don't like it when you look at me with those eyes."

He came back to himself. To her. Claire was gazing at him sadly.

"I don't like it when you look at me with those eyes," she repeated softly.

A faint smile lit Sebag's lips.

"They're my eyes. I don't have any others."

"That's not true," she said. "Your eyes are loving and tender. These eyes are hard and cold. And above all, they're far away. Too far from me."

Gilles's smile broadened.

"Ah, there we are, that's better," said Claire. "As soon as you smile, your eyes come back."

They looked at each other in silence for a few long moments. An immense cold seized his gut and stopped his breath. He saw Claire's lips start to open and then immediately close again. He had the terrifying feeling that they were thinking the same thing. But he didn't want to talk about it, he didn't want to lance the boil. Not now. As long as he could stand the pain he would stand it. All he hoped was that they could very quickly resume the normal course of their love.

Wearing the headset, Séverine was standing next to them. She took Gilles's glass and filled it with water that she gulped down.

"I was thirsty," she said as she went back to slouch in front of the TV.

The moment had passed. Whew . . . Claire was the first to change the subject.

"You must not have had time to work on Mathieu's accident?"

"No, but I brought the file home, and I'm going to have a look at it right now."

"Sévérine expects a lot of you."

"I know."

"But if there's nothing to be found, she'll understand."

"I hope."

Sebag stretched out on the bed and stuck the pillow behind his back. He was beginning to read the file.

Mathieu's accident had taken place the preceding Wednesday. The boy had been on his way home from Perpignan's Olympic pool where he trained every Wednesday afternoon. According to the police report, it was 5:15 when the white delivery van owned by Chevrier Transportation suddenly swerved to its left, striking Mathieu's scooter head-on. There was no trace of skid marks on the pavement. The collision had been violent. As Sebag already knew, the boy had immediately stood up, apparently unhurt. And then suddenly collapsed a little later. Internal hemorrhaging. The emergency team's doctor had recorded the time of death as 5:57.

The driver of the van—Pascal Lucas, 45, the father of two children—claimed he had suddenly swerved to avoid a car that had run a stop sign on his right. The witnesses described a driver who had panicked and clearly showed all the signs of being drunk. Sebag glanced through the documents until he found the medical certificate made out later at police headquarters: 1.2 grams of alcohol in the driver's blood. Further on, he found a copy of the driver's police record. This wasn't a first offense for Pascal Lucas. Three years earlier, his license had been suspended for driving under the influence. It was getting to be a little much. Unfortunately, the case looked like it was going to be very simple.

Claire emerged naked from the bathroom. Gilles followed her with his eyes as she put on a short, cream-colored nightie with a band of pink lace at the bottom. He was still looking at her when she stretched out alongside him. He loved to look at her when she was getting dressed or undressed. He knew that she liked it, too.

Claire pressed her legs against his. The moment for questions was past. Had it ever really come?

"So, this file?" Claire asked.

He shrugged.

"It looks bad for the driver. He's the only one who says that another car ran a stop sign. None of the witnesses mentions that. It really looks like something he invented to reduce his responsibility."

"If you don't find anything, it's not serious. What the family needs is to be sure that the accident really happened the way the police say it did."

"My colleagues don't always do bad work."

"Do you know the one who handled Mathieu's accident?"

"Yes, of course."

"Is he a good cop?"

"Uh . . . a wildcard."

"Ah . . . So it might be worthwhile to dig a little further," she added as she turned out the light.

"Aren't you going to read?"

"No, I'm exhausted this evening. The kids were really unruly today at school. And then Monday is usually a busy day."

She sat up to kiss him.

"Good night."

"Good night."

More than fatigue, Gilles felt a deep weariness. But he tried to go on reading. He looked at the dates and times of the reports. They'd all been made the same day, right after the accident. Cardona had worked late but he'd apparently decided that same evening that there was nothing in the case that required further investigation. A case that had been quickly closed. But had it perhaps been closed too quickly?

Sebag put the sheets of paper on his night table before turning out the light. He lay on his back for a moment, staring at the ceiling lit by the orange light coming in from the street. The shadows of the palm tree in the yard were dancing gracefully. Claire was breathing regularly. She was already asleep.

He closed his eyes but the pages kept passing in front of him. Reports from the ambulance men and the emergency team, witnesses' testimony, Cardona's summary.

Something was bothering him, but he didn't know what.

He turned the lamp back on and quickly reread all the witness statements, compared them. Claire turned over in the bed, disturbed by the sudden return of light. She moaned a little. Gilles paid no attention and continued to go through the documents.

And then he understood.

Yes, the case had been closed too quickly, and there was something to dig into, as Claire had put it. Not much, to be sure, probably just a false lead, but who could tell? It might be the kind of thread that sometimes made it possible to unravel the whole case.

He turned out the light again and soon fell asleep.

# Chapter 5

**Algiers, November 25, 1961**

The three men have been waiting in the Renault Dauphine for half an hour.

"What the fuck is Georges doing, for God's sake?" The driver is getting impatient.

One of the two men in the back seat reprimands him.

"We told you: no names, O.K.? Just the code names. And calm down, Omega. Take Sigma as your model. It's his first operation, but do you see him losing his cool?"

He elbows the young man sitting on his left. The man he's given the code name of Sigma feels tense nonetheless but manages to hide it behind a permanent half-smile.

Omega turns around again to face the men in the backseat.

"Where are we going afterward? Do you know, Bizerte?"

"I have a vague idea, yes, but Babelo will confirm it. He's the boss."

Sigma tries to smoke his cigarette calmly. He draws in long puffs that he lets out slowly. One, two, three, four, five, six . . . He counts silently as he breathes. Today's operation is a kind of test for him: he has to show that he's fit before he'll be authorized to continue the fight.

In the street, boys in short pants are playing with a ball, paying no attention to the world around them. A doomed world. Sigma doesn't feel much older than these kids. He is separated from them by few years, at most, and a few whiskers on his chin. He never imagined that his transition to adulthood would take place with a gun stuck under his belt.

Babelo appears at the street corner, elegantly dressed, as usual. He stops, strokes his thin mustache, and takes the time to look around him before approaching the Dauphine.

Bizerte opens his window and shakes Babelo's hand.

"We're ready. We're just waiting for you."

Babelo gets in alongside the driver. He looks at his watch.

"It's almost noon. We're on time."

Omega turns the key. The Dauphine's engine starts to hum.

"Where are we going?"

"Boulevard de Champagne, the bottling factory. It will soon be time for the lunch break."

Despite his nervousness, Omega drives carefully. He doesn't want to draw attention to himself, even if there is little danger that the cops would dare to stop four men in a car.

A quarter of an hour later they've arrived at their destination. Babelo signals to Omega to stop the car fifty meters from the factory. Shortly afterward, a dozen Arab workers come out of the building. They sit down on the ground in a lane with thin grass, gathered around a shared mess tin.

Babelo gives his final instructions.

"Omega, you'll drive in front of them and turn around farther on. As you're coming back, stop near them, on the right side of the road. Bizerte and I will open the windows, and you, Sigma, will get out of the car and lean on the roof."

Omega restarts the Dauphine. As they pass in front of the factory the first time, Sigma takes care to look toward the other side of the street; he doesn't want to see anyone's face beforehand. Omega drives slowly as far as the next intersection and then makes a U-turn. He comes back toward the factory at a higher speed and stops right across from the workers.

The workers, frightened, immediately get up but Babelo and Bizerte have already lowered their windows. They start firing. Sigma gets out of the car, stands up, and following instructions, braces his pistol on the roof. He aims at a worker who is already running toward the door of the factory. He hits the target. The man collapses. He aims at another one who is standing, petrified with astonishment, in front of his mess tin. He hits him but has a feeling that he is not the first one to do so.

The rest of the shooting is more confused. When Babelo gives the order to stop firing, no Arab is still moving. Bizerte puts away his gun and grabs a bag he's holding between his knees. He gets out, digs in the bag, and pulls out sheets of paper that he throws on the bodies.

Then he gets back into the car. Omega makes the tires squeal as the Dauphine takes off down the boulevard.

"Nice job, men," Babelo congratulates them, a broad smile on his lips. "Now I'm going to take you all to the movies. *Rio Bravo* is playing at the Rex. With John Wayne. A film they say will become a classic in the history of the western."

An intoxicating smell of gunpowder is floating in the car. At the intersection with the boulevard, Sigma meets the eyes of a child. A street kid. Rather well-dressed for a little Arab. The boy has seen everything and is pointing an accusing finger at the car. The Dauphine turns, with another squeal of its tires, and the kid disappears from Sigma's sight. The young man thinks the child will disappear from his life as well. There's nothing romantic about war. Sigma, despite his youth, has just realized that.

In front of the bottling factory, the police count six men dead and three wounded, one seriously. As they carry out the usual routines, knowing they will serve no purpose, they are trampling on the tracts left there by the killers. The tracts that the wind will scatter around Algiers contain only one sentence, crudely printed in black on white:

"The OAS strikes when it wants, where it wants."

# CHAPTER 6

G illes Sebag was waiting in the double-parked car while his partner bought a supply of cigarettes at the tobacconist's shop. The passersby were walking with their heads down because of the wind; the *tramontane* was making an angry return after a few days of rest.

Molina dived into the car and tried to close the door, but a gust beat him to it and slammed the door in his face.

"I almost had a work-related accident," he complained.

"People always say that tobacco is dangerous," Sebag replied mockingly.

"I know, but I can't stop. At my age, I think it's too late."

"No, you aren't going to change now. We're going to arrive late because of the detour that you've just forced us to make."

Sebag started the engine and drove off. He continued to tease his partner until Molina finally interrupted him:

"Turn left, it's here. Rue Joseph Jaume. I have a feeling we're going to spend some time in this neighborhood."

The offices of the *Pied-Noir* Circle were in a small house with a garden, located across the street from the entrance to the Moulin-à-Vent quarter. Constructed in the early 1960s on the heights above Perpignan, this neighborhood of white apartment buildings with red tile roofs had quite naturally taken in many of the French returning from Algeria. And even if the *Pieds-Noirs* had later moved all over the region, many of them still lived in the Moulin-à-Vent quarter or around it. Bernard Martinez's apartment was only three hundred meters from the offices of the Circle.

Guy Albouker had white hair and a beard of the same color. He received them with a smile. Sebag found him astonishingly young despite his snowy hair and the heavy bags under his eyes. The president of the Circle asked them to follow him down a narrow hall that led to what must originally have been a living room but now more resembled a conference room. Looking out on a little garden, the room was furnished chiefly with a few tables and chairs.

"During the Circle's first few years, we had our offices in a building across the way," Albouker explained. "But when we saw that this house was for sale, we took advantage of the opportunity. This place is larger, and, especially important, there's a garden. Once a month we make couscous and when the weather is good, it's nice to eat outdoors."

Albouker's voice was warm and pleasant, and had a slight accent. Only a few drawling stresses on certain syllables betrayed his origins.

"For us, conviviality remains the main thing. Even so far away from our country."

This way of putting it struck Sebag. Albouker had spoken of "his country" as though it had not disappeared more than fifty years before. He refrained from pointing that out. It wouldn't have been a good way of opening the conversation.

"Jean-Pierre!"

Sebag jumped.

"Jean-Pierre!" Albouker shouted again before turning back to the policemen. "My treasurer lives upstairs. He was finally able to get away. I insisted on it; he knows Bernard much better than I do. They belong to the same generation."

The policemen sat down. Guy Albouker introduced the man who had just come in.

"Jean-Pierre Mercier."

The treasurer of the *Pied-Noir* Circle stared at them for a long time before going to sit down at the other end of the room. His austere physique and his grave eyes conveyed no warmth, but the policemen were used to being received coolly. Albouker sat in the middle, with his back to the French window. An awkward silence followed for a few seconds. Sebag put down the little notebook in which he wrote his observations regarding the current investigation. He took out a ballpoint pen and clicked it. For Molina, that was the signal to open the discussion.

"As I told you on the phone last night, Bernard Martinez was found dead in his apartment. He had been murdered."

The two men nodded soberly. Albouker gestured toward the local newspaper lying on a corner of the table. A short article reported the macabre discovery, but made no allusion to the OAS. By common agreement the police superintendent and the prosecutor had not yet told the press about the inscription found at the victim's apartment.

"Today we're pursuing routine questioning of people who knew Mr. Martinez, in order to draw up a portrait of him that is as precise as possible. Have you known him a long time?"

Albouker and Mercier glanced at each other. The president of the Circle answered first:

"So far as I'm concerned, five or six years, I think."

"I've known him for about fifteen years," the treasurer added. "He joined our association when he came to live in Moulin-à-Vent."

"Did you know him . . . well?"

"I can't say that," Albouker replied. "For a *Pied-Noir*, he was rather discreet and reserved."

"He was in fact rather shy," Mercier explained, "but in a small group he was more expansive. I've often been either his partner or his opponent in games of pétanque, and he could be a grumbler and even a very bad loser."

"What did you know about his life?"

"What he was willing to tell us," the treasurer replied. "For thirty-five years, he lived in Terrats, where he owned a vine-yard, but despite all his efforts he never really managed to live off it. I think that was very hard on him. He'd come back from Algeria with a little nest egg he'd saved, an inheritance, I think, and he'd invested it all in the vineyard. He lost everything."

Sebag took notes while Molina conducted the interview. He often looked up to observe their interlocutors.

"Had he never married?" Molina asked.

"No."

"Why?"

"We never talked about it."

"You didn't?"

"We were probably not close enough. And then we belong to a generation that does not easily discuss such personal matters."

"He had a woman friend, I think?"

"Josette Vidal, yes. She used to have a tobacconist's shop in the neighborhood, on the Ramblas du Vallespir. She lost her husband ten years ago. She's been seeing Bernard for a couple of years. But they seldom went out together, they were very independent. And then Mme Vidal is not a *Pied-Noir*, and Bernard always came to our meetings alone."

"Had you noticed a change in Mr. Martinez's behavior lately? Did he seem worried, for instance?"

Albouker and Mercier glanced at each other again, then shook their heads.

"Did he have any enemies that you know of?"

The two men seemed surprised, almost shocked.

"Do you think he might have had some?" said Albouker. "That would surprise me: he was really a very ordinary fellow."

"Frankly, apart from a few pétanque players annoyed by some of his remarks, I can't think of any," Mercier confirmed.

The treasurer of the Circle was beginning to relax. Sebag put down his pen and decided to participate in order to guide the discussion.

"Did he often talk about Algeria?"

"Very often," Albouker immediately replied.

His eyes narrowed, making the bags underneath look even bigger. Then a broad smile came to his lips. He added:

"Very often, yes, but perhaps a little less than most of us."

"And what did he say?"

The question seemed to surprise them.

"Nothing special," Albouker said. "He talked about memories of his childhood, his youth, he talked about the country. Nostalgia is very strong among us, you know. And very often, the older one gets, the more intense it becomes. We've all retained a love for our country."

He struck his breast with the flat of his hand.

"It's still alive here," he added melodramatically. "And so long as we have a breath of life, it will continue to live."

His face closed on his sorrow. Only the corners of his mouth trembled. Sebag had the feeling that the president of the association was having a hard time holding back tears. He was astonished. Albouker noticed.

"Today, there are two things that still bind our community together," the president said after he got a grip on himself. "The first is our love for this lost country. The second is the incomprehension and even the hostility of other French people when they see that this love is still intact."

Sebag felt that Albouker had seen through him, and did not try to hide it. Nonetheless, he continued.

"I'd like you to give us some more details. Do you know what kind of work he did in Algeria?"

"He worked in his father's hardware store in Algiers, in the Bab-El-Oued quarter," Mercier answered. "But he had studied viticulture to some extent. That was already his passion."

"He couldn't stay in Algiers if he wanted to do that," Molina remarked.

"He'd found a job with a colonist in the interior, but his

father wanted him to come back and help him in his shop. His only employee had been killed in an FLN attack. A bomb at the Casino de la Corniche, in June, 1957."

Mercier's voice vibrated under the effect of a rancor that was still trying to find a way to express itself.

"Ten people died and about a hundred were wounded. All of them young people who'd gone there to dance and have fun."

Sebag seized the opportunity.

"What did Bernard Martinez think about the FLN's attacks?"

The two men seemed surprised again.

"He thought as we all do," Mercier replied tartly. "That you had to be a coward to put bombs in public places and kill innocent people that way!"

"And what was his opinion regarding the independence of Algeria?"

"There, too, he thought what all the French of Algeria think. That independence was a stupid mistake and that nobody had the right to make us leave the country where we were born, the country that our parents and grandparents had constructed and made prosperous . . . "

Sebag sensed that Albouker had more reservations. He asked him his opinion.

"Some *Pieds-Noirs* were more moderate than others, however. In my family, for example, everyone belonged to the SFIO.[3] We thought the system wasn't perfect but that it could evolve. We were prepared to accept a certain number of reforms and concessions so that Algeria could remain French. The war destroyed all our hopes. When guns and bombs speak, only the extremists can still make their voices heard."

---

[3] *Section française de l'International ouvrière*, a French socialist workers' party that became the *Parti Socialiste* in 1969.

"And was Bernard Martinez one of those extremists at that time?"

"At that time and still today," Albouker sighed. "He continued to talk in a way that was very . . . uncompromising."

Mercier approved vigorously. Sebag decided it was time to bring up the main question.

"Did Martinez ever talk to you about the OAS?"

Albouker and Mercier looked at each other. They suddenly seemed wary,

"May I ask what that question means?" Albouker retorted. Sebag played dumb.

"My question has no particular meaning. I think it's rather clear. But I can make it more direct: In your opinion, what did Martinez think about the OAS?"

"Is that question really of interest for your investigation?"

Albouker appeared indignant. Sebag tried to reassure him.

"It really is of interest, yes. And I don't understand why this question annoys you."

"It annoys me because for the past half-century too many French people conflate *Pieds-Noirs* with the OAS. According to them, if you were born in Algeria, you're necessarily in favor of the OAS and the extreme right. And we were necessarily rich colonists who were exploiting the Arabs. For people like me, who come, as I told you, from leftist families, I find that insulting."

"I understand, Mr. Albouker," Sebag said, trying to calm him. "My question wasn't general in nature, but specific. I can't tell you anything at the moment, but I need to know whether you think Martinez might have had ties to the OAS."

"Do you mean that there might be a connection between that organization and Bernard's death?" Mercier asked with concern.

Sebag did not reply; instead he leaned back in his chair. Molina understood and took over the questioning again:

"We have to respect the secrecy of the investigation. All we can say is that we are exploring all possible hypotheses. So I'll ask you our question again: so far as you know, did Bernard Martinez have ties to the OAS?"

"I don't know a goddamn thing about it!" Albouker exploded. "We don't talk much about that among us, you know."

"So what do you talk about at your meetings?"

"Politically, we have our demands. They focus mainly on compensations. Some of us had to give up everything over there. Even if we weren't all big landowners, we still had some property that we couldn't fit into our suitcases: an apartment, a house, a few pieces of furniture, sometimes a business . . . "

"And also tombs," Mercier added under his breath.

Since he seemed not to want to say more, Albouker tried to explain:

"Our ancestors are buried over there, in cemeteries that have been abandoned. We'd like to be able to maintain them; that's one of our demands."

The president of the Circle paused before continuing:

"But the goal of our association is not merely to obtain satisfaction on that point, it is also a meeting place for the French of Algeria, a place of memory and the preservation of our culture. During our events, we talk more about cooking than about politics. We exchange memories, reminisce about common friends, and many other things as well. We talk a lot, we talk loudly, we give our accents free rein and let our *pataouète* come out."

"Your pata-what?" Molina asked in surprise.

The *pataouète*! It's our own patois. A mixture of various Mediterranean languages and patois from French regions. It emerged in the suburbs of Algiers and in the interior. People don't realize that the majority of *Pieds-Noirs* were not originally French. Some of them came from Spain, Italy, Switzerland, and even Germany. And then there were quite a lot of Maltese. Today, the *pataouète* still testifies to all these contributions."

Sebag thought all this was pleasant but not to the point. He decided to reframe the conversation. He turned to the treasurer.

"We still have only touched on the question, and I'd like to have your opinion, Mr. Mercier, regarding Bernard Martinez's feelings about the OAS."

The treasurer grimaced. Apparently he'd thought he'd escaped the question and that had suited him fine.

"You want to know if Bernard was a member at the time, is that it?"

"For example."

Mercier reflected. Visibly, he was trying to weigh each of his words carefully.

"Frankly, I can't say for sure that Bernard belonged to the OAS . . . but based on what I recall of the way he talked and what he said, I think it's not impossible."

"What did he say, and how did he talk?"

Mercier let out a long breath.

"I don't remember any particular discussion, but my general feeling is that he must have been pretty close to those ideas back then, yes."

He gestured vaguely toward the president.

"But with the exception of a few families, most of the *Pieds-Noirs* felt close to the OAS. Even if we didn't approve of everything it did, we supported it. It was the only movement that defended our ideas. But . . . how should I put it? Our support was mainly verbal, as we gathered around a bottle of anisette and a *kémia* . . . "

"A *kémia*?" Molina asked.

"It's the equivalent of your *tapas*," Albouker translated.

Sebag was afraid that the conversation would go off track again. Fortunately, Mercier continued his explanations.

"Among us, there was always more palaver than action, and that's probably why we lost the war. However, Bernard spoke differently about the OAS, but without overdoing it, on the contrary, keeping his distance. And he remained fervently anti-Gaullist."

"Did he tell you anything in that regard?"

Sebag had let Jacques take over again.

"His anti-Gaullism was such a gut-level thing that it came out in any political discussion."

"What about the OAS? Did he confide anything to you about that?"

"No, never."

There was a long silence. Molina seemed to have run out of questions, and he kept turning to look at his partner. Sebag was thinking. He was reluctant to reveal the reasons for their interest in the OAS. But Perpignan was a small city, and everything always ended up coming out. Very quickly. So why not?

In the end, he didn't see what divulging this information would contribute to their conversation, so he decided to respect the superintendent's instructions regarding discretion. He scribbled a few more words in his notebook and then looked up and asked:

"Anything else you'd like to say?"

His two interlocutors glanced at one another once again before shaking their heads.

"Fine."

Sebag closed his notebook and put his pen back in his jacket pocket. Molina stood up. Sebag and Albouker did the same. Jean-Pierre Mercier remained sitting, pensive.

"Gentlemen, I'll walk you out," the president suggested.

On the threshold, the three men shook hands. Sebag had one last question to ask, a question that had been bothering him from the outset but which he hadn't brought up, because it had no connection with the investigation.

"May I ask how old you are?" he blurted out.

"I'm fifty-five," Albouker said sadly and then, anticipating the next question, added: "When my parents left Algeria in 1962, I was six years old. I have very few real memories of my native country, but that doesn't change anything. In our association, you will find many *Pieds-Noirs* who were born here in France. They are not necessarily the least passionate, you know, because Algeria is not merely a homeland, the idealized country of our family roots . . . Algeria, our Algeria, is first of all a disease, a cancer, a plague."

"Are you coming to eat with us at the Carlit?"

Sebag had just parked their car in the police station's parking lot. It was barely noon, but Molina was already hungry. The Carlit, a restaurant near police headquarters, served as a cafeteria for them. Sebag declined his partner's offer.

"No thanks, I've got an appointment."

Molina's eyes lit up with hope.

"Well, well, a romantic rendezvous?"

Sebag didn't bother to reply. The joke wasn't new. Jacques did not understand why Gilles had remained faithful to his wife for over twenty years.

"I'll see you back at the office in the early afternoon."

"You're sure you don't need more time?" Molina continued. "I can cover for you if you want."

"I'll be there around 2 or 2:30."

Sebag tossed him the keys to their vehicle and went to look for his own car. On the way, he zipped his jacket all the way up because the wind out of the north made the air feel even colder. This time, there was no doubt about it: autumn had arrived in Catalan country.

At the wheel of his Citroën Picasso, Sebag entered the midday traffic jams. He turned onto the boulevards that ran around the downtown area, drove alongside the Moulin-à-Vent quarter and, after waiting a good ten minutes at the traffic circle in front of the Multiplex movie theater, headed for Argelès. Five kilometers farther on, he took the exit for Villeneuve-de-la-Raho. Pascal Lucas, the Chevrier Company's driver, lived in that community. Sebag had made an appointment with him that morning before going to work.

The old village of Villeneuve-de-la-Raho was huddled around a water tower on a hill overlooking an artificial lake and a sea of modern tract houses. Sebag parked his car at the entrance to a subdivision. Pascal Lucas lived in a little Mediterranean-style house, part of whose attractive, bright yellow stucco façade was hidden behind a wall of plain concrete blocks. That was one of the main architectural blemishes on the Roussillon of the early third millennium. On smaller and smaller lots, people were trying to preserve some semblance of privacy by building veritable perimeter walls. But for lack of money or will, they often left them bare, which made the department's numerous residential subdivisions look perennially unfinished and temporary.

A big, stocky man was waiting for Sebag in front of his house.

"Pascal Lucas?"

"Yes," the man said. His bloodshot eyes owed their condition as much to sorrow as to alcohol. Lucas stepped back to let Sebag pass. Gilles went into the living room and immediately sat down in a large armchair. His host perched on the edge of the sofa.

"I wanted to review a few details with you, but first I have to explain one little thing: my visit is in no way official, and I am not in charge of this case."

Lucas fidgeted and ran his big hand through his thick brown hair. Seeing his astonishment, Sebag added:

"I'm a friend of the family. Mathieu's parents would like to be sure that we know all there is to know about the accident."

The driver suddenly stood up:

"I want this cleared up, too! But your colleagues don't want to believe what I told them!"

He started pacing around the room.

"Since the beginning, I've been telling them that a car ran a stop sign as I was coming along. That's why I swerved to the left, for Christ's sake! Why else would I have done that?"

"Because you were drunk."

Lucas stopped in his tracks. His arms moved instead of his legs.

"I know I'd been drinking, I didn't deny that. But I wasn't dead drunk, either. I remember exactly what happened."

"You had 1.2 grams of alcohol in your blood, that's quite a lot."

"I know it's far too much when you're driving, but I also know what I saw, right? Why won't anyone believe me?"

"Because no witness confirms the presence of that car. What kind of car was it, according to you?"

"Not according to me," the driver said testily and started pacing again. "That car exists, it's a white Renault Clio."

"I don't suppose you got the license number?"

"As if I had nothing to do but that . . . After I hit the scooter, I stopped and rushed back to help the kid. When I saw him get right back up, damn it, I was relieved, I can tell you that. If only I'd known what was going to happen next."

Still pacing, Pascal Lucas told Sebag what was already in the file. Mathieu's sudden collapse. His death. After he'd finished, Lucas calmed down. Three seconds. No more.

"Did you see the car drive away?" Sebag asked while Lucas started walking around the room again.

"No. At the moment, I wasn't thinking about that car anymore. Only the kid mattered to me. When I believed he was O.K., I went back to the van to look for the papers for the accident report, and that's when I realized that the bastard had taken off. The Clio was gone! However, I swear to you that that car exists, goddamn it. Your colleague doesn't want to hear about it, doesn't give a shit. I'd been drinking, I'm responsible, for him that's clear."

His heavy body stopped in front of Sebag. His hands curled into fists and his arm muscles swelled. Lucas had an imposing physique but he was trembling like a leaf. His eyes were pleading.

"How about you, Monsieur, are you going to believe me?"

"Sit down, please," Sebag said. "You're making me dizzy with all your pacing back and forth."

The driver docilely sat down on the edge of the sofa again. He stared at the coffee table in front of him and licked his lips. Sebag noted that the coaster on the coffee table was still damp. Lucas had already been drinking that morning.

"Do you drink often?"

For a moment, the driver covered his face with his powerful hands. Then he gave himself a clap on both his cheeks at the same time.

"I can't stop; I've tried, but I just can't do it."

"Has it been like that for a long time?"

"About ten years, maybe longer, it's hard to say. I didn't walk into a bar one day telling myself, O.K., today's the day I become an alcoholic. It happened gradually, one glass at a time, slowly."

"It was dangerous for your line of work."

"Most of the time I manage not to drink while I'm working, or at least not too much."

"Too much? What does that mean?" "An aperitif and a half-liter of red wine with lunch, but nothing before."

"And nothing afterward?"

"It depends . . . "

Lucas couldn't help standing up again. He took a step but then changed his mind and sat down again.

"You didn't answer my question: are you going to believe me?"

Sebag looked at him for a few seconds before responding. The driver put his hands on his knees, forcing himself to adopt an immobility contrary to his nature. But he couldn't control the constant blinking of his eyes. Sometimes long, sometimes short. Like an SOS.

Sebag got up. The driver bounded to his feet.

"You seem to me sincere, Mr. Lucas, and the primary goal of my visit was to assure myself that you were. It's just that my job is not to believe but to determine the facts. I'm going to try to look into this business of the Clio."

"Thanks," Lucas breathed.

"I'm not doing this for you, but for Mathieu's family. And then, even if I find this car and the driver who goes with it, that will not completely absolve you of responsibility. You were drunk, you didn't retain control of your vehicle, and Mathieu is dead. You won't get your driver's license back, or your job."

"I know that. But as we said a little while ago, what matters is that we know all there is to know, right?"

The driver extended a damp hand that Sebag shook gingerly.

"How are you going to find that car?"

"It won't be easy. First I have to prove that it exists, and a witness will be enough to establish that. But finding the driver . . . "

"Anything you can do will already be great."

Sebag was grateful that Lucas wasn't expecting the impossible. He said to himself that if he only half-succeeded, Séverine wouldn't hold it against him, either. But he wanted more: he wanted his daughter to be proud of her father. And there was only one way to ensure that: he had to find the other driver.

# CHAPTER 7

Abadie, Abdelmalek, Achou, Aguilar . . .
His big, gnarled fingers slipped over the cold marble,
deciphering the names of the dead one by one.
Hundreds of names.

Babou, Bakti, Balaguer . . .

Hundreds of French people living in Algeria hadn't had
time to reach metropolitan France after the war. They'd disappeared without a trace. They were just names in the survivors'
memories. And now names engraved in marble on a wall in
Perpignan.

Berthelot, Bianchi, Bokhtache . . .

They were fathers, mothers, friends, cousins, or maybe
neighbors.

Couraqui, Claus, Delamare, Dominguez . . .

The old man's parched lips silently pronounced the syllables. In his head, the names sang their musical sonorities,
French, Spanish, Italian, German, Arab, or Jewish.

Elbaz, Escriva, Esteban . . .

Hey! His finger stopped for a moment. The old man
smiled, amused by the coincidence.

Gaadoui, Garcia, Hebrard, Humbert . . .

The old man had had a hard time finding the former convent, even though it was located in the city center. He'd walked
past its roof several times before he realized that he had to go
down a stairway to reach its entrance. He'd pushed open the
tall gate and gone up to the wall. Nine marble plaques were

attached to the wall, revealing an endless list of victims, but also a silhouette of a man with a missing heart and a quotation from Chateaubriand that he'd found a little pompous.

Inversini, Janowski, Juan . . .

He stepped to the side, moving to the next plaque.

Lagrange, Lopez, Lorenzo, Maillard . . .

Holding his arm up so long made it hurt. He allowed himself a short break to massage his shoulder, elbow, and wrist. He finished by massaging the compact, knobby form with vague hooks that still served as his hand. He pulled up the collar of his overcoat to protect himself from the wind that was blowing through the courtyard and chilling him to the bone. Then he resumed his litany.

Malleval, Mansouri, Maricchi, Martinaud . . .

His hands looked like those of his grandmother. She too used to suffer from rheumatoid arthritis but had never known its name. At the time, no doctor had diagnosed her problem, her "martyrdom," as she herself called it on evenings when she was very tired. The only moments in her life when she was weak enough to complain.

Melchior, Muller, Navarro, Oubata . . .

He'd never suspected that there were so many of them. What had happened to all these people who had mysteriously disappeared? Had they been kidnapped? Murdered by Arabs or by jealous friends taking advantage of the confusion during the last days of French Algeria? Had they died of starvation or illness in an internment camp? Or had they simply died of old age, alone in an apartment in Algiers, without anyone coming to bid them a last farewell or give them a decent burial and a name on a tomb?

Pacinotti, Palumbo, Pipitone, Pons . . .

Name by name, he was getting there. She couldn't be much farther, now.

Poujade, Pradelle . . . Prietto . . .

My God . . . There were so many Ps.

Prudhomme, Roland, Romero, Rokvira . . .

His fingers caressed the letters. They jumped from one name to the next, more and more feverishly.

Ruiz, Saïd, Sanchez . . .

He was almost there. His lips closed, the names stopped singing in his head, the world fell silent. Just a little further. There, she was there. Grandma Henriette. Not everyone had forgotten her. He choked up as if a mighty hand had gripped his throat. He could hardly breathe.

He retreated to a bench and sat down. A tiny stream of air finally filtered down to his aching lungs. He raised his head toward the marble plaques. From where he was, he could no longer read the name but now he knew that it was there. In raised, gilt letters. He felt his shoulders shake with sobs and his eyes that had been dry for too long began to weep again. Two big tears rolled down his wrinkled cheeks. They bounced off the sides of his chin and fell silently to the tiles of the little courtyard.

The wind was still blowing but he no longer felt it.

# CHAPTER 8

S ebag had spent the afternoon at police headquarters. First he wrote up a report on that morning's interview with the officials of the *Pied-Noir* Circle, and then read his colleagues' reports as they came in. Molina, for his part, was interviewing the winegrowers in Terrats. This task had been assigned the day before to Raynaud and Moreno, but the inseparable duo had ended up working on another case.

Lambert and Llach had talked with Josette Vidal, the victim's woman friend, who had hurried back from Barcelona. Born in Prades seventy-two years before, she had gone to work in one of the Bella doll factories when she was sixteen, and remained there until the firm went bankrupt and closed in 1984. Then she and her husband had taken over a tobacconist's shop in Moulin-à-Vent. That was how she met Bernard Martinez, initially as a customer. After her husband died in 2002, they had naturally become closer and finally became intimate. "Intimate"—the word made Sebag smile. The report said no more about it. The term had probably been used by Josette Vidal herself. Had they been talking to a younger witness, the policemen would certainly have asked her to explain the nature of their relationship more precisely. The question "Were you lovers?" would surely have been asked. But Llach and Lambert had remained very discreet. Sebag didn't hold that against them; he would probably have done the same thing.

Josette Vidal wasn't aware of anyone who might be her

"companion's" enemy. She hadn't noticed that he seemed worried recently, and knew nothing about his past in Algeria, not to mention about any possible ties to the OAS. The lady's statements left hardly any doubt regarding her antipathy toward *Pieds-Noirs* in general—"people who are always brooding on their misfortunes." Martinez was the only one she liked. Go figure. Love has its mysteries, and in that respect, age doesn't change anything.

Llach and Lambert had taken Josette to Martinez's apartment, but she hadn't noticed anything out of the ordinary. Nothing was missing. She was categorical about that.

Sebag reread the report. The policemen's conventional expressions and standard formulas nonetheless conveyed a glimpse of a strong personality, but they told him nothing about the atmosphere in which the conversation had taken place. He picked up the receiver of his office telephone and dialed the number of Llach's cell phone.

"What did you think of our double widow?"

"The old lady's a tough cookie. She doesn't mince words. At first I thought she wasn't upset at all, but that was just a façade. As soon as we got to the apartment, she broke down. Especially when she saw the bloodstain in the living room."

"She really doesn't know anything about the OAS?"

"No, nothing at all. There's no reason to doubt what she says. She dislikes *Pieds-Noirs* so much that when he was with her Martinez must have acted as if he'd been born in Perpignan."

"And where does that hostility come from?"

"I don't know, I didn't ask her."

Llach interrupted himself and paused for a few seconds.

"You know, they *are* a little odd, those people. They left Algeria fifty years ago and they still haven't gotten over it!"

"As a Catalan, how would you feel if you'd had to leave your native country?"

"You can't make that comparison, it's completely different!"

"It is? Why?"

"Algeria wasn't their country!"

"They were born there, and their parents and grandparents, too, sometimes."

"Maybe, but that doesn't change anything: it wasn't their country. It couldn't last. The crusades didn't last either. They should have known that."

Sebag didn't know what to reply. He said goodbye to his colleague and hung up. Then he plunged into Ménard's report.

Ménard had talked with a professor at the University of Perpignan who had outlined for him the Algerian War and more particularly the OAS. Its birth in February 1961. Its historical leaders, Susini, Lagaillarde, Salan, Gardy. The soldiers it lost, Degueldre, Sergent, Bastien-Thiry, and a few hundred more. Its targeted assassinations of French policemen, FLN militants, and *Pieds-Noirs* it considered too moderate. And then above all its blind terrorist attacks: car bombs, plastic explosives, and assaults on Arab immigrants. It even used mortars to bombard a Muslim neighborhood on March 25, 1962: on that day, about forty people died, including women and children.

The OAS had committed its last attacks on territory that was by then Algerian in July, 1962. It had later carried out other actions in metropolitan France, aimed almost exclusively at its sworn enemy, General de Gaulle. Its principal leaders had been arrested; some were given death sentences, others were given long prison sentences. A few had succeeded in going into exile, usually in Spain, but sometimes as far away as Argentina. Finally, in 1968, an initial amnesty had been promulgated, supplemented by a second in 1974.

The name of Bernard Martinez had meant nothing to the Perpignan university professor. But he was not a specialist on the OAS, and had advised Ménard to contact one of his colleagues who taught in Marseille. Thus Ménard hoped to learn more the following day.

Around 5:30, Sebag suddenly felt ravenously hungry. After talking to Pascal Lucas, he'd gulped down only one portion of pizza and a couple of pieces of fruit, but he hesitated to go out to buy himself a treat. Since he'd turned forty, he found that he had a tendency to gain weight. And despite his running, he had to watch what he ate.

The ring of his cell phone provided a welcome diversion.

The call was from Guy Albouker.

"Excuse me for bothering you, but after our conversation I had an idea."

"Did you remember something important concerning Mr. Martinez?"

"No, it's not that. I think I told you everything about Bernard. I didn't know him that well."

"So?"

"It has to do with the common conflation of the *Pieds-Noirs* and the OAS, you remember, I talked to you about that . . . "

"Yes, I remember."

Molina entered the office noisily, threw a paper bag on his desk, and slumped into his chair. Distracted for a moment, Sebag had to ask Albouker to repeat what he'd just said.

"It doesn't matter," the president of the association said, "I think it wasn't clear anyway. In fact, I don't know how to explain it to you . . . I might be sending you on a wild-goose chase, but it occurred to me that since people always lump OAS and *Pied-Noir* together, the murderer might have done that, too."

Albouker stopped there.

"I'm not sure I understand," Sebag said. "Could you explain a little further?"

"Well, I was thinking that the murderer might not have had

it in for Martinez in particular, or even for the OAS, but for *Pieds-Noirs* in general."

This time Sebag understood, and he was beginning to see the disturbing consequences of such a hypothesis.

"Aren't you being a little paranoid, Mr. Albouker?"

"Yes, I know, and it's probably absurd. But I couldn't get the question off my mind and wanted to mention it to you. I don't know whether I should have done that."

"Yes, yes, you did the right thing. We have to explore all hypotheses. Has anything happened recently that would lead you to have such a . . . concern? Threats, hostile letters?"

"No, nothing like that. At least not at the Circle. But we're not the only association of *Pieds-Noirs* in the region, and you'd have to ask the others. You must know that the situation in Perpignan has been rather tense for a few years with all the more or less violent controversies over some of our monuments . . . "

Sebag preferred not to venture onto a terrain that he still didn't know very well. Castello had mentioned the subject the day before, but hadn't given any details, as if everyone already knew all about it. Sebag remembered only that there had been stormy debates about a stele or a wall, he didn't quite know. He'd have to work up the subject for tomorrow.

"Don't worry, Mr. Albouker, we'll look into everything. Besides, we have a meeting tomorrow with some of your opponents."

"Wait a minute, I didn't say that it was they. I haven't accused anyone."

"I know, Mr. Albouker, I know. I've noted your concern and your hypothesis. And for your part, if you hear anything about recent threats made against your community, don't hesitate to let me know."

"Thank you, Lieutenant Sebag, and thanks for your understanding. Excuse me for having bothered you. But we arouse so much hostility each time we speak out that I've always feared that some day we'd be the victims of fanatics or extremists."

"No one can know the future, but for the moment, we have no information that would justify that kind of concern."

"You're right, I'm probably being a little paranoid. Anyway, there's nothing we can do for the moment, so as we used to say over there: *Insha'Allah!*"

Albouker excused himself again and hung up.

In the meantime, Molina had booted up his computer. He looked up.

"What's going on?"

Sebag briefly summed up the conversation.

"Pure fantasy," Molina commented. "And fortunately for us. Can you imagine, if he were right . . . "

"Even if he's wrong, it could cause a lot of problems if that worry spread. All it takes is for certain people to believe it."

Molina grabbed the paper bag on his desk and held it open for Sebag.

"A little pastry?"

"Is that reasonable?"

"It's being reasonable that isn't reasonable. Life is too short."

"You can see where a maxim like that leads," Sebag said, pointing to his belly.

"My name is Jacques, Jacques Molina. Not Maxime."

Sebag chuckled and thrust a hand into the bag.

"I'd planned to go running this evening anyway. So, what did you learn this afternoon?"

"Nothing, or in any case not much. I talked to the mayor and the head of the winegrowers' cooperative in Terrats, and as might have been expected, there was nothing interesting in that direction. When he returned from Algeria, Martinez bought four hectares of vineyards and a little house. He sold his wine to the co-op. He worked alone, except of course for harvest time. He never made much money and was hit hard by the recession in the sector. He went into debt to improve the quality of his wine, but the revenues didn't come in. As we already knew, he sold everything in 1997, the house and the land. He had to pull out the vines."

"That must have been a heartbreaker for him."

Molina shrugged.

"As it was for everybody who had to do it. You know, when I was a kid, there were vineyards everywhere around here. In twenty years the area in vines has been reduced by half or two-thirds. And these last few years it's gotten even worse."

Sebag knew the situation. His usual running paths between Saint-Estève and Baixas passed through former vineyards. Weeds had taken over and were thriving around the giant carcasses of uprooted vinestocks.

"Are you sure, then? Should we drop the winegrowing lead?"

"I don't claim to have your intuition, but I think we can at least put it on the back burner. What's next?"

"We have a meeting tomorrow with members of the CCN, the 'Collective Contra Nostalgeria,' the people who have organized against the monuments to the memory of the *Pieds-Noirs.*"

"'Nostalgeria,' that's a pretty good one. And what were those monuments? I don't quite remember . . . "

"I don't either. I have to bone up on that before I go home this evening, and I'll give you a rundown on it as we're driving there tomorrow."

"That's perfect. If it's okay with you, I'm going to head home now. I've got a date tonight."

Divorced five years before, Jacques Molina was making up for lost time.

"You don't stop, do you? Brunette or blonde?"

"Blonde. And you?"

"What do you mean, me?"

"Your noontime date today!"

"Oh yeah, that . . . Big and hairy!"

Molina looked disgusted.

"Yuck," he muttered as he left the office.

A plastic bag was sailing on the wind, trying vainly to imitate the flight of a turtledove. It slowly rose into the dark sky and was then abruptly blown back to the ground. Its hazardous course ended when it got caught in arms of a gnarled grapevine. With every gust of the north wind, the last vineyard in the area was decorated by such sad garlands.

Sebag quickened his pace. The wind was now blowing in his face.

After giving Claire a kiss, he'd put on his running shoes and sweats and headed for the gravel paths. He'd gone without hesitating, driven by the gusts of wind and the things he had on his mind. Now he had to go home, his mind empty and his legs tired, running into the damp wind. Big clouds were mounting in the sky, heralding the first rains of the autumn. As he was coming home from work, Gilles had listened to the weather on his car radio. Storm warning. Over the next two days, as much water was going to fall as fell on central France in a whole winter. But for all that Gilles, who had worked for several years in Chartres, would not have traded the climate in Roussillon for that of Eure-et-Loir. Rains were like hassles: better that they come all at once, so long as they don't last.

The first drops fell when he reached the Saint-Estève heights. He still had a few fallow fields to cross before going back down toward his home. Under the heavy sky, the piles of uprooted grapevines no longer made him think of giant carcasses but of tiny, ridiculous slag heaps.

Sebag slowed his pace as he entered his street. He picked up his empty trashcan, which the refuse workers had left lying flat on the ground so that the wind wouldn't blow it into the middle of the street.

# CHAPTER 9

The family burial vaults lined the wide paths in the cemetery. They looked like the minuscule houses of a quiet village made of marble. He walked slowly and carefully. He felt deep in his bones the humidity that was spreading over Perpignan, and he had to make an effort not to grimace every time he put one foot in front the other. Fifteen years earlier, rheumatoid arthritis had attacked his hands and then gradually inflamed all his joints. His wrists, elbows, neck, knees, and ankles . . . Even the tiny bones in his feet now hurt him. He knew that he would soon have to start using a cane. For months, his doctor had been advising him to do that.

A calming silence lay over the cemetery. His body was suffering but his mind was at peace. This place pleased him. A natural development, no doubt. As one gets older, one takes pleasure in strolling through one's future garden. One's next resting place.

He wasn't afraid of death. He'd been around it plenty. Sometimes risking it, sometimes causing it. And he was going to do it again one last time.

He'd never taken pleasure in killing. He saw himself as a soldier, not a murderer. It was his mission, his battle. He'd always acted out of duty. And even if he was now acting for more personal reasons, he nonetheless had the feeling that he was assuming a collective responsibility. He was killing out of respect for history.

Someday death would come to demand its due. He would

receive it without hatred or fear. As a judgment that no one could escape. Birth was nothing other than a death sentence. Whatever one did, whatever one said, whatever one thought, death would cut down the heroes and the villains, the saints and the damned.

In front of him he saw a woman bending over the entrance to a vault. She was holding a little watering can and was watering red and yellow flowers with a trembling hand. He thought of Maria. He had loved her so much. Without her, he'd never have had the strength to begin a new life after the tragedy of his youth. If he had passed on before she did, there was no doubt that Maria would have come regularly to take care of his grave. But he'd never returned to the cemetery since his wife was buried there three years earlier. Three years already. He'd never felt either the need or the desire to meditate before her grave. Maria's memory never left him, and when he wanted to talk to her, all he had to do was look at the photos that decorated their dark apartment. He'd never liked cemeteries.

Until today.

He promised himself that once he'd returned to his country after carrying out his mission, he would go sit on the cold stone of Maria's grave. That would be pleasant, it would be sweet. He would take yellow flowers, yellow went so well with the gray marble.

Kneeling down, the old woman began a silent prayer. Her shriveled lips made circles, squares, and lines, executing a daily, divine gymnastics. Her knock-knees were resting on the last step of the vault, next to a plaque engraved with a classic but tender "To my beloved Husband." He slowly approached the widow and was getting ready to greet her politely, but she did not raise her head to look at him.

He continued on his way with the same painful steps. If he wasn't mistaken, he had hardly twenty meters to go.

He came to a wide intersection with a pink star on a circle

of pebbles at its center. He stopped, turned ninety degrees to his right, and found himself facing a dark marble stele erected on a rectangle of gravel. Two dwarf palm trees stood at attention, their fronds pointing toward the sky, guarding the monument on which four pots of flowers were blooming.

There it was! The second stop on his memorial journey. He hadn't been mistaken.

The stele represented a man tied to a stake with his hands behind his back. His body was arched backward under the impact of his enemies' bullets.

The epitaph engraved at the bottom of the plaque left no doubt: "To the men who were shot, to those who died so that French Algeria might live."

Still further down, on the base, four names were inscribed on the marble in large letters. When he saw them, the old man could not control his anger.

# CHAPTER 10

The sky above Perpignan was carrying ill-tempered icebergs whose violent collisions were making cataracts of water fall on the city, cleaning roofs, roads, people's souls. It had rained all night. The gutters on the buildings, acting as open faucets, were spewing their dirty water into the streets. Cold showers were spouting from balconies, and their continuous flow was bouncing furiously off sidewalks that were fortunately empty of pedestrians. The city's storm sewers could no longer handle all this water and puddles quickly became ponds.

Sebag was driving slowly. The old, struggling wiper on the car the police department provided for them was not able to clear the windshield the way it should, and Gilles felt as if he were looking through the glasses of a nearsighted person with weepy eyes. At the same time that he was watching the road, he was giving Molina a summary of the research he'd done the night before.

"There are in fact three monuments to the *Pieds-Noirs* that have aroused controversies in Perpignan over the past few years. In 2003 a stele in memory of OAS combatants was erected in the Haut-Vernet cemetery. Then in 2007, a 'Wall of the Disappeared' was installed at the Sainte-Claire convent; 3,000 names are inscribed on it, French people who are supposed to have disappeared during the Algerian War . . . "

"Why 'supposed to'?" Molina interrupted.

"At least one person whose name is on the list is still alive."

"That seems inappropriate!"

"The person concerned thought so, too. Finally, the third monument was opened recently: it's a museum of the French presence in Algeria."

To make room for a truck that was coming the other way, Sebag swerved to the right. The car drove through a deep puddle and threw up a spray of water worthy of a Japanese tsunami.

"Aren't you going to take the bridge?"

Molina's question surprised Sebag.

"Why? Bompas is this way, isn't it?"

"And how do you think you're going to cross the Têt?"

"By the ford. Do you think that . . . "

"With all that rain last night, it must be closed."

"You're right, I'm stupid, I never thought of that."

Sebag turned around and took the bridge that led to the refuse dump. Molina was correct, the Têt, the river that runs through Perpignan and then into the sea, had swollen in a few hours. The trickle of water had changed into a rushing torrent that was carrying along tree trunks of an impressive size. Despite the eight years he'd spent in Roussillon, Sebag still hadn't managed to get used to these sudden changes in the level of the water. His childhood near Versailles, and then the beginning of his career in the grain-growing desert of La Beauce, hadn't prepared him for the caprices of Mediterranean rivers. He'd discovered the idea of a ford when he moved to Perpignan. Before that, he'd known only bridges that looked down on watercourses and more often on railroad tracks and superhighways.

"So who are we going to see?"

"I told you yesterday: the representatives of the Collective Contra Nostalgeria."

"Yeah, I remember that, but I mean, are we seeing the president, the treasurer . . . ?"

"The president, in fact, along with a few other activists, I think. We're supposed to meet them in a bar in Bompas."

"Do you believe this lead will pan out?"

"I haven't any idea. So far as I'm concerned, it's too early to believe anything at all. Castello asked us to look into these groups, so we're going to do it. At least it will reassure the *Pieds-Noirs* to know that we're questioning their opponents as well."

"Yeah . . . I've got a feeling that we're going to have to watch our step, because these Nostalgeria guys are not going to appreciate our questions."

"Does that mean that you're accusing us?"

Sebag and Molina were facing a dozen offended individuals. Relations with the members of the Collective who had come to participate in the interview had been tense from the outset. Eight men and two women sat in a row on the bench in a bistro. They were activists on the left and extreme left who were obviously not fond of the police.

Sebag thought that for once Molina had shown tact and even subtlety. But their interlocutors were on their guards and didn't let anything pass. When Jacques asked if one of their members might have particular reasons to be angry with a former member of the OAS, the tension had risen another notch.

"Clearly, the police's methods haven't changed," a craggy old activist sputtered, pulling on his white ponytail.

"You can't help accusing everybody without any proof," added a big, bearded man wearing a T-shirt with an enormous "Here we come!" and embellished with a fine grease stain not foreseen by the designer.

Sebag had never understood the reservations, not to mention the hostility, felt by leftists with regard to the police. He'd chosen this line of work in order to defend victims, that is, the weakest people, and he felt himself to be in perfect harmony with the ideas of generosity and solidarity that the left claimed to support. Of course, he wasn't naive, and he knew that there were just as many creeps in the offices at police headquarters as in the bleachers at a soccer stadium, but that was not reason enough to reject a vocational group as a whole. All kinds of prejudice are wrong, he thought, including—*pace* the conventional left—anti-cop prejudice.

Seeing that his partner, as riled up by the activists' comments as a bull is by a *muleta*, was about to lash out, Sebag laid his hand on Molina's arm.

"We're not accusing anyone," he said in a calm but firm voice. "If we had to do that, it would take place not here but at police headquarters."

"Hitting us on the head with phone books to make us confess," a woman sneered. She wore no makeup and was without either charm or age, a sort of Mother Teresa of the secular left.

Sebag looked her straight in the eye.

"Have you often been hit with a phone book, Madame?"

"Uh . . . no, not me personally, but that doesn't mean that we're not acquainted with your methods."

"Better than I am, apparently," Sebag sighed. Then he smiled and added: "I don't have a phone book in my office. When I need to look up a number, I consult the yellow pages on the internet."

"Whoa, our police is state-of-the-art," sniggered a pretty young woman with arched eyebrows that gave her a perpetually astonished expression.

"We can assume that you must have come up with something else," the old activist said in an acerbic voice. "A good old dictionary, for example."

"Dictionaries have solid covers; they do damage and leave marks," Sebag pointed out. "Besides, the administration has not seen fit to provide us with them, the courts never having considered misspelled words on a parking ticket to be procedural errors."

Sebag looked at the activists facing him, one by one. He sensed that they didn't know what to say. Normally, their clumsy provocations made policemen angry. They weren't used to getting no reaction.

Gilles lingered over the emaciated face of a man in his fifties. His thick, black, curly hair fell over his wrinkled forehead. The man sat a little apart, hadn't said anything up to that point, and didn't seem to have any intention of speaking. He limited himself to staring at the policemen with his dark, piercing eyes.

Sebag's last remark had elicited a few smiles here and there. The voice of the old man with the ponytail made them fade immediately.

"So you're the good cop, right? And your partner's the big bad cop?"

"You watch too much television, Monsieur," Sebag replied. "What's your favorite series?"

"I don't watch TV, " the old man vigorously protested.

Had Sebag accused him of molesting little boys the man wouldn't have been more offended.

"It's a routine investigation that we're carrying out," he explained again. "A little old man was killed in Moulin-à-Vent and since it seems that the murder is connected with his past— he might be a former member of the OAS—we're gathering information from the associations that have recently opposed certain monuments to the memory of *Pieds-Noirs* . . . "

"To the falsification of history, you mean," an athletic man in his thirties corrected.

"That's your way of seeing things, the *Pieds-Noirs* see them differently . . . "

"And what's your way of seeing them?" Miss Arched Eyebrows suddenly asked.

"Mine doesn't matter, I'm not paid to choose one side or the other but to investigate without preconceptions. I have to look into everything that might be relevant."

"And so you thought of us, how nice of you," the old activist said mockingly, stroking his ponytail again.

"We can't expect cops to show imagination," the big bearded man added.

Sebag understood that he wouldn't get any useful information out of these people who took childish pleasure in replaying for the nth time the game of "the Resistance against the Gestapo." He realized that he'd made a mistake by accepting to meet them as a group. Individually, all these activists were probably charming and intelligent, but when they were in a group they offered only a caricature of themselves. He wasn't surprised or upset, just a little annoyed. He'd organized this meeting because it was part of the investigation, but he hadn't had high hopes for it. Molina hadn't either; he was fidgeting on his chair, impatient to be allowed to lay into them. It was time to cut their losses.

Sebag suddenly stood up.

"All that remains is for me to thank you for your valuable help. A murderer is on the loose, and he might kill again. If that happens, I'll be sure to let you know."

"If this guy kills only old fascists, I personally have no problem with that," the old activist with a ponytail said, though his gibe didn't receive the approval he'd expected from his companions.

Sebag didn't let that blunder pass.

"I thought you were against capital punishment. I didn't know that you made exceptions."

His retort struck home, and the inspectors took advantage of the resulting confusion to take their leave. Back in the car, Molina gave his exasperation free rein:

"They make me laugh, all those jerks. They think they're

heroes because they didn't answer our questions. But when someday they're attacked by a hoodlum, they'll come to the cop house and cry like everyone else, you'll see. And they'll complain louder than the others if we don't find their attackers fast enough. How can we do our work if too many people refuse to answer the most ordinary questions, for fuck's sake?"

He drove off with screeching tires, Starsky and Hutch style.

Basically, Sebag thought he was right. The French have never liked cops, but in the past at least they tried to get along without them. These days, at the slightest problem—a marital dispute, an argument with a neighbor, a rebellious teenager who has run away—they call the police.

"In any case, I know them all, these leftists," Molina went on heatedly. "I have a pal at the RG,[4] he'll send me their files. I promise you that I'm going to dig into their past and that of their families, and if I find any connection between one of them and the OAS, I'll bring him in right away. And he'd better get a good lawyer. *Em cago en les mares que els va parir!*"[5]

Sebag preferred to remain silent. Molina had sworn in Catalan, and that was a very bad sign. Above all, he didn't want to add to his partner's irritation.

It was still raining with the same intensity, and cars were moving at a snail's pace on all the city's main arteries. Molina calmed his nerves by playing Fangio[6] in the narrow streets of Perpignan, which he knew by heart, as if a GPS had been implanted in his brain at birth. These urban twists and turns ended up giving Sebag the beginning of a headache.

"Papa, you've got an SMS."

Séverine's voice had resounded in the pocket of Sebag's

---

[4] *Direction Centrale des Renseignements Généraux* (Central Directorate of General Intelligence).
[5] "And I shit on the mothers who gave birth to them!"
[6] Juan Manuel Fangio (1911–1995) was an Argentine driver who dominated the first decade of Formula 1 racing.

raincoat. He pulled out his cell phone and saw that there was in fact a message. Claire wrote to tell him that the evening rehearsal for her chorale had been cancelled because of the bad weather. Gilles couldn't help smiling with satisfaction. Blessed be this rain that kept his adored spouse in the family home. Since that terrible last summer, he suffered every time Claire went out without him. A jealous husband, that's what he'd become, and he didn't like himself in that role, because he knew that jealousy fed less on love than on self-love. He didn't want to let the monster thrive in his belly. Claire loved him, he was sure of that. That was what mattered, but he sometimes found it hard to remain convinced of it.

It was one thing to make that decision in his head and another to live it in his gut.

Sebag typed out, "O.K., thanks to the rain," with a clumsy finger before putting his phone back in his pocket.

"Your ringtone is terrible," Molina commented without taking his eyes off the road. He'd turned on the headlights, and their glow transformed the drops into Christmas garlands.

"You think?"

"It's a little stupid, yeah."

"What's your ringtone?"

"Jordi Barre's 'Els hi fotrem.'"

"Don't know it!"

"You don't know Jordi?"

"Of course I do."

Jordi Barre was a Perpignan singer who had recently died at the very venerable age of ninety. A crystalline voice like Tino Rossi's, melodies that were slightly old-fashioned but touched the heart and soul of people who lived in the area. Everyone knew Jordi and Jordi knew everyone. When he died, Catalans felt like they'd lost their grandfather as well as their poet.

"I know Jordi Barre but not that song."

"It's the one they sing in unison at Aimé-Giral stadium

every time the USAP scores a goal. In French it means 'we're going to stick it to them.'

"It certainly isn't Jordi's most poetic song . . . "

"True . . . "

"And you really believe that having put that refrain on your cell phone authorizes you to speak as an expert?"

"That's not silly!"

"It may not be silly, but it's pretty stupid anyway!"

Instead of getting mad, Molina bellowed the refrain, transforming Sebag's nascent pain into a splitting headache.

# CHAPTER 11

**Algiers, December 7, 1961**

The city's breathing is gradually calming down. Its pulse is beating less rapidly. Night is gently falling.

The streetlights are coming on, one after the other. Open windows let the nasal voices of the announcers on Radio Algiers be heard on the sidewalks below. It's time for the news broadcast on the country's main station.

Sigma and Babelo, hidden in the shadow of a streetlamp, are waiting at one end of the street; Omega and Bizerte are waiting just as unobtrusively at the other end. The police headquarters is between the two armed groups. The commando is waiting for Inspector Michel to come out.

Babelo offers another cigarette to Sigma. A mild American one. The young combatant takes advantage of this boon and the two men begin to smoke in silence, surrounding themselves with a mentholated haze. Babelo keeps his eyes on the window of the police station. He's waiting for a signal. Inspector Michel doesn't have many friends among his colleagues. Having arrived from metropolitan France four years ago, he's pursuing indefatigably his investigations into the OAS's activities, believing that despite the growing confusion his work still has meaning. He recently made it possible to arrest two activists in the clandestine organization who were responsible for an attack on an Arab café. The two men spent forty-eight hours in prison before escaping with the help of their guards.

Babelo takes a drag on his cigarette and then throws it in the gutter. The thing was only half-smoked, but he has just spotted a red shirt at the window. He takes out his pistol, cocks it, and takes a step into the light to indicate that he has received the signal. Then he moves back into the shadows. At the other end of the street, Bizerte and Omega have seen his movement. They prepare their weapons. The cop doesn't usually go that way, but just in case, they're ready.

A dark silhouette soon appears on the doorstep of the police headquarters. Inspector Michel hesitates for a moment. To the left or to the right? Routine can be a terrible enemy when you're risking your life at every street corner. But changing your routine every day becomes another routine.

"In any case, you've had it," Babelo murmurs between tight-drawn lips.

The cop ends up making his choice and walks quickly toward Sigma and his boss. The young man feels a cold calm invading him. His senses become ten times more acute. He feels the cold metal of the gun against the palm of his hand, and in his throat, the last bittersweet flavors of the American tobacco. His eyelids squint, and behind them two tranquil pupils watch the target as he approaches them more slowly. The sound of the nailed shoes striking the pavement resounds in his ears. When he discerns in his nostrils an odor of rancid sweat mixed with lavender cologne, he knows that it is time to raise his gun.

The inspector suddenly stops. He turns around and sees Bizerte and Omega following him, revolvers in their hands. Michel takes his hand out of his jacket pocket. He too is armed, he too is ready to fight.

But he doesn't know that now the main danger is behind him.

Sigma's eyes meet Babelo's. His boss makes a face followed by a little movement of his chin, offering Sigma the honor of firing first.

The young man takes three silent steps forward, then hesitates. The target has his back to him, he doesn't like that. His hand grips the gun. He hears Babelo coming up behind him.

"Inspector . . . "

Sigma has spoken in a calm voice. Without fear or impatience. The policeman jumps, then turns around. Their eyes met and understand each other. They both know, before the first shot is fired, who is the killer and who the victim. Sigma fires twice. One bullet in the belly, another in the heart.

Two more shots immediately ring out behind Sigma. Babelo has aimed at the head. One bullet penetrates the right eye, the other makes part of the brain spurt out on the sidewalk. The policeman's body collapses in the gutter.

"Shit! What got into you?" Babelo fumes as Bizerte and Omega run up to them. You scared me! What were you doing, speaking to him before you fired? Have you seen that in the movies, or something? You're not at the movies here, pal, this is real life . . . "

The four members of the commando stand there for a few seconds, fascinated by the sight of their victim's body. There's no hurry. The street is theirs.

"One less son-of-a-bitch," Omega belches before spitting a gelatinous glob of saliva on the pavement.

The sound of a spoon striking a cooking pot comes through a window, soon followed by another, and then another. It becomes a concert. Metallic and deafening. European Algiers is saluting its heroes.

Babelo offers his men a round of American cigarettes. Bizerte holds out to each of them the yellow flame of a lighter. And the four members of the commando take a long drag on their cigarettes before they walk away. No policeman has yet wanted or dared to come out of police headquarters.

"We'll pick up the car and go to the Vox," Babelo suggests. "*One-Eyed Jacks*, a film with Marlon Brando as both the star and the director. I'll treat you to the best seats in the house."

Babelo gives Sigma a thump on the back.

"I sometimes wonder if I'm not making a mistake by taking you to the movies every time. There are people who get a little too excited when they watch westerns. They end up thinking they're John Wayne. One day that'll get you in trouble, Sigma. Be careful."

# CHAPTER 12

The hallways at police headquarters were overflowing with cops in civvies and in uniform. It smelled like sweat and wet dogs. A dense mist stuck to the windows and the lenses of people's glasses. When the rain poured down that way on the Catalan country—once or twice in the autumn, and again in the spring—life stopped throughout the region. The crime rate fell to zero, as hoodlums big and small remained prudently holed up at home. Delightful moments for policemen, with the exception of the least fortunate and those with the worst records, who had to go out into the deluge to help the emergency personnel with their tasks.

Sebag and Molina ran into Ménard on the stairs.

"Any news?" he asked them.

"Not much, no," Sebag said grimly. "How about you?"

"A confirmation: Martinez did in fact belong to the OAS."

"Wow, tell us about it," Sebag said impatiently.

Molina jumped in.

"We're not going to talk about it right here on the stairs, boys. It's almost noon. How about going to grab a bite at the Carlit?"

"It's a little early, isn't it?" Ménard protested.

"So what? We'll be back to work that much earlier."

The conscientious Ménard found Molina's argument persuasive, and the three lieutenants ran across the Avenue de Grande-Bretagne and took refuge in the restaurant. "*Hola, com vas?*" Rafel, the owner of the Carlit, greeted them with a smile. "Fortunately there are cops on stormy days, otherwise I'd just have to close the door and go home. What can I serve you as an aperitif? I've just received a nice little amber Rivesaltes that is going to delight your palates."

"Give us three of those, please," Molina said approvingly, knowing full well that Ménard was going to decline the offer.

"Uh, not for me," their colleague said in fact.

"I'm paying this round," Molina insisted.

"Well, then, a Coca-Cola."

"*Cap de cony!*"[7] belched Rafel. "I don't do chemistry"

"You don't have Coca-Cola?"

"I have Cat Cola."

"I suppose that's not chemical?"

"Yes it is! But it's chemistry from around here. It's less bad for you!"

Rafel, who in his spare time was active in a small group devoted to identity politics, took out of his refrigerator a bottle whose label copied the red and white colors of the famous brand and juxtaposed them with the blood-red and gold of the Catalan flag.

"*És un refresc elaborat amb aigua de deu natural gasificada i extractes naturals vegetals…*"[8]

"You don't have to read me the label," Ménard grumbled. "There are things I can understand, even in Catalan."

The three inspectors hung their wet raincoats on the coatrack before going to sit down at the little table near the bay window. A moment later Rafel came back with a tray and set down three full glasses, two little ones and one big one.

"What's your lunch special today?" Molina asked.

"*Ouillade.*"

---

[7] "Shithead."

[8] "It's a beverage made with sparkling spring water and natural vegetable extracts . . . "

Ménard's eyes opened wide. He was from Picardy, in the north of France, and still hadn't gotten used to the customs and typical dishes of Catalonia, despite his many years in the region.

"It's a kind of hot pot with bacon, blood sausage, cabbage, potatoes, and white beans," Sebag explained. "Dietetic, in other words!"

"Oh, yes! That's right, I've had it before. Right here, in fact, I think. It's very good."

"So we'll all have it," Sebag concluded, knowing Molina's tastes.

He wet his lips with the glass of amber muscat wine, savoring its mellowness with his eyes closed before turning to Ménard.

"So, Martinez and the OAS?"

"This morning I contacted another historian, Michel Sonate. He's based in Marseille and the OAS is his specialty. He has undertaken a study on the former activists—the reasons they joined, what they did, what they think about it now, and so on. He'd met Martinez a couple of weeks ago."

"Great!" Sebag exclaimed. "And what did he tell him?"

"Nothing very specific, unfortunately. He talked about his motivations. In fact, he never really believed that clandestine combat would succeed, he claimed, but at the time he couldn't bring himself to stand by and watch French Algeria being liquidated. He absolutely wanted to do something, anything at all, so long as he acted."

"And what exactly did he do?" Sebag asked.

"He didn't want to talk about that: he limited himself to claiming that he'd managed to take over Radio Algiers's frequencies. The historian acknowledges that he finds it hard to get former members of the OAS to talk about their actions. They all remain very discreet."

"You must be kidding! They're ashamed . . . " Molina interjected.

"I think it's a little more complex than that," Ménard said. "They always admit that they were involved at the time and still show a lot of hostility and resentment toward France in general and toward de Gaulle in particular. In their view, their only possible choice was to keep Algeria part of France."

"So, apart from the confirmation that Martinez belonged to the OAS, we don't have much else," Sebag observed without being able to conceal his disappointment.

He saw Ménard's face fall and understood that he'd annoyed him. He tried to make up for it.

"And . . . that's already very important. We suspected it, but we had to be certain. That was the main thing Castello asked of us. Now we have to find other former members of the OAS in the area. Could your historian give you any names?"

"Not yet. He's questioned an incredible number of people for the book he's writing, but his interview notes aren't classified by the places where they live. Apparently he's a really old-fashioned guy and doesn't computerize anything."

Sebag didn't listen to the rest of what Ménard said. Outside the window he'd just seen Lieutenant Cardona carefully crossing the slippery street in their direction, and when their eyes met he saw trouble coming.

The head of the Accidents group at the Perpignan police headquarters burst into the restaurant. Without greeting the owner, he came and planted himself in front of the three inspectors.

"What the hell are you guys up to?"

Molina sat up straight on his chair, annoyed at this interruption of their conversation.

"Hello."

Cardona looked him up and down and asked his question again.

"What are you up to?"

"What are you talking about, Estève?"

Cardona looked at Molina, then at Sebag, who understood. Trembling with rage, he pointed his finger at Sebag.

"He knows what I'm talking about."

They all looked at Gilles, who tried to smile.

"What's all this mess?" Molina asked.

Cardona ignored him and addressed himself icily to Sebag.

"I had Mme. Grangier on the phone this morning. She's Pascal Lucas's lawyer, you know her?"

"The lawyer? No."

"But you do know her client."

It was not a question. Sebag nonetheless nodded.

"I saw him yesterday."

"And you have no problem with that? You're trampling on my turf without saying anything and you think that's O.K.?"

"Mathieu's family asked me to have a look at the file, just to be sure that nothing had been overlooked."

"And meeting with the person responsible for the accident, that's what you call 'having a look at the file?'"

Ménard's and Molina's eyes jumped back and forth from Sebag to Cardona and from Cardona to Sebag. It was like being at a tennis match.

"I began by examining the accident report and then I wanted to clear up a few points that seemed to me somewhat obscure."

"And you couldn't have talked to me about it?"

"What would you have told me? That it was your business and didn't concern me!"

"Probably . . . "

"Well then, you see . . . There wouldn't have been any point to it."

"It's my case," Cardona said heatedly. "You had no business messing around in it."

His face was getting beet-red, accentuating the flamboyance of his blond, greasy hair combed straight back on his head.

"The family want to be sure that the investigators . . . I mean, the investigation didn't neglect certain aspects of the case."

"And you think that you're authorized to supervise my work? I don't neglect anything."

"I just wanted to be sure about this business regarding the white Clio."

"There was no such car, goddamn it. Lucas is the only one who saw it. None of the witnesses confirms what he said! The guy is trying to protect himself, that's all, we can't be naive here. I don't have time to waste on all this nonsense . . . "

They fell silent for a moment. Molina and Ménard held their breath. Sebag looked his adversary in the eye and said in a steady, calm voice, trying to avoid aggravating matters:

"My daughter was very close to young Mathieu. I promised her that I would check out all the leads. And I'm going to do that."

Cardona banged his fist on the table, knocking over the glass of Cat Cola. All the conversations in the restaurant had stopped.

"If you go on that way, it's going to turn out badly. Who do you think you are, to give me lessons and tell me what to do? I'm warning you, I'm not going to let some good-for-nothing Parisian shit all over me. Is it because I'm a Catalan that you think I can't handle a case properly without your help?"

"I never said that, that's utter nonsense!"

Molina slowly rose to his feet and rolled his former rugby player's shoulders.

"You're beginning to cross the line, Cardo. And it's a Catalan who's telling you to shut up now."

"I'm not talking to you, Molina . . . "

"Yes, but I'm the one who's hearing you and you're hurting my ears."

Cardona cranked his tone down a notch. He'd also played rugby, but wasn't nearly as hefty as Molina.

"Are you O.K. with what he did?"

"If it's a promise he made to his daughter, there's nothing to be said, it's sacred."

"Do you think our bosses would say the same if they knew?"

"Are you going to snitch?"

Sebag got up as well. It was time to calm things down.

"I'm going to make you a promise, too, Cardona. If I find something, you will be the first to hear about it. And you can take all the credit."

He let a few seconds pass. Cardona still didn't seem convinced but didn't say any more.

"Think about it carefully, because if you decide to file a complaint, I'm going to pursue this no matter what, and if I find something, you're the one who's going to look bad."

Cardona still kept silent; he was weighing the pros and cons. But Sebag was confident. The carrot and stick tactic was as old as the hills, but it still worked.

"Sounds to me like a fair deal," Molina said. "You've got nothing to lose, in the end, and everything to gain. Because Gilles may be a Parisian, but he's also an ace detective, and if there's anything to be found in this case, you can be sure he'll find it."

"There isn't anything," Cardona grumbled, and then looked at them one by one, including Ménard, who had kept out of the discussion.

Rafel came to wipe off the table and replace the spilled cola. One at a time, conversations started up again in the restaurant.

"Do you want something to drink, Estève?" Rafel asked.

"No, I don't have the time."

Sebag and Molina sat down again and swallowed a big mouthful of their amber muscat. Cardona shook his head and his face gradually relaxed.

"O.K., I'll let it go this time, and we'll handle it the way you said. But no stabs in the back, O.K.?"

"Don't worry. I'm not doing this for the glory, only for my daughter."

Cardona snorted.

"Yeah, sure, and it's too bad for her and for you, too, because you won't find anything."

"If there's nothing to find, I won't find anything, we can agree on that."

"Don't say I didn't warn you. Don't come crying to me."

"No chance of that," Molina interrupted. "That's not how we do things here."

"So, *tot va be*," Cardona concluded. "*Adéu*." He turned on his heel and rapidly walked away.

"*Adéu*, you poor jerk," Molina said in a low voice.

Cardona left the restaurant and went back to headquarters. It was still raining hard: it was as heavy and dusky as a dark beer drinker's piss. The three inspectors finished their aperitif, looking out at the rain without talking.

Rafel brought three bowls full of *ouillade*, hot and fragrant. It was only after the third mouthful that Molina broke the silence.

"All the same, that was a dirty trick you played on him."

Sebag shrugged.

"I wouldn't have liked it if you'd done the same thing to me," Ménard added.

"Except I wouldn't have done it to you," Sebag assured him. "I wouldn't have doubted your investigation."

"So that was what the big bald guy, your date yesterday at noon, was about?" Molina asked.

Sebag admitted it with a wink.

"You could have told me about it."

"I didn't want to get you involved in a risky business."

"It's okay. We almost paid for a *ouillade* twice today."

Sebag smiled but Ménard sat there stone-faced. He hadn't understood the play on words.

Molina deciphered it for him:

"In Catalan, a *ouillade* is also a fight. It's the term they use in rugby matches when the players' blood is up."

Molina suddenly looked at his empty glass.

"Didn't Rafel forget something?"

He called out to the owner:

"Hey, Rafel, bring us a bottle of Canon du Maréchal to decorate the table. With this lousy weather, we need more color here."

"I'm sorry to have gotten you mixed up in this thing with Cardona," Sebag said.

"I'm not. He's been annoying me for years, that guy. We played together on the USAP's junior team and he's never pardoned me for making the first team whereas he ended up in the amateur league."

He stuffed a big forkful of bacon and cabbage in his mouth and went on:

"In any case, I hope you haven't gotten into this without knowing what you're doing, because he's not going to cut you any slack. He's a nasty one."

Sebag just gave him a smile that he hoped was enigmatic, but Molina was not fooled.

"Damn, could you be any more sure of yourself than that? Then you'll just have to pray that he fucked up his investigation. On the other hand, it's entirely possible that he did. Cardona's as stupid as he is nasty. But what can I say? He's not even a real Catalan. His father came from Andalusia!"

"Gentlemen, I have asked you to come to my office so that we can proceed more quickly. I have to take a plane for Paris at 6 P.M. and don't have a lot of time. I'll be concise and ask you to do the same."

Superintendent Castello was in a foul mood. He had to attend the big annual meeting of the departmental national security directors at the Ministry of the Interior. They were all supposed to compare their crime statistics, and those of the Perpignan headquarters were not good. Castello was going to be reprimanded in front of all his colleagues and that made him furious. Especially since he boasted of being the only one who hadn't falsified his figures.

"I've just received the last results that hadn't yet come in. First of all, the autopsy: Bernard Martinez was in fact killed by a bullet shot at point-blank range and his death occurred last Wednesday, probably in the afternoon. I'll spare you the bullet's trajectory and the damage done to the brain's vital functions; you can find all that, if you want, in the copies of the medical examiner's report that I will have sent to you."

He caught his breath before continuing.

"The ballistics expert also confirms that Martinez's murderer was standing behind his victim when he fired. From the angle of the shot, our experts conclude that the murderer is of . . . medium height, between 5'9" and 5'10". You will see the importance of this fundamental advance in the investigation! Otherwise, the weapon used was a Beretta 34 9 mm short, a weapon that came out in the 1930s and was used especially by the Italian police up until the early 1980s. But it circulated widely in Europe, especially after the Second World War, because it was also used by the Wehrmacht. There, that's about all I had to say to you."

"What about the white hair Pagès found?" Ménard asked, eliciting a smile from Molina.

"The DNA analysis is still underway. It may take a while because it wasn't considered a priority. It's mainly our head of the forensic police who seems to take an interest in it, and our friend is on reduced time for a few days. Since he didn't retire as planned, he's taking days off!"

"He could be usefully replaced by his assistant," Molina said ironically.

"Thank you for that brilliant comment, that really advances

our work. You don't have any new information to give us about the investigation?"

Molina reported with persistent bitterness on the morning's interview with the activists from the Collective Contra Nostalgeria. Castello then gave the floor to Lambert and Llach, who had interviewed almost all the tenants in Martinez's apartment building without gleaning any interesting information. In fact, Ménard was the only one who had contributed something new. Castello started pacing around the room, circling his team.

"More than ever, then, it's the lead of an old settling of political accounts that has to be followed. Any objections?"

No one responded. The inspectors all remained stock-still, not far from standing at attention. Sebag thought again about Albouker's telephone call the day before and his paranoid notion, but didn't think it would be useful to mention it.

Castello abruptly stopped walking.

"Gentlemen, forgive me the expression, but we're in deep shit!"

The superintendent looked at them one by one. Ménard, Molina, Sebag, Lambert, and Llach. As usual, Raynaud and Moreno were "busy" with another case.

"We're in deep shit because this first answer leads us to immediately ask ourselves another question: is this settling of accounts over and done with, or do we have to fear that there will be other victims? Gentlemen, your opinions?"

People exchanged grimaces. To compensate for his inefficiency that morning, Sebag decided that for once he would be the first to speak up.

"We might think so, and even fear it, but we don't want to complicate matters too much, because the investigation has turned up nothing that allows us to give a categorical answer to that question."

"That's my feeling as well," Castello said, without waiting for the others' opinions. "Whatever happens over the following days, we'll need a kind of map of the *Pied-Noir* milieu: I want to know who, here in Perpignan, used to belong to the OAS. Ménard, you get back in contact with your historian and make him cough up all this information."

"It won't be easy . . . "

"Why? Is he another one who doesn't want to collaborate with the police? We're going to have to find another word—'collaborate' is necessarily pejorative."

"Cooperate?" Ménard suggested.

"*Voilà*, that's perfect, cooperate. So, your historian François, he doesn't want to . . . cooperate?"

"That's not the question, it's just that there's a practical problem: he's based in Marseille."

"So?"

Ménard was caught off guard and stammered:

"Well . . . it's that . . . I . . . I'm in Perpignan."

"Do you have something against trains?"

"Uh . . . no. Absolutely not."

"Then find one for tomorrow morning and by noon you'll be there. Other objections? Do you want me to help you look up the departure times?"

Ménard blushed and frowned.

"No, that's O.K. Thanks, Superintendent."

"Great."

Castello turned to Sebag.

"Gilles, you're going to completely immerse yourself in the *Pied-Noir* community in the area, I want you to meet each of its members. You, too, will have to find out who used to belong to the OAS and who knew Martinez's past. You will remain in permanent contact with Ménard and as soon as he gives you a name, you will meet with that individual. But don't wait for his information, start fishing on your own end."

Sebag, as a good soldier, approved with a nod of his head. Castello then addressed Jacques.

"Molina, you will sift through this milieu of anti-*Pied-Noir* leftists. Quietly at first. Inform yourself about each of them, but I want a list ready by tomorrow evening. This case is going to get out, and we have to be ready to react. Lambert will help you."

Sebag saw his partner's face close up. The first part of his assignment pleased him, the second much less. The superintendent finished the distribution of tasks with Llach.

"Joan, up to this point we've been operating on the principle that this affair began a few days ago in Perpignan, but we can't exclude the possibility that it is only one geographical and chronological stage in a larger case. So you will carry out a search at the national level: I want to know where and when another *Pied-Noir* has been murdered in, let's say, the last three years."

"That's an enormous job," Llach protested, "especially since the victims are never classified by the community they belong to. '*Pied-noir*' doesn't mean anything; I'll never find anything that way . . . "

Castello swept the argument aside with a gesture.

"You'll start with the date and place of birth, that's not so hard. A victim who is of French ancestry and was born in Algeria before 1962 is a *Pied-Noir*. Period. It's not that complicated.

"Still . . . "

Molina winked at Sebag. He wasn't going to miss the opportunity.

"I can get along by myself. If Joan needs help, he can take Lambert with him."

"That's a good idea," Castello said.

Llach couldn't repress a grimace, while Molina grinned. Lambert was delighted to feel that he was indispensable.

"This is a kind of double-or-nothing case. It's going to make people talk about us, and that's worth all the statistics in the world. On the condition, of course, that we succeed in solving it. Otherwise . . . "

Castello rubbed the tip of this nose vigorously:

"Otherwise, as I said, we're in deep shit! Gentlemen, dismissed."

# CHAPTER 13

He was walking slowly through the streets of the old Spanish village of La Jonquera. He'd thought it prudent to put a border between him and the police investigation being conducted in Perpignan. On this side of the Pyrenees, the rain had stopped in the late afternoon and he could take his daily walk. The doctor had warned him a thousand times: given his condition, inactivity was the worst possible thing for him. In spite of the pain, he had to move.

He approached a small shop whose display window was decorated with small posters in bright colors. They boasted about unbeatable telephone rates and listed a series of exotic places one could call: Caracas, Manila, Lima, Mexico City, Buenos Aires . . . Exotic for someone from south Catalonia, but not for him.

He opened the door of the shop, making a bell ring softly. Behind the counter, a young man smiled at him warmly.

"*Bon dia*," he said in Catalan.

"*Bon dia*," the old man replied.

This was his sole concession to the second official language of south Catalonia. He didn't recognize the Spain where he had lived for a few months, long ago. Franco had unified the country, what a stupid idea it had been to want to go backwards. And then Spanish—Castilian, as some people treacherously preferred to call it—was such a beautiful language. When had it supplanted French in his heart and on his lips? He no longer remembered. As early as the 1970s, perhaps.

And certainly after the birth of his daughter, thirty-three years ago. He'd never uttered a single word of French in front of Consuela, and she didn't know a single word of the language of Voltaire.

She didn't even know who Voltaire was.

He'd found his return to his native language disappointing. After so many years, he'd been afraid he would feel a terrible nostalgia. But he didn't feel anything. Nothing at all. The French that people spoke today in the streets and in the media had nothing in common with the language he'd spoken earlier. And the Perpignan accent did not have the charm for his ears that the accent of his youth had had. A matter of music and tempo. And also of passion.

He gave his daughter's number to the young man, who pointed him toward a booth. It was 10 P.M. in La Jonquera, 5 P.M. where his family lived. Gabriella had just come home from school. He took great pleasure in hearing her voice again. It was difficult to go several days without talking to his grand-daughter. It hadn't been like that with Consuela. Maybe that was one reason for their estrangement.

The tinkle of a marimba came over the line for several long seconds. Then the ring. So close and yet so far.

"Hola."

Consuela's voice sounded happy.

"Hola, it's Papa."

"   . . .   "

"Are you O.K.?"

"   . . .   "

"I'm fine. I'm still traveling in the old country but I often think of you and Gabriella. Is she O.K.?"

The connection was good but the receiver pitilessly conveyed the echoes of a hostile silence. He hadn't been able to communicate with his daughter for ten years, and that had nothing to do with the caprices of modern technology.

"Could you put Gabriella on the line, please?"

The disagreeable sound of a telephone slammed down on a table broke the silence and attacked his left eardrum. The pain soon stopped under the caress of a soft and melodious voice.

"Hello, Grandpa."

Spanish was really the most beautiful of languages when it was spoken by his granddaughter.

"Good evening, my little Gabriella."

"Good evening?"

"Yes, here it's late, you know. It's night already. How are you doing?"

"Very well. Today I got an 18 in math. Aurelia only got a 15. How are you?"

When she asked that kind of question, he realized that his granddaughter was growing up. A few months earlier she would never have inquired about his health.

"I'm fine."

"Your bogeyman's hands aren't hurting you too much?"

"From time to time, yes, but it's bearable. What's hard is being so far away from you."

"Then you shouldn't have left, Grandpa. I miss you, too."

"How's your mother?"

"She's fine. She often says that she's tired out by her work, but I think it's going O.K."

"Do you think she misses me, too?" Gabriella hesitated to reply and her loving grandfather was immediately sorry that he'd involved her in their adult quarrels.

"I don't know, she never says so. Why don't you get along?"

"It's complicated. Grown-ups' problems are always complicated, you know."

"Then I don't want to grow up. Never. I don't want to not get along with you."

He reassured Gabriella and turned their conversation

toward the trivial subjects that constitute the daily life of an eight-year-old girl. Friends, games, meals, school.

Then he regretfully said goodbye and hung up.

On the way back, he thought again about the rest of his mission. The first part had gone as planned. He'd hit his first target, and located the others. He just needed a little patience. But he'd never lacked that quality.

The second target would soon be back. Soon he would be within his grasp. There had been a little problem. Without importance. He even thought that this unforeseen delay would ultimately make his task easier. But he wasn't wasting his time because he had begun to prepare the third part of his mission.

The most delicate one.

He returned to the hotel and had a snack brought up to him. Two slices of bread rubbed with garlic and tomatoes. *Pa amb tomàquet.* Delicious and more than enough. Since Maria's death, he'd lost the habit of eating in the evening.

After this frugal dinner, he took his sleeping pill and then his medicines for blood pressure and rheumatism. He liked to go to bed early, and he wasn't used to staying up so late. The time difference had forced him to make this exception, but he didn't regret it. The voice of his little Gabriella was still singing in his head. For once, sleep came immediately.

# CHAPTER 14

S ebag had finished shaving and was looking at his face in the mirror. He gently ran his finger over the vertical wrinkle that had been developing between his eyebrows for several years. He got that from his father.

He didn't like it.

He detested everything that came to him from that man who had betrayed them, left them, him and his mother.

"What are you thinking about?"

Claire had pressed herself up to his naked back. He hadn't heard her coming.

"Nothing."

"Liar . . . "

She pinched his cheek.

"Do I know her?" Gilles couldn't keep from pouting. Claire, who was watching him in the mirror, noticed it. Gilles turned around and took his wife in his arms.

"We've been together for almost twenty years and there has never been anyone but you," he said, looking deep into her eyes.

"And . . . you're beginning to find that a long time?" Claire said evasively, smiling.

"When you're in love, you're always twenty."

"That's nice . . . "

"What about you? Does it seem a long time to you?"

She put her lips on his. Their mouths opened and their tongues caressed each other. A few seconds of eternity. Despite the taste of peppermint toothpaste that they exchanged.

"Did you like my response?"

"It was nice, too."

It was hard for them to part from each other.

"I'm going to be late," she said.

Gilles watched her put on her makeup. Here nascent wrinkles didn't come from anyone. Or maybe from her joyous heart and her good nature. He admired his wife and especially he envied her. He loved her steady temper, her easygoing ways, and her *joie de vivre*. She knew how to take things as they came without letting herself be invaded by pointless fears and useless worries. In contrast, he was often melancholic and uneasy. It had always been like that. But it had become even more pronounced since he'd started down the other side of forty. And even more since he'd started being suspicious last summer.

In the kitchen, Gilles allowed himself a second cup of coffee. The children had given him a professional espresso machine for his birthday, the kind that made coffee that turned an Italian green with jealousy. He opted for a mocha that he stirred with his eyes closed.

Claire's purse started to vibrate. She had set it open on a corner of the table. Gilles approached it as if he were dealing with a wild animal. He spotted the telephone stuck between the card holder and the coin purse. The temptation was strong. These days, cell phones were the best confidants but they were also the worst traitors. In the call list, the text messages, and the e-mails, secrets were often hidden, the little and intimate ones, the serious and more painful ones. He was in a position to know that people showed no prudence with this new accomplice, which was as featherbrained as it was indifferent. How many cases had been solved just because the criminal hadn't been careful enough in cleaning out an electronic memory? And how many adulterous affairs had been revealed by a simple indiscreet manipulation?

It would be so easy. Just tap a key and consult her phone.

If Claire had had a lover, she probably wouldn't have erased all the text messages. She would have kept at least one, for the ecstatic pleasure of remembering. If Claire had had a lover, she would never have thought to erase the repository of all the calls. If Claire had had a lover, she would surely have mentioned him somewhere in her messages to her girlfriends.

The telephone finally fell silent. The temptation remained.

All the questions he'd been constantly asking himself for weeks had their answers in the circuits of this damned telephone! He just had to make a move. A simple move.

He quickly retreated before this ferocious beast that was taunting him.

Outside, the sky was continuing to weep hot tears. Its sorrow had known only short pauses during the night, and the earth could no longer soak up all that sadness.

Lost in his thoughts, Sebag was no longer paying attention to where he was going and he set his foot in a mud puddle as he was getting into the car.

"Shit!"

He used the bottom of the car's body to scrape as much of the mud as possible off the sole of his shoe and especially around it. Then, fairly annoyed, he started the car.

The radio helped him calm down. He'd turned it to a continuous news station. Always the same tone, often the same rhythm, sometimes the same words. Similar voices with identical intonations. He was no longer listening. Whatever the subject, the journalistic logorrhea lulled him better than the sweetest of melodies.

The Arago bridge leading to the center of Perpignan was already almost bumper to bumper. Why was it that the more the speed of the water passing under a bridge grew, the more that of the cars passing over it slowed? He tried to concentrate on the investigation, but only partially succeeded.

Parts of the case passed through his mind without really sticking there. He'd just turned right after crossing the bridge when his cell phone rang.

"It's Castello. Where are you?"

"I'm on my way to headquarters. I'll be there in a couple of minutes."

"No point in going any further. I need you to go to the Haut-Vernet cemetery right away. Our guys are waiting for you there."

"What's going on over there, Superintendent?"

"You'll understand when you get there. I don't have time to tell you more. I'm in Paris and I'm going into a meeting. And hang up quick—you're not supposed to be on the phone when you're driving, it's dangerous!"

Surprised by the facetious tone his boss had adopted just as he was about to go into an important meeting in the course of which he was supposed to be reprimanded, Sebag made a U-turn in front of police headquarters and drove back over the Arago bridge.

He noted with pleasure that it was easier to go upstream in traffic than in a rising river. "Hmm, I'm becoming facetious myself," he mumbled to himself, astonished by his change in mood in the course of a few minutes at most. He recalled a famous quotation whose author he didn't know: "Humor is the politeness of despair." He turned the sentence over and over in his head before finally deciding to reject it. It couldn't be suitable for his reality, it was too exaggerated. And then his marital situation was in no way desperate. It was just dreadfully banal.

As for his humor . . .

He was at that point in his reflections when he arrived at the entrance to the Haut-Vernet cemetery. A young police officer in uniform was waiting for him under the entry porch. He came up to the driver's-side window. With his index finger, Sebag lowered the glass.

"You can drive your car in," the policeman suggested. "With

this weather, that will be more convenient. My colleagues are already there. You can't miss them."

He turned around to point the way:

"You see that fork there? Take the right-hand lane, and afterward it's straight ahead."

Sebag thanked him, closed the window, and went ahead. He drove slowly about a hundred meters to reach a large traffic circle where a police car was already parked. He grabbed the raincoat on the passenger seat and put it on before going out into the downpour.

The door of the other car opened at the same time as his. An umbrella came out first, then a stocky silhouette. Next Sebag saw coming towards him a face that looked like a stunted grape. Officer André Ripoll. His whipping boy. The only one. His favorite!

Ripoll greeted him rapidly and came to stand next to him in the praiseworthy intention of letting him share his umbrella. Sebag's nostrils immediately took in an acrid odor of gamy meat. Instinctively, he took a step backward. He found himself back in the rain and took out an old running cap. With his free hand, Ripoll pointed to a dark gray marble stele.

"That's the monument to the memory of the men who were shot," he explained, taking a step forward to put his superior back under the protection of his ridiculous bit of fabric. "It's called the OAS monument."

Followed by Ripoll's umbrella, Sebag went up to the damaged monument. The vandals had attacked the man's face, which had completely disappeared, probably under the blows of a hammer. Despite other damage here and there, the rest of the design was recognizable: it represented a man with his hands tied behind a post. The names of the former combatants for French Algeria must have been inscribed on the base, but the furious hammering had made them illegible. On both sides of the monument, the vandals had broken flower pots.

"You didn't cordon off the area," Sebag remarked.

"We stayed here, it really wasn't necessary," Ripoll said. "And then no one has come into the cemetery since we've been here—who would want to come here with this weather?"

"All the same, it would be better," Sebag insisted.

The stunted grape grew red. Ripoll had trouble controlling his annoyance. He puffed noisily before yielding to authority:

"Whatever you say."

As he was returning to his car, Sebag called Elsa Moulin on her cell phone.

"Castello already informed me, I'm on my way," she said. "I'll be there in five minutes."

"See you in a moment. I hope you've brought along an oil-skin."

"Oilskin, boots, and hood. I spent my last vacation in Brittany, and I'm fully equipped."

He hung up and then put his cell phone in the pocket of the jacket he was wearing under the raincoat. Water was running down the headstones and Sebag said to himself that this year even the least well-maintained of them would be shiny for All Saints' Day. The monument, on the other hand, was ruined, and this act of vandalism was in danger of setting the whole city on fire.

The monument had always aroused a lot of opposition. Ever since it was erected in 2003, every June 7th an extremist association of *Pieds-Noirs* tried to organize a ceremony in honor of the OAS's former combatants, invariably provoking a call for a counterdemonstration. To avoid any incident, on each occasion the prefect issued an order forbidding both the ceremony and the demonstration. Sebag thought he also remembered that the monument had already been the object of vandalism. But at the time that act had not been preceded by a man's murder.

However, did that mean that this new defacement was necessarily connected with Martinez's murder? Sebag thought again about Albouker's recent statements. The president of the *Pied-Noir* Circle had wondered whether the community of former French of Algeria wasn't the real target of this murder. Gilles had immediately rejected that notion. Perhaps a little too quickly, he now said to himself.

Officer André Ripoll, his hands full of stakes, stood at attention in front of him:

"Where should we put them?"

"Cordon off a space of thirty square meters around the monument and that will be fine."

"Yeah, yeah," Ripoll said, scratching his skull under his cap.

Sebag added in an ironic tone:

"Let's say, a space about six meters by five."

Ripoll went away mumbling a few words, half in French, half in Catalan. Sebag had annoyed him, he was well aware of that and fully satisfied by it. God alone knew why, the old officer irritated him and he took a malicious pleasure in needling him every time they met. These were the only times in his life when he abused his hierarchical position that way, but it always relieved him.

With the help of another policeman, Ripoll quickly set up a few stakes and then attached the traditional yellow tape to them, making use of a few nearby tombs as well. He came back toward Sebag.

"What I especially wanted to tell you a little while ago is that this cordon of yours isn't going to be of much use. With all the rain that fell tonight and is still falling, the forensic guys are not likely to find many clues here."

"That's possible, but it's our job. Now you can go back and stay dry in your car."

Ripoll looked at his soaked uniform and then murmured:

"Stay dry, stay dry, it's a little late for that . . . "

Another car came down the lane and parked near the others. Despite the mist on the windows, Sebag recognized Elsa Moulin's cheerful face.

The young woman got out of the car dressed in a banana-yellow oilskin zipped up to her chin and strawberry-red plastic boots. As soon as she emerged, she put her curly hair under an apple-green cloche. She looked like a mischievous little girl.

"Hi!" she cried out joyously.

He thought Elsa looked splendid, and told her so.

"I thought I wasn't going to see the sun today."

Elsa seemed surprised. Sebag was usually very reserved with women. She smiled and her eyes lingered on him for a few moments. Then she walked over to the monument.

"You're not wearing your usual outfit?"

She replied as she looked at the monument.

"It would be better but I'm not sure it's waterproof."

"By the way, is Pagès still on leave?"

"Until the end of the week, yes."

She returned to her vehicle and opened the trunk. First she took out an umbrella that she opened and balanced on her shoulder. Then she hung her camera around her neck.

"First a few pictures . . . " she said when she came back to Sebag. "Could you hold my umbrella for me, please? It's mainly to keep the camera dry."

He obeyed with pleasure. Together they began by backing up to take general views of the traffic circle. Then they approached the monument little by little. Medium-range views and then close-ups. Elsa even went so far as to almost glue herself to the monument to photograph the impact of the hammer blows in detail. Sebag conscientiously held the umbrella over the young woman and the camera. Water was running off the plasticized fabric and onto his soaked cap. A few drops occasionally ran down his neck.

When Elsa had finished taking her pictures, they returned to the car. Sheltered by the umbrella and by the open trunk lid, the young woman carefully put away her equipment in a bag. Then she took out a heavy case.

"Could you help, me, please? It's what I'm doing that has to be protected. My sweet little face doesn't matter."

He went with her to do the tedious work of collecting evidence. His thoughts very quickly turned elsewhere. If Castello had sent them here so rapidly, it was because he didn't want to think it was a coincidence. But how could this act of pure vandalism be connected with a cold-blooded murder? For Sebag, that didn't make sense. At the same time, the proximity of the two events couldn't be completely random.

Elsa's work took a good hour. At one point, she held her tweezers before his eyes. She'd just found a white hair on the gravel. They grimaced simultaneously.

"This isn't yours, is it?" Elsa joked.

"Not yet."

She put the hair in a plastic bag that she labeled in the shelter of the umbrella. Despite his raincoat, Sebag felt soaked to the skin. His shoes had long since ceased to be waterproof and every step he took was accompanied by a ridiculous sucking sound. After Elsa left, he went back to the police car. As he approached, Ripoll rolled down the window, revealing his shriveled, anxious face.

"I think you can go now," Sebag told him. "Leave the area cordoned off at least until tomorrow and keep a man at the entrance to the cemetery to watch for any suspicious movement."

Ripoll nodded, reassured. He was the leader of their group and he had already decided to delegate the work to the youngest member while he went to dry out his uniform in front of the radiators at headquarters.

"I'd like the man who remains here to be experienced," Sebag added treacherously. "I want you to do it, Ripoll."

The old policeman's face shriveled up again. His mouth and

nose came closer as if they were going to fold inward, and his eyes half closed. Ripoll gave a military salute laden with cold hostility. Sebag walked away, a smile on his lips. He really didn't understand the sick pleasure he took in tormenting this poor cop. But he didn't care. He felt no remorse. He felt good. Relaxed. And he didn't even feel annoyed when he once again stepped in a hole full of icy water as he was getting into his car.

He started the car and turned the fan on maximum to clear the fogged windows. He drove slowly as far as the gate to the cemetery but stopped there to talk to the caretaker. The man had fallen sound asleep, lulled by the beating of the rain on the roof of his lodge. He'd discovered the damage early in the morning, when he'd taken advantage of a brief letup in the rain to make his daily rounds through the tombs. Sebag saw that he wouldn't learn anything from the man, and didn't linger.

Before starting down the avenue to the hospital, he took out his cell phone and punched in a number. His day was going to be entirely occupied by this new event, and he had to cancel the appointment he'd made for the afternoon in connection with his investigation of Mathieu's accident. Too bad. Séverine would just have to wait a little longer. He left a message on the cell phone of the witness with whom he was supposed to meet and suggested that they postpone the interview until the following morning.

On his way to headquarters, he made a detour to stop at his home. He changed clothes, but the only footwear he found was running shoes. With slacks and a raincoat, it wasn't the look he would have chosen. Considering himself in the mirror, he thought he looked almost ridiculous. Oh, well, just once won't matter, he told himself philosophically.

Pascal Lucas, the driver of the van, called him on his cell phone while he was alone in his office, writing a report on the destruction of the monument.

"Hello, Inspector. I've just remembered something important. The car, the Clio, had Spanish license plates!"

The driver's voice was vibrating with excitement, but his slurred voice left little doubt that he had been drinking.

"That could be an interesting detail," Sebag said coolly. "Assuming that I can really count on it. Tell me the truth, Mr. Lucas, have you drunk quite a bit today?"

"No more than usual," the driver said sullenly.

"But no less, either."

On the other end of the line, Pascal Lucas replied, almost inaudibly, "No."

"And how did you come to have this . . . revelation?"

"I was watching a series on TV and there was a car with a Spanish license plate, and that was what made me think of it."

"Fine, fine, I've noted that down, Mr. Lucas. I'll see what I can do with it."

Sebag hung up, puzzled. Could alcohol have the same effect on memory as hypnosis? Could it also make thoughts we assumed had been erased reemerge from the black abyss of our brains? He remained skeptical, but he had hardly any choice but to pretend to believe it.

He realized that his witness hadn't yet called back. He dialed his number again, and this time immediately got him. The guy could talk with him the following morning, and they agreed to meet at the site of the accident.

"But watch out, Lieutenant," the man warned him amiably, "if you have to cancel this time it will be several days before I can talk to you. I have to go to Spain for my work."

Sebag crossed his fingers as he hung up. He hoped that there wouldn't be another unexpected impediment. Too many days had already passed since the tragedy, and the longer it was, the more memories were likely to fade.

He thought again of Lieutenant Cardona's rage and glimpsed for a moment the malicious pleasure his colleague would take if he failed to find a new lead. And above all, he imagined Sévérine's disappointment. Gilles could handle anything but that.

That white Clio had to exist.

He had to prove it.

He had to identify the driver.

"Well, gentlemen, we really didn't need that."

Castello's tone was not in any way facetious. He'd abruptly left his summit meeting of superintendents in Paris to catch the first afternoon plane.

"Since the ministry is already not very happy with us, I can tell you they'll be keeping a close eye on us. Moreover, I expect the arrival of the director of the prefect's cabinet any minute now."

In the meeting room, Sebag, Molina, Llach, and Lambert were physically present, while Ménard was participating via conference call from Marseille.

"Where are Raynaud and Moreno?" Castello said with concern.

Without waiting for an answer, he picked up the telephone in front of him and asked his secretary to call the two members of the team who were late.

"Tell them that if they aren't here in five minutes, I'll cancel all their overtime pay for the last month."

He hung up angrily.

"Normally, I like to begin our meetings by laying out the facts and the first evidence collected by the investigation, but just for once I would like to begin with conclusions. Before the cabinet director arrives, I want to take up right away the question that seems to me essential: Should we connect the act of vandalism against the OAS monument with Martinez's murder? Gilles?"

Sebag had been expecting Castello to ask him to speak first. He'd thought about it all afternoon.

"The coincidence is disturbing, I have to admit, but I have a hard time imagining that the same individual is responsible for these two acts. A murder and an act of vandalism have nothing in common. And then the timing doesn't work, either. If everything was planned by a single individual, I think the acts would be committed in ascending order. Here, we start off with a murder . . . "

Sebag looked at his boss and then at his colleagues. His arguments hadn't hit home. They all remained perplexed. He wasn't surprised. He himself probably wouldn't have been convinced. He always had trouble putting into words what he felt regarding certain investigations.

Joan Llach spoke up:

"All the same, 'OAS' written on a door at a crime scene and a couple of days later, the destruction of a monument erected in honor of that organization is disturbing, to say the least."

"That's true, but we could very easily explain that coincidence by the fact that the murder of Martinez might have aroused hostilities between the *Pieds-Noirs* and their opponents," Sebag replied.

"We could . . . if we'd mentioned that 'OAS' was written on Martinez's door. But I remind you that we didn't release that information. We didn't give it to the media."

Sebag rejected Llach's argument.

"Right, but we all mentioned the OAS when we talked with the people close to Martinez. And also in our interviews with the left-wing activists we met. In a little city like Perpignan, information travels fast."

"The leftists were very tetchy yesterday," Molina pointed out. "Besides, on that subject . . . "

The door of the meeting room opened, interrupting Molina.

Raynaud-Moreno, the brotherly duo, made an entrance they would have liked to have been more discreet.

"Good evening," Moreno said in his barely audible, sepulchral voice. Raynaud limited himself to making a vague sign with his hand.

"Finally!" the Superintendent said angrily. "May I ask what you were working on today that made you so late?"

The two inspectors sat down, taking care not to make their chairs squeak. They glanced at each other as they always did, and it was Moreno who spoke for both of them.

"We're still working on the holdup at the pari-mutuel bar on Rue Foch."

Three weeks earlier, two armed and hooded individuals had held up a bar, seriously wounding the manager. Probably the same ones who had then engaged in several other holdups in the neighboring department of Aude.

"And are you making progress?"

The two acolytes of the "laughing brigade"—that was the nickname the other inspectors sometimes gave them—exchanged glances again.

"Not much," Moreno recognized.

"Then for the moment you'll put that case on ice and, for once, you'll work in the team. I mean 'team' in the broad sense—I'm not referring to you two."

The two men reluctantly acquiesced. Castello turned to Sebag.

"Do you have anything else to say about what we were talking about?"

"For my part, no."

"Does anyone else want to say something?"

A metallic voice rose in the room. All eyes converged on the flying saucer that had been set on the table. Ménard was speaking from Marseille.

"Are we completely giving up the idea that the two crimes are connected?"

"We never exclude anything, you know that very well," the

superintendent replied. "And, unfortunately, I don't think we'll have a choice this time. Everyone is going to push us in that direction. The *Pied-Noir* community is going to be indignant, even worried, and more than ever we're going to be walking on eggshells. We need to make rapid progress."

"Exactly . . . " Molina began.

Two loud knocks on the door interrupted him. Castello got up immediately. He opened the door and stood aside to let a woman enter. She was as young as she was severe-looking. Sebag, who had already met her, knew that she was only twenty-five years old, and had just graduated from the ENA.[9] The post as director of the cabinet of the prefect of Pyrénées-Orientales was her first, and if she lacked a sense of humor and flexibility, she had already shown herself to be very efficient. She smoothed out her straight skirt before sitting down.

Castello introduced her to his men more out of politeness than necessity:

"Mlle. Sabine Henri, who is representing the prefect here."

The young woman took the time to look carefully at each of the inspectors. She wore glasses with rectangular lenses and black frames.

"Good evening, gentlemen. I won't conceal the fact that the prefect is very concerned about the turn these events have taken. He fears that the situation will degenerate very quickly, and demands rapid results." The inspectors silently nodded their assent. They were being respectful and docile, but none of them was fooled: they knew that a police investigation requires work, rigor, and sometimes luck, but it always requires patience. Results couldn't be produced by a movement of her chin.

---

[9] École nationale d'administration, a prestigious school that trains people for careers in government.

Castello took the floor again.

"Before you arrived, we were talking about the vandalism at the monument in Haut-Vernet. Lieutenant Sebag was there this morning. Lieutenant?"

Sebag circulated the photos Elsa Moulin had taken.

"The forensic team didn't find much around the monument. No fingerprints, no footprints. It has to be said that the surfaces in the cemetery—mainly asphalt, with some gravel here and there—don't really favor prints. The weather conditions didn't make their task any easier, either. Despite everything, however, they did find a white hair on the gravel."

While he was giving this last bit of information, he'd given Molina a little kick under the table to warn him not to make any inappropriate jokes. His partner got the message and limited himself to repressing a groan of pain. Sebag went on:

"The initial observations suggest that the instrument used to damage the monument was a sledgehammer of the usual size, the kind that can be found in every home improvement store in the region."

The cabinet director was listening and observing him neutrally.

"The gate to the cemetery is closed at night, but the perimeter wall is not even two meters high," Sebag explained. "Thus, it would be easy to get over. On the west side, it is sheltered by a row of trees that can be climbed without anyone noticing."

Sebag stopped abruptly. He didn't know what else to say. The young woman's smooth, oval face came to life. Her delicate lips opened.

"In a cemetery, white hairs must not be very rare. In short, you haven't got anything that would allow us to identify the perpetrator or perpetrators?"

The words had been uttered without aggressiveness. As a simple observation. But Sebag felt as if he had been slapped.

"We'll have a DNA analysis of the hair made anyway, since

we've already found one in the victim's apartment that seems not to have been his own. Otherwise, in view of the easy access to the cemetery and the simple nature of the tools used, we can assume that an individual could have acted alone. Even a relatively elderly individual."

"Do you really believe that we're dealing with an elderly vandal?"

Sebag weighed his words:

"I don't believe, I investigate. I'm looking for clues or proofs, and sometimes I'm able to find them and solve a few cases."

Sabine Henri did not react, but Sebag saw her round chin tremble. He felt that the young woman was trying to use her coldness to compensate for her lack of experience. That it was no more than a pose adopted to impose her authority, in spite of her age and her sex, in the very masculine universe of the prefecture. The cabinet director managed to put a very discreet smile on her lips.

"I've heard about you, Lieutenant Sebag."

She slowly turned toward the superintendent.

"And in the other case, the murder, have your men made progress?"

Castello coughed:

"Uh . . . I don't know yet, we haven't yet had time to take up the question. I sent one of my men to Marseille to consult with a historian specializing in the OAS. He's the one who confirmed that the victim did in fact belong to the organization—Hello, Ménard, are you still there?"

The flying saucer began to emit a few broken sentences.

"Michel Sonate . . . interviewed . . . Bernard Martinez in January . . . 2011 in Perpignan for the pur . . . pose of writing a book about . . . the former members of the OAS. I was . . . able to listen to the whole inter . . . view but Martinez didn't mention . . . his motivations. At no time . . . "

The sentence was lost in a terrible burst of static. Castello shook the flying saucer.

"We couldn't hear you very well, François, could you repeat the last things you said?"

"Martinez had nothing . . . to say about the actions he'd led in Algeria."

"And your historian has no idea of what Martinez might have done at the time? Or about the identity of any of his victims?"

"For the moment . . . no. But he's doing research and . . . correlating his data. The hardest part is that . . . members of the OAS . . . used . . . pseudonyms for each other."

Sabine Henri seemed astonished.

"Do you mean, Superintendent, that you think the motive for the crime might go back to the last years of the Algerian War?"

"That's one of the hypotheses, yes. I must say that it's even the only one."

"But that's so far back . . . If it's a question of revenge, why so long afterward? It's fifty years this year!"

Sebag began to smile. Obviously to a young woman of twenty-five, the 1960s seemed almost prehistoric.

"Some hatreds recognize no statute of limitation," Castello explained.

"But why wait so long?"

Sebag found that question pertinent. Plunging straight ahead, he hadn't yet asked it himself. One of the keys to the mystery might lie in the answer to that question. He wrote down this idea in his notebook and didn't hear Castello's response. The superintendent had already moved on to another aspect of the investigation.

"Since the murder appeared to be connected with the victim's membership in the OAS, and thus with the community of the former French of Algeria, we wondered if there hadn't been other murders of *Pieds-Noirs* elsewhere in France, other settlings of accounts. I assigned Joan Llach and Thierry Lambert to look into that possibility. Gentlemen . . . ?"

Lambert held back to let his colleague take the initiative. Llach didn't have to be asked twice.

"We searched the national data banks of the police and the gendarmerie, and up to this point we've found three murders of French nationals born in Algeria at the time of the French occupation: a pharmacist in Cannes, a retiree in Paris, and a restaurant owner in Nantes."

From the tone Llach had adopted everyone had understood that no great revelations were to be expected. But since all police work requires a detailed report, he was allowed to continue:

"The pharmacist in Cannes was killed during a holdup of his dispensary a year and a half ago, the retiree was stabbed to death by his wife, and the restaurant owner in Nantes, who was probably connected with the mafia, was shot down by henchmen whom the local police have not yet been able to identify. In these three cases, no reference to the OAS was found at the scene of the crimes."

"Do you think you've dealt with this question, or do you need to continue?" Castello asked.

"I lack a few bits of information, but I should be able to finish up alone tomorrow. Uh . . . I'll no longer need Thierry."

"Fine, fine. That's it, I think . . . Ah no, wait, Molina . . . Usually you open your mouth to say absolutely nothing, and this time you haven't said anything much at all. Can I hope that when you keep quiet, it's because you have some new evidence to give us?"

"I just might . . . "

Molina had a satisfied look on his face that intrigued Sebag.

"I made my little investigation into the activists in the Collective Contra Nostalgeria and I found a guy whose profile is particularly interesting: Émile Abbas was born fifty-four years ago in Algeria, of an Arab father and a French mother."

To make the greatest effect, he took the time to look around his audience. Normally, Castello would have been irritated, but the presence of the cabinet director led him to show patience.

"You're keeping us waiting, Monsieur Molina."

"Émile Abbas's father was murdered in Algiers in February 1962 by an OAS commando," the inspector finally said.

"Well, well, that's certainly interesting," the superintendent conceded. "Have you called him in?"

"Yes, for tomorrow morning at headquarters, but I don't know if he'll agree to come. For the moment, he and his friends have not been very cooperative."

"He'll have an interest in being more flexible. He's a simple witness now, but he could become a suspect. If he doesn't come, Molina, go pick him up at his home or at his workplace."

The cabinet director nodded in agreement, but added a little cautionary note.

"Be careful not to go too far. Let's avoid handcuffs, for example. That might make us look bad if he's not the right man."

With that incitement to be prudent, Sabine Henri abruptly stood up.

"I beg you to excuse me, but I have to leave you. I can't stay any longer. The whole region, as you know, is on severe storm watch because it's supposed to rain until 10 P.M. today and I have a press conference at the prefecture's crisis center. Let's not make our friends the journalists wait. They haven't yet gotten excited about this matter of the monument, and that's so much the better."

The young woman made a little sign with her hand and left. Castello had only to conclude the meeting, which he did by assigning everyone a task for the following day. He ended with Sebag:

"Gilles, you'll be with Molina tomorrow to receive Abbas."

Sebag hid a grimace. Shit! Molina had mentioned 9 A.M., and that was precisely the time he had a meeting with Clément Ollier, the witness to Mathieu's accident. Castello's tone was categorical, there was no way he could get out of it. Too bad! He didn't have a choice. Once again, he would be obliged to play truant. It wasn't the first time, and it certainly wouldn't be the last. Molina would understand perfectly, Sebag had no doubt of that. They'd worked together and arranged the tasks to suit them for so long that they'd lost count: it was impossible to know which of them was indebted to the other.

CHAPTER 15

**Algiers, December 12, 1961**

It's slowly getting light in Algiers. The day before, a gentle rain fell on the white city, but this morning it has finally given way to the sun. The timid rays lick the pavement and make the dampness rise from the ground. The gardens of the villas on Rue Sévérine are exhaling in abundance their aromas of cypress, boxwood, and pine.

The commander of the OAS has put one of the villas under high surveillance because a dozen suspect individuals are in it. Cops, soldiers, or simple civilians—it isn't yet entirely clear— they arrived from metropolitan France two weeks before and have since been conducting clandestine actions against partisans of French Algeria. Two cafés have been destroyed by attacks that this time had nothing to do with the FLN. Degueldre, the leader of the OAS commandos, has been clear: there is no question of letting those scum act as they want in Algiers.

Sigma shivers. He has spent the night in the Dauphine, accompanied by Bizerte and Omega, dozing off from time to time. His body is stiff with cold despite the blanket he threw over his shoulders. At dawn, Babelo joined them, bringing coffee and fresh bread. As well as his famous American cigarettes. He has handed them out generously to his buddies and thick smoke is now stagnating in the car.

Shortly after nine o'clock, they see a figure slip through the junglelike garden of the villa they're watching. A man in his thirties opens the gate and comes out cautiously. He has no difficulty spotting the Dauphine and its four phantoms. He puts his hand inside his jacket to make sure his gun is there.

Another man soon joins him, a gorilla well over six feet tall and weighing nearly two hundred and fifty pounds. The two men exchange a few words as they look toward the Dauphine. Then the colossus walks off and gets into a big Mercedes.

A delivery van passes the two cars and stops about fifty meters farther on. The driver gets out and immediately disappears into a nearby house. The driver of the Mercedes puts the car in reverse and slowly backs up to get the second man. Now they hesitate.

The van is still blocking traffic, and Rue Séverine is too narrow to make a U-turn. They decide to back up all the way to Rue Mangin.

Everything is going as planned.

The Mercedes backs down the street. As it passes the Dauphine, its two occupants are paying no attention to the OAS men. The car reaches the intersection, where it can finally turn around. Omega wipes the condensation off the windshield and starts the engine. Babelo, Bizerte, and Sigma cock their submachine guns. They're ready. Omega drives slowly and stops ten meters from Rue Mangin.

In the middle of the intersection, the Mercedes is no longer moving. They know why. Another car is blocking its way. Babelo and Bizerte roll down their windows while Sigma gets out of the car and lies down on the street.

The submachine guns start firing.

Their heavy fire echoes that of the other commando unit positioned on Rue Mangin. Despite the crossfire, the occupants of the Mercedes fire back. The younger of them jumps into the street and fires in their direction. Sigma takes refuge in the car. Babelo throws a defensive grenade, but not far enough, and it explodes on the street without damaging the Mercedes.

Before the street fills with smoke, Sigma has time to see the massive silhouette of the driver slump behind his steering wheel.

Omega rapidly backs the car into Rue Séverine. As if by enchantment, the van has disappeared. Omega takes advantage of a wide place in the street in front of a luxurious villa to make a quick turnaround and the Dauphine takes off. It soon resumes a normal speed in the streets of Algiers.

Shortly afterward, Omega finds a parking place in the Rue Michelet. The four men hide their submachine guns in the trunk of the car and walk to the Otomatic. A hangout for activist students, the bar's terrace on the sidewalk is shaded by young plane trees. They sit down at a free table and despite the early hour order four strong anisettes.

For a long time they remain silent, each of them reliving the emotions of the battle. A second glass of anisette loosens their tongues and the first laughs ring out.

"A film with James Stewart and Richard Widmark this afternoon, what do you say to that?" Babelo suggests. "*Two Rode Together* is playing at the Modern Cinema."

"Is it good?" Omega asks. He's getting a little tired of westerns.

"Is it good? The truth is . . . It's by John Ford, the greatest director of them all!"

"Well . . . if it's by John Ford!"


At 4 P.M. they meet at the Modern Cinema. When they come out, they learn that their action that morning, despite the risks they took, was only partly successful. Wounded in the left arm and the stomach, the driver of the Mercedes was taken to Maillot Hospital, but will live. The other man, one of the leaders of the group, escaped with only a few scratches. The people at the villa in Rue Séverine moved out that afternoon.

"Don't worry," Babelo reassures them. "They're going to set up somewhere else, but we'll soon find out where they are. The battle is just beginning."

# CHAPTER 16

S ebag was drinking a lousy coffee in a little bistro in Moulin-à-Vent. He was early for his meeting and was taking the opportunity to read the newspapers. The local paper's big headline was about the bad weather. In addition to the fords, several roads had been cut, notably along the coast between Collioure and Cerbère. In Canet, about thirty houses in a subdivision had been evacuated and their residents put up for the night in the community center. The destruction of the monument did get a half-page on the inside of the paper. Illustrated by photos, the article described the damage caused to the monument and then quoted members of the association that had erected it, their opponents, and, finally, the mayor. The state prosecutor, however, had refused to make a statement. Below the article, a box recalled the polemic that had exploded when the monument was put up and the tensions that persisted every time a memorial ceremony was planned there.

Fortunately, the journalists had not yet made a connection with the murder of Martinez. And for good reason: the information regarding the "OAS" painted on the apartment door had not yet been divulged.

But it was only a matter of days, or even hours.

Sebag finished his excessively bitter coffee, paid without leaving a tip, and left. Outside, the clouds were beginning to stop dripping, and under the impact of a vigorous north wind, bits of blue sky were starting to colonize the sky. Sebag chose to walk to the place where he was to meet the witness. He liked to walk in the Moulin-à-Vent quarter. The broad *ramblas* had pleasant median strips planted with immense palm trees. Regularly re-stuccoed, the apartment buildings were aging well and their white walls naturally harmonized with the green lawns on which prospered not only palm trees but also majestic parasol pines.

Sebag walked fast and soon arrived in front of the church of Saint Paul, a triangle of concrete covered with white stucco and topped with a tuft of red tiles. Built in the late 1960s, this religious edifice might have been confused with an ordinary community center if its pediment hadn't been decorated with a big cross and the square in front of it provided with a campanile with two bells.

A little bald man was standing across from the church, waiting. The witness.

"Mr. Clément Ollier, I presume?"

"Yes, that's me."

"Lieutenant Sebag. Thanks for having agreed to meet with me despite all the hitches, and especially for having been willing to come here."

The witness shrugged.

"I live right nearby, in fact. I'll go to work afterward. It won't take long."

"No, I don't think so. What do you do for a living? I read in the file that you were a sales rep for an import-export firm. That means everything and nothing."

"That's true," Ollier acknowledged. "I work for a firm at the Saint Charles market that imports fruit and vegetables from Spain. I'm leaving this afternoon for Andalusia."

"On a Friday? Don't they know about weekends in your business?"

"Oh, but they do," Ollier replied with a sly gleam in his eyes. "I have to be there on Monday and I'm taking advantage of the trip to spend a weekend with my wife."

"When it's possible to combine business and pleasure . . . "

"I see that policemen have a sense of humor . . . "

"Yes, I know, too many people think a sense of humor is incompatible with the job."

Clément Ollier refrained from commenting. He was probably not far from sharing the general opinion. And then he must have thought that the polite chitchat had gone on long enough and that it was high time to get down to brass tacks.

"Tell me what happened, please," Sebag asked.

"I wasn't working the Wednesday of the accident, and I had gone out to buy cigarettes. I saw a van coming up the street at a rather high speed. It passed by me and then suddenly swerved to the left. That was when it hit the scooter that was coming in the opposite direction. Bang! The boy went flying and landed three meters farther on. I can still hear the sound. It was a real shock, I can tell you that. In every sense of the term. I still get shivers behind my knees when I talk about it. Poor kid . . . "

Clément Ollier expressed himself with the accent of a southern area other than Catalonia. Sebag would have bet on somewhere around Toulouse. Ollier's bald head made him look older, but he was probably not much over forty.

"In your opinion, why did the van swerve like that?"

"I heard on the local radio that the driver claimed that a car had run a stop sign."

Ollier didn't add anything more. Sebag was forced to ask him to be more precise.

"Did you see that car?"

"Me? No, I didn't see anything. Just the van and the scooter. Nothing else."

Sebag made a disappointed face. Clément Ollier was, in fact, the only eyewitness to the accident, everyone else in the file having rushed to the spot only after the collision. That was the main weak point that he had noted in Cardona's investigation, the only bone he had found to gnaw in the hope of finding something new. But this slender hope had just evaporated. The accident had happened near the church in front of which they were standing, right on the other side of the street, about fifteen meters further on. Thus nothing could have escaped Clément Ollier.

"Were you standing right here at the time of the accident?"

"Not far away, yes."

Sebag recovered a little hope.

"Where?"

Ollier made a vague gesture.

"A couple of meters away."

"Could you show me exactly?"

Followed by Sebag, Ollier walked down Foment de la Sardane Boulevard. To the policeman's great surprise, he went past the site of the accident and then continued a good twenty additional meters.

"I believe I was here," he cried.

He took two more steps before pounding on the pavement.

"Precisely here!"

Sebag contemplated the site from their new position. The perspective had changed radically: they were now on the left rear of the van.

"I had a ringside seat, so to speak. The kid couldn't do anything, it all happened so fast!"

The inspector closed his eyes, trying to imagine the scene and especially to judge the angle of view. When he reopened his eyes, he was sure: at the moment of the collision, Clément Ollier was behind the van. He could very well not have seen the infamous white Clio coming toward the right front side of the van. On the other hand, he could have seen it when it continued on its way and took off.

"And then . . . after the accident, what did you do?"

"I rushed over to the kid. I was a volunteer fireman for ten years, so I wanted to make myself useful. At first, we thought all the damage was to the van, the kid was very pale but seemed not to have been hurt. If only we'd been able to guess . . . "

Sebag was no longer listening. Hurrying to help Mathieu, Clément Ollier had stopped looking at the street. His attention must have been entirely focused on the victim. It was possible that he hadn't seen the car. Pascal Lucas's claim became credible.

"Of course, even if we'd guessed earlier, we couldn't have done anything. Internal bleeding . . . Still, it was bad luck."

Sebag was wondering what he was going to be able to do with this new information. It was a long way from the credible to actual proof, and Cardona wasn't going to help him get there. He needed another witness. He looked up at the apartment buildings surrounding him. The white façades were adorned with loggias with wooden railings and trellises made of round tiles. After the rainy period of the last few days, it was warming up again and here and there Sebag could see people through the open windows. If that damned car existed, someone must have seen it. Must have.

"Papa, I know you have a lot of work. If you can't deal with Mathieu's accident, it's O.K. I won't be mad at you."

Gilles had come home late the preceding evening. Séverine had watched him out of the corner of her eye and her father's preoccupation hadn't escaped her. She had joined him on the terrace when he'd gone out to sip his coffee. He could drink coffee at any time of day, it had never prevented him from sleeping. Séverine had come up quietly behind him, put her arms around his waist, and laid her head on his back.

"I'm fourteen years old, I can understand . . . "

He hadn't known what to say. In any case, he had a lump in his throat and couldn't have talked. He'd savored his coffee down to the last drop before turning around to face Séverine and take her in his arms.

Then his voice and his words came back to him.

"Thanks, sweetheart, but don't worry: I'm going to be able to find a little time. And as I told you from the beginning, if there's something to find, I'll find it."

He was now up against the wall, in both the literal and figurative senses. Across from him, two rows of apartment buildings with five stories each. He was going to have to go door-to-door. That was the part of his job that he hated the most.

He said goodbye to Clément Ollier, thanking him warmly. Then he called Molina on his cell phone.

"So, is he there?"

"One second, hang on."

He watched his witness get into his car parked in front of the church. Clément Ollier started to drive away and waved as he passed in front of him. Molina's voice resounded again in his ear.

"Excuse me, I was with Abbas."

"He came after all, then?"

"Yes, he was on time. I was the one that made him wait half an hour before seeing him. Llach lent me his office."

"What did he tell you?"

"Nothing, for the moment. We've just started. We're still getting his vital statistics."

"Do you need me?"

"Do you think I can't handle this by myself?"

"It's not that. It's just that Castello wanted us both to work on it."

"You'll join in later. Whatever happens, I'm not going to let this guy go anytime soon. I'm going to teach him some manners, after all! You can just come by for dessert. Are you getting anywhere?"

"I've got something new, yes."

"Enough to annoy Cardona?"

"Not yet. But enough to hope I can."

"O.K., go for it, I'm counting on you, champ! I've got to let you go, I've got a client on the grill."

During the following two hours, Sebag knocked on fifty-two doors. Thirty-seven of them opened up. More or less spontaneously. Each time, he tried to question every member of the family. In all, he obtained a total of a hundred and twelve negative opinions: seventy-five persons were out at the time of the accident, thirty-four had looked out their windows only after hearing the sound of the collision or the emergency vehicle's sirens, and the last three, though present, had heard nothing at all.

Thus there remained fifteen apartments, fifteen closed doors that he'd have to try to get to open up another time. Luck was on his side. Mathieu's accident had taken place less than three hundred meters from Martinez's apartment; he could always claim to be working on one case while he was working on the other.

However, it was now time to get back to headquarters to help Molina. As he drove down the boulevards toward the city center, through a gap in the clouds he caught a glimpse of Le Canigou towering against the blue sky. For the first time this season, a fine white powder had covered the summits, but after two days of heavy rain the peak was as blotchy as cokehead's nose.

Sebag found Molina alone in their office, playing on his computer.

"Well, how did it go with Abbas?"

"It's happening . . . "

Silence. Jacques didn't take his eyes off the screen.

"Well?" Sebag insisted.

"Mr. Abbas is not exactly a motormouth."

Another silence. Molina remained absorbed in his game.

"That makes two of you, then," Sebag commented.

Molina grimaced. He must have been in a particularly delicate phase of his game.

"Two what?"

His fingers gripped the mouse. He clicked nervously twice and then pushed it away and swore. He'd lost.

"Two what?" he asked again, this time looking up at Sebag.

"Two motormouths. Words have to be extracted from you with forceps, too."

"The computer helps me relax, and I needed it," Molina explained. "Abbas immediately agreed to give his identity, but then nothing more! He just kept repeating that he'd talk only in the presence of his lawyer."

"He really said nothing at all?"

"I'm exaggerating a little. He said—I'm summing up—that the OAS was nothing but a bunch of fascist, racist assholes, and that he was glad that some courageous guy had finally decided to massacre the monument."

"What about the murder?"

"There, he was more moderate. He said that the Algerian War was very far away and he didn't understand how anybody could want to take revenge at such a late date."

"Did you talk to him about his father?"

"Obviously. That's when he shut up. Fortunately, I'd gotten a few details thanks to an early morning phone call from Ménard. He's really a hard worker, that guy. Apparently he stayed all night in his historian's archives. Of course, he hasn't anything else to do in Marseille."

"And so?"

"And so Émile Abbas's father, first name Mouloud, was a doctor at a hospital in Algiers. He worked in the emergency room and is supposed to have secretly treated several FLN activists. In any case, that's what the OAS accused him of, but I think it was mainly the fact that he was a doctor and an Arab that really bothered those bastards. In short, a commando burst into the hospital in the middle of the day—it was in early January 1961, I think—and shot him in cold blood, a dozen bullets to the body, right in front of patients and nurses, and then calmly walked out."

"How old was Abbas then?"

"Four."

"And when you questioned him, did he really have nothing to say about his father's murder?"

"No. Just something to the effect that it was just like the police to confuse victims with perpetrators."

"And how did you react?"

"I remained very Zen. Yes, I did, I did . . . You should've seen me, you'd have been proud. I asked my questions, he didn't answer. I calmly asked them again, and since he still wouldn't answer, I left."

"Still calmly?"

"Yes. I gently closed Joan's office door and went down to drink a cup of espresso in the cafeteria."

"Great!" Sebag said ironically.

"Of course, I did kick the coffee machine. Mustn't be too Zen . . . "

"Ah, now you're reassuring me."

"Were you worried?"

"Not really. No one has ever seen an old rugby fullback become as Zen as a Tibetan monk from one day to the next. And since then you've been letting Abbas stew?"

"Exactly."

"How long has it been?"

Molina glanced at his watch.

"Almost an hour and a half."

"Not bad. Then what?"

"I'm going to have to go back."

"And say what?"

"I'll ask my questions again. Still calmly."

"And since he'll continue to refuse to answer, what are you going to do?"

"I don't have any idea," Molina said, annoyed. "As people say, 'that's when it starts to get complicated . . . ' Now, either we put him in custody or we let him go."

Sebag noticed the sudden use of "we" at the point where an important decision had to be made. Molina was bringing him back into the game.

"I suppose he didn't allow you to take his fingerprints?"

"Are you kidding?"

"And he didn't say anything about what he was doing on the night the monument was damaged or on the day of the murder?"

Molina just shrugged.

"So we don't have anything! Not against him, or for him, for that matter . . . And in that case there's no point in hoping for a second that the prosecutor will authorize us to search his home."

Sebag sank into his chair and turned on his computer.

"We've put the cart before the horse. It would have been better to investigate this guy before we called him in. Either we would have found nothing and we'd have let it drop, or we'd have something useful and we could question him more precisely. And then even if he didn't answer, it would mean police custody and all the rest."

"It's a little late to see that now!"

"Yes, I know. But we couldn't foresee that he wouldn't give us anything at all. And then yesterday I was obsessed with the witness to the accident."

"What happened, by the way?"

Sebag summed up what he'd discovered, the absence of real witnesses, and told him about his failure to find other witnesses.

"So you haven't won yet, then?"

"Not yet."

"O.K.! What about Abbas?"

"So far as Abbas is concerned, I'm going to take my turn and have a little conversation with him."

"Good luck! And what am I going to do in the meantime?"

"Play another game?"

Molina didn't have to be asked twice. His hand was already on the mouse, and his eyes immediately flew back to the screen. In front of the door to Joan Llach's office, Sebag took a deep breath before entering.

"Hello."

Émile Abbas didn't respond to his greeting and watched impassively as he sat down in front of Llach's computer. Sebag shook the mouse to wake up the machine. He resumed the session Molina had left open.

"So . . . Your name is Émile Abbas. You were born on November 28, 1957, in Algiers. Your father, Mouloud Abbas, was a doctor, and your mother, Geneviève Fontaine, was a nurse. In the same hospital?"

Émile Abbas sighed.

"Is that important?"

The two men looked at each other for a few seconds. Abbas had a lean, hard face with hollow cheeks. His long, pointed nose plunged toward a large, thin mouth. His delicately framed upper lip was supported on a more generous lower lip. Under his straight black eyebrows his eyes shone with a dark light.

Sebag sighed in return.

"No, it isn't important. But we have forms we have to fill out, you know. And since you don't want to talk about anything else, we have to do something."

"I haven't done anything, and so I don't have anything to say, anything to justify."

"And I'm supposed to believe that just because you're such a nice guy?"

"That's your business."

Sebag looked at his watch.

"You could have been outside a long time ago if you'd cooperated. Especially if, as you say, you haven't done anything."

"I don't even know what you're accusing me of. Your colleague mentioned the destruction of the OAS monument and the murder of a *Pied-Noir*. The one you already came to see us about at the Collective, right?"

"And you really helped us out a lot that day . . . "

"We don't much like 'collaborating' with the police."

"We've changed, you know, since the Second World War. The Resistance, the Gestapo, that's over. Even kids no longer play that game during recess. The only people still playing that game are a handful of old-fashioned activists."

"The police can't change, it's genetic."

Sebag didn't want to prolong a debate that would benefit no one. He shook his head several times while Abbas looked at him. Then he lowered his eyes and looked at the computer screen.

"You're a teacher of technology at the Pablo Picasso Lycée. You are married to Chantal Abbas, née Vila, and you have two children, Samira and Didier. They are both grown-up and have left the family home."

Abbas sighed again. More loudly.

"Whenever you want, we can talk about more serious matters."

Abbas did not reply.

"We'd just like you to tell us where you were on the night the monument was destroyed and on the day of the murder. If you have an alibi, we'll check it out and if it holds up, we'll let you go. It's as simple as that."

"And if I don't have an alibi? I go directly to jail? And all that because my father was murdered by the OAS fifty years ago? For you, that's enough to harass decent people and you claim that the police have changed?"

"We're only human," Sebag acknowledged. "We have our flaws, and first among them is a cruel lack of imagination. We work in a basic way. For a crime or misdemeanor, we look first for the motive. Here, it's not money, it's not a woman, it's politics. We have reasons to think that Bernard Martinez, the victim, was killed because he used to belong to the OAS. So yes, the murder of your father and the fact that today you're an active opponent of the former supporters of French Algeria make you . . . "

"The ideal suspect!"

"I would say rather a person we absolutely have to question, a lead we can't ignore. If you were a suspect, you'd be in custody, you'd be handcuffed and we'd be searching your home. And all that with the permission of the state prosecutor. We live in a state under the rule of law."

"My father was murdered, and at the time, the police didn't make any effort to investigate, and you call that the rule of law?"

"You just said 'at the time.' Today, the war is over. The Algerian War and the Second World War. And then, in case you didn't know it, French policemen were killed by the OAS for having tried to do their jobs."

"They were a minority!"

"I'll grant you that, but they died all the same. They deserve your respect."

Abbas pressed his lips together and said nothing. Sebag had the impression he had scored a point.

"You've never found out who killed your father?"

"It was the OAS. The men who did it don't matter."

"Yet you have just said that you wish there had been an investigation."

"It's hard enough to lose your father. But then to see that no one gives a shit is even worse."

"I understand."

"No, you can't understand," Abbas replied with scorn. He sat erect on his chair, his hands on his thighs. Sebag saw no hatred in him, nothing but rage. A furious rage capable of spoiling a life but not of killing. Especially not fifty years afterward.

"You've never tried to find out who killed your father?"

The scorn in his dark eyes grew.

"If you think I don't see you coming with your hobnailed boots! I didn't know this Martinez and I didn't kill him."

"Why are you active in the Collective Contra Nostalgeria if it isn't to settle accounts?"

"I want to settle accounts only with History. No question of letting killers pose as martyrs. That monument in honor of the OAS is already a scandal. The fact that it could be put up in a public place is a scandal. The people whose names are inscribed on it—do you know what they did?"

"The principal names were crushed with a sledgehammer."

"Bastien-Thiry, Degueldre, Dovecar, and Piegts, those are the names! Four killers sentenced to death by the French Republic and shot, some of them for having tried to assassinate General de Gaulle, and others—well, precisely!—for having killed cops. Do you think it's O.K. that today monuments to them are put up with the complicity of the public authorities?"

"No."

This direct response threw Abbas off balance. Sebag continued, blowing cold after blowing warm:

"But destroying that monument is nonetheless a crime. If you weren't the one who did it, where were you the night it happened?"

"Duty is duty, right? I told you the police would never change. You claim to be against this monument, but you're prepared to arrest and put in prison the person who destroyed it. That was the logic used by your predecessors who helped deport the Jews in 1940. In thirty years of activism, I've learned to mistrust the police. I know it's better not to say anything. First you demand an alibi, then it will be my fingerprints—your colleague already asked for them, moreover—and finally a sample of my DNA. And once I'm in your files, anything can happen."

Sebag patiently listened to this anti-cop diatribe. For someone who didn't talk much, Abbas was beginning to talk a lot. Words eliciting words, it was better to let them come out.

When Abbas finally stopped, Sebag slipped in amiably:

"It's certain that your fingerprints would make our job easier. Martinez's murderer left us some beautiful ones. All we need to do is compare them to prove your innocence."

"And did you find any on the monument?"

Sebag had to admit that they hadn't.

"You see," Abbas said triumphantly. "That's not enough to clear me of everything you want to blame on me. If you want to hassle me, nothing will keep you from continuing to do it."

"Except the alibi . . . "

"Does it seem to you that we're going around in circles?" Abbas retorted.

Sebag rubbed his eyes, then suddenly relaxed.

"O.K., you're right. We're going to end this. Do you want something to drink? How about a glass of water, would that do?"

Abbas hesitated before turning down the offer with a wave of his hand.

"If you don't mind, I'm thirsty," said Sebag, getting up.

The lieutenant left the room and went to get a cup of water at the fountain in the middle of the corridor. He ran into a young woman cop in uniform and for a few seconds remained so spellbound by her blue, almond-shaped eyes that he forgot to respond to her greeting. He drank his water, threw the cup in the bin, and filled another one. Back in his office, he set the cup in front of Abbas.

"Just in case . . . "

He moved back toward the door.

"I'm going to get my colleague for the official report on your testimony."

Molina was already deep in his game. Sebag waited patiently in the doorway.

"You couldn't get anything out of him, either?" Molina asked, without raising his eyes from the screen.

"No, it's pointless to waste any more of our time."

Molina consented to pause his game.

"Do you think he has nothing to do with our two cases?"

"Objectively, we have no reason to implicate or clear him."

"And subjectively?"

"I may be mistaken, but I don't see him as a killer, and especially not as a cold-blooded killer. And then he's married, has children, a job, and friends . . . No, I just can't imagine it. Obviously, if the investigation into Martinez's past proves that the little old man played a role in the murder of Abbas's father, I'll reconsider my view."

"What about the monument?"

"He chose collective action in broad daylight, and I'd find it odd if he suddenly started attacking the monument with a hammer at night."

"But somebody did it! Somebody who wasn't fond of the OAS!"

"Are you fond of the OAS?"

"No, but I don't see the connection . . . "

"I mean that so long as we're not sure that the damage is linked to the murder and vice versa, I don't give a damn who destroyed that monument. It was ugly, anyway . . . "

"I'm not sure they see things that way at the prefecture."

"It's true that to keep the peace between these communities, it'd be better that there be no more acts like that one. I'd forgotten that aspect of things."

Molina got up and joined Sebag in the hallway.

"To sum up, in your view Abbas is pure as the driven snow?"

"That's how I see it, yes."

"If Madame Irma says so . . . "

Molina trusted his partner's intuitions, but never missed a chance to make fun of them. When they entered Llach's office, Sebag noted with satisfaction that the water cup was empty. He let Molina sit down in front of the computer. Jacques reread the report out loud, occasionally looking up to see if Abbas agreed. But Abbas remained motionless on his chair, his fingers drumming on his thighs. When he finished reading, Molina hit the print button.

He collected the printed sheets to present them to Abbas. He handed him a pen as well.

"I don't want to sign it."

Molina took back the report.

"What you said committed you to nothing, but O.K.," he said with annoyance. "That's your right. You can go now, we have nothing more to say to each other."

Then he added, wanting to sound threatening:

"For the time being."

"I understood that."

For the first time, he'd smiled. Sebag opened the door for him.

"Take the stairway at the end of the hall. At the bottom, just push the button on your right to open the door."

He stepped aside to let Abbas pass. Abbas started to hold out his hand and then thought better of it. He left the office, but once he was in the hallway, he hesitated.

"I . . . if . . . you . . . "

Abbas looked down at his feet.

"If by chance in the course of your investigation . . . "

He looked up at Sebag. His eyes were no longer so dark.

"If you discover that this Martinez or one of his buddies played a role in my father's murder, would you tell me?"

Sebag no longer had in front of him a ferocious and battle-hardened activist but a kid whose father had been taken away from him too soon.

"Of course!" He grinned. "Then you'd be our prime suspect."

"Of course, how stupid I am . . . "

He turned on his heel, went down the hallway, and disappeared.

"Go ahead, give him a big kiss while you're at it!"

Molina, standing up, was furious.

"That guy has been screwing with us for four hours and you whisper sweet nothings to him? It won't hurt too much, do you want a little Vaseline? And on top of that, you give him a glass of water. Why not a cup of coffee? Oh, yeah, that's right, you think the coffee here is too disgusting!"

Molina went to grab the cup and throw it in the trashcan. Sebag shouted:

"Stop!"

Jacques froze before he'd touched the cup. Sebag pointed to the desk.

"In the bottom drawer on the left: Llach always keeps plastic bags there."

Molina, taken aback, obeyed without saying a word. Sebag took the bag and slipped the paper cup Abbas had used into it. Molina let out a long whistle: he'd just understood. Sebag handed the plastic bag back to him.

"Here, you've got his prints if you want them, and also a bit of his DNA."

"You could have taken the opportunity to pull out one of his hairs, while you were at it," Molina laughed. He was in a better mood.

"So far as that's concerned, we don't need to do an analysis. The guy still has brown hair, despite his fifty-four years."

Molina wrote a made-up name on a self-adhesive label.

"All this isn't very legal, Lieutenant Sebag."

"So? And if it ends up definitively removing Abbas from our list of suspects, he won't hold it against us. But then of course he'll never know anything about it."

"And if we find that they are the murderer's prints?"

"Then we won't be able to use these prints as evidence, but we'll have no trouble getting others. But frankly, I don't think he's the killer. And neither do you."

"Unfortunately, I don't."

Molina stuck the label on the plastic bag.

"I'll take care of this right away. It's Friday; if we want to have the result before Monday . . . "

Sebag went back to their office. He sat in front of Molina's computer and finished his game. He enjoyed it, and started another one.

The analysis of the prints came in quickly and confirmed their views. Abbas hadn't killed Martinez. Sebag immediately informed Castello. Then he began giving serious thought to his weekend. The weather report predicted a very pleasant Saturday—sun, mild temperatures, and moderate wind—but another big storm was supposed to come in on Sunday.

# CHAPTER 17

Y*alla*, René, I don't want to annoy you, or criticize people from Oran, I had plenty of friends in Oran, but the truth is . . . the *calentita* was good only in Algiers. That's to be expected: it was the capital, after all."

"Shut up, Roger, the real name of that dish is not *calentita* but *calentica*!"

A long table filled the whole of the *Pied-Noir* Circle's main meeting room. About thirty people were lined up along it, including Gilles and Claire. Once a month, the members of the association recreated the atmosphere they'd known in Algeria long enough to eat a couscous.

In the old days. Back there. The Sebags, who knew nothing about Algiers before independence, felt as if they'd been thrust into a film by Alexandre Arcady. The setting was colorful, the ambiance extremely enjoyable, and the actors excellent, even if they hammed it up a bit.

Claire's neighbors were pursuing their culinary squabble. Sitting across from Gilles, Guy Albouker's wife gave them a quick explanation:

"A *calentita*—in Oran, they call it a *calentica*—is a kind of flan made with chickpea flour and olive oil. It's eaten steaming hot, usually between two slices of bread."

She turned to her neighbor on the left, the aforementioned Roger:

"It took me years to make a *calentita* that more or less resembled the ones we ate back then."

"You succeeded? My word, you're the woman I should have married, my poor Josiane has never been able to make a good one."

"And do you know why?"

"No, but you're going to tell me, I'll bet."

"I don't know . . . "

"*Yalla*, don't make me wait . . . "

"Well, just because it's you . . . The secret, in fact, is the chickpeas. I used to buy them at the supermarket, but they're not the same. When I ate the *calentita* made by my sister-in-law in Montpellier, it was so good that tears came to my eyes. And do you know why?"

"Well, no, I don't! You haven't yet told me, for heaven's sake."

"My sister-in-law buys her chickpeas from a little Arab who imports them directly from Algeria. Since then, every time I go to Montpellier, I come back with several kilos of chickpeas."

"Give the address to Josiane, I don't want to die without having eaten that again!"

"Who's talking about dying," another guest three seats farther on shouted at him. "You're always the one who talks the loudest, you'll bury us all."

Guy Albouker had invited Sebag to come to the couscous party this Saturday evening. The lieutenant would have liked to decline the invitation, but he'd been afraid that his refusal might rub the officials of this influential association the wrong way. In the current context, that wouldn't have been very smart. And then Claire had been immediately enthusiastic about it.

Another bowl full of couscous was set down on the table. Gilles accepted a second helping. He'd never eaten such good couscous.

Claire declined a second helping but nonetheless picked choice morsels off her husband's plate. Guy Albouker came and joined them. He'd spent half the meal moving around to talk with everyone. He gave his wife a little poke with his elbow.

"Marie, you're failing to do your duty, our guests' glasses are empty."

Without asking, he filled their glasses with a Sidi Brahim as dark as blood.

"Didn't you like it?" he said anxiously when he saw that Claire's plate was empty.

"It was delicious, but I'm no longer hungry."

She added, stealing a chickpea from Gilles's plate:

"But you see that I'm still eating a little more out of pure gluttony."

"My daughter doesn't like couscous," René from Oran said, a wine-laden sob in his voice. "She likes the vegetables all right, but she won't touch the semolina. She doesn't like *calentica*, either."

"Oh, dear, that sounds like a psychological problem," Marie Albouker said.

"Yes, yes, yes, I know it's psychological . . . And that's exactly why it's so sad. For my daughter, our Algeria is like the castle in Sleeping Beauty, she stopped believing in it when she grew up."

"She might change her mind, you know," Albouker said, trying to reassure him. "I was the same way until a few years ago. I didn't want to hear anything about Algeria. How many times I argued with my parents and told them they had to figure out how to get over it. And then from the day my father died, I picked up the torch. Without having thought about it before. It came all at once. After the burial, I accompanied my mother back to their house, and there were a couple of magazines put out by *Pied-Noir* associations lying around. I took them all home with me, and a few days later I transferred the subscriptions to my own name. And you see, now I'm here with you."

"Yeah, with you it's different . . . You lived in Algeria."

"So little. I was six years old."

"Nonetheless, that matters. My daughter was born in 1971 and she has always lived here. She feels more Catalan than *Pied-Noir*."

"That's what she tells you to drive you crazy. And who knows, she probably says something entirely different to her own children."

For a moment, René gazed silently at the rest of the wine in his glass. He turned it around with a little movement of his wrist. Then he went on:

"It's true that my grandsons know our history surprisingly well. They have often astonished me. Do you think their mother talks to them about Algeria?"

"Certainly," Marie said encouragingly.

René finished his glass and held it out to Albouker.

"Po po po, go ahead, son, give me a little more sun and life."

Albouker poured him more wine. The culinary discussion resumed immediately. This time it was about *créponnet*. A kind of sherbet, Sebag seemed to understand.

"The best of all was in Bab-El-Oued, I tell you," Roger from Algiers said. "I'm not sure about who made it, but the name was something like Grosoli."

Since Albouker was not participating in this discussion, Claire asked him a question.

"Your rejection of Algeria for so many years is astonishing. Why did you change your mind so late and so suddenly?"

"I think that at first it hurt too much, and in order to avoid suffering, I denied it as much as I could. And then I also wanted to belong here, I refused to be a *Pied-Noir*, I wanted to be French like everyone else. But that was impossible: those of us who returned from Algeria can't be French people like the others."

"Why not?"

"Most of my friends who are here will tell you that it's because we loved France too much and it betrayed us, but I think that's a little simplistic. In fact, we loved a France that wasn't the true one. We were living far away and we lived France as a fantasy. My parents were both born in Algiers and the first time they set foot in metropolitan France was in 1962. They really didn't know anything about this country."

He poured himself another glass of wine. He forgot to fill Gilles's glass but not Claire's.

"Our France was the eternal France of our history classes in elementary school, but it was very close to our hearts. Our France was the France of the 1930 centenary celebration of the conquest of Algeria. At that time, the colonization of Algeria was the glory of France, and the colonist was seen as a courageous and hardworking man, a hero, a veritable cowboy of the Far South. Those of us who lived in Algeria saw things that way in the autumn of 1954, when the war began, and we still did in 1962, when the war ended. We didn't understand the changes that had taken place so rapidly in the other France, the true France, your France. For the metropolitan French, we were no long heroes but rich exploiters, unjust and racist. The glory of France had become its shame. And this biased view has become a historical truth. We'd like a more complex understanding of our history: that's why we're so attached to the monuments that celebrate this memory."

Claire, who was bored by remarks that were too general and political, brought the discussion back to a more personal level.

"What about you? Returning to France must have been really wrenching."

Albouker gave her a sad little smile. The bags under his eyes swelled up like lungs.

"You see, you've just involuntarily illustrated the difficulty we have in explaining our unhappiness to metropolitans. You said 'returning to France.' But for us, there could be no return because we hadn't ever been here! For the same reason, many former French of Algeria reject the term 'repatriates' that is often used to refer to us, because for them, their country was Algeria, not France. In any case, not this France . . . "

He put his hand on Claire's and tapped it gently.

"But to answer your question more precisely: it was more than wrenching for me, even more than a rupture, a genuine mourning."

Gilles was listening to their conversation but trying to look elsewhere. He felt that Albouker would talk more freely with a woman.

"For me, there will always be a before and an after. I have the feeling that I was never the same after . . . after our departure. Oh, of course I've been happy here. I was able to pursue the studies I wanted, and I would probably not have been able to do that over there. I met a woman whom I love, I have children and a beautiful house. Nothing to complain about. Yes, I've been happy, but . . . "

He took the time to find the right word to express the vague feeling that possessed him.

"Yes, I've been happy, but I think I've never again been . . . joyous. Yes, that's it, joyous. Joyous and carefree. In fact, at the age of six I stopped being a child."

He had been looking down at the table as he spoke, as if he were searching for his words and feelings among the scraps of food that stained the tablecloth. He raised his eyes and stared at Claire.

"You're not Catalan?" he asked her abruptly.

"No, I was born in Yvelines."

"Are you attached to your native region?"

"No, not really."

"Then it will be impossible for you to understand our passion for Algeria. I believe that only people of Catalan origin can understand us. Because they, too, love their country, their culture, their language . . . "

"Explain that to me."

"That's just it, it can't be explained, it's ineffable. One feels these things in the depths of oneself. They can't be translated by words. Words aren't strong enough. Words don't convey feeling enough. I could tell you about Bab-El-Oued, the assemblies, the balls, the festivals—people took every opportunity to throw a party—but no matter what I said I don't think my words would succeed in making you share anything at all. The only way to transmit something is through emotion. But when we *Pieds-Noirs* let ourselves be emotional, watch out! We get out of control, and right away it's too much and it becomes laughable."

"Ah, that marvelous wonderland that we've lost," Marie Albouker broke in ironically.

Her husband discreetly wiped away a tear that was lingering in the corner of his eye. He also sighed, because he knew what was going to come next; they'd had this conversation countless times before.

"All *Pieds-Noirs* weren't unhappy to leave Algeria, you know. For my mother, for instance, it was a liberation."

Claire didn't hide her surprise.

"You can't imagine the archaic and macho side of *Pied-Noir* society back then," Marie Albouker explained. "In that respect, our families were no better than the Arabs. My mother wanted to work, to have a job, but she was never able to do that. Not until she came to live in France."

A new light shone in her eyes.

"And I will always remember the pleasure she took in shopping in the streets of Marseille, where we lived during the first years after Independence. She marveled at the slightest thing. I don't think I ever heard her express any regret at having had to leave Algeria. Except perhaps at the very end of her life."

"And you, how do you feel about it?"

"I have mixed feelings. Inevitably. It's always been hard for me to find a position between my father's sorrow and my mother's relief, a relief that she took care not to express in front of her husband and her family. She talked about it only with me. But she often told me that I didn't know how lucky I was to grow up in metropolitan France."

"And what are your memories of Algeria?"

"There, too, I find it hard to talk about them. I was three years old in 1962. I'm not even sure that my memories are my own."

"What do you mean by that?"

"That I can't distinguish the authentic memories from the recreated ones. People talked to me so much about Algeria—my father, my grandparents, my brothers, too; they were four and seven years older than I was. Every year, on the anniversary of our departure, my parents would get out the photo albums. They told stories and wept."

Roger, who had been listening to the discussion for a few minutes, took the opportunity to put in his two cents.

"*Yalla*, my little lady, if you want someone to tell you about Algeria, you don't want to ask these kids. I'm seventy-eight, and I was almost thirty when I left Algeria. So you can imagine that I had time to get to know it. I could tell you all about it, the excursions to the beach at Padovani or the one at Sidi Fredj. We spent whole weekends there. We set up our tent on the sand and caught fish for our dinner. We fished with the water up to our knees and we caught little fish that we took off the hooks and threw directly into the frying pan. The fish were still alive and flopped around in the oil; a little glass of rosé with that. With next to nothing, we made ourselves a paradise."

He looked around at the other guests and smiled, delighted to have captured everyone's attention.

"I'm permeated with that country down to the marrow of my bones. I'll tell you, little lady, Algeria still runs in my veins. When I talk about it, all I have to do is close my eyes to hear it and smell it." He closed his eyes and drew in a rapturous breath.

"The miserable thing is that I'm there . . . I've got my feet in the water, the waves are caressing my knees; I feel the fishing rod quiver, I set the hook, and the fish is caught. Bingo! I throw it to my buddies behind me and immediately I hear it frying in the pan. My pals have tossed spices on it. I can smell them as if I were there."

His friend René sniggers:

"The spices are easy enough . . . with the remains of the couscous on the table, I can smell your spices even without closing my eyes."

Roger smiled but went on, undeterred. He kept his eyes closed:

"I hand the rod to a pal and sit down on the sandy beach. The sand at Sidi Fredj is warm, I slip my feet in, it almost burns them. Somebody hands me an anisette in a glass with two big ice cubes. The pal to whom I gave the rod continues to angle and the fish pile up in the pan. The first ones are already cooked, and they're as golden as wheat, appetizing, we're hungry, we're going to be able to start eating. One by one, we pick fish out of the pan . . . "

"Watch out, it's hot," René joked.

"Yes, it's hot and we pay attention," Roger went on, speaking even more loudly. "But above all, it's delicious. It's no longer fish but velvet, I tell you, it's silk, it's . . . "

"Hey, watch out for bones!"

"The fish in Algiers didn't have bones, never. Algiers was paradise on earth, and moments like that were explosions of happiness. We watched the sun disappear over the horizon in the direction of the Strait of Gibraltar."

"You had good eyes in those days," René laughed. "Gibraltar is a long way off."

This time Roger stopped and suddenly reopened his eyes.

"Damn, the guy's just not going to stop. Obviously, poetry was never your strong point in Oran. Any more than *calentita*."

"It's not *calentita*, it's *calentica*, I tell you!"

"And I'm telling you what I'm telling you and it's the truth . . . "

The two old men were resuming with shared pleasure a quarrel that seemed to have bound them together for years. Guy and Marie Albouker watched them indulgently.

"Have you never been tempted to go back there?" Claire asked.

Albouker glanced at his wife before deciding to reply:

"Of course we have. Many *Pieds-Noirs* have gone back. For better and for worse. Some of them have returned delighted, others completely depressed."

"What about you? Don't you want to go back there?"

"Our 'back there' no longer exists, it's another country now. Our 'back there' now lives on only in us, and that's the one that has to be preserved. I lived in Algeria for only the first six years of my life, and I have memories that are very strong but also very vague. I'm afraid that the images of it today might erase the ones from yesterday."

"It might also be a way of healing the wound!"

Albouker held his hands out toward Claire and made a cross with his index fingers.

"*Vade retro, Satanas*."

He put his hands back on the tablecloth as a shrill little laugh escaped his mouth.

"What did you say there, wretched woman? I don't want to be healed. The *Pied-Noir* carries within him a deep and painful wound that is at the same time his strength, his cross, and his soul. He preserves this wound, he cherishes it, and he doesn't want to lose it. That is exactly what many French people reproach us for. Because they don't understand. They don't know that if we were healed, not only our Algeria would disappear but also ourselves, I mean we would disappear as a community. That will happen soon enough, believe me. We exist only through the memories that we carry within us, but every year, those who lived in Algeria are fewer and fewer. It's a little like old men in Africa; do you know the proverb?"

"Every time an old man dies, it's a library that burns."

"Precisely. Well, it's the same with us: every time a *Pied-Noir* dies, part of our memory disappears, part of our history sinks into oblivion. In ten to twenty years we'll all be dead and that will be the end of our community. That's what I understood, I think, when my father died: I had to pick up the torch, transmit the heritage."

Albouker tried to pour them some more wine but the bottle was empty. He had only to reach over and grab a full one, two guests farther on.

Marie Albouker put her hand on her husband's shoulder and massaged it affectionately.

"I know somebody who's not going to sleep again tonight," she finally said. "Every time he talks about the approaching disappearance of the *Pieds-Noirs*, he can't sleep. He was deeply affected by Bernard's murder. One night this week he didn't sleep a wink. He even went out for a walk, despite the rain." She put her hand on her husband's arm, who seemed to be embarrassed by her revelations.

"I understand," Claire said with compassion. "I know somebody else who's prone to insomnia: every time he has a case that's hard to solve."

Guy Albouker took advantage of the opportunity to change the subject:

"What a thing, that murder! And the vandalism, too . . . I heard that you have a lead?"

"No, I really can't say that we do," Sebag replied a little curtly.

"Oh? I thought you'd arrested someone," Albouker persisted.

"We're just carrying out routine questioning. For the moment, no one has been arrested, or even placed in police custody. It's going to be a difficult case, I think."

Silence fell around them. The whole group was waiting to hear what Sebag would say. It was a time to speak very carefully. But what should he say? He would have preferred to leave that role to the superintendent or the cabinet director: they had been trained for it.

"I think people shouldn't panic. We have two isolated acts here. Their proximity is a disturbing coincidence but at this stage in the investigation, it's still only a coincidence so far as we're concerned."

About twenty perplexed faces remained turned toward him. At the other end of the table, Jean-Pierre Mercier spoke up:

"Without violating the secrecy of the investigation, Lieutenant, I'd like you to tell us what we should think of a persistent rumor that's been circulating for two days in the neighborhood."

"Please tell me about it."

The treasurers' ceremonious tone made him uneasy.

"It's said that the letters 'OAS' were found written on the walls of Bernard Martinez's living room. Is that true?"

What should he reply to that? He quickly realized what he had to say: he'd been asked to reassure the members of the *Pied-Noir* community, and he decided he couldn't do that by lying to them.

"It's true, yes. More precisely, they were painted on a door."

Exclamations all around the table. Half surprised, half angry.

"In an investigation there are always elements that the

police keep secret," Sebag said. "It's a question of effectiveness. And sometimes, I admit, of diplomacy."

"Then why do you continue to say that the murder has no connection with the destruction of the monuments?" Mercier demanded.

"Because the acts are not of the same nature, and the weapons used aren't either. There is only the proximity of the events."

"The connection with the OAS isn't enough for you?"

"The same teams are working on both acts. We're not excluding the hypothesis of a common perpetrator. We've put the maximum number of men on these cases, which are a priority for us because we are well aware of the emotion that they are going to arouse in the city."

Gilles saw Claire looking at him with amusement. She knew he was a cop but was taking unconcealed pleasure seeing him play this role as a diplomat.

"What if the true connection wasn't with the OAS but with the *Pied-Noir* community itself?"

Guy Albouker had spoken in a soft voice, but one that all the guests could hear. A shiver ran around the table. Sebag took this remark for a stab in the back.

"I know, you mentioned that concern on the telephone the other day. It seemed to me to be without foundation. It still does."

"However, I find it credible," René added. "Most of the little bastards who constantly oppose the things we try to do don't make the distinction. For them, 'OAS' and '*Pieds-Noirs*" are synonyms."

These remarks elicited general approbation. Sebag got up and handed out his card.

"You shouldn't be excessively worried," he tried to reassure them. "But I'm giving you the number of my cell phone. Never hesitate to call me."

"Well, that promises to give you some sleepless nights," Marie Albouker said to Claire.

"I'm afraid you're right."

"*Insha'Allah*! O.K., I'm going to get the pastries. That will cool down the atmosphere."

She returned almost immediately with an immense tray covered with sweets that she listed with pleasure: gazelle horns, *tcharek* with dried figs, vanilla shortbread cookies, and many others whose names Gilles and Claire didn't even try to remember. The hubbub soon became deafening, still mixed with laughs and shrieks. Sebag gave Marie Albouker a grateful smile.

Claire took advantage of this moment to take her husband's hand under the table. She squeezed it very hard, at the same time looking elsewhere and seeming to be very interested in the conversation. Gilles pressed his thigh against hers and simultaneously smiled at another explosion of his neighbor Roger's anger. He liked nothing better than these moments of intense intimacy. Alone in the world, the two of them amid the crowd. Then he imagined that Claire wasn't his wife but his mistress, a secret liaison, unknown to all the guests around them.

But the moment was spoiled by a sudden nausea. He would so much have liked to persuade himself that he'd always been her only lover. He felt Claire's hand squeeze his even harder.

# CHAPTER 18

The old man was driving slowly down the avenue bordering the long beach at Canet. The Mediterranean, normally so calm, was roaring under the driving rain and throwing up heavy, foamy waves onto the quiet sand. Battered by the wind off the sea, the high, straight palms flailed their torn arms as if they were trying to keep their balance. Before he arrived at the marina, he turned first to his left, then left again thirty meters farther on. He found a parking place and took it.

Now he had to wait.

A thick mist gradually covered the windows of his little car, hiding him from the eyes of the people who lived on the street. The car radio was playing golden oldies at low volume. The man massaged his painful hands. The Catalan autumn wasn't a season for him.

His target lived in an opulent house in the residential quarter of Canet-en-Roussillon. Pink stuccoed walls, blue shutters, Mediterranean tile roofs, pink and red oleander hedges behind an unstuccoed wall. A little bit of paradise. Even with all this rain.

He kept his eyes on the big white gate, hardly a hundred meters in front of him. He was waiting for it to open.

His target was returning from a week's vacation in Tunisia. He'd made an appointment with him before he left and they had agreed to meet as soon as he got back. He'd introduced himself under a false name and claimed that he was putting together a collection of testimonies on the French of Algeria, but he had at first met with an absolute refusal. He thought he'd understood that his target had just been approached by a historian making the same request and that he had rejected it.

He'd had to argue for a long time, but he'd finally succeeded by explaining that his work would not be a neutral history: he wanted to produce a militant book that would do justice to the courageous fighters for French Algeria.

"Come see me on Sunday morning, as soon as I return," his target had agreed with a sudden enthusiasm. "My wife has to go to her yoga class. I prefer her not to be there: she doesn't like me to talk about certain pages of our history."

"That will be perfect," he had replied. "If you want, you don't even need to tell her that I'm going to visit you."

"We'll have an hour and a half to talk, will that be enough?"

"I think so. Otherwise we'll meet again later."

"Thanks for your understanding."

Luck was on his side. The bad weather made the headlines and journalists seemed already to have lost interest in Martinez's murder. His second target probably suspected nothing.

Besides, he wondered if his target had been afraid when he heard the news. For these bastards, this all happened a long time ago. Did they even remember everything they'd done at that time?

He saw an orange light flashing on the wall of the house that he'd been keeping an eye on for a good half hour. The heavy gate slowly opened to allow a luxurious Audi to pass through it. He waited another five minutes before starting the engine. He drove around the neighborhood once and then came back and parked in front of the house.

Getting out of the car, he pulled up the collar of his raincoat. What weather, he sighed as he walked up to the gate. On the first floor of the house, the lights had been turned on and he could see the living room through the large picture window without curtains. He saw a stooped figure and stepped back. He pulled his raincoat's hood over his head.

The old man was ready to put his gnarled index finger on the button to ring the doorbell when he jumped. Behind the window, a second silhouette came into view. Small, joyful, and bouncy. A young child. He swore. There was a kid in the house. A young kid. Less than ten years old. Hardly any older than his Gabriella.

He'd have to postpone the operation.

He returned to his car, simultaneously disappointed, annoyed, and touched. Gabriella . . .

He thought about his target again and gripped the steering wheel with his hands, triggering an acute pain all the way back to his wrists. An idea occurred to him. He took out his cell phone and called the house.

"Hello, it's Mr. Malpeyrat. I'm sorry, but something has come up at the last minute and I won't be able to come this morning. Could we possibly meet this afternoon?"

"The problem is that this afternoon my wife will be here."

"Oh, yes, that's true."

"Next week?"

No, the next week was too far off. It would become increasingly dangerous. He could take some risks for his third target, but not now.

"Unfortunately, that would be too late. My editor is pressuring me, he wants me to send him the manuscript as soon as possible. It's too bad; your testimony would have been invaluable."

"It's really too bad, yes . . . "

He said no more and waited. Not for long.

"I could meet you somewhere else tomorrow if you want."

The old man grimaced. He was ready. It was supposed to be today. Tomorrow would be too complicated. Too risky.

"Sorry, my plane leaves early tomorrow morning."

Another pause.

"I can arrange it for this afternoon, I'll find a pretext."

"How about 5 P.M.?"

"Fine. Where?"

"On the beach road between Canet and Saint-Cyprien, for example. I happen to have an appointment not far from there. What kind of car will you be driving?"

"A blue Audi A8. And you?"

He hesitated. It had to happen in the target's car.

"I don't know yet. But I'll be able to find you easily."

"That's for sure, with this weather there won't be anyone at the beach."

"Then we can do what we need to do without being disturbed," the old man concluded, a predatory smile on his lips.

His little SEAT Ibiza was buffeted as he drove down the road between the Mediterranean and Canet Lake. The wind off the sea was blowing a sticky mixture of water, salt, and sand onto the windshield. White with anger, the waves merged with the sky not far off the coast.

The old man hunched over the steering wheel, leaning far forward to see the road. In spite of the poor visibility, he had no trouble spotting the blue Audi, the only car parked that Sunday morning on the ten-kilometer stretch between the seaside resorts of Canet and Saint-Cyprien.

He stopped his car next to the Audi. He was late, but on purpose. It was important that his target get there first, that he be comfortably settled in his car, and especially that he stay there. That was also why he hadn't said what car he'd be driving. If the target had any doubts, even small ones, regarding who was in the car that stopped alongside his, he wouldn't venture into the storm to find out.

Once he'd gotten out of the SEAT, the old man looked quickly around. He could pick out the headlights of another vehicle coming toward them. He walked up to the Audi and looked at the backseat before knocking on the passenger door. The door opened. He got in. The other car with its lights on passed by them and disappeared in the direction of Canet.

Once he was inside the car, he held out his hand to his target. He hadn't changed much, despite his features deepened by age and swollen by good food and luxury. The target hesitated for a second, then mechanically shook his hand while he sifted through his memories.

"It's funny, your face seems familiar, but I don't think we've already met. Your name doesn't ring a bell: Jean Malpeyrat, that's it, right?"

André Roman was still looking at him trying to recognize his face disguised by the mask of time. His memory was slowly coming back to him.

He opened his eyes wide, and then his dumbfounded mouth murmured:

"It can't be . . . "

His eyes slowly moved from the old man's face to his hand. It was already holding a gun. A Beretta. His astonishment increased.

"It must be a dream . . . "

"A nightmare, you mean."

"What do you want?"

"To kill you. I've come a long way to do that."

"But . . . why?"

"You know very well why, you bastard."

Fear crept into André Roman's eyes.

"That was so long ago . . . "

"Not that long, really."

The rain was drumming on the car's roof, and like a metronome, it emphasized the sobriety of their conversation. Their mouths were emitting vapor that clung to the windows in an opaque shroud.

"What about the others?"

"One of them is already gone."

André's eyes narrowed and his mouth puckered.

"Who?"

"You'll find out soon enough. You're going to see him in Hell."

Roman's breathing accelerated, this was serious. But there might still be hope. He had money, he was rich, he'd invested his nest egg well.

He didn't have time to make an offer. He heard a voice from the past, dry and determined.

"I don't want your money."

This time, André understood that there was no way out. In a few seconds, the light was going to go out forever. He squirmed on his seat and managed to slip his left hand discreetly into the pocket of his overcoat. He'd have liked to be able to warn his former boss, but the latter had long since burned his bridges. Feeling his way, he tapped in the shortcut for his home phone. He could also have called the police, he said to himself afterward. Too late. He wouldn't be able to try again.

The old righter of wrongs had seen what he was doing but didn't care. He was in control of the timing, and the hour had rung.

"Adieu."

Without waiting for a response, he fired.

André opened his eyes wide. He took his hand out of his overcoat pocket and put it on his torn belly. Strangely, it didn't hurt, but a terrible cold was overtaking him. He lifted his eyes toward his killer and then his head sank. He would have liked to understand.

The shooter raised the barrel of his gun slightly. A car passed close to them on the coast road. He waited until it was far away before firing a second time. Right in the heart.

Roman's body collapsed, held upright only by his seatbelt. An odor of gunpowder filled the car.

He took a deep breath.

A child's voice made itself heard in the Audi.

"Hello . . . Grandpa? Grandpa? My Dédé?"

The voice moved farther away.

"Mama, it's my Dédé, he's not saying anything."

He went through his victim's pockets, found the cell phone, and turned it off. He had trouble swallowing. War didn't do you any favors. Not now and not in the past, either.

He took out his can of spray paint. He still had to sign his act.

Then he got back into his own car. He'd completed the second part of his mission. The third would be more difficult because now the target was more likely to be on his guard. Even if he didn't succeed in killing the last criminal, he knew that his life was already over. Fear would haunt him right to the end.

In a bar that was open in the port of Saint-Cyprien, he drank a pastis, shivering. In the late afternoon, he crossed the border again.

# CHAPTER 19

Gilles allowed himself a second cup of coffee before leaving. The last reprieve before going to work. He closed his eyes to savor the delight of the Ethiopian mocha.

"Well, is it good?"

He opened his eyes. His son was smiling at him. A smile and a four-word sentence, two miracles at once. Sebag was about to respond with a good-natured quip when he noticed that Leo had his helmet under his arm.

"Surely you're not planning to take your scooter today?"

"Why not?"

"Have you seen the weather?"

"It stopped raining."

"Yes, but the wind is back. You'd be better off taking the bus to school."

"Some of my teachers won't be there, I get out at 3 P.M. I'm not going to wait for the school buses."

"You can take the city bus."

"Are you kidding? It would take me almost an hour to get home."

"Yes, but at least you'd be sure to get here."

"You shouldn't have given me a scooter, then."

"I remind you that I was against it."

"We're not going to go through all that again . . . "

"We might if you don't obey me."

"I always obey. But you haven't forbidden me to do anything: you just said it would be smarter to take the bus."

Gilles took the time to look at his son. His features had gotten coarser with adolescence, and a few ugly pimples studded his cheeks. But when he joked like that, the last embers of his childhood still burned in his eyes. Like the light of a star that manages to reach us many years after it has died.

"Are you taking courses in rhetoric at school?" Gilles asked.

"Courses in what?"

"Rhetoric, it's the art of debate. Too bad! At least you'd have good grades in that subject."

"I've got some good grades in other subjects this year."

"Sports?"

"Not only. In French and math, too, I've been working a little harder this fall, you'll see it on my report card."

"I can hardly wait."

"Besides . . ."

Léo hesitated, then went ahead.

"Besides, if I can get home earlier, I can do a better job of reviewing for my test tomorrow."

Sebag couldn't help snorting.

"Are you really trying to convince me that if you take your scooter it's in order to do more work? Look your father straight in the eyes, you know that you can't fool me. If you're lying, it looks like . . . your acne in the middle of your face."

Léo laughed, for purely tactical reasons. Sebag finished his coffee while he waited for his son to try again. He didn't have to wait long.

"So, is it yes?"

"Let's say that it's not no."

"Yes!"

Léo held out the flat of his hand. Gilles slapped it.

"Be careful, though."

"I'm always careful."

"I hope so, son—one burial a month is more than enough for me."

\*

Contrary to what Léo had said, the rain hadn't completely stopped. The wind was driving great black clouds through the sky and blowing them out to sea. "Terrible time to put a dog or a scooter outdoors," Sebag said regretfully as he got into his car.

As he drove, he turned on the radio. It was time for the news on France Bleu Roussillon. After a report on a concert given by young local singer who had earlier been the star of a reality show, he listened attentively to a news flash about Martinez's murder. As he expected, this time the information had filtered through to the news bureaus: the journalist mentioned the letters on the door of the living room and talked about the victim's membership in the OAS, but didn't indulge in wild speculations. On the whole, the report seemed to him pretty good.

Once he'd arrived at headquarters, Sebag stopped for a moment at the office that handled emergencies.

"Anything happen last night?"

"There was an altercation at the exit from a nightclub, a fight in Bas Vernet, and an attempted burglary at a depot in the Saint Charles market," Lieutenant François Ravier replied. "The usual, in other words! And you, how are things going?"

"Well, I had a little argument this morning with my son about the dangers of scooters . . . The usual!"

"I hear you. My son's sixteen and we've never agreed to buy him one. He worked this summer and he'll probably soon buy one with what he earned, but that'll be his business: if Louis has an accident with the vehicle he bought for himself, it won't be our fault. That said, we're crossing our fingers all the same!"

"*Insha'Allah*, as they say!"

"Ah? Do you say that too?"

"Sometimes, yes."

Climbing the stairs to his office, Sebag reflected on the expression he'd just used. *Insha'Allah* . . . It sounded good, he thought. Better than that: it sounded right. Fatalistic at first sight, it radiated calming vibrations as soon as it had been said. Trusting in God could sometimes be good. Because whatever we say about it, in life we don't control anything. Thinking was illusory. Worse than that, thinking meant setting the bar too high and taking on too many responsibilities. In life we can dream, wish, hope, act, try, find a way to do what we want to do, and then events end up making the decision for us. The events? A fig leaf that conceals chance, destiny, and perhaps even God, everyone being free to choose his own word to designate the inexplicable. In life, we have to act in accord with our feelings, at the moment that we have them, and afterward there's no longer any need to cogitate, ruminate, or bother oneself about it. Afterward? *Insha'Allah*, yeah, that might be enough. And it was not just an expression, it was the best of all philosophies.

Before he could figure out how to apply his newfound wisdom to his personal life, Sebag had reached his office. It was time to go to work, because *Insha'Allah* had its limits. To solve a case, first you had to roll up your sleeves, and in this case that meant picking up the telephone. He dialed the number of the president of the *Pied-Noir* Circle.

"Hello, Mr. Albouker. Lieutenant Sebag here. I didn't want to bother you about it Saturday night during the very convivial couscous dinner, but I need to contact rather urgently other people who also belonged to the OAS."

There was a heavy silence at the other end of the line.

"Mr. Albouker?"

"I'm afraid I can't help you. The members of our association are not classified by their former political associations, or by the current ones, for that matter. I don't need to tell you that that would not be legal."

"You know your members, and you know who might have acquaintances with that organization."

"Being acquainted with it doesn't mean belonging to it."

Sebag was getting annoyed all the more quickly because he still resented Albouker's having spread panic at the dinner. He didn't find that very responsible.

"If you're going to refuse to help me, tell me right away, that will keep me from wasting my time."

Another silence. Then Albouker spoke again in a more conciliatory tone.

"In fact, I'm not the best person to help you. As I already told you, in my family we were on the left. So I'm not the person others confide that kind of information to. Contact Mercier."

Sebag wrote down the cell phone number Albouker gave him, hung up, and called the treasurer. He repeated his question and was met with the same reluctance.

Along with a touch of hostility.

"You're going to awaken painful memories, hatreds and angers that are still open wounds, and that's not good."

"You have to make up your mind. If you think a concerted, hostile action is currently being carried on against former members of the OAS, you have to help me. And then I have a hard time understanding your reluctance. No one is taking responsibility for what happened among you, is that it?"

First he heard very loud breathing in his phone.

"We take responsibility, Inspector, I assure you, we take responsibility," Mercier replied. "But we're tired of people constantly sending us back to a very precise period. The history of the OAS lasted one year. Just one year, that's very little when you know that France remained in Algeria for a century. But it's always for that same year that we have to take responsibility. We'd so much like to talk about other years . . . "

"I know, I was at the couscous dinner on Saturday, I remind you. And I heard you talk about your happy years in Algeria. But Sunday is over and now it's Monday. I've got an investigation to conduct, I'm doing my job, that's all. I understand your resentment, but it's not my fault. It's the killer who made the choice, not me. I was born after the Algerian War and I've never had any interest in history. If you see some other way to conduct my investigation, don't hesitate to tell me, I'll be glad to hear about it."

Sebag stopped; his argument had left him breathless. Like Albouker just before, Mercier took the time to reflect before giving out any information.

"I'll see what I can do. I'll call one of my brothers, Gérard. He was . . . he knew certain members of the OAS in Algiers. He now lives in Paris. I'll let you know."

While he waited, Sebag opened his inbox and consulted the log for the weekend. Mercier quickly called back.

"My brother is making inquiries. He promised me he would phone you in the course of the morning."

Sebag occupied himself by rereading all the reports on the case. As soon as he started in on the first one, he screwed up his face and kept it that way all morning. Really, he'd never get used to the formatted, conventional language of these reports, his own as well as those of his colleagues. Police reports always left him unsatisfied. They filtered reality to give it the smooth, even appearance of objective and rigorous information that he considered stupid and sanitized. The police report is to sensible, complex reality what industrial food is to French cuisine.

The formula pleased him and he wrote it down in a corner of his blue notebook.

Around 10:30 his telephone rang. Gérard Mercier had kept his word.

"I'm able to confirm that Martinez was in fact a member of our organization and that he was not a simple activist but a combatant."

Sebag knew that already. He expected more. Mercier must have sensed his disappointment.

"I wanted to get back to you as quickly as I could, and I haven't had time to collect a lot of information."

"What I need is a list of former members of the OAS who live in Perpignan. If possible, people who were part of the group to which Martinez belonged, for instance."

"You're asking for a lot. Even those who haven't repudiated their convictions aren't very fond of talking about those years."

"I know, your brother already explained that to me at length a little while ago. We aren't getting very far this morning. I didn't think it would be so hard. What I'm looking for is not simply a witness, it's a potential victim!"

To shake up his interlocutor, he'd deliberately painted a dark picture.

"Do you think the murderer is going to attack other activists?"

Gérard Mercier had taken the bait. Now Sebag didn't need to go any further.

"To tell the truth, I don't know. It's a hypothesis we're working on because we can't yet exclude it. When I know what the killer's motives are, then I'll be able to say whether he has targeted other people. But in order to know more about his motives . . . "

" . . . you have to meet with people from the OAS!"

"Precisely!"

Mercer paused, and to Sebag that seemed a good sign. In more than twenty years on the job, he'd never met a witness who could give a cop names without taking time to think it over, even if only for form. This held true even when it was a matter of drawing up a list of possible victims rather than suspects.

"A friend gave me one person's name. I haven't been able to check it out, and I don't know whether he was part of the same group as Martinez, but he will be able to tell you that. Especially since, according to my friend, the guy lives rather close to Perpignan. His name is André Roman."

"Where exactly does he live?"

"I don't know, near Perpignan, that's all my friend knew. But you should be able to find him easily."

"Probably, yes."

Sebag suddenly felt in a hurry to hang up.

"I have one last thing to ask of you, Mr. Mercier. Could you continue to gather information about this group for me?"

Gérard Mercier chose to reply frankly and directly:

"The case interests me and I definitely plan to talk to all my contacts to find out more about it. I will continue to gather information, but first of all for myself. I don't guarantee to tell you everything I find out: that will depend on how events develop and how you conduct your investigation."

Sebag thanked him and hung up. He had no trouble finding Roman's address and phone number on the internet. The man lived in Canet. Sebag immediately dialed the telephone number. A woman's voice answered. He asked to speak to André. The voice broke, and Sebag understood.

"André? No, I . . . I can't put him on the line . . . "

The flat voice was replaced by another, more male and more assured."

"Why do you want to talk to André Roman? Who are you?"

"Gilles Sebag, Perpignan police."

"Sebag? We know each other! This is Lieutenant Cornet of the gendarmerie. We met last summer in Collioure."

"Yes, I remember it well. How are you?"

The question had slipped out even though he'd understood that this was no time for polite chitchat. Anyway, Cornet didn't give him any news about his health but instead confirmed what he had feared.

"André Roman has been murdered. I'm at his home. I'll wait for you here."

A navy blue car from the gendarmerie was parked on the

sidewalk in front of the gate to the villa in Canet. Sebag pushed the button twice and waited. The door of the house opened and Lieutenant Cornet's tall, slender figure came out. The head of the gendarmerie's criminal investigation unit came to meet him. He extended a long and delicate hand.

"I'd tell you how glad I am to see you again, but I'm not sure that would be fitting, under the circumstances."

Cornet was only twenty-five, but his brown hair was already starting to go gray.

"Would you mind if before we talk about what happened to Roman, I ask why you called him?"

"Not at all."

Sebag told him about Martinez's murder and gave him a complete account of the main lines of the ongoing investigation. Something in the lieutenant's sparkling eyes and his tone of extreme politeness led him to think that the gendarmes had already connected the case with the information that had appeared in the press. It was better to be open about it in order to obtain full collaboration.

After he'd finished, Cornet made no commentary. He limited himself to an invitation.

"Roman was not killed in his home but in his car, on the road to Saint-Cyprien. Shall I give you a ride?"

As they drove there, the two men exchanged a few banal observations on the weather. Sebag didn't want to rush his colleague. The time for questions would soon come.

They soon saw, at the end of the long, straight stretch of road, two spots of blue: a gendarmerie van, and next to it, André Roman's lighter-colored Audi. Cornet parked his car nearby. The gendarmes had finished their investigation and the body of the victim had been taken away. The two officers still watching over the vehicle greeted them. Sebag examined the surrounding area. He spotted tire tracks in the soft sand.

"Given the amount of rain that fell yesterday morning,

these tracks must be recent," Cornet explained. "We took casts of them, and I hope to have the results before the end of the day."

Sebag cautiously approached the vehicle. He walked slowly around it without seeing any sign that it had been broken into.

"We found Roman's body in the driver's seat. We think he let his murderer get in the car. They must have had a rendezvous."

"A rendezvous that required discretion," Sebag remarked. "There can't have been very many people who passed by here yesterday."

"Mme. Roman contacted us yesterday evening. Her husband had not come home; she'd had a telephone call from him that afternoon but there was no one on the other end of the line. She tried to call him several times but couldn't reach him. She got worried. But you know how it is when a grown-up doesn't return to the conjugal home . . . Usually, it's a matter of an inconsequential escapade. We called the hospital emergency rooms, and since there hadn't been an accident, we tried to reassure her and recorded her call. This morning, a resident of Saint-Cyprien who was going to work in Canet spotted the car and in particular a dark form slumped in it. He notified the local brigade of the gendarmerie, which sent out a patrol car."

Sebag would have liked to open the door to inspect the interior of the car but the seals had already been put on it. He squinted through the passenger side window.

"It's especially the headliner that you need to look at," Cornet advised him.

Sebag bent his head. The inside was dark but he could easily read the three white letters on the headliner: OAS. Sebag shivered. There was no doubt: this was the beginning of a series.

On the way back to Roman's house. Lieutenant Cornet was more talkative.

"It appears that the murderer took no precautions, and the prints we took from the passenger side of the car are probably his. It won't take long to compare them with the ones you found in Martinez's apartment."

A gust of wind shook the car. The tramontane was clearing the sky, and the sea, far offshore, was gradually regaining its blue color.

"André Roman was shot at point-blank range, once in the stomach, and once in the heart. The ballistic analysis will tell us if the same weapon was used. A 9 mm Beretta 34, I think?"

Sebag confirmed what Cornet said and was glad he'd been frank with him, since he seemed to know the Martinez case well.

"He probably died late yesterday afternoon," Cornet continued. "After 5:12."

The young lieutenant was amused by Sebag's astonishment.

"That's the time of the call Roman made to his home. The cell phone was found on his body. I'm inclined to think that Roman called home just before he died. He probably dialed the number without his murderer noticing."

"Why didn't he call the police?"

"He probably acted automatically, he didn't have time to think. In any case, it was too late, it wouldn't have changed anything."

They were coming to the first apartment buildings in Canet, and Cornet slowed down. The road turned away from the beach to go around the town. The lieutenant from the gendarmerie continued his account.

"Roman has his papers on him, his credit card, and cash. The motive was not money, but you already suspected that. The body was transferred to the forensic lab. The autopsy is supposed to take place tomorrow."

At a traffic circle, Cornet turned right and headed back toward the sea. He had to stop at a crosswalk for a couple of retirees being dragged along by two dogs.

"The widow, Mathilde Roman, is in shock. She hasn't yet told us much. Except that they had just come back from a vacation in Tunisia. They go two or three times a year. They have a small family house over there."

Cornet parked his car in front of the Romans' villa again. Then he led Sebag down the garden path. When they got to the front door, he knocked softly before opening it.

"Mme. Roman, it's the gendarme again. I'm coming in."

Sebag followed him to a large, opulent living room where an elderly lady was slumped on a tawny, leather-covered sofa. Her dyed blond hair, green blouse with a little collar, and her bent head made her look like a faded sunflower.

"Mme. Roman, I'd like to introduce you to Lieutenant Sebag of the Perpignan police. We have a few questions to ask you."

Mathilde Roman looked up at Gilles with empty and indifferent eyes. She furtively blew her nose on the tissue she held in her hand. Cornet sat down alongside her, but Sebag remained standing, looking at the numerous photos hung on the wall. He lingered a few seconds in front of a group portrait that had probably been taken in the summer on the beach at Canet. He counted twelve persons lined up in a row, clearly arranged by age. At one end the two grandparents seemed to be happy and beaming. He realized that he was seeing for the first time the face of the victim.

"You have a fine family, Mme. Roman," he said.

"Yes. We have three children: two boys and a girl. And we have seven grandchildren. That photo dates from a few months ago. This summer we were lucky enough to be able to bring them all together at the same time. That's not always possible: our elder son lives in Montpellier, the other in the United States, and our daughter has been living in Toulouse since she married."

"Seven grandchildren, that's very good," Sebag complimented her. "They must also keep you busy, don't they?"

"Not as much as I'd like. Since their parents don't live in Perpignan, we don't see them very often."

"What are their names?"

Mathilde followed Sebag's finger as it moved from one face to the next on the photo.

"Bénédicte, Léon, Martin, Camille, Chloé, Lucie, and Antoine. Antoine is the baby, he's five years old, my daughter's second child. We often take care of him."

She sniffled noisily before continuing in a more muted voice.

"He had been with us for two weeks. We took him with us to Tunisia. My husband lived part of his childhood over there and we often went back. Once again, we had a wonderful vacation. If we could have known . . . Antoine loved his grandpa so much. He called him 'my Dédé,' a nickname he invented all by himself. He started calling him that when he was still very young. It was Antoine who picked up the telephone yesterday when André called for the last time. He thought it was a game and I still haven't had the heart to tell him what happened. I left him with a neighbor this morning. Laurence, his mother, is supposed to come this evening from Toulouse to pick him up and to . . . help me. She'll have to be the one to tell him. I won't have the strength."

Sebag decided this was the right time to begin a more professional conversation. He sat down on the chair opposite the sofa.

"So your husband lived in Tunisia. I thought he was a *Pied-Noir* from Algeria?"

Mathilde Roman laid her tissue on the coffee table and took out another one from a packet that she kept clutched in her hand.

"Yes, he was born in Algiers, but his father was a government official who was later assigned to Bizerte, in northern Tunisia. The family found that country calmer and more hospitable, and they would have liked to stay there. That's why they bought a house, the one we inherited. But eventually André's father was transferred back to Algeria. That was a few years before the war began."

She spoke quickly and volubly about the past, with the unconscious hope of forestalling the policemen's other questions. The ones that would certainly plunge her back into this dreadful present.

Sebag met Lieutenant Cornet's eyes and signaled to him to take over. The gendarme gladly accepted the invitation.

"A little while ago you told me, Madam, that your husband had a meeting and that was why he left the house shortly before 5 P.M. Is that correct?"

Mathilde Roman took the time to blow her nose before nodding her head in assent.

"A meeting with a writer, you said?" Cornet persisted.

"Yes, that's correct, with a writer, for a book . . . "

"A book on what subject?"

"The Algerian War."

Sebag took out his notebook and starting writing in it.

"What was this writer's name?"

"I don't recall, but I saw that André wrote it down in his appointment book. He didn't say any more about it because I don't like him to talk about that past in front of me."

"Where is the appointment book?"

"Probably on his desk."

She started to get up but Cornet stopped her.

"We'll look into that later. In any case, it's surely not the man's real name."

She gave the gendarme a terrified look.

"Do you think it was that man who . . . "

She didn't dare say more. Not giving expression to the unbearable is a classic defense mechanism that seeks to deny the inevitable. Sebag decided to help her confront reality.

"Yes, we assume that your husband's murderer contacted

him under this false pretext." He had uttered the word "murderer" very slowly and distinctly. Mathilde Roman bent her head, resuming the position of a faded sunflower. In alternation with Cornet, Sebag asked the usual questions, even though he already knew the answers. Had André Roman seemed uneasy lately, did he feel threatened, did he have enemies? She limited herself to replying by sadly shaking her head.

Sebag finally decided to get to the heart of the matter:

"Did you know that your husband had belonged to the OAS?"

Mme Roman looked up at him.

"Do you think that is related to . . . to his . . . "

This time, Sebag didn't help her out. But she stopped and didn't utter the word.

"We have every reason to think so, yes. Did your husband often talk about the OAS?"

"Never. Never in front of me."

"Why?"

"I told you that I didn't like him to talk about Algeria in front of me. I even forbade him to do so."

Mme. Roman's voice grew stronger.

"The Algeria we knew is dead, and I moved on a long time ago."

"Were you born over there, too?"

"Yes. I met André on the boat that was taking us from Algiers to Port-Vendres."

"What do you think about the fighting he did in Algeria?"

"Nothing. At the time, I considered him a hero. Now I don't know. No one here in France sees things as we did then. So I don't want to think about it anymore."

"Does it surprise you that his death might be connected with that past?"

"I don't know. Yes and no . . . It's all so long ago. But on the other hand, what else could it be? André has been retired for ten years. We belong to a Scrabble club and go to a gymnastics class twice a week. Sometimes we also help out at the Catholic Aid Society. What could anybody hold against André in all that?"

"Your husband was a car dealer before he retired, right?" Lieutenant Cornet asked.

"Yes."

"In Perpignan?"

"In Perpignan, and the regions of Pyrénées-Orientales and Aude. He had several dealerships."

"Did sell everything when he retired?"

"No, only part of it. He still owned certain dealerships even though he had stopped managing them."

Seeing that Sebag was not following him in this direction, Cornet suddenly fell silent and made a face excusing himself. The inspector responded with a broad smile signifying that he was not bothered by this interruption.

Collaboration between the police department and the gendarmerie was working well in this investigation, for the moment, but it was better not to rub anybody the wrong way.

Sebag resumed the questioning:

"Do you know what actions your husband carried out in the name of the OAS?"

"No. I never asked him. As I told you, I considered him a hero as soon as we met, and yet I never wanted to hear about it. It was as if I had already sensed that horrible things had happened."

"André had committed horrible acts?"

"That war was terrible, and each side did horrible things."

"So horrible that they might lead someone to take vengeance for them so long afterward?"

Mathilde Roman shrugged her shoulders.

"Except for a few persons like me, the *Pieds-Noirs* have never wanted to forget about that time. On the contrary, they love to scratch their painful wounds. They remember everything and everyone."

"Had your husband maintained contacts with other former members of the OAS?"

"No, I don't think so."

She wiped her nose with her tissue.

"But if he did, he wouldn't have told me about it."

Sebag looked intensely at her for a moment. Something in the widow's attitude put him on alert. For the first time, he had the impression that she was not telling him the whole truth.

"Did you know Bernard Martinez?" he asked.

"No."

She had replied a quarter of a second too fast. When you don't recognize a name, you take a moment to think before you answer.

"Are you sure, Madame?"

She wiped her nose and looked up at him.

"I didn't really know him . . . "

"What does that mean, 'not really'?"

She put her tissue on the coffee table next to the first one and took a third from the package.

"I happened to see that name in my husband's appointment book."

"So did they see each other from time to time?"

"I suppose so."

"And he never talked to you about him?"

"No, never."

"So you imagined that he was connected with this past of your husband's that you don't want to hear any more about?"

She nodded.

"And that's why you don't want to talk to us about it?"

She gave him an embarrassed smile to thank him for understanding.

"Yes, excuse me, it's stupid. But I've been avoiding this subject for such a long time . . . "

"Bernard Martinez was murdered a week ago in his apartment in Perpignan."

Sebag had deliberately told her this without warning. He felt that Roman's wife was holding back part of the truth and he wanted to blow hot and cold. Mathilde, stupefied, opened wide her eyes reddened by weeping.

"Did your husband know about Martinez's death?" Gilles asked.

"I don't know. No, certainly not."

"Would he have been saddened by it?"

"Probably."

"They were that close?"

"I think so."

"Would that death have worried him?"

"I don't know."

"But you think so?"

She looked at him, disoriented by this sudden burst of questions. Lieutenant Cornet also seemed surprised. But Sebag hadn't finished.

"Bernard Martinez used to belong to the OAS. Was he in the same group as your husband?"

"I don't know."

"You no longer want to remember it, Mme. Roman, but you know. What did your husband write in his appointment book when he was supposed to see Martinez? 'Meeting with Bernard'?"

"Yes, that's it."

"Just 'Bernard'?"

"Yes."

"Not 'Martinez'?"

"No."

"But you knew that it referred to Bernard Martinez?"

"Uh . . ."

"In any case, when I asked you if you knew Bernard

Martinez, you didn't imagine for a moment that it might be another Bernard."

Mathilde Roman collapsed. She put her head on her knees and burst into tears. Long sobs. Cornet put his hand on the widow's shoulders and gently massaged them as he gave a questioning look to Sebag, who was also beginning to wonder if he hadn't gone at her a little too hard.

To find out, he had to go on a little further.

"André and Bernard were part of the same OAS group, weren't they?"

She made a brief movement of her shoulders that he interpreted as a confirmation.

"What exactly did they do to defend French Algeria? You know. You have to tell us. It will help us arrest your husband's murderer."

Mathilde went on sobbing for a long time before she slowly sat up and showed them a face ravaged by tears. Then Sebag understood the intensity of her suffering. In this painful time she would have liked so much liked to remember only an affectionate husband and a thoughtful grandfather.

"Yes, André and Bernard Martinez were active members of the OAS," she said in a monotone voice. "They killed. They set bombs and machine-gunned people. FLN combatants but also defenseless Arabs. Also a French police officer. Women and children too, I suppose. I don't want to know anything about it. It was horrible. The whole time was horrible. How could they go so far as that? The Arabs were our friends . . . "

She interrupted herself to blow her nose.

"The only good and brave thing they did was to combat the *barbouzes*."[10]

The *barbouzes*. For Sebag, this term aroused mainly memo-

---

[10] French secret agents working against the OAS.

ries of a film made by Georges Lautner in the 1960s. With Lino Ventura, Bernard Blier, and Francis Blanche, if he remembered correctly. A spy film, it had nothing to do with Algeria. He had to get to the bottom of this right away.

"Who else belonged to their group?"

Mathilde's reddened, swollen eyes looked into those of the inspector.

"I don't know, sir, truly I don't know. They alone could have told you. Bernard Martinez was the only person from his past with whom André had kept in contact. He didn't see anyone else."

"Do you know how many of them there were?"

"No, really not, I'm sorry."

Sebag didn't persist. He was ashamed of having gone so far, but it was his job. He had to do it. He got up, and Lieutenant Cornet immediately did the same.

"You shouldn't be alone, Mme. Roman . . . " the gendarme said gently.

"My daughter should arrive soon from Toulouse."

She glanced at a clock attached to the living room wall.

"She should be here any minute."

"You sent Antoine to be with a neighbor, you said?"

She sniffed a barely audible "yes."

"We'll take you to her house," Cornet said.

Without giving her a chance to protest, he took her arm and forced her to get up. Then he led her to the door. Before he followed them, Sebag picked up the package of tissues that had remained on the coffee table. Mathilde Roman would still need them.

# CHAPTER 20

Sebag was walking rapidly through the streets of Perpignan, gulping down a sandwich. Serrano ham, peppers, lettuce: delicious. He had come back from Canet too late to get the daily special at the Carlit and had had Rafel make this *entrepa*[11] to order. He took advantage of his lunch break to get a little exercise, because he knew that it would be a long afternoon and that it wouldn't be possible for him to engage in his traditional evening run. Informed of André Roman's murder, Castello had redeployed his teams and called another emergency meeting for the end of the day.

Sebag stopped on Cassanyes Square to drink mint tea in a little Moroccan *bouiboui*.[12] Located between the North African and Gypsy quarters, Cassanyes Square had a colorful outdoor market every morning. But today, in the early afternoon, there was not much left to testify to that, only empty crates and rotting vegetables left lying on the asphalt. The air was still warm, despite the humidity that oozed from the walls and rose from the ground. Sebag quietly sipped his hot, sugary tea on the terrace. A street-sweeping machine was noisily going about its work, surrounded by a horde of little men in green who picked up the bulkier waste.

Around 3 P.M., he set out at a quick pace toward police

---

[11] Sandwich (Catalan).
[12] Restaurant or café of mediocre quality.

headquarters. He had brought five cartons full of documents to his office. The Romans didn't have a computer, and Mathilde had let him take everything he wanted from her husband's office, while Lieutenant Cornet agreed to turn a blind eye to what Sebag was doing. The judiciary and administrative procedures being what they were, the gendarmes had not yet relinquished the case, and in theory Sebag didn't have the right to investigate this second murder.

The first thing he took out of the cartons was the family list of telephone numbers. He went through it quickly without finding anything noteworthy. He would have preferred to be able to examine the victim's cell phone, but Cornet hadn't been willing to let him take that major piece of evidence. Procedure would have to be respected. The head of the investigative unit at the Perpignan gendarmerie had promised to act as quickly as possible and keep him informed.

In the victim's appointment book, Sebag had found three dates, three meetings with "Bernard." February 15, May 23, and July 20. In each case a different restaurant's name was written next to "Bernard." At first glance, there was nothing mysterious about these meetings, just two old men who must have shared, as they ate good meal, their memories of war and infamy.

Sebag set aside for the time being a few files he'd brought along on principle but which he did not think had priority: insurance, tax returns, bank statements, etc. Instead, he took out an old photo album. He had left Mathilde the family albums and had taken the one from André's childhood in Algeria and Tunisia.

He opened it with great care.

The black-and-white snapshots had the stiff and formal charm of rare photos celebrating the great events in a person's life. André as a baby, nestled in the arms of a young couple standing in front of two older couples. André, still a baby, in a church for his baptism, and then another, taken twelve years later, during a communion. Between the two, André at six posing, probably with a brother, in front of an artificial backdrop of a snowy mountain; then André and the same boy smiling before a Christmas tree. As the children grew, the photos began to show more intimate scenes in their daily life: a soccer match in a vacant lot, swimming in the sea, a family meal.

Only the last pages interested Sebag. Two photos in particular. Roman as a young adult, leaning proudly on a white Dauphine with a friend in the driver's seat. Then Roman and three other young men, including the same friend, surrounding a soldier about forty years old with a long, solemn face. The young men were smiling broadly, but the soldier was staring at the camera with all the gravity that went with his rank. The photo had been taken in a small room without much distance.

Sebag carefully removed them from the album before also taking out a tract and an article clipped from a newspaper. The article was about an armed commando's murder of a French policeman in 1961, and the tract proclaimed, in bloodred letters, that the OAS would strike where and when it wanted. Taking along all these documents, Sebag went immediately upstairs and entered the office of Castello's secretary.

Jeanne greeted him warmly, a pleasant smile on her full lips. Gilles showed her his hands full of documents, and explained:

"I need to make a few photocopies and scan these documents . . . "

"Go ahead, Monsieur Sebag. Do you know how to use the machine?"

"Uh . . .yes, at least for the photocopies."

Standing in front of the machine, Sebag quickly realized that he'd been presumptuous. He put the two photos on the sheet of glass and tried to understand the machine's control panel. It would probably have been easier to take off in an Airbus than to force this photocopier to carry out the elementary task for which it had been designed. Sebag tapped at random on a few illuminated buttons, but nothing happened.

He turned around to ask Jeanne's help, but saw that she was already standing behind him. She was wearing a belted black dress that harmoniously emphasized her figure.

"We've just received this new model, but I'm the only one who knows how to make it work. Normal or reduced size?"

"Enlarged, if possible."

"Mmm . . . with pleasure."

She tapped three buttons in succession. The long, white-lace sleeves of her dress enhanced the velvety quality of her arms.

"There we go."

The photocopier actually started up and spat out its first sheet. Sebag handed Jeanne the newspaper article and the tract.

"Normal size will be fine for these."

"Normal size? Good. After all, normal size is the best . . . "

Sebag couldn't help blushing at the double entendre. Jeanne liked to tease the men at headquarters, but she never went any further.

"Will that be all for you, Monsieur Sebag?"

"Would it be going too far to ask you to scan them, too?"

"Go too far, Monsieur. Sebag, go too far. It's a pleasure to serve you."

He couldn't help admiring the lines of her dress when the secretary went back to her desk. The fabric stopped at her mid-thigh and her white, transparent stockings echoed the motif of the lace.

"I'll scan them on my session and send them to you by e-mail. Will that be all right?"

"You are perfect, truly perfect."

Jeanne clicked several keys.

"There, they're underway. As soon as they're done, I'll send them to you. You can take back your documents."

"Thanks, Jeanne. What would we do without you?"

"I don't dare even think about it," she said, still bantering.

Back in his office, Sebag took time to examine the photos in detail. The old snapshots were a little fuzzy but he would have bet that one of Roman's companions was none other than Martinez. From there to thinking that he had in front of his eyes all the members of a single action group, it was only a small step.

His cell phone rang. It was Lieutenant Cornet.

"The fingerprint analysis is categorical. It is in fact the same killer. I've just talked with the prosecutor: the two cases are going to be joined. Obviously, they will be assigned to you."

"Sorry about that."

"So am I, but that's how it is. Before the end of the day, I'll send you all our reports and initial analyses. At least I know that the investigation is in good hands."

"I thank you for your confidence."

"You're welcome, really."

"I'll keep you informed."

"That would be very nice of you."

There was a brief silence. Sebag smiled.

"Aren't we laying it on a little thick here?" he asked his interlocutor.

"Maybe," Cornet replied.

Then the lieutenant from the gendarmerie broke into a sincere and merry laugh.


"Gentlemen, I have to tell you: this is a grave hour. If we don't want to be the laughingstock of all France, the overseas departments and territories, and the whole Mediterranean basin, we're going to have to seriously raise the level of our performance."

Although the tone was intended to be Churchillian, the vocabulary was more like that of a minor-league Raymond

Domenach.[13] But that wasn't the point: to galvanize the troops, the music is sometimes more important than the words.

In the meeting room at police headquarters, no one said a word. Everybody was present, including Raynaud and Moreno. There was even a little new recruit. Sebag recognized the young woman he'd passed in the hallway that same day, the female cop with eyes the color of the Mediterranean.

Castello introduced her:

"We have Julie Sadet with us. She comes to us from the capital. She is preparing to take her examination to become a lieutenant. She's going to help us in our investigation."

"Hello," the aforementioned Julie said in a firm and level voice.

The policemen responded to her greeting, both happy and intimidated to have a woman in their ranks for the first time.

Castello continued his introductory speech:

"So now we have a second corpse to deal with. A single killer, a single weapon, and probably a single motive connected with the victims' involvement in the OAS. Gilles has put before you the first evidence produced by the gendarmes' investigation. I've just had a look at it, and it's good work, but incomplete, of course, and it will be up to us to finish it. Gilles is going to outline it for you."

Sebag briefly summed up what he had learned that morning and what Lieutenant Cornet had communicated to him via e-mail in the late afternoon.

"Pending the autopsy and the ballistics analysis, we can say with a high degree of probability that André Roman was killed yesterday, around the middle of the day, hit in the heart by a 9 mm bullet. There were numerous fingerprints in and on the

---

[13] Celebrated former soccer player and coach of the French national soccer team.

car, but the freshest ones correspond to those we found at Martinez's apartment. The tire tracks found nearby come from a Kleber model usually put on small cars such as a Renault Clio, a Peugeot 206, or a SEAT Ibiza. The neighborhood canvass made this morning around the Romans' villa in Canet has not yielded any results as yet, but many of the neighbors were not there today. Concerning the car in which the crime was committed and that of the killer, we do not currently have any witnesses, unfortunately. You all know that road . . . "

He stopped and smiled his excuse to their new colleague.

"Almost all of you know that road along the coast; for several kilometers there are no houses except a few old fishermen's shacks near the lake. The gendarmes were planning to put out a call for witnesses, but obviously the ball is in our court now."

"I've talked with the prosecutor, and he has okayed that," the superintendent added. "The appeal will be put out tomorrow in the newspapers and on the radio. For once the journalists will be useful to us, and we've got to take advantage of that. A few words about the victim, Gilles?"

"André Roman was born in Algiers in 1939. His father worked for the post office and his mother was a housewife. André began work at the age of sixteen, as a mechanic in a garage. When he arrived in France in 1962, he took over a car dealership in Perpignan. He sold Simcas, a brand that later became Talbot, and was then absorbed by Peugeot-Citroën. His business did well, and when he retired in 2005, he owned a dozen garages in Perpignan, Prades, Leucate, and Narbonne."

"He managed better than Martinez did," Llach commented.

"You could say that, yes. André Roman had, in addition to his fine villa, a twenty-one–meter boat moored in the port at Canet, an apartment in Font-Romeu, and a small house in Tunisia. He inherited the latter . . . "

Castello was getting impatient.

"Is there anything else, Gilles? You have photos, I think."

"Yes. These." He circulated copies.

"I've e-mailed them to you," he explained.

"What are they?" the superintendent asked.

"In the first photo, I think the two men are André Roman and Bernard Martinez, but the second one is the more interesting. There we see four young men—including Roman and Martinez, grouped around a soldier."

He turned to Ménard, who had returned from Marseille over the weekend.

"François sent them to his historian, who had no difficulty identifying the central figure . . . "

Ménard put two handwritten pages on the table. He looked at the first.

"It is in fact the notorious Lieutenant Degueldre," he confirmed. "Born in 1925 in the north of France, he was a young resistance fighter under the German occupation, then a hero of the war in Indo-China, decorated with the military medal for bravery. Having become a lieutenant in the first foreign regiment of paratroopers, he participated in the Algerian conflict before going underground and operating within the OAS to lead the redoubtable Delta commandos. He was arrested in 1962, sentenced to death, and shot by firing squad."

"The name Degueldre was inscribed on the monument that was destroyed at the cemetery," Sebag added.

"Four men around this Degueldre," Joan Llach said. "Were Martinez and Roman thus part of a single group that is supposed to have included two other members?"

"At least two other members, in any case."

"Then we've got to find these two guys quick," the Catalan policeman concluded.

"That is in fact our priority," the superintendent reminded them. "This second murder tells us that our killer is not striking blindly just any *Pied-Noir*, or even just any former member of the OAS: he has an account to settle with a precise group that included at least four men. With Roman, we were unlucky. If it had happened twenty-four hours later, Gilles would have gotten in contact with him before the killer did. We have to get there first the next time."

"Except that the killer probably already knows his targets," Molina interrupted. "That's a major advantage."

"But he may not have localized them all yet. We have to remain optimistic, Lieutenant Molina. Besides, at this very moment the prosecutor is giving a press conference on this case, and we have to realize that we can't get along without the media at this point. The prosecutor is going to reveal what we know about the commando, the two victims, and the two other potential victims. The press conference won't be attended solely by the local press; correspondents from the big national media will also be there, and the case will soon become known throughout France. Wherever the two other members of the group live, they will soon know what's happening and we can hope that they will make themselves known."

"They may already be dead," Llach dared to say. "I mean, they might have died of natural causes."

"That is also a possibility, and it would make our job easier, in a way. In that case we could still hope that their relatives would recognize them and get in contact with us anyway. However that may be, we have to move forward. And fast. We know our job and we're going to treat this case like a normal case, without forgetting the fundamentals of the profession."

He bent over a sheet of paper on which he had written his instructions before the meeting:

"Starting tomorrow, there will be an investigation around Canet and along the coast road. The gendarmes didn't find anything today, we've got to go back there. Llach and Lambert, you will take care of that. You have new evidence, since the tire tracks lead us to look for a small car. Sebag and Molina, you will follow the call for witnesses and compare the testimonies. Ménard, you and Julie will follow up the leads connected with the past . . . "

François Ménard raised his hand and the superintendent gave him the floor.

"On that subject, Gilles also asked me to look into the battle against the *barbouzes* Mathilde mentioned."

"Oh yes, that's right, the *barbouzes* . . . I think that was one of the most incredible episodes of the Algerian War," Castello recalled.

Ménard agreed and consulted his second page of notes.

"The term *barbouzes* designates the agents of a secret, parallel police force sent to Algeria in late 1961 to wage a kind of antiguerrilla war on the OAS. Two to three hundred men in all, including a handful of Vietnamese karate champions who didn't go unnoticed. Initially assigned to gather intelligence, they also blew up bars and restaurants frequented by members of the OAS. But they were soon identified and the houses they were occupying in Algiers became in their turn targets for attacks organized mainly by Lieutenant Degueldre's Delta commandos."

"To which our four guys belonged," Castello added.

"Probably. The OAS won that episode of the Algerian War because almost half of the *barbouzes* were killed, and the survivors were brought back to France during the emergency of March, 1962."

A profound silence followed. The inspectors remained perplexed. This plunge into a recent, violent history troubled them. How could they untangle the ties linking the past to their double murder?

"You've got your work cut out for you, Ménard. Among the *barbouzes* who survived the war, a few may still be alive and want to take revenge on former members of the OAS. That should give us loads of suspects. And we mustn't forget, either, the French policeman who was killed. Get his name and find his descendants. There's work to do! Also talk to Sebag, who seems to have a good contact with a former member of the OAS."

Finally, the superintendent turned to the pair of friends who hadn't said a word since the beginning of the meeting.

"Raynaud and Moreno, you will concentrate on the affair of the monument, which mustn't be neglected. Personally, I still have trouble understanding what that act of destruction is doing in our double murder case. If our killer is settling a particular account with a precise group in the OAS, I don't see him vandalizing a funeral monument at the same time. On the other hand, another element common to the two cases has been added today: Lieutenant Degueldre. There, I have to admit that I don't know quite what to say."

He stopped to survey his inspectors, but none of them had a hypothesis to offer. They all took care to look elsewhere.

"By the way, that makes me think again of that matter of the hairs found on the site of the first murder and near the monument: we need to accelerate the analysis of those. Pagès is back, and he'll be glad to look into that again. Raynaud and Moreno, you talk to him about that. And then you will go back and investigate the leftist milieus hostile to the *Pieds-Noirs*. Just because we couldn't prove anything against Abbas doesn't mean that his whole group is cleared. O.K., good evening to everyone, see you tomorrow."

The inspectors immediately stood up with a shrill concert of chairs screeching on the linoleum. The superintendent had called them by their last names rather than by their first names. That was a sign. A very bad sign.

# CHAPTER 21

**Algiers, December 29, 1961**

Night has fallen in two stages on the Rue Faidherbe. The first time gradually, after the pale winter sun disappeared over the horizon. The second time more suddenly, when the street-lamps went out all at once.

Since then, a dense silence has reigned on the sidewalks.

A few timid fireflies still pierce the dark from time to time. One of them leaps from the hand of a phantom and goes to die as a cigarette butt in the dirty dampness of a gutter.

A cool wind is blowing down the street, forcing the men lying in wait to pull up the collars of their overcoats. The OAS's men all keep their eyes on the façade of the Villa Dar-Likoulia. Soon, they'll be warm. Soon, daylight will return. Soon, the tempest will succeed the silence.

Babelo's hobnailed boots ring on the pavement. They advance about fifty meters and stop in front of a car. One of the windows is slowly rolled down in the back, letting out damp, polluted air. Despite the darkness, Babelo recognizes on the back seat the massive silhouette and oval face of Lieutenant Degueldre. He makes a vague salute that is more respectful than military.

"Everybody is in position, Lieutenant. There are six commandos, including a team with the bazooka on the terrace of a neighboring apartment building. There are twenty-four men in all."

"Are there people in the house?" the leader of the Delta commandos asks.

"According to our two sentries, who have been there since this morning, there are at least fifteen *barbouzes*. We cut their telephone line in the early afternoon: they have not been able to warn anyone."

"Perfect."

Degueldre opens the door and gets out; he is immediately flanked by two bodyguards.

"Is your commando there as well?"

Babelo raises his arm. Sigma, Bizerte, and Omega step out of the shadows. One of the Lieutenant's guerillas gives each of them a grenade.

"You will come with me," Degueldre orders in a cheeky voice in which a heavy northern accent makes itself heard.

He strikes a match and holds it up to look at his watch, illuminating at the same time his craggy old paratrooper's face. His rectangular forehead is framed between a bar of thick eyebrows and a strict military haircut. His desertion from the army hasn't changed him in any way. A soldier he was, and a soldier he will remain. Until death. It's not a matter of a uniform or paycheck but of genes and guts.

"11:15, it's time," he announces without emotion.

He gives the roof of the car two brisk taps. The driver responds by briefly flashing his headlights twice. Three seconds later, a streak of lightning crosses the area and thunder descends on the street. Behind the villa's façade, an explosion resounds. The first shot has hit its target, striking a stock of munitions inside the building.

The bazooka fires again six times before Degueldre gives the order to attack. About twenty men, armed with submachine guns, move toward the main entrance. In the villa, the last intact windows are broken out with gun butts, and barrels appear that spit lethal sparks. The OAS men take shelter behind the trunks of trees in the garden and fire back.

Lieutenant Degueldre takes Babelo and his commando

toward the back of the building. They walk slowly through the brambles and weeds. Without difficulty, they approach to within ten meters of the house wall.

Degueldre signals them to wait and stay in the shelter of the pine trees. He rests his left arm on a tree trunk. Then he puts his right hand, holding a pistol, on it.

He fires.

The light in a window goes out. Degueldre fires a second time. Another lamp is out. Calmly, the former legionnaire puts out the lights in the *barbouzes'* house. Between shots, he takes a long breath.

Degueldre reloads his weapon, then orders the men to advance. But the Delta group can't go far. A burst of stars suddenly illuminates a dormer window. The sound of the volley reaches them with a slight delay. Omega, hit, is already down.

The men in the commando dive into the weeds. Degueldre is the first to fire back. The others quickly do the same and bullets make brick fragments fly all around the little window. The *barbouze* is still firing. He fires in brief bursts and then takes cover again. His volleys are aimed by guesswork but they're on target.

"The bastard is good," Degueldre comments without anger. "And on top of that he's an acrobat. He must be standing on a toilet seat to be able to fire through that window."

After a few seconds of lying motionless on the ground, Omega has crawled warily behind a large palm tree. Bizerte goes over to him. He gives his comrade a questioning look. Omega points to his bloody leg. The wound is not serious, the bullet having only gone through the fleshy part of his calf.

The firefight lasts a good quarter of an hour. After being surprised, the *barbouzes* have quickly regrouped and their fire continues unabated. They probably have large stocks of munitions inside the house. Degueldre orders his men to throw their grenades to cover their retreat. The storm redoubles in fury for a few seconds, and then slowly dies down.

Bizerte and Sigma help Omega walk as far as the street. A small van stops near them. The side door slides open and a man gets out to lift Omega inside. The driver floors the accelerator and the little van speeds off. It will take the wounded man to a doctor who can be trusted. There is no lack of such doctors in Algiers.

Degueldre puts his hand on Babelo's shoulder.

"Good work. Just one man wounded on our side and probably several dead on theirs. Their hideout is finished. Stay here and keep an eye on the area for a few minutes. You never know."

The lieutenant-deserter turns on his heel, still followed by his bodyguards. Bizerte goes off to get their Dauphine, which is parked in a nearby street. He returns shortly afterward. Babelo gets in the front seat and Sigma in the back.

They don't have to wait long.

The garage door on the villa opens noisily and a black Peugeot 404 roars out with two men in it. Bizerte follows them at a prudent distance. The *barbouzes* are driving at breakneck speed through the dark, deserted streets of Algiers and finally stop in front of another villa in the Rue des Pins. Another hideout.

"What a bunch of degenerates," Babelo chortles. "If they give away their hideouts that easily, I don't think they'll last a month before they're on a ship back home. We're going to have these guys for lunch!"

# CHAPTER 22

Sebag's office was disappearing under the spread-out pages of French newspapers. Most of them mentioned the double murder in Perpignan, but only the local paper, *L'Indépendent*, connected it with the destruction of the monument and echoed an increasing anxiety in the *Pied-Noir* community. At the bottom of the page there was an appeal for witnesses who might have seen cars parked along the coast road on Sunday afternoon. The radio had conveyed the same information in its morning news broadcasts.

There was nothing more to do but wait for the first phone calls.

Molina opened the office door. He was holding a coffee cup in his hand.

"I didn't bring you any," he said, holding up his cup.

"Pouah," Gilles said in disgust. "How can you drink such dishwater?"

"I don't know anything about coffee, this or any other, I don't give a damn so long as it's black and hot. Apart from liquid shit . . . "

"Well, precisely!" Gilles interrupted.

"Why don't you give me a real coffee-maker and put it on a table in here? And at the same time you could educate me about coffee . . . "

"I'd rather give up right away: you've been impossible to educate for years!"

"You sound like my ex-wife. But seriously, why don't you buy the same coffee-maker you have at home?"

"Because I'd drink coffee all day long and that wouldn't be good for my health. And then good coffee is expensive. I'd spend half my salary on it."

"It's true that we're not paid very much . . . You're right, drinking the cafeteria's coffee allows you to save money."

"Especially since I don't drink it."

"Reasoned perfectly," Molina concluded, emptying his cup in a single gulp without making a face.

He quickly flipped through the national press and then took the *Midi Olympique* out of his jacket pocket and sat down at his desk.

Their desks faced each other. Sebag was looking at the photos that Jacques had put up behind him. They all dated from June, 2009, the year the local rugby team had finally won its seventh national championship after fifty-four years of trying. One of the pictures particularly impressed Sebag. It showed the team's return to Perpignan the day after its victory: an enormous, dense crowd of fans in red and yellow was massed in front of the Castillet. A human tide to celebrate a people's heroes. On that day, Sebag had been working and was helping the uniforms maintain security in the streets. Faced with the fervor of this familial, friendly crowd, he'd been sorry not to be Catalan. He was even almost annoyed with himself for not liking rugby. That's how much this moment had moved him . . .

Molina looked up.

"By the way, has anyone called yet?"

He didn't wait for a reply before plunging back into his reading of his paper. Sebag was still looking at the photos of his colleague. Once again, he said to himself they ought to reverse their walls. Molina had his back to his own world and Sebag to his: photos of Claire, Léo, and Séverine, in swimsuits at the beach, in ski clothes in the mountains, or sitting at a table on the terrace at home. It would be logical to change things around, but he didn't propose it. Because people didn't put their memories on the walls to admire them but rather to assert their personalities: this is my place and here are my tastes, my passions, and the people I love. It all seemed as puerile as it was universal. Some days he thought it was ridiculous, even pathetic. But he always ended up telling himself that after all, it was a more civilized way to mark territory than pissing on the ground.

His telephone rang, tearing him away from his reflections. The switchboard was connecting him with the first call. He listened, asked a few questions, and took notes. When he hung up, he met the questioning eyes of his partner.

"It was a resident of Saint-Cyprien who passed by there on Sunday. Apparently at the time of the murder. He saw a white car parked next to a blue Audi. A SEAT, he said."

"He didn't get the license number, obviously?"

"Obviously."

"But it's interesting for a first call."

Sebag and Molina received a dozen phone calls that morning. Most of them were of no interest. In addition to the first, they gave serious consideration to only one other, from a young woman who had gone to see her mother in a retirement home in Canet on Sunday afternoon. This second witness offered no further information regarding the model of the vehicle, which she described as "a small white car," but she seemed to remember that the license plate was foreign, maybe Spanish.

"She remembers or she thinks she remembers?" Molina groaned.

"We work with what we have," Sebag said, philosophically. "Now we have to find out what Llach and Lambert learned from Roman's neighbors."

"Do you think it was worthwhile sending them down there? He wasn't killed at home."

"It's not impossible that the killer did some reconnaissance near his house. He might even have planned to kill Roman at home, and then, seeing that it was too dangerous—because of neighbors who were too curious, for instance—decided to lure him to the Saint-Cyprien road instead."

"Well, that seems to me a little complicated . . . "

Sebag shrugged.

"The boss told us not to forget our fundamentals. Investigating the nearby area is part of that."

"Nearby what?" Molina persisted. "Because he wasn't killed in his house."

Sebag was no longer listening to his partner's quibbles. He had just picked up his phone to call Llach. He repeated out loud he information Joan conveyed to him.

"Concordant testimonies, you say. How many? We also had two. They mentioned a small white car. No certainty regarding the model. One of them mentioned a Clio or a SEAT. The other one mentioned a Spanish license plate. Hey, that's great, man! Wait, I'm writing down the names and addresses."

As he hung up, Sebag couldn't help having a gleam of victory in his eyes.

"O.K., O.K.," Molina grumbled. "But small white cars, even if licensed in Spain, are not exactly rare around here. In fact, they're very common. That's not enough to give us a lead. If at least we could be sure about the model . . . a SEAT or a Clio . . . "

Sebag suddenly froze. The last word had shocked his neurons and triggered fleeting images in his mind. The area around Martinez's apartment. The Moulin-à-Vent quarter. A white care licensed in Spain. He took the file on Mathieu's accident out of his drawer. As he flipped through it he asked Molina:

"Do you remember the estimated date the medical examiner gave for Martinez's death?"

"Uh . . . no, I don't recall, a Wednesday or a Thursday,"

Molina said, surprised. "What does that have to do with what we were saying?"

"Could you find me the exact information, please. The estimated day and hour?"

Jacques was going to protest when he saw on Gilles's face the signs of the inspired prophet that he had learned to recognize. Sebag clenched his teeth, frowned, and hardly breathed. His eyes shone with a strange light. He seemed to be in an altered state. Molina would not have been surprised to see him start levitating over his desk,.

"You're red-hot. You're onto something there."

"No, I don't know," Sebag said in halfhearted denial as he went compulsively through the pages of the file on the accident.

"That's right, that's right, play me for a fool, too . . . " Molina scoffed, but in a low voice to avoid disturbing his partner.

Sebag found what he was looking for and put his finger on a specific line.

"Well?" he said impatiently.

Molina clicked his mouse nervously several times.

"It's all right, I'm looking for your information, I'm opening the file. There . . . The medical examiner's report. O.K., I found it: The death of Bernard Martinez is estimated to have occurred on Wednesday, probably in the late afternoon."

"Shit . . . that's not possible!"

"With you, everything is possible."

"5:15—do you consider that already late afternoon?"

"It might . . . "

"Holy shit!"

Molina was getting impatient in turn.

"Are you going to tell me someday?"

Sebag looked at his colleague without seeing him. Beyond Molina, he was seeing Moulin-à-Vent, the street where Mathieu had lost his life. He grimaced as he imagined the collision.

"Hello?" Molina was waving his hand before Gilles's eyes. "Hello? Madame Irma, are you with us?"

Sebag suddenly shook himself.

"Yes . . . "

"Are you going to explain it to me now?"

"Mathieu, my daughter's friend—his accident took place that same afternoon at 5:15."

"And so?"

"In the same Moulin-à-Vent quarter, next to the Saint Paul church."

"Well, now . . . "

"That's only two hundred meters from Martinez's apartment."

"Do you think . . . "

"The driver of the van said he had to swerve because of a car that had suddenly appeared on his right."

"Fascinating."

"According to him, it was a white Clio licensed in Spain."

Molina immediately stopped his mocking comments.

"What are you suggesting there? That Martinez's killer caused that accident?"

Put so crudely, the hypothesis seemed outlandish to Sebag as well. But in his heart of hearts he felt it was plausible.

"Well, why not?" he finally said. "Does that seem too far-fetched?"

Molina thought for three seconds.

"It's just that it would be a very odd coincidence, after all. The medical examiner's window was pretty big: 5:15 is the very beginning of 'late afternoon.' And then, this morning's only witness who was fairly certain talked about a SEAT. Those who said 'Clio or SEAT' were the ones who weren't sure."

"So in short you don't believe it?"

"When I try to judge the facts objectively, it seems to me pretty shaky, but . . . "

"But?"

"When I look at you and see you that inspired, I want to believe it."

Sebag stood up.

"So, O.K., let's go have a look around in Canet, then!"

"Shall we interview Llach's witnesses ourselves?"

"Yes. And also one of the people who called us this morning. The one who saw a SEAT works in a tavern there."

"Where?"

"Place de la Méditerranée."

Molina glanced at his watch.

"Perfect! I'm beginning to get a little peckish."

"You're always peckish. And thirsty."

"I wouldn't have anything against some nice cool rosé, in fact."

"With you, one knows where it begins, but never when it ends. Do you know the proverb?"

"*Aïe!*"

"Eating makes you thirsty."

"So, here's to your health!"


Sebag and Molina were basking in the sun on the tavern's terrace. The meal had been acceptable, not great. Gilles had had filet of hake with vegetables and Jacques prime rib with shallots. The table in the tavern spread out over the paving stones of the main square in Canet-Plage. Wearing dark glasses, the two inspectors ate side by side, facing the sea and the sun. There were only a few small cotton balls still floating in the blue sky over the Albera Range.

Sebag spoke to the waiter when he put the bill on their table.

"Are you Sébastien Puig?"

"No. Sébastien is working inside today."

"Could you ask him to come out, please?"

The waiter hesitated for a moment, then obeyed. A second waiter soon came to stand between the inspectors and the sun.

"What can I bring you?"

Sebag showed him his card and asked him to sit down.

"This concerns your phone call this morning."

"If I'd known you were going to show up at the place where I work, I wouldn't have called."

"We're very sorry but it's urgent."

Sébastien smiled sardonically as he looked at their faces reddened by the sun.

"I can see that, yeah."

Sebag sat up.

"This won't take long. I'm the one who had you on the phone a little while ago and I need to know one more thing. You told me that you'd seen a car on the road between Saint-Cyprien and Canet. A SEAT, right?"

"Yes."

"Are you sure?"

"Uh . . . is it important?"

"It could be."

"The problem is that I no longer remember very well. I didn't pay that much attention. But there weren't many cars on the road on Sunday, and it did seem to me that it was a SEAT, yes. I was coming home from work, we hadn't had many customers for Sunday at noon. But with the rain that was pouring down, that was predictable, there was nobody out anywhere. And also a blue Audi parked alongside the beach. I think it was a SEAT, yeah, but I couldn't swear to it."

The policemen didn't persist. They thanked the waiter and paid the bill.

"The wine's on me," Sebag said.

"You hardly touched it . . . "

"Precisely, that makes up for it."

"That makes no sense!"

"I know, but I'll pay."

Molina didn't try to understand. He headed for the car.

"We could walk there, it's only two steps away," Sebag suggested.

"But afterward we'd have to come back. Two steps plus two steps, that makes four steps. It would waste our time. I'm just saying, this is about work, right?"

"You must be joking . . . O.K., I'll walk there and you meet me with the car."

Five minutes later, Sebag was approaching a small blue house while Molina parked the car. At the window, he saw a curtain suddenly drawn shut. He'd had time to glimpse the thin face of a woman around seventy years old. The mailbox bore the name of Madeleine Bonneau. They rang the bell but the echoes of a harmonious carillon were not followed by any sound of footsteps or a door opening in the house. They saw only a slight quiver behind the curtain.

Sebag looked at the notes Llach had given him. Madeleine Bonneau had been an English teacher in Niort, she'd been retired for ten years, and she spent half the year in Catalonia. In the file Sebag found a landline telephone number and dialed it on his cell phone. This time a metallic cooing sounded inside the house. Only three times.

"Hello?" an alert but unfriendly voice answered.

"Hello, Mme Bonneau, we're two policemen from Perpignan. We're waiting in front of your gate. We'd like to talk to you."

"I already talked to policemen this morning."

"Yes, we know. But we'd like a few further details."

"I have nothing more to say."

"Then we won't take much of your time."

He hung up immediately to accelerate the process. The sound of a key turning in a lock was heard. Followed by the sound of two bolts being slid open.

"Well . . . " Molina commented.

The door opened partway and two piercing eyes scrutinized the street for a few seconds. Finally it opened completely and Madeleine Bonneau consented to come out of her bunker. She was wearing a faded mauve nylon blouse decorated with pink flowers that seemed to have withered with time. She walked toward them at a slow pace, carefully sliding her furry slippers over the uneven pavement of her tiny courtyard. She stopped in front of the gate.

"Please excuse me for making you wait, but these days a woman living alone can't be too careful. Especially since I was already a little apprehensive . . . Since Mr. Roman's murder I've been literally terrified."

Despite her excuses, she didn't open her gate and left the policemen on the sidewalk.

"What can I do for you, Messieurs?"

"I'd like you to talk to me about the car that you saw on this street the other day."

"I told your colleagues everything."

"Could you tell me again, please? One never knows: an important detail might come back to you."

The former English teacher looked him up and down as if she were dealing with a particularly stupid student.

"It was Sunday morning. I saw that car for the first time around 10:30. It was driving down the street very slowly. That was already astonishing; these days, people drive so fast, even in residential zones . . . Then hardly an hour later it went by again and stopped a little farther on."

"Did you see the driver when he got out of the car?" Sebag asked, full of hope.

"Of course not," she replied with scorn. "You don't suppose that I spend my days spying on my neighbors? After ten minutes, nobody had budged, so I left the window."

"And when the car passed in front of your house, did you see anything or anyone inside it?"

"Don't you remember what the weather was like on Sunday? A genuine deluge. The windows of the car were all fogged up, I couldn't see anything."

"You described a small white car to our colleagues. Can't you say any more about what kind of car it was?"

"If I could have, I would have. I don't know anything about cars. But I know the license plate was Spanish."

Sebag noticed that Molina was getting angry. He thanked the old bat, who immediately turned around and slipped back toward her cavern.

"I hope the next witness will be friendlier," Molina commented. "Who is it?"

Sebag consulted his notes.

"Gabriel Coutin, at number 12 on this same street."

Leaning over his bicycle in his driveway, the other neighbor was adjusting his dérailleur when they approached. Gabriel Coutin stood up, displaying before them a cyclist's jersey more covered with ads than a screen on a private Italian television channel.

"It was a SEAT, not a Clio. Since your colleagues came by, I've checked on the internet. I compared the cars, and it was a SEAT Ibiza."

"Are you really sure?" Sebag asked, disappointed. "The two cars look quite a lot alike, after all."

"I know, and that's what fooled me, because I don't know a lot about cars. I can distinguish a Campagnolo from a Shimano dérailleur with my eyes closed, but so far as cars are concerned, nothing, absolutely nothing, I don't like them. But I informed myself, I looked at photos, and now I no longer have any doubt."

From the back pocket of his jersey he pulled out some tattered papers.

"Here, I've still got the photos on me."

He unfolded them and showed the policemen.

"See, the front of the two cars is very different. The grille, for instance, is much bigger on the SEAT. And the car that I saw the day before yesterday had a big grille. "

Molina asked him a few more questions while Sebag moved away a few steps to call Pascal Lucas. But his hope was short-lived. The van driver turned out to be an expert on car bodies and he remained absolutely certain.

"The car that ran the stop sign was a Clio, and even a rather recent model."

Molina came up to him just as he was hanging up. He saw his disappointment.

"You can't win 'em all, champ. That doesn't change anything: you're still the best."

They got back in their car. Molina drove.

"I suggest that we now go look around Moulin-à-Vent. Since we think that Roman's killer is driving a white SEAT with Spanish plates, we'll go ask Martinez's neighbors. And we'll ask about the Clio as well as the SEAT. You never know. If they don't remember the killer's car, with any luck they'll have seen the reckless driver's car."

He drove away, slowly for once. From the fast road that took them back to Perpignan, the view of Le Canigou was sublime. Heavy snow had covered the summit with a layer of powdered sugar. Just as they were leaving the interchange and were about to head for the heights of Moulin-à-Vent, Sebag received a call from Ménard.

"You don't know the best news?"

"Not yet, but I can hardly wait."

"I tracked down a former *barbouze* who might be a good suspect. There aren't many *barbouzes* still alive, apparently. After the Algerian War, my guy, Maurice Garcin, was a member of the SAC, a sort of parallel police for the Gaullist party that was dissolved in 1981. He wrote a few books about his memories of his combat activity in Algiers, and he was always very hard on his former adversaries. Julie even found a text of his on the internet, and it's pretty virulent, close to defamatory. Garcin was also a member of an association for victims of the OAS. In 2008 they got a court to require the destruction of a monument in Marignane identical to the one in Perpignan."

"And what's the best news?"

"Castello doesn't want him interviewed on the phone, he wants me to meet with Garcin in person. And do you know where he lives?"

"Is this a riddle you're asking me to solve?"

"Absolutely!"

Sebag didn't need to reflect for very long.

"It's easy, right?"

"Tell me and we'll see."

"Your Garcin attacked a monument to the OAS in Marignane. So we can assume that he lives in a town near the Mediterranean?"

"Not bad . . . "

"A large city?"

"You could say that."

"And Castello wants to send you there hoping to kill two birds with one stone?"

"Meaning?"

"He'd like you to take advantage of this to say hello again to one of your buddies over there, a pal who's a historian?"

"Bravo, you're the best."

"Well! I hope you'll begin to appreciate pastis and bouillabaisse, and that you've found a good hotel over there."

"You never cease to amaze me. You're the king of puzzlesolvers. If only you could find a better suspect before I leave . . . "

"What time does the next train to Marseille leave?"

"4:52."

"It's going to be close, but we'll do our best. If not, *bon voyage!*"

After hanging up, Sebag saw that Molina had a smile on his face.

"Ménard is off to Marseille again?" he asked. "The lucky bastard . . . I hope he has found a little mistress over there."

"He's not the type . . . "

Molina sighed, discouraged.

"Do you think you have to be a certain type to have a mistress? And just what would that type be, in your opinion?"

Fortunately, they had arrived in Moulin-à-Vent. Molina found a parking place on the Ramblas a short distance from Martinez's apartment and Gilles took care to forget his partner's question.

Sebag spent a tedious and interminable afternoon. He was having a hard time getting over his recent disappointment. And above all, he couldn't accept it. Why had he been so sure about this business of the cars? A white Clio or a SEAT of the same color, Spanish plates: in the end, wasn't that simply a coincidence?

The work that he was doing didn't distract him. Making neighborhood inquiries was the kind of thing he hated most about the routine of his job. Neither at law school nor at the police academy had he ever imagined that he would some day have to develop a sales rep's techniques and qualities in order to get someone to open the door of an apartment. It had been a long time since just showing his police card was enough to convince people to listen to him and let him enter their homes. He always had to explain, persuade, convince. And sometimes to accompany the argument with a quick course in French law: crammed with American cop shows, people often demanded to see a warrant just to return a friendly greeting.

So Sebag and Molina walked for hours up and down the streets and stairs of Moulin-à-Vent. To save time, they'd split up, but the work just seemed even more tiresome.

Around 5 P.M., when he was beginning to despair, Sebag received a text message from his partner: "Got something. Meet me at no. 2, Rue du Perthus."

He put his phone back in his pocket and said a quick goodbye to the little old lady who had just started telling him the story of her life, from her childhood in Cerdagne to her retirement in this neighborhood that she hated. He ran down the stairs of her building two at a time and came out on the Avenue Amélie-les-Bains. All he had to do was turn to his left. Then he saw Jacques a hundred meters away, talking to a little man with a paunch.

Molina quickly introduced them to each other:

"Charles Mercader lives on the third floor of this building, and he loves to do crossword puzzles on his balcony."

The man stroked his mustache with satisfaction.

"Monsieur, please tell my colleague what you told me."

Charles Mercader folded his pudgy hands on his belly and gladly obliged.

"The other day I was sitting on my loggia when I saw a car parked just below take off as if it had been the start of a Formula 1 race. The guy made his motor scream and then his tires squealed on the pavement. At the next corner he turned in the direction of the Saint Paul church, and almost immediately afterward, I heard what sounded like a collision. I thought it was probably just a fender bender, and I went on with my crossword, but about ten minutes later I heard the sirens of the emergency vehicles. Then I went down to see. At that moment, I obviously thought that driver must have caused the accident, but I was wrong: it was a van that had hit a scooter. And what's more, the boy, poor kid, died."

Molina kept him from launching into extended lamentations.

"And what could you tell my colleague about that car?"

"It was a little white Clio with Spanish license plates."

Molina smiled happily, very pleased with his witness.

"I know a little Séverine who is going to be very proud of her dad."

Sebag closed his eyes and imagined his daughter's delighted face. But strangely, he didn't feel relieved. Molina was showing more joy.

"Moreover, we discovered this testimony by working on Martinez's murder," he exulted. "Cardona won't be able to accuse you of trying to make him look bad, and so you don't owe him anything! He's going to be very disappointed, that asshole."

Charles Mercader's mustache quivered and its extremities turned down. Molina's remarks worried him.

"Is something wrong?" he asked. "I'm not going to have problems, am I?"

"No, absolutely not, Mr. Mercader, you've been great. Everything suggests that your driver was the cause of the accident that led to that boy's death. His parents will be happy to know the truth."

The tips of the witness's mustache rose with astonishment.

"Do you really think so? A little old man like him?"

"What?" the two policemen said in unison.

"You saw the driver?" Molina asked.

"I saw him before he got into his car. I was leaning on the railing of my balcony. Don't tell my wife, but let it be said in passing that I was smoking a little cigarette when I saw the old geezer walking. Actually, I shouldn't call him an old geezer, he must be about my age, but all the same, he was more bent over."

"Pardon me for asking, but how old are you?" Molina asked.

"Seventy-two," Mercader replied proudly. "And I can tell you that I get around much better than he does. He seemed to be wanting to run but couldn't really do it. Age affects us all differently, doesn't it?"

Sebag abruptly cut him off.

"Where was this individual coming from?"

"The Avenue Amélie, like you. He turned this way, coming from the right. Just as you did."

"And you're sure it was a Clio?"

"Absolutely! I've been driving one for the past ten years. If I couldn't recognize one it would be serious, wouldn't it?"

Sebag, puzzled, took out his notebook and wrote down this latest information. They took the witness's statement, had him sign it, and drove back to headquarters.

It took them half an hour to cover the two kilometers between Moulin-à-Vent and the city center. For the past few months, Perpignan had suffered from traffic jams worthy of a regional capital. In particular, it was very congested around the train station every evening. Sebag was tempted to leave his partner to his sad fate and walk the rest of the way to headquarters, but instead he just asked him to turn off the radio so he wouldn't have to listen to the buffoonery that was broadcast at that hour.

Jacques reluctantly switched off the radio so Sebag could concentrate on their case. But he wasn't able to fit together the way he wanted to all the new information they'd gathered that day.

They finally pulled into the parking lot at police headquarters. They'd hardly entered the building before Molina insisted that they go immediately to "say hello" to Lieutenant Cardona. Sebag didn't want to annoy his partner, but he sensed that it wasn't a good idea.

They found Cardona sitting in his office, smoking a cigarette next to a partly opened window.

"Well, here are the Perpignan police's ace inspectors! The ones who claim to solve all puzzles, including the ones that don't exist."

"You don't know how right you are," Molina replied.

He summed up in a few belligerent words their meeting with Charles Mercader. Cardona thought for a moment before answering.

"Do you think I'm a fool, or what? That's your big news?"

"Our witness saw the car the van driver is talking about," Molina argued.

"Your witness saw a car, sure, but he didn't see the accident."

"You're quibbling," Molina retorted. "He saw a car roar off in the direction of the accident. Then he heard the collision."

"Hearing isn't seeing. Your witness saw the car but not the accident. My witnesses saw the accident, but not the car. It's stupid!"

"Only one of your witnesses was present at the time of the accident," Sebag broke in, "the others got there just afterward. And from where he was standing, the single eyewitness couldn't see the car coming from the right toward the van."

Molina continued:

"And don't you think it's a strange coincidence that Mercader happens to have seen a white Clio with Spanish plates exactly like the one the van driver described?"

Far from seeming convinced, Cardona let a mocking grin spread over his lips. He opened a drawer and very slowly took out a file. He slammed it down on the desk.

"And can you tell me where it says in this file that your famous Clio had Spanish plates? I've got the report on the interrogation of Pascal Lucas right here. Go ahead, find me any mention of Spanish plates!"

Molina was struck dumb and turned to his partner.

"Pascal Lucas didn't mention it in his first interrogation," Sebag explained. "He gave me that information."

Cardona pounced.

"And he gave it to you in a casual conversation that you were not supposed to have with him, didn't he?"

"That's true, but it doesn't diminish the importance of that information. You can't just set it aside like that."

"No, of course not," Cardona laughed. "Lucas didn't tell me everything, but naturally, he told you the whole and exact truth. That guy is drunk all day long. He found a sucker willing to believe anything at all, so he started saying what worked for him. But look out, Sebag, that guy's making a cuckold of you!"

Cardona's bad faith had annoyed Sebag and this last comment electrified him. To his great surprise he felt his blood boil in his veins. He realized that it was ridiculous for such a vulgar, common remark to have that kind of effect on him. But Sebag, who was ordinarily so levelheaded and so calm, was seized with a mad desire to take Cardona by the collar. He couldn't resist. He reached over the desk, grabbed Cardona's shirt and gave it a good quarter turn. Cardona tried to protest but Sebag's closed fist was compressing his larynx.

"Listen to me, you asshole, we've just handed you a significant bit of testimony, and even if it may not be decisive, it's important. It's going to be in our file because we obtained it in the course of our investigation of the double murder. So it's completely legal. Do you understand? LEGAL!"

His right hand hurt but he tightened his grip further and slowly lowered his arm, forcing Cardona to bend down over his desk.

"So I'm going to write an official note to the effect that I did in fact transmit this testimony to you. Now I advise you to take up the investigation again and this time carry it all the way through without neglecting anything. Because I'm also going to continue it. Whether you like it or not, that car exists and I might find other witnesses. If I do, I'm going to transmit the information directly to the big boss, have you got that?"

Bent over forward, Cardon tried to raise his head to give Sebag a black look. Sebag tightened his grip even further for a few seconds and then gradually let go.

Cardona sat up and massaged his neck. His cheeks were crimson, but his forehead was a little green. Pushing back a greasy lock of blond hair, he raised a threatening index finger.

"Never do that again, Sebag. Never."

"I'll promise you that, Cardona. But never talk to me like that again. Never."

Molina silently followed Sebag to their office. Once the door was closed, he couldn't help breaking into laughter.

"Damn, you really told that son of a bitch where to go!"

He put his jacket on the coat hook behind the door and then added more seriously:

"I think he was surprised by your reaction. I was, too, for that matter . . . "

He waited for a response that didn't come.

"I've never seen you like that."

Sebag shot him a vague grimace.

"Did it make you feel better, at least?"

Sebag collapsed onto his chair. He put his feet on the desk and rested his arms on the armrests. Then he slowly nodded his head.

"A little, yes."

"You see, that's what I've been telling you for years: you've got to let yourself go sometimes."

Sebag was watching the city's streetlights come on. It was only 6 P.M., but they had just gone off daylight saving time and that had abruptly shortened the afternoons. He wondered if he should tell Séverine about the progress of his investigation into Mathieu's accident. After thinking about it, he decided not to. It wasn't over yet, it was better to wait. And if she asked questions, he would limit himself to telling her that things were moving forward and that he now had hope of getting somewhere.

Images of white Clios and SEATs began to pass through his

head. He tried to think about something else but couldn't. The telephone on his desk rang at the same time as Molina's. Jacques picked up more quickly. He didn't say a word, just listening and grimacing.

"Shit," he said soberly as he hung up.

"Is it serious?"

"Pretty. The president of the *Pied-Noir* Circle was attacked, with a knife. He's been taken to the hospital. Before escaping, his attackers left him a note."

Molina got up, grabbed his jacket, and put it on.

"The note said something like: "Death to *Pieds-Noirs*.""

"Shit!"

"That's what I just said, yeah . . . "

"It's a good summary of the situation, in fact!"

# CHAPTER 23

In a cubicle at the Perpignan hospital's emergency room, Guy Albouker was grimacing in pain on his stretcher. His frightened eyes had withdrawn into their round, swollen pockets.

Sebag gave a questioning look to the young woman doctor, a petite brunette with wavy hair kept in check by a series of multicolored elastic bands. They knew each other by sight because they had encountered one another on several Sunday mornings while running errands in the area. The young woman's name was written in black on her white blouse. Doctor Morgane Davier showed Sebag the wound on Albouker's abdomen.

"The blade went in here. A few centimeters, no more. It didn't hit any organ, just a little fat. In my opinion, the aggressor just wanted to scare him."

"So far as that goes, he succeeded," Albouker groaned.

The young doctor put her hand on his shoulder.

"I'm going to give you a prescription and sick leave for three days. Then you can go. Your wife has just arrived, she'll take you home."

She held out her hand to Sebag.

"I'll let you question him now. See you one of these Sundays, maybe?"

She went tripping off. Another patient was waiting for her. The nurses had mentioned an accidental wound caused by a chain saw. Sebag shivered.

"She's nice, isn't she?" Albouker said.

The wounded man was feeling better.

"And competent," he added, caressing his bandage. "It looks to me as if she did that very well. I probably won't have a big scar."

Sebag turned to him.

"Tell me what happened."

"I'd just left Mme. Chevalier. She's an old lady who lives in Bas-Vernet and has belonged to our Circle for forty years. She's sick at the moment and can't leave her apartment, so I had gone out to buy three articles for her. I took them to her apartment and it was as I was coming back down the stairs that I was attacked. In the lobby; they must have been waiting for me."

"They?"

"Two men, so far as I could see. But it all went so fast . . . "

"What did they look like?"

"Medium height, both of them, about 5'9", I'd say. One was heftier than the other, and had a beard. Under their jackets they were wearing sweatshirts with hoods."

"Could you describe their clothes in greater detail?"

"The bearded one had a leather jacket and red sweatshirt, the other a cloth coat and a gray sweatshirt with a series of English words on it. Decorative words, not meant to have a precise meaning. You know the kind I mean?"

Sebag knew very well. His son wore the same kind.

"Were they young?"

"Fairly young, yes, but I'm not real sure. Everything happened very fast. I was taken by surprise, I didn't have time to understand what was happening before they'd already left. And then they were wearing sunglasses that hid their eyes."

"Did they say anything?"

"The bearded one shouted something like 'dirty *Pied-Noir*' while the other one stabbed me with his knife. Afterward I collapsed on the floor of the lobby. They kicked me a couple of times before taking off."

"What time was it?"

"Around 6 P.M."

At that point Molina came into the cubicle. He'd just been talking with the paramedics who had taken care of the wounded man. Sebag continued his questioning.

"They left you a note, a letter, I don't know what to call it . . ."

Albouker pointed to his jacket hung on the back of a chair.

"In the right inside pocket."

Molina was closest. He dug around and pulled out of the pocket a wrinkled sheet of paper. He carefully unfolded it and handed it to Sebag. It contained three lapidary sentences and two spelling mistakes. It was written with letters cut out of a newspaper and glued to the sheet of paper. Not very original. Sebag though he recognized the typeface of the local newspaper. He read the message out loud:

"You were driven out of Algeria. You should have all been killed, you gang of murderers. It's not too late. Death to *Pieds-Noirs*."

"I'm not happy about that, but it shows that I wasn't entirely wrong," Albouker commented, with an apologetic smile on his lips. "They've got it in for *Pieds-Noirs* who were killers, that is, for the OAS. More people who have fallen for the simplistic amalgamation. And when I think that they attacked me—a guy whose parents were active in the SFIO . . ."

Sebag remained pensive. He didn't know how to interpret this latest event. Or especially how to relate it to the others. The two murders and the destruction of the monument. Did there absolutely have to be a connection?

"Had you already received threats of this kind?"

"Personally, no. But at the Circle we've received some disagreeable mail over the last few years."

"Did you keep it?"

"No, I don't think so. If we'd had to worry every time . . . "

"To come back to the men who attacked you today, can you tell us anything more about them?"

Albouker hesitated.

"It's just that . . . "

"It's just that what?"

"I don't know how to put it. Unless I borrow the comedian Coluche's famous line: 'They weren't downright shady but they were downright dark-skinned.'"

"Were they North Africans?"

"Probably. I had the impression that they also had the accent."

"They didn't say very much . . . "

"That's why I spoke rather of an impression."

"What did you do after your attackers left?"

"I called the emergency services and then the police."

"Why didn't you call me, too? I'd given you my card."

"I didn't have it on me."

Sebag turned to Molina:

"Did the emergency service tell you anything?"

"They received the call at 6:07 and they got there at 6:16. They didn't notice anything unusual. They found Mr. Albouker alone in the lobby, leaning on a step of the stairway. He was lucid and didn't seem to be suffering too much. They saw right away that the wound was superficial."

"Any news from the police patrol that was sent?"

"It arrived in the area at 6:27. They didn't see anything suspicious but it was probably too late. They didn't find anything abnormal in the lobby, either. Do you think we need to bring in the forensic team?"

"That would be pointless. After the emergency team, our colleagues, and probably a few residents of the building, they won't be able to do anything significant."

A nurse's aide came into the cubicle with the prescription and the sick leave form signed by the doctor. Marie Albouker appeared immediately afterward. Her face was haggard and she collapsed in her husband's arms.

"Papa, you've got an SMS."

Séverine's voice coming out of Sebag's pocket startled everyone. Molina stared at his partner as if he had farted. Sebag excused himself and took out his phone. He had a message from Claire asking when he expected to be home. "In about an hour," he wrote with his clumsy index finger.

Albouker was patting his wife's back.

"Excuse me," the president of the Circle implored her. "I'm sorry to have given you such a fright . . . "

Marie Albouker sat up to blow her nose.

"It's not your fault, for heaven's sake."

"No, of course not. But when I see you like that, I feel guilty."

"You're an idiot."

"You took a long time to notice that."

Sebag cleared his throat to remind them of his presence.

"I think we've bothered you long enough," he said. "I'll write up the report on the attack tomorrow morning and bring it by for your signature. Will you be home tomorrow?"

"I'm on sick leave, I'm not going anywhere."

"I'll give you a call first, just in case."

Back in the car, Molina didn't miss the opportunity to tease his partner.

"So, when are you going to change your ringtone?"

"Did you change yours?"

"No, why?"

"Guess . . . "

Molina discussed again, and at length, the merits and defects of their respective ringtones. But Sebag let him talk. He finally had the impression that he was beginning to understand where this business about the car might lead. Clio, SEAT. And what if it wasn't a coincidence? An idea had sprouted and he let it grow before daring to contemplate it. Yes, of course, it was possible . . . They'd stupidly failed to see the obvious and today's hypothesis still seemed to him valid.

However, fearing that Molina's sarcastic remarks might extinguish it like the flame of an ordinary candle, he decided to keep it to himself. He still had to think about it, support it, argue it. Tomorrow, things would be clearer.

Yes, tomorrow would be the time to talk about it again.

# CHAPTER 24

He was walking painfully through the steep streets of the village of Cadaqués. To admire an opening onto the Great Blue between two white façades and to catch his breath before beginning a stretch dangerous for his old legs, he paused on the path to the Santa Maria church. Gray schist paving stones lay on the ground, but when the slope got steeper, they gave way to pieces of slate set in cement. The architects had come up with that idea to prevent pedestrians from slipping on rainy days. For the old man, however, these random asperities represented so many traps and possibilities of falling.

It would be pretty ridiculous of him to break something now!

The sun was going down fast. It would soon disappear behind the mountain barrier that had for centuries isolated Cadaqués from the rest of Catalonia. Up until the 1950s, the village could be reached only by sea.

He finally came to the square in front of the church. The view proved disappointing. He'd hoped for a 180-degree panorama, but had to make do with a little opening bordered on one side by terraces and canal-tile roofs. In the distance, he could still make out a brown, pointed rock that rose out of the water like a single canine tooth in the mouth of a poor man.

Jean sat on a bench and warmed his face in the last rays of the sun. When the light dimmed, he got up and went down toward the port.

At the seaside, the terraces of the cafés were still bathed in sun. A few French, Spanish, and German tourists were savoring the return of good weather after a week of wind and rain. On the pebble beach, a young dog was pushing a ball among the beached fishing boats. The old man strolled down the beach and then continued walking east down the road that ran along the seacoast. Four-story houses, all lined up, gleamed in all their radiant whiteness. Regularly whitewashed, they testified to the present prosperity of the village, which had become a prime tourist site on the Costa Brava.

He enjoyed seeing the place, even though the reasons for his coming here had nothing, absolutely nothing, to do with tourism.

The street wound along the coast. He walked with more assurance on the asphalt. He consulted a map affixed to a wall. He had already passed *Es Poal*, then the *Playa es Pianc*. The *avinguda Rahola* wasn't far away.

He stopped in front of the slender metal figure of a woman. With a jar on her head and her hair blowing in the wind like a banner, the statue faced away from the houses and looked out toward the sea. He sat down on a broad stone bench that was still warm from the sun. Huddled around its church, the village rolled up on its butte was awaiting the night. The man took out of his coat pocket the little camera he'd bought in La Jonquera before leaving. He started rapidly shooting pictures around him.

After taking a dozen snapshots at random, he stood up and started walking up the avenue again. But this time he stopped often to take photos. Not of the sea, not of the village, but of the houses along the road.

He'd arrived at the swankiest part of the village. The continuous wall of narrow, white façades had given way to luxurious villas partly hidden by high walls made of flat stones. These residences for the wealthy had sumptuous second-floor terraces with priceless views of the sea.

Jean pretended to be admiring a splendid prickly pear that raised its thorny leaves as high as ten feet. He took numerous photos, moving little by little toward the neighboring villa. One of the most fashionable in the area. The apartment he occupied in Buenos Aires would have filled only a third of its terrace.

The old man spotted three surveillance cameras around the building, which must also have a sophisticated alarm system. This confirmed what he'd already expected: he wouldn't be able to strike his third target at home. He wouldn't be able to get in here as easily as he'd gotten into Martinez's apartment. And this target, he knew, would be much tougher than the other two. Whether or not he knew about what had happened to his former accomplices.

His mouth and his lips opened in a malicious smile. He had a backup plan. Obviously. The war years had taught him foresight. A single weapon in his hand but all the solutions in his head, that had been the key to his success. Yesterday in the streets of Algiers, today in those of Cadaqués.

And then he was ready for anything. To be sure, he would have preferred to carry out this last mission without problems so that he could go die—as late as possible—alongside his beloved Gabriella. He'd so much like to see her grow up . . . But nothing could weaken his determination. It was a question of honor. He owed it to all the companions in arms that these bastards had betrayed.

He owed it to their memory.

He owed it to his ideals.

He owed it to his youth.

He owed it. Period.

# CHAPTER 25

This is quite a change from the meeting room at headquarters, isn't it?"

Molina was proud of his idea. Sebag congratulated him by raising his espresso to him. Castello was in Montpellier for a regional seminar for superintendents, and Molina had proposed to his colleagues that they hold their morning meeting at the Carlit.

"After all, our bosses are having their big wingding in a luxurious hotel, so we can certainly have our meeting in a little bistro," he'd argued.

Llach, Lambert, and Sebag had approved the idea with enthusiasm, Julie Sadet with reservations, and Ménard, who was still in Marseille, had not been able to contest it. As for Raynaud and Moreno, they would surely not have been opposed to it, but faithful to their habits, they were taking advantage of the boss's absence to play hooky.

Sebag swigged with undisguised pleasure the excellent mocha Rafel had made. Then he took the floor. Everyone thought it was natural that he lead the discussion in Castello's absence.

"The officers sent yesterday to the site of the attack on Albouker found nothing. No material evidence, and no testimony about the two perpetrators, either. Examination of the message left by the attackers yielded nothing; only Jacques's prints and those of the victim were found on it."

"Clearly, we're floundering here," Joan Llach lamented.

"Hard to disagree with you there," Sebag admitted.

He chose to take up immediately a question that seemed to him indispensable for what was to follow.

"In what way does this attack change our ongoing investigations?"

"In no way," Llach replied frankly. "Apart from the fact that the victim is a *Pied-Noir*, this attack with a knife has nothing in common with the double murder we're working on."

"In the message the attackers left, there is, however, a direct allusion to . . . to the OAS," Lambert said.

"An indirect allusion, rather," Joan corrected. "If the message mentioned the OAS, it would be a direct allusion. But it refers only to 'murderers,' and that's an indirect allusion."

"You can always quibble, but that doesn't change anything in what I mean," Lambert insisted.

"And what exactly do you mean?" Molina asked bluntly. "That everything is connected?"

"No, I don't know. I just mean that we have to be careful before rejecting everything. I mean before excluding the possibility that all these cases are connected."

"But we have to try to see things more clearly," said Llach, irritated. "And we won't be able to do that by mixing everything up."

Julie Sadet spoke up in her calm voice.

"Everything is connected, in fact."

Skillfully, she waited until all eyes were on her before continuing.

"I believe we have before us, on the one hand, a double murder, and, on the other, people who are trying to take advantage of this case to sow discord in Perpignan. The two cases are distinct, but they are also connected: without the murders, there would probably have been no attack on Albouker and no destruction of the OAS monument."

The silence that followed showed that the inspectors found their new colleague's argument pertinent.

"The other day we had trouble understanding the coincidence, which seemed strange to us," Molina reflected out loud. "But on your hypothesis, it wouldn't really be a coincidence."

"I find that interesting," Llach confirmed, seeking approval in Sebag's eyes.

Sebag nodded pensively. Yes, he found the idea attractive. But one thing bothered him. A question of chronology. Martinez's murder had been discovered on Monday and revealed by the press on Tuesday. The monument had been destroyed on Wednesday night, before the news about the painted letters OAS that had been found in Martinez's apartment had circulated in the city. If people wanted to sow panic in the city's *Pied-Noir* community, they had been well-informed and had acted very quickly. Sebag preferred to keep his reservations to himself, and took up the other subjects. He conveyed to his colleagues the reports that Castello had left for him. André Roman's autopsy confirmed that he had been killed by a bullet to the heart—the second bullet fired, and the ballistics analysis certified that the weapon used was in fact a 9 mm Beretta 34, the same weapon that was used to kill Martinez.

"In addition, I reviewed the situation with François this morning, on the telephone. There's a new development in Marseille: François was supposed to meet with his *barbouze*, but the guy disappeared several days ago."

The policemen opened their eyes wide in surprise.

"Let's not get excited too fast: Maurice Garcin is eighty-one years old, suffers from Alzheimer's, and it was from the retirement home where he lives that he disappeared. Or rather wandered away. It seems that he does that often. According to his two sons, whom François contacted, Garcin is coping very badly with his decline. Whence his repeated escapes."

"So if the guy is senile, he's no longer a suspect?" Llach asked.

"He was never really a suspect, he's a witness like many others. Well . . . I mean, among many others. We don't have as many as it seems. Isn't that right, Julie?"

"That's right," the young woman acknowledged. "Among the former *barbouzes* who are still alive that François and I have identified, Garcin seems to us the only one who has retained a robust hatred of the OAS for the past half-century."

"Since he can't talk to the father, François is going to meet with the two sons today. He'll find out from them what Garcin's exact state of health is. Alzheimer's is a progressive disorder, one doesn't become senile from one day to the next. Above all, I believe there are now treatments that attenuate its effects."

"What if he isn't sick at all," Llach suggested. "Can't one simulate that illness?"

"I'm not very well-informed on that subject," Sebag admitted. "I don't know whether there are irrefutable tests or clinical examinations."

"That may also depend on the degree of the illness," Julie pointed out. "You said that he was still fairly lucid."

"That's the impression I got from François, but if the guy is in a retirement home, it's because he's actually sick.'

"He could be the one," Lambert ventured. "At eighty-one, he'll necessarily have white hair."

"He could also be completely bald," Molina countered. "We'll have to ask Ménard to check."

"Send him an SMS right away," Sebag proposed. "Then it'll be done."

Molina took out his cell phone and tapped on the keyboard. Gilles thought this was the moment to bring up the question of the killer's car. He hadn't stopped thinking about it since the day before. He wanted to see if some of his colleagues, with new eyes, would arrive spontaneously at the same conclusions as he had.

"Concordant testimonies gathered yesterday allow us to think that Roman's murderer was driving a white SEAT with Spanish plates. The problem is that on the day of Martinez's murder residents of Moulin-a-Vent saw not a SEAT but a white Clio with Spanish plates."

"Are the witnesses reliable?" Llach asked. "The two models are pretty similar, if I'm not mistaken."

"We can assume that they are reliable, yes. We checked."

"That's strange," Lambert commented.

"I don't see what's strange about it," Julie Sadet said. "The murderer could have simply changed cars. It's unlikely that he used his own vehicle."

Sebag smiled. Castello's recruit was proving to be a good one. She'd avoided the trap that he and Molina had stupidly fallen into the preceding day.

"So according to you, where did he get his cars?"

"From a rental agency on the other side of the border, of course."

"But why would he choose two models that are so similar?"

"He didn't necessarily choose. Maybe in each case he opted for a widely-sold model and color in order to avoid making himself conspicuous."

The idea struck the inspectors as judicious. Sebag was jubilant.

"That's exactly the conclusion that I arrived at last night. The similarity of the models and the Spanish license plates in the two cases prevented us from immediately seeing what now seems obvious to us. At first, we thought that the witnesses were mistaken, and that it must be the same car. Then when we understood that the witnesses were right and that there were in fact two distinct vehicles, we were incapable of imagining this solution which is ultimately very simple."

"So the killer rents his cars in Spain?" Llach summed up.

"Affirmative," Sebag confirmed. We can even imagine that that's where he lives between crimes."

"Hop, hop, hop," Molina interrupted vigorously. "Aren't we moving a little too fast there? You're now assuming that the old man with the Clio, who was probably responsible for the accident that killed your daughter's friend, is also the murderer?"

"Yes, I think that's possible."

"What old man, what accident?" Llach interrupted.

Sebag rapidly told them about Mathieu's death.

"Charles Mercader, a resident of Moulin-à-Vent, told us that he'd seen a man at least seventy years old get into the Clio. We can imagine that the murderer was a little nervous after committing his crime, and that in hastening to escape, he ran a stop sign."

"An old man? That would be Maurice Garcin, then!" Lambert exclaimed. "The *barbouze*!"

"Hold on, hold on, let's calm down," Sebag said. "The fact that the murderer is old doesn't prove anything. Even if he might want to take revenge for something that happened more than fifty years ago, Garcin isn't the only survivor of the Algerian War.

"So we're back to the infamous white hair, then," Llach remarked. "Did Castello look into that?"

"I don't know, I'll have to talk to Pagès."

"An old gunslinger and hot-rodder who leaves his hair lying around everywhere like Tom Thumb's pebbles . . . Isn't all that a little implausible?"

Molina didn't conceal his ill humor. Sebag hadn't taken him into his confidence and he was mad about it.

"We have to beware of drawing hasty conclusions," Sebag conceded. "But it's by following leads that we make progress."

"Or go off on the wrong track!"

"Last night, I still had serious doubts about this business of the car, and that's why I didn't talk to you about it. But this morning, I'm practically convinced. And even if I'm moving a little fast by attributing to the murderer the responsibility for the accident, that doesn't mean that it's stupid to think that our man rented two similar cars from Spanish agencies. And I remind you that I wasn't the only one who arrived at that hypothesis. Julie did, too. And without my having said a word about it to her."

"We're going to be wasting our time," Molina grumbled again. "There are thousands of car rental agencies in Spain."

"If, as Gilles says, the murderer is living in Spain, he's probably based not far from the border," Julie said.

"So what? Between Le Perthus and Girona, there are at least several dozen agencies . . . And over the past two weeks, each one of them must have rented dozens of Clios and SEATs."

"But they must not have many customers who rented a Clio and then a SEAT."

"If our guy is being careful, he wouldn't have gone to the same agency twice."

"That's true," Julie conceded.

"And in any case, it's not going to be easy for us to get the information in Spain. We'll have to go through official channels, and that will take days and days."

Llach, who had kept silent as they talked, sat up on his chair.

"One of my wife's cousins works for the Mossos. He could give us a hand. Unofficially, of course. We've already done each other some favors when we needed to move fast."

Sebag turned to Julie, who didn't seem to understand.

"The Mossos is the police force in South Catalonia. Its full name is *Mossos d'Esquadra*."[14]

"Isn't the Spanish police the Guardia Civil?"

Sebag, Molina, and Lambert smiled. Julie Sadet had just

---

[14] Lit. "squad lads." It is one of the oldest civil police forces in Europe.

committed her first big blunder. Llach sighed but agreed to give her a quick explanation.

"The Guardia Civil is in fact the Spanish police, yes, but in South Catalonia it has gradually been replaced by the Mossos. The process has been going on for over twenty years. Today, the Guardia is involved only in matters of terrorism and immigration. All the rest, including criminal cases, is in the jurisdiction of the Catalan police."

Llach added, not without pride:

"It's one of the oldest police forces in Europe. It was created at the beginning of the eighteenth century."

"Fine, fine, I'll go to bed less ignorant this evening. Thanks, Joan."

"Should I call my cousin in the Mossos, then?" Llach asked.

"That would be good . . . "

"And I suppose that I should bring in Charles Mercader to do an Identikit picture?" Molina asked reluctantly.

"If my hypothesis is valid, Mercader is the only person who saw the murderer. I'm going to try to get a photo of Maurice Garcin. We have to show it to Mercader. We'll ask François to dig us up one."

Sebag gave the signal for dismissal, while Jacques sent another text message to Ménard. Llach, Lambert, and Julie Sadet stood up, but the young woman cop didn't follow her colleagues out the door.

"Did you have something else you wanted to say, Julie?" Sebag asked her.

"I had an idea. A hypothesis, to use your vocabulary."

"Let's hear it, please."

"It occurred to me that the killer could have taken his car back to an agency different from the one where he rented it. That's a pretty common practice."

"Yes, it happens quite often. But why would he have done that?"

"I don't know. Because it was convenient, or to try to hide his tracks."

"That's possible. And where does this line of argument take us?"

"We might imagine that he returned his vehicle to a French agency."

Sebag's eyes narrowed. His brain was calculating all the consequences of that supposition.

"That means that we could follow that lead right away, without waiting for the help of our colleagues in South Catalonia. It also means that we won't be flooded with suspects: there can't be too many customers who rent a car in Spain and return it in France. Bravo! You should be the one to look into this, of course. Ask Llach or Lambert to help you."

Julie turned on her heel and joined her colleagues in the street. Molina put his cell phone back in his jacket.

"She's pretty good, our new recruit," Sebag remarked.

"Yeah."

Sebag looked hard at Molina. He was expecting further comments, but none came.

"You're either pouting or you're getting old!"

"I'm not pouting."

"So you must be getting old!"

"What do you mean, getting old? What are you talking about?"

"You have nothing more to say about our young, pretty Julie? No comments on her lovely eyes, her nice little ass, and God knows what else?"

"It's just that . . . well, no!"

"That's exactly what I said, you're getting old: you're not even trying to put moves on her."

"I'm not that heavy-handed. I don't shoot at anything that moves, after all."

"In any case, you try . . . "

Molina laughed.

"Yes, it's true, I'm a little heavy-handed sometimes."

"But here, nothing! What's going on?"

"I don't know, I'm not feeling anything."

"Why? Don't you like her?"

"Are you kidding? She's super hot."

"What then?"

"I don't know. The old hunter's instinct, probably. She's not in my league."

"She's too good for you?"

"Oh please, don't give me that. I've had some who were just as good, or even better. But I'm not getting any vibes off her: she's not on the market, that's all!"

"That's a very classy way of putting it . . . "

"That's how I see things. And I'm saying it as best I can. She's very . . . not distant, no, it's not that, she's just . . . withdrawn. You can't understand, you haven't tried to pick up a woman since you met Claire at the university, but those of us who do can sense these things. In my opinion, Julie's got a boyfriend and she's very much in love. And she's probably very faithful. If you see what I mean . . . "

"I have some vague sense of what you're driving at, yes," Sebag replied.

He suddenly wondered when Claire had . . . put herself back on the market, what signals she might have sent out and what "predator" had picked them up. A pang of jealousy bored into his stomach followed by another even more treacherous—a pang of fear. And what was the situation now? Now that her summer fling seemed to be over—if it ever existed— was Claire on that infamous market again?

He suddenly raised his hand to order another coffee. One more little treat and he'd immerse himself in the investigation again. That would be more useful than his eternal, painful, sterile ruminations.

\*

Around the middle of the morning, he telephoned Gérard Mercier.

"I was just about to call you," the brother of the *Pied-Noir* Circle's treasurer said. "The photo you sent of our two boys with Lieutenant Degueldre helped me. I talked to some of my contacts—they're old friends—and I've got new information for you. Do you have something to write with?"

Sebag was sitting at his desk, with his notebook lying open in front of him.

"Go ahead, I'm all ears."

"There were in fact four of them who made up what was called the Babelo commando, after the name of their leader, or rather his nickname. Around Babelo we see Sigma, Bizerte, and Omega . . . "

"You have only pseudonyms?" Sebag said with concern.

"Omega was Bernard Martinez. Sigma was a young guy named Jean Servant, and Bizerte . . . I suppose you've guessed who Bizerte was?"

Sebag remembered that André Roman spent part of his childhood in the city of Bizerte, in northern Tunisia.

"They didn't go to a lot of trouble to find their pseudonyms," he said.

"It was more a game than a necessity. Especially since among the *Pieds-Noirs*, everything always came out anyway. But the pseudonyms gave certain groups the feeling of being in the Resistance."

The comparison startled Sebag but he refrained from making any commentary that might annoy the former member of the OAS.

"What about Babelo?"

"That comes from Bab-El-Oued, which means 'Door of the River.' It was a working-class European neighborhood in northern Algiers. It was also one of the bastions of the OAS. The leader came from there."

"And do you have his real name?"

No response, only silence.

"Hello, are you still there?"

"Yes, yes, I'm here."

"Do you have his name, or didn't your 'contacts' give it to you?"

"Yes, they gave it to me. According to them, Babelo wouldn't like being bothered by the police for such old matters."

"Nonsense! Did you tell them that it was chiefly a matter of saving his life?"

Mercier chuckled.

"They weren't impressed; they told me he could take care of himself."

"That's ridiculous. I have to contact him. You have to give me his name."

Gérard Mercier resisted.

"I don't have to do anything! I told you at the outset that if I helped you it would be mainly to protect our guys. And anyway, Babelo is not in your jurisdiction: he didn't return to metropolitan France."

"Where does he live?"

"Elsewhere . . . Don't worry, I'll try to contact him myself and he'll be on his guard."

Sebag conceded defeat for the moment. He had to avoid antagonizing his interlocutor because he had other questions to ask him. He reread his notes.

"And the last guy—his name is Jean Servant, right?'

"Yes, that's right. But he isn't in your jurisdiction, either."

"Come on!" he replied, overcome by annoyance.

"He didn't return to France either, after the war," Mercier explained. "He didn't have the chance to. He died in Algiers. He was killed in the bombing of a bar in June, 1962."

Sebag noted down this information. The investigation was coming to an abrupt end: there was now only one potential victim and he couldn't do anything to help him. He felt both disappointment and relief.

"O.K., then! Let's see if we can find out a little more about the murderer's motives. Do you have any idea of what the Babelo commando did back then?"

"The Babelo group was one of the famous Delta commandos that were under the direct control of Lieutenant Degueldre, the OAS's chief operations organizer."

Mercier's voice trembled slightly as he uttered Degueldre's name.

"It was a very active group that carried out spectacular, daring actions . . . "

"I got that impression, yes," Sebag said ironically.

Horrible things, Mathilde Roman had said before talking about the murder of the French police officer and innocent Arabs. Mercier pretended to not to have heard what Sebag said.

"They began by taking over Radio Algiers. We liked that kind of operation. We cut the programming of the official radio station and replaced it with our own. That way our compatriots got real news that was very different from what the government told them."

"But the Babelo group didn't limit itself to that, right?" Sebag interrupted.

He immediately sensed discomfort at the other end of the line. He had to encourage Mercier to go on again.

"Hello, are you still there?"

"I'm still here. I'm thinking about how I can explain to you something that you can't understand."

"I can try."

"I don't doubt your goodwill," Mercier sighed, "but it's always a matter of putting everything in its historical context. Even if it wasn't acknowledged as such, the Algerian War was a real war, a kind of civil war, and especially a terrible war."

He paused to take a breath.

"Let us recall first that it was the FLN that started the fighting in November 1954. And the *fellaghas* never limited themselves to military targets. They killed civilians, women, and children, too. Slit their throats, disemboweled them. You must have seen lots of corpses in your work, but how many have you found with their testicles in their mouths? By damn, that makes one hell of an impression, believe you me."

He spoke faster and faster.

"Personally, I was twenty-two when I got in contact with the OAS. At the time, I was full of hatred, we all had someone close to us who'd been killed by the FLN. That doesn't encourage clemency, I can tell you that."

His *Pied-Noir* accent took over as he grew more heated.

"It was war. And in wartime points of reference and values are not the same as they are in peacetime. When everything's calm it's easy to have generous ideas and great moral principles. But during a war, it's entirely different."

"All this in order to say what?" Sebag pressed him.

"To say that the Babelo group didn't commit just nice actions like taking over the radio."

"Did it kill a French police officer, for example?"

"For example. I see that you are already well-informed."

"I don't know his name, or the date."

"It was Inspector Michel. Executed in Algiers in December 1961."

Sebag noted the choice of terms: "executed." That was something quite different from "killed" or "murdered."

"They also 'executed' defenseless Arab workers."

Gérard Mercier was breathing heavily.

"I told you that you couldn't understand."

"I'm having difficulty, in fact."

"I think I know what operation you're referring to. In November 1961, Babelo's men waited for workers at the exit from a bottling factory and shot them down without warning. There were six dead. The workers were unarmed, they weren't necessarily members of the FLN. But they were Arabs, and at the time that was enough for us."

He took a deep breath.

"There were lots of operations like that one, and some that were even worse. Women and children were killed in the same way. It's true that all that mattered to us was that they were Arabs. Just as to fire on us, it was enough for the *fellaghas* that we were Europeans. I told you: it was war. For my part, I booby-trapped cars and put bombs in Arab cafés. I was caught, tried, and went to prison. I paid."

Mercier cleared his throat before going on.

"Because we did pay, we all paid. We lost our battle, and as a result, History has decided that we were in the wrong. History is always a bitch for the losers. It has made our actions crimes and those of our adversaries great military feats. The former *fellaghas* have become cabinet ministers and our fighters have become pariahs who don't even have the right to have public monuments to their memory in France. But we did nothing that was worse than what the FLN did."

"Eye for an eye, tooth for a tooth. It's pretty classic, after all," Sebag summed up. "You began by talking about spectacular, daring actions. Up to now, I haven't seen anything like that."

"The Babelo group was in the forefront of our battle against the *barbouzes*. You've heard about the *barbouzes*?"

"Only recently, but now I know who they were."

"Battle-hardened veterans with powerful weapons. They bombed our bars, killed our fighters, tortured some of us. They gave us no quarter . . . "

"You didn't give them any, either."

"That's true," said Mercier, with intact pride in his voice. "They didn't stay in Algiers long. Three months after they got there—and despite reinforcements—they all went back to metropolitan France."

"Those who were still alive."

"The others, too," Mercier said mockingly. "I can guarantee you that their bodies weren't buried over there."

Sebag noted down a few more words, and then rapidly reread what he'd written since the beginning of the conversation. Next he asked Mercier what the Babelo commando could have done that could have elicited such a belated vengeance.

"In my opinion, nothing. Or else everything! What I mean by that is that I don't see anything in particular in their acts that could explain it."

"Can you envisage it as revenge taken by former *barbouzes*?"

"Had you asked me that question forty years ago, I would probably have answered yes, but today! Why today?"

"Some *barbouzes* are still angry at the OAS."

"Just as we are still angry at de Gaulle and the FLN. It's always in the camp of the losers that you find the people who want revenge. But I ask again: why today?"

"Because before, the murderer didn't know that Martinez, Roman, and other . . . 'Babelos' were responsible!"

"That wasn't known to everyone, but it wasn't a secret, either. And even if it was! That was half a century ago! Who can still harbor such a tenacious hatred after so long a time? No, if you want my opinion, the only really tenacious hatreds are found . . . "

Gérard Mercier suddenly stopped.

"Yes?" Sebag asked.

"No, nothing. I'm letting myself get carried away by passion and I was going to say something stupid."

"Go ahead, say it. I'll tell you what I think."

"These are only speculations that are of no interest."

"Not necessarily."

"Yes, necessarily. If I'm wrong, it's stupid. And if I'm right, it's even stupider."

Mercier tried to snigger, but his laugh sounded false.

"Don't leave me hanging," Sebag tried again.

"Don't insist. I believe I've already helped your investigation quite a bit. You've gotten more out of me than I intended. You're redoubtable, Lieutenant Sebag. Goodbye."

With that cheap flattery, he hung up. Sebag, perplexed, wrote a series of question marks at the end of his notes. Then he took the photo of the commando's four men and looked again at the infamous Babelo. Older than his three accomplices, he wore with pride—and perhaps a certain self-importance—an elegant, fashionable suit. A light-colored kerchief poked out of one pocket. His oiled hair, slicked back in waves, revealed a broad, triangular forehead. Straight eyebrows, a long nose squeezed between protruding cheekbones, and a thin mustache protecting a winning smile. The guy had an obvious charm and charisma. Sebag made himself a promise:

"My dear Babelo, whoever you are, wherever you are, and whatever you think, I'm going to find you. I just hope I find you before you die."

Later that morning, Sebag received a call from Ménard.

"I've just spoken with Garcin's sons. They confirm that their father has never completely gotten over the Algerian War and is still angry at *Pieds-Noirs* in general and the OAS in particular. They have always heard him say that the criminals of French Algeria got off too easily, that the Republic had been too lenient with them, and that it should have shot a lot more of them. But they also say that's just talk, and that he'd never have actually done anything. And in any case, he's now physically incapable of it."

"Who says that? His sons?"

"Yes, of course."

"You should go talk with the doctors at the retirement home and get their opinion. Find out, for instance, whether it's possible to pretend to have Alzheimer's."

"O.K., I'll try to see them this afternoon."

"Does the old man wander off frequently?"

"Apparently."

"How long has he been gone this time?"

"Three days."

"So, since Sunday, the day Roman was assassinated. About what time?"

"He didn't come to breakfast, which is served at 7 A.M."

"And at the time of Martinez's death, were you able to find out where he was?"

"He was gone then, too."

"For a long time?"

"No, just one day."

"He takes off that frequently?"

"Three or four times a month, on average. Sometimes a few hours, sometimes a few days."

"Those are long walks, in fact."

"You could say that."

"We're laughing but we still can't exclude the possibility that these walks lead to murders. Were you able to get a photo of him?"

"Yes, his sons gave me a picture. The most recent one. I'll photograph it with my iPhone and e-mail it to you. The quality isn't great but it will be useful all the same."

"That's fine. I'll be waiting for it."

A miracle of modern technology, the photo appeared on his computer screen only three minutes after he hung up. Despite his age and his illness, Maurice Garcin had retained a slender figure and a certain presence. The flames of strong passions still burned in his pale blue eyes. His square, wrinkled face was framed by white hair thinned by age.

Sebag immediately called Ménard back. He'd forgotten one detail.

"Try to get one of Garcin's hairs while you're at the retirement home. Maybe you'll find one on the pillow of his bed or on a comb in his bathroom. Then we can compare his DNA with that of the hairs we've already found."

The hair or the hairs; were the other two from the same man? Sebag tried to call the head of the forensic team. Since there was no answer, he left a message. But he knew that he'd have to try again; Pagès never called back.

Sebag printed the photo. Molina could show it to his witness Charles Mercader that afternoon. He hadn't been able to meet him this morning, the retiree having a longstanding appointment with his cardiologist. Sebag stretched and then got up. He went to the office next door where Llach and Julie were calling car rental agencies.

"We've already done all the agencies in Perpignan," Julie explained. "Now we're starting in on the agencies in Narbonne. We decided to follow the rail line: we figure that after he'd turned in his car, the killer would have no choice but to take the train to get back to Spain."

"That seems me an excellent supposition."

With that compliment, Sebag left them. He took the police vehicle to go to find out how Guy Albouker was doing. He found the president of the *Pied-Noir* Circle comfortably settled in a large armchair, his feet resting on an ottoman. He'd put on a dressing gown over his shirt and pants, and was reading a magazine for the *Pied-Noir* community. He seemed to be recovering quickly from his attack.

"The night was a little difficult. The wound hurt every time I turned over in bed. But this morning it's better. I was able to take a little walk around the neighborhood."

"And psychologically, you're O.K.?"

Albouker's wife answered for him.

"He's less affected than I'd feared."

Albouker grimaced as he sat up in his chair. His face hardened.

"My body is all right and my mind, too. It's my heart that hurts. I thought all that was over—the hostility, the resentment, the hate. You'd think that time hadn't changed anything. History still casts us as the bad guys."

Marie tried to calm him: "Stop, there's no point in stewing about all that,"

"Stop, stop . . . Precisely, I'd like all that to stop some day. But we're still the victims of the same ostracism. So I get stabbed, I can handle that, it's only a flesh wound, it'll heal up; what I can't stand is being called a murderer. No one in my family killed anybody."

He put his hand on his stomach.

"We're often accused of brooding on our bitterness, but do you know why we can't heal, Mr. Sebag?"

"Yes, you told me last Sunday. To heal would be to die. To die as a community."

"Did I say that? Damn . . . Sometimes I say stupid things."

He refrained from smiling, he hadn't yet vented his anger.

"Do you know what makes our tragedy unlike any other? Yes, I know I'm exaggerating . . . Let's say what makes it so different from many other tragedies suffered by many other peoples? Well, it's that today, History hasn't changed. It remains fixed. We're the bad guys, and the bad guys we'll remain. The truth has not been restored. People don't want to see that we are victims first of all. Granted, some *Pieds-Noirs* did terrible things, but collectively we're victims. France has to do us that justice. We weren't racist colonists, and still less murderers. It's not de Gaulle who betrayed us, it's France! And today it's still going on."

Marie Albouker sat down alongside her husband and took his hand without saying a word. She knew that if she spoke she would only make things worse.

"We have to express our anger again and again. Otherwise we'll all die from holding it in. My father died of that. An ulcer and cancer. A marvelous combination. Thanks, France! I still often mourn my father, because I don't even have a grave where I can go and think about him. And do you know why?"

Sebag shook his head. He also preferred to remain silent.

"My father, like many *Pieds-Noirs* of his generation, did not want to be buried in the earth of the country that had betrayed him. We cremated my father's body and I scattered his ashes in the Mediterranean. That was his last wish. He hoped that the current would carry him to the shores of Algeria. And I want to think that that's what happened. Because if there is no justice in this world, we have to believe that at least there will be justice in the next world."

He leaned back in his chair, exhausted. His diatribe was finally over. His wife gently patted his hand.

"You know that Mr. Sebag is not to blame."

"Yes, I know the inspector's not to blame. But he's the one who's here, so too bad for him."

Marie Albouker gave Sebag a little smile of excuse.

"You probably haven't heard yet?" she asked shyly.

"Heard what?"

"About this afternoon."

"What about it?"

"The demonstration . . . "

"The *Pied-Noir* associations have organized a rally at 5 P.M. in front of the Castillet," the president of the Circle explained. "I'm not the instigator but I didn't disapprove of it. Jean-Pierre Mercier, my treasurer, met yesterday with the officials of other *Pied-Noir* associations and they agreed to demonstrate our dissatisfaction. You understand . . . with two murders of *Pieds-Noirs*, the destruction of the monument, and now the attack on me, the community owes it to itself to react."

Sebag was not happy about the rally. It was not the kind of thing that was likely to calm people down.

"Has the prefecture been informed?"

"This action is largely spontaneous, largely improvised. Everything was decided at the last minute. But I think that by now, yes, the prefect has been informed."

"Do you think that this kind of demonstration will calm things?"

"That's not necessarily the goal."

"Thank you for recognizing that. And you think that reacting collectively to attacks directed essentially against the OAS is going to help people make the distinction between your community and, as you put it, that criminal organization?"

Albouker scowled.

"For the past fifty years, no one has wanted to make that distinction! So a little more or a little less, it's all the same."

"I hope at least that in your condition, you're not going to take the risk of going there."

"Don't worry," Marie Albouker told him. "He's going to stay right here."

Sebag said a rapid goodbye and left. Out on the sidewalk, he called the prefect's cabinet director on her cell phone. Having been informed by the RG, Sabine Henri already knew about the rally.

"We're going to take steps to prevent this demonstration from degenerating. The organizers have asked to be heard. The prefect himself will receive them. In the absence of Superintendent Castello, I'd like you to be present at this meeting to tell us about the progress of the investigation. There has been progress, hasn't there?"

"Let's say that we're moving forward step by step and that we're following promising leads."

The cabinet director laughed.

"I hope you will be able to present the case in a more attractive way. And especially present your work in a more positive manner. You're not unaware that these days policemen also have to master the art of communication."

"I've heard that said, yes, but making things known too often substitutes for knowing how to do things."

"Bravo for the formula. I hope you'll find more of those before this afternoon. And especially more appropriate ones. I doubt that one would be suitable for our interlocutors."

"I'll do my best."

"I'm counting on it, Lieutenant Sebag, I'm counting on it. And the prefect is, too. See you in a little while."

Sebag hung up and couldn't help swearing.

"Fuck it to hell!"

Nearby, an old lady who was letting her dog defecate under the parasol pines jumped. She shot him a furious glance and rapidly walked away. Her dog followed her reluctantly, dropping behind him a smelly series of Tootsie Rolls.

# CHAPTER 26

**El-Biar, March 15, 1962**

The two cars are speeding down the Ben-Aknoun road that connects the village of El-Biar with Algiers. A black Peugeot 403 is in the lead. Inside it, Omega is driving silently, his hands gripping the steering wheel. Every time he's involved in an operation he gets more nervous.

In the backseat, Sigma is constantly asking himself questions. One of them finally makes it past his lips:

"Why them?"

Babelo, sitting next to the driver, turns around:

"The welfare centers were established by a communist, their members are all propagandists. They're spreading the FLN's message to the villages. It's people like them who have made it possible for the insurrection to reach the whole country."

"There are Europeans with them . . . "

The commando leader's mouth twists into a scornful sneer:

"Communists, Gaullists, and liberals. In other words, traitors!"

The cars leave the main highway and take the long avenue lined with palm trees that leads to the Château Royal.

"The negotiations in Évian are progressing too fast," Babelo goes on. "De Gaulle is getting ready to sell Algeria to the *fellaghas*. Our orders are clear. We have to hit hard and in every camp. General Salan reminded us again yesterday: war isn't waged with choirboys."

He looks hard at each of his three companions and adjusts the kerchief in the breast pocket of his jacket.

"We aren't choirboys!"

The two cars stop in front of the old buildings of the Château-Royal. Babelo, Sigma, and Bizerte get out of the 403. Three more men get out of the second vehicle, a beige 203: Richard Caceres, Paul Tanguy, and Antoine Hernandez. Men who can be trusted—they're not choirboys, either—and who participated a few weeks earlier, along with Degueldre and the Babelo commando, in the attack on the *barbouzes*' villa.

The drivers make a U-turn to get into their starting positions. It's 10:30 A.M.

Armed with pistols and submachine guns, the six OAS combatants enter the courtyard serving the various buildings of the Château-Royal. They meet an employee who is coming down the stairs. He's carrying a heavy load of files in his arms.

"What are you doing here?" the employee demands without getting flustered.

"We're here to check papers," Babelo replies.

"But there's nothing to check here!"

Tanguy and Caceres threaten him with their guns and order him to follow them. The man doesn't hesitate for long and allows himself to be led to a French door above which there is a sign: "Administrative Offices."

"Nobody moves, and nobody gets hurt," Tanguy tells the three secretaries sitting at their desks, while Caceres, without saying a word, pulls out the lines of the telephone switchboard. Babelo, Bizerte, and Sigma go down a long hallway. They have prepared their mission well, and they know where they're going. They stop in front of a door behind which a meeting of the inspectors of the social services and education sector is being held. They throw open the door.

"Stand up, hands in the air, against the wall," the leader of the commando orders in a firm but cordial voice.

There are about twenty inspectors. They obey. Sigma makes sure none of them is carrying a weapon. Babelo looks at them one by one and then, smiling, says:

"Don't be afraid: we aren't going to hurt you. We just want to make a recording."

The inspectors think that they are simply going to be forced to take part in a clandestine radio broadcast as part of one of the many takeovers made by the OAS. As planned, the atmosphere immediately becomes more relaxed. Babelo brushes a bit of dust off his jacket before taking a sheet of paper out of his inside pocket. He begins to read a list of names:

"Mouloud Feraoun. Max Marchand. Marcel Basset . . . "

Seven names in all, six of them are present. Only one is not there.

"We're waiting for him," one of the inspectors says, "He's late."

"No problem," Babelo says. "You're going to follow me, please."

One of the six men raises his hand as if he were in school.

"Can I take my glasses?"

"Of course," Babelo says courteously.

The inspector, an Arab about fifty years old, grabs a pair of glasses lying on the conference table. He puts them in the vest pocket of his jacket. Then the six men follow the commando out into the courtyard.

Antoine Hernandez has set up two machine guns on their stands at opposite ends of the courtyard. Perfect for a crossfire. When the inspectors understand what awaits them, it's too late. They can no longer escape. Babelo, Sigma, and Bizerte drive their prisoners forward. Tanguy and Caceres have joined them. They take their places behind the machine guns.

Babelo orders the inspectors to stand with their backs against the wall. The six doomed men obey.

And the firing begins. It is long and intense. The furious staccato of the machine guns covers the cries and pleas of the inspectors.

Tanguy and Caceres deliberately aim low. They hit the legs first, and when the bodies collapse, they strike the abdomens, then the hearts. Mouloud Feraoun is the last to fall. The Algeria that has not yet been born in Évian has just lost one of its greatest writers.

When the firing finally stops, Babelo holds out his hand to Sigma. The young man hands him his pistol. The leader of the commando approaches the bodies. Calmly, he gives each of the victims a superfluous coup de grâce. Then he gives the smoking gun back to Sigma.

The police, arriving long after the commando has calmly departed, pick up more than a hundred 9 mm cartridges in the courtyard of the Château-Royal, about twenty bullets per man killed. As they roughly haul off the body of the Arab inspector they hear a faint cracking coming from a pocket in his jacket. The policemen have just broken a pair of glasses that has somehow miraculously survived the gunfire.

# CHAPTER 27

T wo hundred and fifty *Pieds-Noirs* were loudly express-
ing their anger and their concern on the Place de la
Victoire in Perpignan. The brick walls of the Castillet,
the ancient medieval gate to the city, resounded with their slogans, giving body and magnitude to their eternal demands:

"Justice for the repatriates!"

"No to the distortion of History!"

"Compensation!"

"Have pity on our cemeteries, our tombs, and our monuments!"

Happy and proud to feel their strength, the former French
of Algeria seemed ready to shout their lungs out until they
died.

Standing at a certain distance, Sebag observed the scene
from a small stone bridge that looked down on the River Basse.
From that vantage point, he saw nothing but white hair or bald
heads floating and shining under improvised banners. He
thought again of what Albouker had said during the couscous
dinner: "In ten to twenty years we'll all be dead and that will
be the end of our community."

Sitting at a table on the terrace of a café, a few young adults
were watching the demonstration with unconcealed curiosity.
In the shade of a bus shelter, several North African boys were
looking on scornfully. Sebag saw an inspector from the RG discreetly approaching to keep an eye on them. A single spark
would suffice to reignite the ancestral hatred.

Since that morning, Sebag had been constantly thinking about the meeting that was to take place at the prefecture in the late afternoon. He had been regularly calling his teams, but no progress seemed to have been made in the course of the day. Julie and Joan had contacted all the car rental agencies in Narbonne, Béziers, and Carcasonne. Without result. They were continuing to follow the rail lines, one toward Toulouse, the other toward Montpellier. However, their energy and conviction were diminishing as they moved farther and farther away from Catalonia.

Molina's talk with Charles Mercader had not been successful, either. The witness was proving to be unhelpful. Jacques had shown him a dozen photos of elderly men, and after hesitating for a long time he'd finally pulled the portrait of Maurice Garcin out of the pile. But the hope had been short-lived. "It's possible," "I can't exclude the possibility," "This is the one that comes closest," he'd said, before concluding with a disappointing: "I don't know anymore." Then Molina had tried to have him work up an Identikit image, but his memories were too fragile and allowed him at most to come up with a square face with a short, powerful nose and brown eyebrows, despite the white hair. Police rigor alone would have prevented them from calling this vague sketch an Identikit portrait. But that was nonetheless how Sebag was preparing to present it to the prefect.

The setting sun was lighting only the top of the Castillet, its crenellated terrace, its little tower, and its Catalan flag. There were now almost three hundred *Pieds-Noirs* there, and they were beginning to organize themselves. They put the largest of the banners at their head. On a white cloth attached to two broom handles, the words "*Honneur et Justice*" were written in red and black paint. Prepared with enthusiasm and haste, the second "n" in "*honneur*" had been crossed out. Behind the banner rose a dozen posters, some of them carrying the demonstration's main slogans, others proudly displaying the ancient coats of arms of the cities of French Algeria.

The demonstrators started to move down Boulevard Clémenceau. It had been agreed that the procession would make a small loop around the Place de Catalogne and then return to the prefecture. It was at that point that a delegation would be received by the prefect.

Sebag recognized Jean-Pierre Mercier at the head of the procession, flanked by René from Oran and Roger from Algiers, the sparring partners from the couscous dinner. All three of them had somber faces and a grave manner. They gave the lieutenant only a solemn nod; the mood was no longer one of feasts, polite remarks, and culinary disputes. The cortège moved with slow and heavy steps in front of the amused smiles of curious onlookers. More accustomed to demonstrations by government workers and farmers, the people of Perpignan watched the procession pass with derisive indifference, as if it were a quaint, old-fashioned event.

For the tenth time that day, Sebag tried to reach Jean Pagès, both at headquarters and on his cell phone. In vain. He was tempted to call Elsa Moulin, but he knew she was off duty, and he didn't want to bother her.

The demonstration turned in front of the Dames de France. This tall, prestigious, modern building, constructed at the beginning of the twentieth century on the site of former ramparts, had been the home of prosperous stores and employed as many as three hundred people before it had to close its doors in the 1980s. The entrances had remained blocked for more than ten years. Then the building was bought by the city and renovated with private funds. Since 2003, a magnificent glass dome lighting the interior had sheltered many fashionable stores, including a large FNAC.

After they passed the Place de Catalogne, the demonstrators relaxed a little. Slogans ran out of steam and were replaced by friendly conversations and even a few bursts of laughter here and there. The pleasure the repatriates took in being together, in feeling their numbers and strength, made them forget for a few moments the reasons for their anger.

The relaxed mood changed abruptly as they approached the prefecture. Then the demonstrators remembered their demands and started chanting them again in loud voices. A slight cold wind was blowing as night began to fall on the Quai Sadi Carnot. A car with its headlights on stopped near the crowd. A demonstrator left the group to open the trunk. He took out old saucepans and big spoons, which he began distributing. An infernal metallic concert immediately broke out in front of the austere prefecture building. Like Algiers in the old days, Perpignan began to resound with anger.

Sebag didn't hear his cell phone but he felt it vibrate in his pocket. Julie Sadet's name appeared on the screen. The racket made by the saucepans drowned out her voice and prevented Sebag from understanding what she was telling him. He was able to pick out just one word. A word full of hope and promise. A key word that was waited for in every police investigation.

"We've got something new," Julie repeated after Sebag had moved some fifty meters away from the demonstration. "After Narbonne, Béziers, Sète, and Carcasonne, we finally have a lead in Montpellier. On Sunday evening, at a rental agency near the train station, a man named Manuel Esteban turned in the vehicle—a white SEAT—he had rented in Figueres the preceding evening."

Sunday . . . the day Roman was murdered.

"Since it was Sunday," Julie went on, "the agency in Montpellier picked up the vehicle the next morning. No one was able to see the customer and they had no details on him. So Joan contacted the agency in Figueres. He just did it, without worrying about the rules. The Catalans didn't make a fuss about it: they told him what they knew. That Manuel Esteban was born on April 25, 1942, and that he had presented a driver's license issued in Madrid in 1962."

"Where was this Esteban born?"

"Also in Madrid."

"So he's a Spanish citizen?"

"Absolutely. Is that a problem?"

Gilles didn't reply immediately. He felt a slight disappointment. He wasn't expecting that. He'd imagined that the suspect would be a French citizen and that he would have an obvious connection with colonial Algeria. What if they'd been on the wrong track? Maybe Julie's idea wasn't so good after all. But a white SEAT . . . rented the day of the murder. It couldn't be just a coincidence.

Julie had followed the drift of his questions

"Since this morning, we've contacted sixty-five car rental agencies. Only three of them had received a car rented in Spain. But neither the model nor the date corresponded."

"Had Manuel Esteban rented other cars from the agency? A white Clio, for instance?"

"No. If he's really our man, he must have changed agencies, as Jacques suggested this morning. Now that we have his name, it shouldn't be too hard to find the other agency."

"Unless he gave them false papers!"

"Even if he did . . . that won't necessarily prevent us from following the lead. He probably doesn't have dozens of different identities. He might have rented a Clio with the same false papers."

Julie Sadet was a go-getter and didn't allow a few questions to paralyze her. Sebag liked this quality in her; he often thought himself too hesitant.

"You're right. It's a real lead. The first one. In a few minutes, I'm going to report on the investigation at the prefecture. This comes at the right time, we'll have no trouble getting the prefect's help in accelerating things with Spain."

"It also comes at the right time for you."

"It's good for everyone if the prefect is happy. But the most important thing is that we finally have a hope of wrapping up this case. We've got to find this Manuel Esteban. The ball will also be in the Spanish police's court."

"The Spanish police and the South Catalonia police. The *Mossos d'Esquadra!*"

"That's right, you learn fast."

"I spent the day with Joan, that's like taking an accelerated training course," she explained. "Speaking of Joan, he took the initiative and he's on the phone with his pal in the Mossos. The investigation of Manuel Esteban is supposed to begin unofficially tonight on the other side of the Pyrenees."

"That's great. You guys are champs!"

"Thanks, boss," Julie replied with a touch of irony.

Before putting down his phone, Sebag put it on mute. He didn't want it to ring at the wrong time during the next few minutes. He said to himself that Jacques might ultimately not have been wrong to insist on his changing his ringtone. Séverine's voice crying "Papa, you've got an SMS" in the middle of a meeting at the prefecture would hardly encourage people to take his report seriously.

About thirty *Pieds-Noirs* were still on the Quai Sadi Carnot, waiting for their delegation to come out. Gilles Sebag heaved a great sigh of relief as he left the wood-paneled halls of the Prefecture of Pyrénées-Orientales. He thought he'd done pretty well.

Twenty people sitting around a big square table had listened with attention for half an hour. Among those present were the officials of the repatriates' associations, the prefect, his cabinet director, and a few government officials whom he knew by sight only. Sebag had not sweated under his shirt like that since he took his French oral for the baccalaureate degree.

But he hadn't wasted his time. Summing up for all these people the case that had been occupying his mind for almost two weeks had allowed him to review it for himself as well: he had the feeling that he now saw things more clearly, especially since he had been obliged to eliminate from his vocabulary and his thinking the question marks, "maybes," and "probablys" that always encumbered his arguments.

Thus, as former OAS combatants, Bernard Martinez and André Roman had been murdered for crimes committed fifty years earlier, during the tumultuous last months of French Algeria. A victim or someone close to a victim was now seeking vengeance, though the reason for its belatedness remained unknown. The murderer, a man at least seventy years old, had achieved two of his three objectives. The third and last target had not yet been identified, but it was already known that he did not reside in France. Thus there was no longer any reason to fear another murder in Perpignan. Sebag had then silently congratulated himself on having mentioned this point rather early in his presentation. A wave of relief had run through the room and on both sides of the table people's jaws unclenched.

The murderer had established his home base in Spain and had made at least two trips to France. To get around, he'd rented a vehicle in Spain. In the case of Roman's murder, he had rented a car from an agency in Figueres, under the name Manuel Esteban, and he had returned it in Montpellier. From there, he'd taken the train to cross over to the other side of the Pyrenees. Sebag had discussed this new lead at considerable length. "The most promising one," he had said, not mentioning that it was also the only real one. After the meeting was over, the prefect had promised to exert all his influence on the Spanish authorities to get them to issue a wanted notice for Manuel Esteban.

Sebag had also mentioned Maurice Garcin's name. He no longer had much faith in that lead, but its existence lent substance to their investigation. He had implied that it was not necessarily incompatible with the Esteban lead, because one could very well imagine that the former *barbouze* was acting under a false Spanish identity.

In the course of committing his first crime, the murder of Martinez, the killer had—perhaps in the grip of panic—caused a fatal accident in the Moulin-à-Vent quarter. Sebag had not concealed all his reservations regarding this hypothesis, which still had to be verified. To do so, it would suffice to track down the place where this Manuel Esteban rented a white Clio.

The atmosphere in the room at the prefecture had grown tense again when he came to the destruction of the OAS monument and the attack on Guy Albouker.

"At the present stage of the investigation, nothing allows us to connect these deplorable events with the double murder." As he uttered those words he'd felt a kind of pinch in his stomach: he would have liked to have the DNA analyses of the hairs before going that far out on a limb.

"If your suspect is not responsible for these other acts, then who is?" Jean-Pierre Mercier had asked, addressing himself to the prefect rather than to Sebag. And the representative of the state had just handed the question over to the lieutenant.

Sebag had recognized that the investigation of those events was not making progress, that there had been no witness to the vandalism in the Haut-Vernet cemetery, and that as for the attack on Albouker, the latter's statements had not yet made it possible to identify the perpetrators. He declared with a rather forced assurance that in his opinion these acts were committed by individuals whose goal was to create concern in the *Pied-Noir* community and discord in the city. He had then slipped in an appeal for calm. The prefect had appreciated that and had seized the opportunity to take the floor to expand on that subject.

As he crossed over the Basse near the central post office, he heaved another sigh of relief. He so rarely felt satisfied with himself!

He remembered that his cell phone was still on mute. Toward the end of the meeting he'd noticed a vibration. The screen confirmed it: there was a message.

The call came from Martine, the young woman cop on the reception desk at headquarters. She asked if he could come by headquarters before going home. A lady was waiting for him. Although he was no more than five minutes' walk away, he called Martine back.

"I'm on my way. Who is this lady?"

"Mme. Vidal. She wanted to see Lieutenant Llach, but he has gone home. I was able to reach him on his cell phone, but he told me it would be good if you could talk to her yourself."

Sebag was about to reply that he didn't know this lady and that he preferred to postpone the conversation when he remembered: Josette Vidal was Bernard Martinez's woman friend. He walked faster and was soon crossing the headquarters' threshold.

A small brunette lady was waiting for him in the lobby. She stood straight as an arrow on her high-heeled shoes. Her dyed hair and her made-up face made her look a good ten years younger than she was. She held out an emaciated hand. Rather than take her to his office, Sebag decided to have her sit down in a cubicle near the lobby where the policemen received complaints. He introduced himself and sat on the corner of the desk.

"With my colleague Joan Llach, I'm working on the murder of Bernard Martinez. May I ask what brings you here, Mme. Vidal?"

"I can't figure out who owns Bernard's apartment."

Her velvety Catalan accent attenuated the dryness of her tone.

"It's very annoying, I've got piles of papers to deal with and

I don't know what to do," she explained. "And moreover, I thought he owned it. I wouldn't want someone to demand back rent from me a few months from now. With my little pension I couldn't pay it, and what Bernard left me certainly isn't enough. Poor fellow! He didn't have much to live on . . . "

"You must have found receipts for rent payments among his papers?"

"No, otherwise I wouldn't be here bothering you."

"And you're sure that he wasn't the owner?"

"Yes, of course I'm sure. The notary told me, and the building manager confirmed it."

"But the building manager must know who owns it."

Sebag felt himself getting irritated. He didn't see how all this was his concern. Josette Vidal was also beginning to get annoyed as she saw the policeman's indifference to her problems.

"The manager referred me to some kind of corporation whose telephone number and address I don't have. Just a post office box in Spain. I wrote to it giving my contact information, but I've still had no response. So I'm getting worried. Will Inspector Llach be here tomorrow? He was very nice . . . "

Unlike you, Sebag understood.

He huffed for a long time. He'd always hated paperwork. At home, Claire took care of it. He didn't see why he should take an interest in Josette Vidal's administrative problems on the sole pretext that she was the girlfriend of a murder victim. This business of the apartment was not in the jurisdiction of the police, but rather in that of the notary and the property manager. He was about to send Josette Vidal away with all the politeness and respect owed to her age when she laid down before him the paper on which she had written the name of the company that owned the apartment.

Sebag saw it. He grabbed the paper and feverishly reread the name. He couldn't believe his eyes. He abruptly stood up.

He suddenly took a passionate interest in Mme. Vidal's problems. The old lady noted with pleasure and surprise the policeman's sudden change of heart. Sebag politely accompanied her back to the lobby and told her in a reassuring voice:

"Don't worry, Mme. Vidal, I'll take care of everything."

# CHAPTER 28

S ebag was drinking his morning coffee on the terrace of his house. Dead leaves covered the tarp protecting the swimming pool. They came from their apricot tree and the neighbors' cherry tree. The north wind was making them fall and then blowing them into a corner of the garden. A pile of leaves was already forming near the fence, and would have to be cleaned up the following weekend. Everything was a matter of timing. In Catalonia, the caprices of the wind made Sunday gardeners fatalistic and lazy.

Gilles shivered.

He glanced at the thermometer. It was still above 14 degrees, despite the advance of autumn, but that was only one indicator among others of the mildness of the weather. The north wind also had something to say about it. And it often expressed it. This morning, it was even shouting at top volume.

Gilles wrapped his hands around the hot cup of coffee and closed his eyes to listen to the wind's lament.

It was humming in hoarse, powerful gusts through the heavy branches of the cedar that bordered their garden on the west, alternating deep silences with thunderous blasts. It was carrying in its nets the sounds of the neighboring subdivision: Gilles could hear a car door slam, the screech of a shutter being rolled up, and then the crying of a child on his way to school. Sometimes the wind conveyed to him, through the opening of a door or window, the empty chatter of a television set.

When the wind came off the sea, it produced a different

music. Blowing out of the east, it slipped through the frail stalks of the bamboo, whistling a merry air despite the humidity that it brought along with it. The sea wind blew toward Sebag's house the heavy, metallic noise of the Saint-Estève industrial zone. Not to mention the annoying beeping of trucks backing up.

Gilles heard the sliding door open behind his back. He recognized Claire's walk.

"Aren't you cold?" she asked

"No. So long as the coffee's hot . . . "

He knew, before she asked it, what the next question would be.

"What are you thinking about?"

He slowly turned around and began a smile.

"I'm not thinking, I'm daydreaming."

Claire's delicate eyebrows rose.

"I don't see the difference."

He sipped his coffee before explaining.

"When you're in a canoe, letting yourself be carried along is not the same as paddling."

Claire agreed with a movement of her head that made the beads on her earrings tinkle. Hmm, he'd never seen those before. She must have bought them recently. Or someone had given them to her. A farewell gift, perhaps.

Claire moved her slender neck toward him and offered her lips. Gilles made her drink a sip of his coffee. A drop of coffee slid down her round chin. He wiped it away with a finger that he then put in his mouth. Claire smiled at him with her shining green eyes bordered in black.

She was wearing a belted dress and black stockings. He found her beautiful. Too beautiful to be happy. He finished his coffee in a single gulp.

"I'd have liked to have some more," Claire complained pleasantly.

"I can make you some more."

"I'm going to be late."

"It won't take long."

"Let it go—it won't have the same taste. I'll have one when I get to school if there's time."

"From the machine?"

"Yes, it isn't as good as yours but it's not bad, either."

"Pouah, you disappoint me . . . "

"I know, my love, I know . . . "

His cell phone clamped between his shoulder and his ear, Sebag wrote down a name in his notebook. At the same time, through the open door to the meeting room, he was watching the superintendent, who was sitting in his usual place, reading the reports from the day before and in particular Sebag's presentation at the prefecture. His hand, nervously tapping on the table, betrayed his impatience. Sebag, who knew him well, was aware that he always came back in a very bad humor from these consultations with the upper hierarchy of the police establishment. So he tried not to make the conversation any longer than necessary.

"Thanks, Didier, for this information. I don't doubt that it will be of great help to us. Call me if you find out anything else, O.K.?"

Sebag hung up and went into the meeting room. Standing near the window, Joan Llach was looking at the snowy slopes of Le Canigou. Up there, the north wind was blowing the snow, making a plume for the sacred mountain. Molina, Julie Sadet, and Lambert made their appearance and sat down around the table, spreading around them effluvia composed of tobacco smoke and perfume.

Castello gathered the papers scattered around him and surveyed his troops.

"As usual, Raynaud and Moreno are not here," he observed

grumpily. "Where have those two clowns gone now? This time, it's too much. I'm canceling their overtime pay and I'm giving them a warning. Enough is enough."

He took the pile of papers and tapped them on the table to make a neat stack.

"I've read your reports, but I'd like you to sum them up here in person. That's often clearer and more precise."

Sebag discreetly signaled Julie to encourage her to speak up first. The young woman explained the research she'd done the day before, her intuition, and its results. She received the superintendent's warm congratulations:

"Bravo. I knew we had to inject a little new blood into this team. And a little feminine intuition, too."

Llach spoke next. Between calls to car rental agencies, he had also examined the calls Roman had made on his cell phone, a task that had been assigned to him at the outset but which he hadn't yet had time to carry out.

"Up to now, I've looked at the calls for just one week. I didn't notice anything abnormal. Except that André Roman had a mistress."

"I don't see anything abnormal about that," Molina commented.

"All the same . . . at his age," Lambert remarked.

"Precisely! Maybe he thought that at his age, it was time to live a little."

"Molina, we can do without your commentaries," the superintendent broke in. "Go on, Joan."

"Unfortunately, I don't have anything else."

"Too bad."

Castello nervously scratched the end of his nose before continuing.

"I don't think it would be very useful to contact that woman or even to mention this affair to his widow. For the moment, we'll let that subject alone. Thierry, you go back to studying

Roman's calls, you never know. Joan's plate is going to be full today. He's the only one of us who's trilingual."

Castello bent over toward the flying saucer that was still sitting on the table.

"And you, François, anything new in Marseille?"

Lieutenant Ménard's voice filled the room with a metallic echo.

"Maurice Garcin still hasn't returned to his retirement home. His sons are beginning to get worried and have requested that a search for him be organized. But our colleagues there aren't very eager to do that."

"I imagine they've got other things to do up there," Castello said. "Uh . . . what did you say, François?"

Ménard hadn't heard the superintendent's interruption and had continued to talk.

"I was saying that I'd found a few of Garcin's hairs on his comb in the bathroom. But I don't know what to do with them."

"Just mail them to us, that will probably be the simplest way to go."

"The simplest way isn't necessarily the fastest way. I was thinking that I might be back before the package arrived."

Castello immediately threw cold water on his lieutenant's hopes.

"I still need you to be there. First of all, in case Garcin suddenly reappears. And also because we haven't yet found all the surviving *barbouzes*. Have you asked your historian whether the name Manuel Esteban means anything to him?"

"Not yet. But I've got an appointment with him early this morning. As for the rest, I was thinking . . . there's a midafternoon train, and I was hoping I could take it."

"What a homebody you are, François! The administration offers you a free stay in Marseille and you think only of coming home to Perpignan. For a native of Normandy, you're sure acting like a true Catalan."

A protest garbled by static followed:

" . . . from Picardy, Superintendent . . . not Normandy."

Castello shook the flying saucer.

"This thing works when it wants to . . . It's a little like Dario Moreno . . . uh . . . I meant to say like Raynaud and Moreno. Why did I say Dario Moreno? Who was that guy, anyway?"

"An actor and an operetta singer, I think," Llach replied.

"He was big in the first half of the twentieth century," Molina added. "He had some famous hits, like 'If You Go to Rio' and 'Coucouroucoucou.'"

"Ah yes, I see. Someone else who helped create the great French song tradition, so to speak."

Castello was gradually recovering his spirits. For him, contact with work in the field was always the best mood regulator.

"I'm glad to see that my cops have culture," he joked. "Apart from that, anything else, François?"

"Just a little medical detail that might be of some importance. At Gilles's request, I questioned the retirement home's doctors about the way in which they arrived at a diagnosis of Alzheimer's. In fact, there is no single test for that illness, and the doctors render their verdict on the basis of a set of neurological tests and clinical and radiological evidence. Although they acknowledge that diagnostic errors occur from time to time, they doubt that someone could fake it."

"In short, Maurice Garcin is not a very credible suspect, but he still can't be crossed off the list?"

"More or less, yes—to my great regret, moreover!" Ménard sighed.

"I understand, François," Castello assured him. "No need to push too hard. I promise you a humanitarian repatriation as soon as possible, but I'd like you to remain there a little longer. We'll talk about it again tomorrow."

"As you wish . . . "

Castello sat up and massaged his neck. He saw Sebag raise his hand but didn't immediately give him the floor.

"Just a minute, please. With his complaints, François almost made me forget the DNA analysis of the hairs. I still haven't read Pagès's report." He picked up the telephone and asked his secretary to find the report and bring it to him. Then he turned back to Sebag.

"Did you have something to say?"

"I've let everyone sum up their work so that we could see things more clearly, but I think I've got something new. Something important."

He told them about his conversation with the late Bernard Martinez's woman friend and showed them the piece of paper, which he had kept. Alongside the number of a post office box, Josette Vidal had written the name of the corporation that owned Martinez's apartment: Babelo, Inc.

"Babelo . . . " the Superintendent repeated out loud.

"Like the pseudonym of the head of the OAS commando, yes. Obviously, last night I tried to find out more about that corporation but I wasn't successful, so I entrusted the research to a colleague in the financial unit in Montpellier. He's the one I had on the phone just before the meeting. He hasn't yet been able to locate the box exactly—we know it's in Spain—but he did discover the name of its manager—a certain Georges Lloret."

"Georges, are you sure?" Joan Llach asked.

"Yes, why? Do you know him?"

"No, not at all, but 'Lloret' is a Catalan patronym and since the guy seems to live on the other side of the Pyrenees, I'm astonished that he has a Gallicized first name. The name ought to be Jorge if the guy is Spanish, or Jordi if he's Catalan."

"Unless he's actually of French origin," Sebag suggested. "A former *Pied-Noir* who went to live in Spain after the war, for example. It's not necessarily too much to think that the owner of that company is none other than the former head of the commando . . . "

Llach was astonished.

"A *Pied-Noir* with a Catalan name?"

An incomprehensible spitting sound replied.

Castello shook the flying saucer vigorously

"Could you repeat that, François? We couldn't understand you."

"I was saying that contrary to what most people think, . . . . *crhcrh*, the majority of the *Pieds-Noirs* did not come from France. *crhhch* . . . many Spaniards *crhhch* . . . and thus necessarily also Catalans . . . *crhhch* . . . independence, some preferred . . . *crhchr* . . . the country of their origins. Especially since . . . *crhhch* Franco's régime . . . *crhhch* . . . Gaullist."

"That's enough, François. We have a very bad connection. We'll continue this history lesson later. If you have nothing more to say that is indispensable for the investigation, we'll let you go."

" . . . *crhhch* . . . *crhhche* . . . "

"Right. You have a good day, too!"

Castello slammed the audioconference box down on the table. He pushed on a button to turn it off.

"If I understood correctly what François was trying to say, we can imagine that after the war, this Georges Lloret preferred to return to Franco's Spain rather than to France under General de Gaulle."

The superintendent turned over one of the sheets of paper lying in front of him and took a few notes on the back. Then he looked up.

"So, what does all that tell us? Decidedly, it's still toward Spain that we have to turn our attention if we're to have any hope of completing this investigation successfully. But we're not going to limit ourselves to hoping that our colleagues will be quick and efficient, we're going to move ahead by ourselves. We're going to find out if this Georges Lloret has a police record, and whether he has a residence or even some kind of position in France. We're also going to find his telephone number so we can warn him as soon as possible. And then . . . "

Castello suddenly interrupted himself to stare at Julie, who had been bent over her phone for several minutes.

"Is everything O.K., Mademoiselle Sadet, I'm not bothering you, am I?"

Julie, surprised, quickly raised her head.

"No, not at all . . . "

When she saw her boss raise an eyebrow she realized that her spontaneous response was close to insolent.

"Excuse me, Superintendent, but I thought we could probably find important information about this Lloret person on the internet, and I began to search for it on my iPhone."

Castello's face immediately relaxed.

"Very good, very good. And?"

"Well, I found several Georges Llorets. In the Gard and in the Marseille region, but their profiles don't fit: they're too young. Ah, here, I've got another one . . . I don't have his age, but he lives in Spain!"

She had fixed her eyes on her cell phone again and was skillfully slipping her finger over the tactile screen.

"He's involved in subdivision projects. It seems that he's a real estate developer. He has an agency in Roses, and another one in Figueras . . . "

"Figueres," Llach corrected.

"And still another in Cadaqués. Hmm . . . apparently this is an article in a newspaper, *El Punt*, does that mean anything to you?"

"It's a Catalan newspaper," Llach explained.

"I'm opening it . . . There, it's obviously in Catalan, but there's a photo. Just a minute, the connection isn't great . . . Ah, there we are! This could be our man: he's no longer young but he still looks pretty good."

Julie handed her iPhone to her colleagues. The device made a rapid tour around the table.

"A real computer in this meeting room wouldn't be a luxury," Castello remarked. "Remind me to have one installed."

The telephone came around to Sebag. Georges Lloret did in fact have a certain presence. He was wearing an elegant black suit with a red silk kerchief in the breast pocket, and he stood as ramrod straight and proud as a soldier at attention on July 14. His white, wavy hair stood out against the blue sky.

"We'll have to read the article," Gilles said, handing the cell phone back to its owner.

"No problem, I can enlarge the text a bit and Joan will translate it for us."

"We could all go to my office, it would be easier to read on a PC," Llach suggested.

Castello stood up, giving the signal, and all the policemen walked downstairs to Llach's office. Sebag stopped at his own office to get his file. When he arrived at Llach's office, he found him seated in front of the computer. Castello had taken another chair and was sitting alongside him. All the other inspectors were crowded behind him.

Sebag compared the article's photo with the one in the file found among André Roman's affairs. The photo in which the four men of the commando posed alongside Lieutenant Degueldre.

"The same figure, the same hairdo, the same ideas of elegance. That could be our man. Babelo. He has just shaved off his mustache since the Algerian War."

Llach had started to scan the article in silence.

"It's him. No doubt about it."

With the mouse, he moved to the end of the article. Then he went back to the beginning.

"In fact, the article is the third one in a series on the great fortunes of South Catalonia. I'll sum up the gist of it for you.

Georges Lloret is a self-made man who got rich in the 1970s by promoting developments for tourists on the Costa Brava. He opened his first real estate agency in Cadaqués, and then very quickly opened others all along the Catalan coast."

Llach was following the lines of the article with his finger. He was translating and summing up at the same time.

"But it's mainly as a developer that Lloret made his money. He invested large sums in the construction of big tourist complexes in most of the resorts along the coast: Rosas, L'Escala, Palafrugell, Palamos, and others, some of the most famous and especially the ugliest. He is, it seems, a very discreet, even secretive man who does not give any interviews. The author of the article was not authorized to meet him, and he says that he had a great deal of trouble confirming rumors that circulate regarding Lloret."

Llach stopped to catch his breath. His index finger was still following the article as it moved down the screen.

"This is where it gets interesting . . . Lloret was born in Algiers in 1933, where his grandfather had emigrated in 1898. Georges is supposed to have fought for French Algeria—on that point, the article gives no details, too bad for us—before taking up residence in Spain after Algeria became independent. He formed close friendships with members of Franco's party and with a few other wheeler-dealers who had good contacts in the government. Which probably explains in part his business success."

"Sounds like a really nice guy," Julie commented.

"He's also just barely scraping along," Molina remarked. "Another one! Poor French of Algeria. They never stop whining about their fate but there are a lot of them who have rebounded very well after leaving their native country. Roman was also rich."

"On the other hand, Martinez ended up living on welfare."

"Because he was probably less talented—or less fortunate—than his former buddies. Nonetheless, when he returned to France he had enough to invest in a vineyard . . . "

Castello raised his hand to put a stop to these digressions. He addressed Llach.

"Doesn't the article say anything else?"

"Yes, it does. Politically, after Franco's death Lloret got involved in the center-right again. In particular, he is supposed to have financed the CDC, the Convergencia Democratica de Catalunya, one of the parties that has governed Catalonia since 1980. Otherwise, the journalist also mentions a few things about his private life. Notably his remarriage, some fifteen years ago, to a young actress, which led to a break with his daughters, who no longer speak to him."

Llach let go of the mouse and sat back in his chair.

"That's all there is."

"Well done," Castello congratulated him. "We're still going to need you: we have to contact this Lloret as soon as possible."

Julie still had her cell phone in her hand.

"I'm going to give you the phone numbers of his real estate agencies; I think the main one is in Rosas."

Llach and Sebag each began writing down the numbers as Julie dictated them. Castello got up and put his hand on Gilles's shoulder.

"I'm going back up to the meeting room with the others, but you and Joan stay here to get in touch with this Lloret. That's the top priority."

Sebag sat down in the chair freed up by his boss, who left the office followed by Julie Sadet, Molina, and Lambert. Llach picked up his landline phone and dialed the first number. Several minutes of tedious, long-winded conversations followed: Joan was speaking in brief bursts separated by silences. His successive interlocutors apparently weren't impressed. Sebag quickly stopped listening. He had learned a few rudiments of Catalan during his first months in Perpignan, but this conversation was going much too fast for him.

After twice knocking softly on the door, Jeanne opened it a little and showed her pretty face.

"Monsieur Sebag, the superintendent wants to see you right away in the third-floor meeting room."

The request surprised the inspector. He left Llach to his telephoning and followed Castello's secretary. He walked behind her, his eyes fixed on her high leather boots and her jeans tightly molding her little round butt. Jeanne ignored the elevator and took the stairs. She climbed the first few steps and then stopped. She put both hands on her buttocks and explained:

"Apparently it's good for your figure."

"You're the living proof of that," Sebag choked out.

He left the secretary in front of her office and continued down the hall to the meeting room. An embarrassed silence prevailed. Castello, without a word, handed him the DNA analysis of the hairs. Sebag had to start over several times before he understood what he was reading. The words and the figures danced before his eyes and every time they stood still, Sebag read the same thing: the white hair found in Martinez's apartment belonged to the same person as the one discovered in front of the OAS monument in the Haut-Vernet cemetery.

# CHAPTER 29

He was walking leisurely through the streets in downtown La Jonquera. He'd taken a liking to walking. Even if his illness made every step painful. In any case, on his bad days everything made him hurt anyway. Opening a door, holding a pencil, drinking a glass of wine, eating. On bad days, he couldn't do anything. Just breathe and watch television. On the condition that he not use the remote too much.

His doctor had advised him to be active. Whatever he did. Walking, swimming, cycling. He mustn't allow the illness to deposit its calcium on his bones. But he'd never liked water—except the clear, warm water of his Mediterranean—and cycling scared him since he had felt his sense of balance growing weaker.

So he walked every time he could. And as he walked he had the feeling that he was leaving his arthritis behind him.

He arrived at the edge of the commercial zone. One of the ugliest, most hideous, most shameful he'd ever seen. The luminous signs and the enticing advertisements flayed the retina of his poor old eyes. Here began the country of discounts and debauchery.

La Jonquera had developed in the 1970s around the autoroute, but it had really taken off when Spain joined the European Economic Community, the village having easily profited from the flaws in the structure of the EEC. The difference in taxation between France and its neighbor made life in Spain cheap. La Jonquera was now three hundred shops, about twenty supermarkets and service stations, a hundred bars, a large number of them frequented by prostitutes. Since 2010, the commune could even boast that it had the largest brothel in Europe. Open every day from 5 P.M. to 4 A.M., the Paradise offered without blushing its "Lesbian shows," its 120 prostitutes, and its 80 rooms.

The French flocked in droves to La Jonquera, as many as twenty-five thousand of them a day, in couples or in families, in order to fill up shopping carts that jingled through the aisles of the *supermercatos*. Others came at night, alone or in groups, to have sex with girls from Eastern Europe or Latin America.

Jean turned back toward his hotel. His cardiac rhythm accelerated as he passed in front of the Guardia Civil building. However, he knew that he had nothing to fear. His false papers were in order, and on the other side of the Le Perthus pass, the police were not on his trail. He'd been following their investigation step by step by regularly reading the French newspapers and listening to a local radio station in Roussillon that he could get in his room: he knew that the investigators were on the wrong track. He'd tricked them without doing it on purpose. By signing his crimes, he'd led them astray.

His last target probably didn't suspect anything, either. He'd established contact with him. It hadn't been easy. The last of the three bastards had become an important person. Somebody who couldn't be approached that easily.

But he'd succeeded in doing it.

They had a rendezvous.

Soon the old accounts would be settled once and for all, and he could go home. To his adopted country. With great relief, he'd see his Gabriella's gracious smile again. It had been three days since he'd called her. He missed his little girl terribly.

He entered his small hotel, an inconspicuous establishment

in the center of La Jonquera, where the village still resembled other villages in the rest of Spain. Miguel, the owner, welcomed him with a broad smile.

"Hi, how's my Argentinian?" he asked in Castilian.

"Tired, but no more than usual. At my age, you're always tired."

"And your pain?"

"Also the usual. The day I don't have pain will be the day I'm dead."

Miguel broke into a cheerful laugh and patted him softly on the shoulder.

"It's great to be an optimist, huh, Argentinian?"

The old man laughed in turn. But not for the same reasons. His Spanish fooled everybody. It was in that language that he thought and expressed himself most easily. And if there were traces of an accent in his Spanish, they came from the South American inflections he'd acquired, not from his French origins. He now found it difficult to operate in his native language. He often had to search for his words, and didn't always find them. In this small hotel where he had settled in, no one had been able to guess that he'd been born on French territory seventy-two years earlier.

His cover was definitely perfect.

He returned to his little hotel room and took off his overcoat. He opened the armoire, took out a hanger, and hung up his coat. He ran his big hand over the collar to brush off a few white hairs. Lately he'd begun to lose his hair. That dismayed him: he already had so many reasons to feel that he was getting old.

# CHAPTER 30

Llach slammed down the receiver.

"They just don't want to understand. Even though I explain that I'm a cop and that it's a question of life and death, they just keep saying that they have strict instructions and can't give me their boss's cell phone number. And then they tell me that they're going to convey the message with my telephone number and that Lloret will call back if he thinks it necessary. By the way, I gave them your number."

"That was the right thing to do," Sebag replied distractedly.

"Lloret must speak French, you won't need an interpreter."

Sebag smiled at him. He hadn't heard what Llach said.

"I called the office in Rosas and the one in Cadaqués. Shall I try the others?"

"Uh . . . yeah."

"You're right. It's worth a try. You never know . . . "

Llach picked up his telephone and repeated his requests to new interlocutors. Gilles couldn't seem to concentrate and was lost in the contemplation of a map hanging on the wall behind Joan.

It was a map of southern Europe. A green line ran from the north of the department of Pyrénées-Orientales to the southern extremity of the province of Valencia in Spain and marked off the zone where Catalan was spoken. There were also the Balearic Islands and a little area on the northwest coast of Sardinia, around the city of Alguer. Sebag remembered having read that the king of Aragon had installed several families from Barcelona there. That must have been in the sixteenth century.

Llach hung up with the same angry gesture.

"I didn't get any more out of them in Figueres. They promise to leave a message but don't even assure me that their boss will call us back. This Lloret seems to be a pretty shady character!"

"Sure looks that way."

Llach stared at him.

"You look like there's something wrong with you. What was that quick trip upstairs about?"

Sebag told him what he had just learned.

"Son of a bitch!" Llach said, banging his fist on the desk.

"My feelings exactly."

"That means that the murderer of Martinez and Roman also destroyed the OAS monument."

"Looks like it . . . "

"That's not at all what we thought!"

"What I thought."

"Why just you? We'd all excluded that possibility."

"But I'm the one who said yesterday at the prefecture that it couldn't be the same person."

"True, that might come back and bite your ass."

Sebag shrugged.

"Too bad. That's not necessarily the worst part. What's really unfortunate is that at this point we're on the wrong track."

"But what difference does it make, in the end? It's almost logical, when you think about it! The guy is so pissed at the OAS that he demolishes anything connected with it."

"We thought he was taking personal revenge on three specific people, not on the OAS in general. We were mistaken about his psychology and maybe also about his true motives."

"Mustn't throw the baby out with the bathwater. You're the

one who likes proverbs, you can trust that one. Our murderer is out to get Martinez, Roman, and Lloret, and while he's at it he also messes up a monument in honor of an organization he detests more than anything. I don't find that completely incoherent."

"Except . . . "

"Except what?"

"Except that you're forgetting the attack on Albouker!"

"Shit, that's right."

Llach thought for a few seconds, and then he banged his fist on his desk again.

"In my opinion, that still doesn't change anything! We thought that certain malicious persons had taken advantage of the double murder to piss off the *Pieds-Noirs*. That hypothesis remains valid, maybe not for the monument, but for the attack on Albouker. Not too bad an argument, no?"

Sebag had to agree: the idea wasn't stupid. But he needed time to reflect on it. He sometimes had flashes of intuition, but it generally took him a while to think them through.

"Let's go back for a moment to Georges Lloret. What else can we do to get in touch with him?"

"Apart from going through the Catalan police, I don't know . . . And there, my wife's cousin can't do anything. This Lloret guy is a pain in the neck and he won't respond to an unofficial request."

"Speaking of your cousin, do you have any news from him? Has he started calling the car rental agencies?"

"He promised me yesterday that he would try this morning. Do you think it's going to take very long to get our colleagues to collaborate in the regular way?"

"I thought you were the expert on cross-border collaboration."

"Not in the least: I'm only the expert on cross-border improvisation."

Sebag laughed heartily. He hadn't often had occasion to work with Joan and was pleased to find that he was an efficient colleague.

"O.K., what do we do now?" Llach asked.

"We wait for the phone to ring. Lloret may call back some-day."

Sebag had hardly finished his sentence before his cell phone vibrated. He took it out of his pocket.

"Here we go," he said, taking the call. "Hello?"

"Hello, Lieutenant Sebag. This is Jean-Pierre Mercier."

"Hello, Monsieur Mercier. Have things been going well for you since we met at the prefecture?"

"I have to admit that they were going better yesterday."

Mercier sounded worried. His voice was trembling slightly:

"I've taken the liberty of calling you because this morning I found a letter in my mailbox. A threatening letter. If you could come to my home right away, I'd greatly appreciate it."

Sebag immediately stood up and signaled to Llach to do the same.

"Don't touch the letter again, Monsieur Mercier, just leave it where it is. I'll be there right away with one of my colleagues."

Llach parked the car on the Place de l'Europe in the Moulin-à-Vent quarter. As he got out of the vehicle, he said to Sebag:

"We've got a few seconds, let me show you something."

He led Sebag to the middle of the traffic circle, which had been made into a public garden, and pointed to a block of concrete set up between two benches. They went over to it. Sebag saw that it was a panoramic table. He looked for the known reference points and was disoriented for a few seconds. There was no mention of Spain, Le Canigou, or any of the peaks of the Pyrenees. There were only the names of cities more distant in space and time: Algiers, Oran, Bône . . .

"Did I tell you these people don't want to let bygones be bygones?" Joan sighed. "They still need to locate themselves in relation to places they left long ago. As if they hoped to go back there someday. I really don't understand it . . . "

They rapidly walked back and rang the bell at Jean-Pierre Mercier's apartment. He opened the door to the building's lobby.

"It's on the third floor," Mercier explained on the intercom.

The two inspectors didn't wait for the elevator and climbed the steps two at a time. Jean-Pierre Mercier met them on the landing.

"Thanks for coming so fast."

He led them down a little hallway to reach the living room. A warm, generous autumn sun was coming in through a French door that opened onto a balcony. Mercier showed them the letter, which lay on a writing desk right next to the opened envelope.

The message read: "We're going to get you, too. You can be scared now."

"As I said on the telephone, I found it this morning, along with the mail in my box."

Sebag took plastic gloves out of his jacket pocket to pick up the letter. It was a simple, white, normal-sized piece of paper. There was nothing written on the back. It had been folded in three lengthwise so that it would fit in the envelope. Like the one left by Albouker's attackers, the message consisted of letters cut out of the local newspaper. This method seemed to him very archaic. He put the letter down and examined the envelope. There was no address on it, only Mercier's name. That was what worried him the most.

"They came themselves to put it in the box."

Sebag agreed but said nothing.

"I have coffee ready, would you like some?"

The inspectors gladly accepted his offer, and Mercier went

into the kitchen. Shortly afterward he returned with a colored tray on which he had arranged a full coffee pot, three cups, three spoons, and a little bowl of sugar. He put the tray on the hexagonal coffee table covered with terra cotta tiles. Llach and Sebag sat down on a tawny leather sofa with rounded armrests while Mercier filled their cups.

"What time did you find the letter this morning?" Sebag asked.

"Around ten o'clock. That's when the postman comes. He had just been here."

"And the last time you opened your mailbox was when?"

"Yesterday, at about the same time."

"You didn't check it again in the meantime?"

"No, why would I do that?"

"Sometimes people put flyers in the box."

"I put a notice on my box: 'No advertising please.'"

"Have people other than you touched this letter?" Llach asked while Sebag was noting down the first information Mercier had given them.

"No."

"Your wife, maybe?"

"I'm a widower."

"Ah! I'm sorry," Joan said with embarrassment.

"It's all right. It will be ten years next month. Cancer."

Sebag continued:

"Is this the first time you've received threats?"

"Personally, yes. But we've received quite a few at the Circle office."

"But at your home, you've never received threatening letters or phone calls?"

"No. But I wasn't paying attention. I'll be more vigilant now. After what happened to Guy, I think I shouldn't take these threats lightly."

"No, and it would even be preferable to be careful and

never go out alone. Do you have children who live in Perpignan?"

"My daughter lives in Cerdagne, but my son is here."

"Could you stay with him for a while?"

"I don't think my daughter-in-law would much like that . . . "

"If you explain the seriousness of the threats, she'll understand."

Mercier didn't seem convinced.

"The more serious she thinks it is, the more she'll think that I should stay away from her children. I'm going to call my brother Gérard instead. He's been promising forever to come visit me . . . If he's not too busy working for you."

"I don't think he can do much more for us. We got some valuable information from him even if he didn't give it to us."

Sebag grinned, and his mouth hinted at a faint smile of complicity.

"Yes, I know, he kept me informed. I told him that he could trust you but that wasn't enough. The old habits of secrecy . . . "

Sebag touched his lips to the coffee and struggled to keep from grimacing. The beverage was hardly stronger than flavored water.

"Are you still convinced that these threats have nothing to do with the murders of Bernard and André Roman?" Mercier asked.

Sebag hesitated and his eyes met Llach's. Joan replied in his stead and with more assurance than he could have mustered.

"We don't see how all these facts are connected, unless we suppose that the more the murderer killed, the more frightened he became. He killed two people first, slightly wounded a third, and then limited himself to threatening a fourth. Do you find that logical?"

"I don't know. You're probably right. Moreover, that's what I told Guy last night when he stopped by here after our meeting at the prefecture. But he still thinks there's a kind of conspiracy against us."

"Your president's a little paranoid, isn't he?" Sebag joked.

"A little, yes. He was already that way before, and being attacked hasn't made it any better. He's very upset, and as a result he's a great cause of concern for the future."

"Come now!"

"He thinks that we're wrong to try to assimilate and that we have to remain a strong community, tightly knit and militant. Rather like the Jewish community. He actually drew an elaborate parallel with the history of the Jews in France, who, according to him, have never been as persecuted as when they sought to integrate themselves into the French nation."

"You astonish me; I hadn't thought he was so extremist."

"'Extremist' isn't the right word for him. He's even rather moderate regarding most of our financial demands, and he has no liking for the old activists of the OAS. Besides, I've always taken care not to introduce Gérard to him when he comes to visit me. It's only on questions of cultural identity that Albouker can prove more intransigent: our history, our culture, our roots. But 'intransigent' isn't the right word either: I should rather say 'passionate.' Yes, that's it: Guy is a passionate man!"

Not very interested by their conversation, Llach stood up, intending to bring it to an end. He walked over to the desk with a plastic bag in his hand. He pointed to the letter and the envelope.

"Can I take these documents?" he asked.

"Of course," Mercier answered. "Do you think you can do something with them?"

Joan shrugged.

"We're not likely to be able to find fingerprints other than yours, but we'll have to try anyway. And then they're better off in our file than in one of your drawers."

"A file that must be getting pretty thick."

"That's for sure."

Mercier's landline resounded in the living room.

"It's a little loud," the Circle's treasurer said apologetically, "but I can't seem to adjust it."

He got up to answer it:

"Hello. Ah, it's you, you got my message. Yes, I'm fine, everything's O.K. I'm trying not to worry too much. The police are here, including Inspector Sebag, whom you know . . . "

He turned to Sebag:

"It's my brother."

Then he went over to the bay window. Llach came and sat down next to Gilles. He noticed that Gilles's coffee cup was still full.

"Aren't you going to drink it?"

"Are you kidding? It's revolting."

"Yeah, it's *aïguette*, as they say here, plain water. But that doesn't bother me. May I?"

He seized the cup without waiting for a reply and drank it dry.

Sebag went over to Jean-Pierre Mercier and whispered in his ear:

"Could you let me talk to him when you're done, please?"

The treasurer nodded. He was talking with his brother about the train schedules late in the day. Sebag opened the French door and went out onto the balcony. He leaned on the railing. The wind was still blowing hard. In the street down below, an old man was riding his city bike with his head down like Bernard Hinault in the last stretch of a race against the clock. Nonetheless, he was being passed by two boys running along the sidewalk.

Jean-Pierre Mercier came up behind Sebag and handed him his phone. Sebag took it and began to talk.

"Hello, Monsieur Mercier."

"Hello."

The former OAS man seemed wary. He must have feared that the policeman was trying to make him say what he'd tried to keep to himself the day before. But Sebag had moved on since then and told him so at the outset:

"Did you succeed in contacting Georges Lloret?"

Silence at the other end of the line. Sebag tried to imagine Mercier's crestfallen face before realizing that he'd only talked to him on the telephone and had no idea what he looked like.

"Are you still there, Monsieur Mercier?" he asked. "We haven't yet been able to reach Babelo. I wanted to know if you'd been able to speak with him."

The silence continued for another few seconds and then Mercier decided to reply.

"Very good, Lieutenant Sebag, you're really very good. Bravo. May I ask how you managed to find Lloret?"

Sebag savored the compliments and especially the implicit confirmation that accompanied them: If he'd still had any doubts about Babelo's true identity, Mercier, without realizing what he was doing, would have just dissipated them.

"We all have our secrets, you know. I think the main thing is that one of us be able to alert our man to the danger he's running at the moment. You haven't been able to contact him then?"

"Not yet, no."

"It's really not easy to get in touch with this man. Not more for his former companions in arms than for the French police. Too bad. Especially for him."

"I'm doing all I can. I've reached out to several people close to him."

"We're doing everything we can, too. All that remains is to cross our fingers."

"*Insha'Allah*."

"*Insha'Allah*, yes, you're right."

A silence followed: Sebag was letting Mercier digest his little defeat. The former OAS member was the first to speak again.

"I hope you're going to protect my brother. I don't much like this business of threats."

"Neither do I. But I don't think your brother is in any very great danger."

"He told me that you thought the writer or writers of the anonymous letters had nothing to do with the murderer."

Sebag tried to seem convinced:

"Yes, that's what we think. They just want to scare people."

"I hope you're right."

Sebag refrained from saying, "Me too."

"Are you going to give Jean-Pierre police protection?"

"We don't have the means to do that. And then, if we really had to take threat seriously, we'd have to provide protection for all the *Pieds-Noirs* in Perpignan. The best thing would be for your brother never to be alone. Are you planning to come down here?"

"I'm currently arranging to do that."

"Good."

Sebag hesitated. He didn't think he'd managed to establish a climate that encouraged Mercier to spill his guts, but he nevertheless hoped to take advantage of the opportunity to obtain new information. He gave it a try.

"Now that we all know who Babelo is . . . maybe you could tell me more about his career? I know only its broad outlines."

This time the silence didn't last.

"I think you've earned that," Mercier replied, a smile in his voice. "But I'm far from knowing everything. He's a very private man. What I know is that he was born in Algiers in 1933 and that his parents ran a bakery in the Bab-El-Oued quarter. He joined the ranks of the partisans of French Algeria very early on. In particular, he was in the forefront of the fighting during the week of the barricades."

"The what?"

"Excuse me, I was forgetting that you're not a specialist in history . . . The week of the barricades was an insurrection that took place in Algiers at the end of January and the beginning of February 1960."

Then Gérard Mercier gave Sebag an account of Lloret's involvement with the OAS and his escape to Spain after the end of the war. Sebag learned one thing new: that during the first years of his Spanish exile Georges Lloret had lived under a false name. He'd taken back his real name only after the amnesty laws were passed in 1966.

"I was also able to gather new information regarding our fourth member of the commando . . . Does that interest you?"

Sebag didn't want to annoy his precious informant.

"Of course, go ahead."

"Sigma, alias Jean Servant, was only nineteen when he became a member of the OAS. According to a guy who knew him at the time, he was a real hardliner, a genuine idealist despite his young age—or maybe ultimately because of it. He was the last to join the Babelo commando and the only one who got killed. Anyway . . . I mean . . . the only one who was killed during the war. Are you also interested in the circumstances of his death?"

"Yesterday you mentioned the bombing of a bar."

"That's right, yes. But what I've learned since is that it was Sigma himself who blew up the bar. He'd been surrounded by French gendarmes who were trying to arrest him."

"I thought I understood that at that time the police force wasn't really trying to track down the members of the OAS."

"It's true that we had many sympathizers among the police. But the antiriot police waged an implacable war on us, especially after the ceasefire of March 1962. Once France had put an end to the struggle against the FLN, the army focused all its attention on us. You've heard of Mission C?"

"Never."

"It was a team of about a hundred security police and anti-riot police specially assigned to fight the partisans of French Algeria. They arrived in Algeria in the wake of the *barbouzes* and carried out more secret and especially more effective missions against us. In the case that concerns us, they obtained information to the effect that our four commando members were supposed to meet in a cafe to plan their future actions. The information came, I'm told, from the FLN . . . Apparently it didn't bother them, those Mission C guys, to arrest Frenchmen on the basis of information provided by the enemy! Anyway, we're not going to rewrite history! But the fact remains that they maintained surveillance on the cafe, a surveillance that paid off, but not as much as they'd hoped because there were also leaks on their side: it was possible to warn Babelo, Omega, and Bizerte in time. Sigma, however, came to the rendezvous as planned. The back room of the bar also served as a depot for explosives. He blew everything up so that he wouldn't be taken alive. I told you, he was an idealist. May he rest in peace."

Sebag gave Mercier three seconds to honor the memory of his hero.

"And then what happened to the commando? Did it continue its actions?"

"June 1962 was already three months after the signature of the ceasefire accords in Évian. The French army was completing its withdrawal and the exodus of the French was beginning. French Algeria was dead. Lloret, Martinez, and Roman took the boat in early July. They landed at Port-Vendres. Lloret took off for Spain; that was more prudent because the French police knew his identity. Martinez and Roman took up residence in Perpignan. There, now you know everything. Everything I know, anyway. It remains only for us to do everything we can to protect Lloret from the murderer."

"That's all that remains . . . Yes!"

Sebag went back into the living room and put the telephone back on its base.

"Would you like another cup of coffee?" Jean-Pierre Mercier asked kindly.

"I'd love to," Sebag lied. "But we have to go now. We've got work to do."

Llach stood up, smiling. He was still holding the plastic bag with the letter and its envelope in it.

"Don't hope too much that we'll find the writers of this letter," Sebag warned. "That's virtually mission impossible. Our priority remains the identification of our murderer and preventing him from doing any further harm. When we've caught him, I think everything else will immediately stop and the situation will calm down."

He noticed a photo on the writing desk in the living room. Two smiling, elderly men against a background of palm trees. He recognized Jean-Pierre Mercier and the view one had from his balcony. He put his finger on the second man.

"Is that your brother?"

"It is. The photo was taken two years ago. The last time he came down here."

The man had an oval, rather jovial face, and he was completely bald. Sebag gave the photo a little salute.

"Delighted to make your acquaintance, Gérard," he joked.

He put the frame back on the desk.

"Don't go out alone," he recommended again. "I'm going to ask for more frequent patrols in this area for a few days, particularly around your building. I'll also contact the city police and suggest that they be more vigilant as well. And don't hesitate to call us if you see anybody suspicious-looking."

He held out his hand to Mercier, who shook it.

"But don't worry too much. I really think you're in no great danger if you're careful. You know, the most dangerous dogs are not the ones that bark the loudest."

"Very true. I wonder if that isn't an Arab proverb . . . " Mercier reflected.

"In any case, it's not Catalan," Llach commented.

# CHAPTER 31

Three telephone calls punctuated Gilles Sebag's afternoon. First there was a call from Sabine Henri, the young director of the prefect's cabinet.

"What's this I hear, Lieutenant Sebag? You were completely wrong about the OAS monument?"

That question had been haunting him all day. He served up Llach's theory. But that way of seeing things didn't entirely satisfy him, and the young woman sensed that.

"You don't sound very convinced," she said.

He decided to lay his cards on the table.

"I admit that I'm puzzled. Really. I still feel sure that the same individual was not responsible for the double murder, the destruction of the monument, the attack on the president of the *Pied-Noir* Circle, and the threatening letters. We're dealing with a murderer who kills two men in cold blood to avenge something that goes back half a century. He also has a third target to hit in Spain. So I can't see him fooling around distributing threatening letters and stabbing a quiet director of a *Pied-Noir* association, any more than I can see him using a hammer to destroy a monument in a cemetery, even if it was a memorial to the OAS."

"I understand your reservations about the threats and the knife attack, and I'm tempted to share them. But I don't agree regarding the monument. Our murderer is settling accounts with three men, but also with the OAS in general. We have to operate on that assumption, I think."

Sebag did not immediately reply. As usual, he didn't know how to explain what he was feeling.

"All I can tell you is that for me that just doesn't ring true. If I attribute all the crimes to one person, he no longer makes sense to me!"

Sabine Henri giggled.

"Superintendent Castello has told me how much he admires your intuition, and I'd like to believe you, but I'm much more rational. I need better arguments to be convinced. And I'm afraid that this so-called intuition actually conceals an inability to recognize your own mistakes . . . "

Sebag sighed.

"I don't have any other arguments," he had to admit.

"That's a problem. And all the more so because it makes me doubt another one of your . . . theories. Yesterday you claimed that the murderer and the person responsible for young Mathieu's death were one and the same, but I don't recall that you provided any proof whatsoever for that, either."

"I don't have any proof, in fact, but I've got a cluster of assumptions."

"That's much better than a simple intuition," the cabinet director scoffed. "But what really bothers me here is that this afternoon the prefect gave that information to the press. If you're mistaken, we're all in trouble."

"I wasn't mistaken," Sebag said stubbornly, though he was less and less sure of himself. "In any case, there's only one way to find out who's right and who's wrong, and that's to arrest the murderer."

"And have you made any progress today?"

"I don't know. Everyone is working on his own assignment. Since Superintendent Castello is here today, I'm not coordinating things, he is. All I know is that I have two colleagues who have been authorized to go to South Catalonia this afternoon to follow the rental car lead."

"Fine, I'm going to call Castello."

Sabine Henri didn't hang up right away. She paused to think for a moment and then added:

"Don't get me wrong, Lieutenant Sebag. It's my job to put pressure on you. Even if you haven't convinced me today, I have confidence in you. Arresting the murderer is in fact our top priority. Do that and we'll accept the rest."

These last words were hardly any relief to Sebag, who was already thinking about something else. And especially about someone else. Sévérine.

Up to this point the lack of certainty had prevented him from telling his daughter about the developments that had occurred in the investigation into Mathieu's accident. He was willing to take the risk of having to take back something he'd said in front of all the *Pieds-Noirs* and all the cabinet directors in the world, but not in front of her. Now he no longer had the choice. The information was going to appear in the newspapers, and Sévérine had to hear it from him first.

He called her on his cell phone. It was Thursday, it was 5 P.M., school was out.

Sévérine took the news properly, with prudent and restrained joy. She promised to transmit the information to Mathieu's parents with the necessary reservations.

"I'm going to write them an e-mail and I'll let you read it before I send it to them. In any case, they're not here right now. They couldn't bear staying home any longer without Mathieu . . . They're in Andalusia, in a house some friends lent them."

Her voice trembled when she mentioned her friend.

"We're going to find this reckless driver-murderer," her father promised her. "I'm going to go all out."

"I'm proud of you, Papa. I've always known that you're the best."

As he put down his phone, in the reflection on his computer screen he caught a glimpse of a silly grin that stretched from ear to ear. Good thing Jacques isn't here, he said to himself.

Late in the afternoon, Sebag's cell phone rang. Unknown number. It was late. He shouldn't answer. The caller would leave a message if it was urgent.

Finally he answered.

"Georges Lloret here. You've been trying to reach me, I think."

The tone was dry and direct, the voice grave and deep.

"Uh . . . yes, absolutely," Sebag stammered.

"You've been hassling my secretaries, I hope it's important."

"It is, in fact."

"You said it was a matter of life and death."

"Yes, that's right, and I wasn't exaggerating."

"I'm listening."

There was no trace of concern in Lloret's voice, only impatience.

"Monsieur Lloret, I'd first like to know if a certain Gérard Mercier has already contacted you."

"I know that like you, that man has tried to reach me several times today. But I respect the laws and the police, and I called you first."

"That's very kind of you . . . "

"No, I'm not kind, and I'm sure you've already figured that out. Now let's get to the point, please, otherwise I'm going to hang up and call this Monsieur Mercier."

Lloret seemed to be one of those men who see life as a permanent battle and who conduct all their affairs the way one launches an attack. Sebag understood that he wouldn't be easily impressed. He had to hit hard.

"Did you know André Roman?"

A silence followed. Then Lloret showed that although he'd been living in Spain for years, he hadn't forgotten the nuances of the French language.

"Did I know him?"

The fish had taken the bait. Now it was a matter of not giving him too much slack.

"Excuse me, Monsieur Lloret, I didn't quite understand your answer. Did you know André Roman?"

"Did something happen to him?"

"If that matters to you, I assume that means that you knew him?"

Lloret bristled. He was used to giving orders and especially he was used to being obeyed.

"Don't play games with me, you'd lose. All I have to do is make a certain call in France to find out everything you don't want to tell me. You tried to reach me to warn me, apparently. I'd like you to tell me, Lieutenant, exactly what is going on, and stop beating around the bush. Lieutenant who, by the way?"

"Lieutenant Sebag, Gilles Sebag. But I'm not beating around the bush, I'm asking questions, that's my job. I would like to be sure that I'm talking to the right person."

"You know very well who I am . . . "

"Your name is Georges Lloret, but are you the Georges Lloret born in Algiers in 1933?"

"Yes, I am."

"Thus you knew André Roman?"

"You're stubborn, aren't you? Yes, I knew him. That was a long time ago. In Algeria, precisely. But I haven't seen him in years. I've closed the door on that past. So, has something happened to André?"

Sebag decided that he could make a few concessions, but not too many.

"Yes, he's dead."

"Was he killed?"

"Why do you ask that question? André Roman was an ordinary retiree, why would you immediately think he's been killed?"

"Don't take me for a fool! You're the police, you bother me for a so-called question of life and death, and you tell me that one of my boyhood friends is dead. You don't have to have gone to the police academy to draw the conclusions. Especially since if you've connected him with me, that's because you know about our past and you know that before he was an ordinary retiree, as you call him, André fought alongside me in the ranks of the OAS."

Sebag decided to fire his second bullet without waiting any longer:

"Did you also know Bernard Martinez?"

"Bernard? . . . Has Bernard been killed, too?"

For the first time, Lloret's voice betrayed concern.

"How did it happen?"

"Omega was murdered in his apartment two weeks ago, and Bizerte in his car last Sunday. If we also count Sigma, who died in an explosion fifty years ago, you're the last survivor of the Babelo commando: that's why we're calling you today."

"I understand better now," Lloret admitted.

His voice remained just as cavernous but had become less harsh, almost soft. But that didn't last.

"I understand, but it's stupid," he replied in a tone that was sharp again. "All that stuff is so far in the past, it doesn't interest anyone anymore. Not even those who lived through it, and not even me, though I loved Algeria so much. You're on the wrong track, it's ridiculous. And then I haven't been in contact with André and Bernard for years."

"However, Martinez was living in an apartment that belongs to you."

"I see that you are well-informed," he said, "but I had

almost forgotten that. Bernard contacted me about ten years ago, when he went bankrupt. He'd had to sell everything to pay his debts and no longer had a penny. I bought that apartment so he could live under a decent roof. That wasn't a problem for me. Since I didn't want my name to be connected with that operation, I set up a small corporation just for that purpose. Its address is a simple postbox that I never look at. I did everything long-distance, and I didn't even meet with Bernard about it."

"What a generous and disinterested thing to do," Sebag ironized.

"Generosity can't be judged in the abstract: it's a function of the sacrifice that the donor makes. For me, there was no sacrifice involved. And if I've closed the door on my past, that doesn't mean that I've forgotten anything. Bernard would have given his life for French Algeria, he didn't deserve to die homeless on the streets."

"His murderer didn't forget anything, either."

"You're mistaken, Lieutenant. The murders of André and Bernard have nothing to do with the battle we waged."

"We haven't found any connection between the victims other than this shared past. They saw each other only now and then, just for a meal in a restaurant, and did no business together. And then . . . "

Sebag decided it was time to reveal the main bit of information to Lloret.

"And then, after each of these crimes, the killer left a message, a kind of signature, on a door at Martinez's apartment and on the headliner of Roman's car. But it wasn't really a message, it was an acronym. A three-letter acronym."

"A signature, you say?"

"Yes."

"FLN?"

The suggestion surprised Sebag.

"No. OAS."

"OAS," Lloret repeated pensively. "Then it wasn't a signature."

"Not really, you're right. Rather a mark of infamy. Like the fleur-de-lys branded on the shoulders of convicts back in the old days."

"OAS a mark of infamy? You'll allow me not to share that point of view . . . "

"It's that of the murderer. Not necessarily mine."

Sebag was immediately annoyed with himself for making that stupid remark. He would have liked to add "Although . . . " but he decided it was pointless to stupidly provoke an interlocutor whose animosity he'd taken so much trouble to allay.

"Now you probably understand better why we considered it urgent to find you and warn you."

"You think I'm next on the list?"

"Everything leads us to think that."

"That's incredible . . . Who could . . . ?"

Lloret didn't finish his sentence. Sebag gave him a little time, but nothing came.

"Yes, who? That's certainly one of the questions we're asking. The other being: Why?"

"Do you think I know?"

"Who else would know?"

"Maybe El Azrin," Lloret sighed after a few seconds of silence.

"Excuse me?"

"El Azrin, the Angel of Death among the Arabs."

"You think the murderer is a former member of the FLN?"

A loud hissing sound tickled Sebag's ear. Lloret must have blown noisily into the receiver.

"No, I was only saying that . . . It was an expression we used to use. I'd forgotten it, and it just came back to me . . . As for the reasons for this belated vengeance, frankly I don't see . . .

As I believe I told you a moment ago, that all seems so far away."

"You made enemies as well as friends back then," Sebag insisted.

"That's for sure."

Gilles perceived a certain satisfaction in Lloret's tone. The former OAS activist continued:

"But precisely, that was 'back then.' Why bring it up now? We're all so old."

"Obviously, we've asked ourselves that question, too. The best answer we've come up with is that the murderer must have learned something new recently. Maybe he didn't know your identities before . . . "

An idea was born in his mind.

"Or perhaps he didn't know that he had something to hold against you. Maybe he learned recently that you played a dirty trick on him back then."

Several periods of silence had already occurred since the beginning of their phone conversation, but the one that now began was far thicker than the others. Sebag had no basis for imagining Lloret other than the photo and the sound of his voice. He couldn't see either his gestures or his facial expressions, but like a blind man, he hoped to somehow sense them.

He closed his eyes.

The silence seemed dense and compact. The idea he'd thrown out had reimmersed Lloret in his Algerian past. He'd almost stopped breathing. The man was reflecting. He was probably reliving scenes, reviewing his friendships, revisiting his fantasies, his crimes, his boasts.

"No, really . . . I don't understand."

The powerful voice had lost its assurance. It had lingered too long on certain words.

"I'm sorry, Lieutenant. And . . . for your part, do you have any good leads?"

"Leads, yes, but it would be too much to call them good leads. We're looking in particular at former *barbouzes*."

"I see . . . That's not stupid. We didn't give them any quarter at that time. Of course, they didn't give us any either. They tortured and executed some of us in cold blood."

"In your opinion, are there *barbouzes* who might have something against your commando in particular?"

"*Aïwa*! More than one, for sure."

"Does the name Maurice Garcin mean anything to you?"

"Absolutely not. But you know, we never took the time to introduce ourselves to each other."

He gave a loud, sonorous laugh, then immediately stopped.

"At the time, neither side was very sociable, you know," he joked.

"I see that the threat hanging over you hasn't frightened you too much."

"It isn't the first. I've never been a very popular person. That is, in fact, not the least of the things that I'm proud of."

Sebag was convinced that Lloret had had an idea that he preferred to keep to himself. He hoped that by reminding him of the dangers facing him he'd be able to get the former OAS man to reveal it.

"My job is to keep you from getting killed, and the threat is real. I have the feeling that you're not telling me everything, Monsieur Lloret."

"Come now!"

"If you want us to be able to protect you, you have to tell us everything. Even if the idea that occurred to you seems completely preposterous."

"No idea occurred to me, really."

His denials rang false.

"According to our information, the murderer is already in Spain. The threat is not only real but imminent."

Lloret took time to think for a moment before asking:

"How were Bernard and André killed?"

"A bullet in the head for Martinez, one in the stomach and then in the heart for Roman."

"So they didn't have time to suffer . . . Do you think they understood before they died?"

"Understood what?"

"Who was killing them and why?"

"For Martinez, I'm sure of it. For Roman, I think so."

"What weapon was used to kill them?"

His voice had changed slightly. A half-note higher with respect to its normal timbre. Lloret had asked the question casually, but Sebag sensed that he attached great importance to it. Nonetheless, he replied directly:

"A 9 mm Beretta 34."

Lloret's breathing stopped. A leaden silence followed.

"You know . . . " Sebag began. "You know who killed them!"

"No... I don't know anything."

"I don't believe you, Monsieur Lloret."

"I don't give a damn what you think, Lieutenant. With all respect, I don't give a damn."

Sebag knew that he was wasting his time, but he had to insist.

"We have to arrest this criminal before he strikes again. Before he kills you."

"At my age, you have to die of something. You know, I've had three passions in my life: Algeria, women, and business. Algeria—I don't have to draw you a picture—I lost fifty years ago. I have now had to give up women as well. There, too, I don't have to draw you a picture. As for business . . . my doctor keeps urging me to retire definitively. My heart, it seems. Eighty is a good age to bow out, don't you think? And then dying by a bullet coming from such a marvelous and distant past—it seems to me that would have a certain style, no?"

Sebag didn't know what to say in response to this foul-mouthed millionaire. If he wanted to die, that was his business. Sebag's problem was to arrest the criminal before he made it three in a row.

"Think about the families of the other victims. They have a right to know who killed their relative."

Lloret snorted loudly.

"Please, Lieutenant, don't give me that. Not me. And then, stop thinking that I know the criminal. You're mistaken about that, I assure you."

"You may not be sure, but you've got an idea."

His senses on the alert, Sebag had the feeling he'd heard Lloret smile.

"No idea, Lieutenant, no idea at all. Just an old dream."

CHAPTER 32

**Algiers, March 24, 1962**

This time, it's war. Since this morning, tanks have been
, moving through the streets of Bab-El-Oued. They're firing
without scruples on French people. The residents are holed up
in their apartments and the few OAS combatants who weren't
able to leave the quarter in time hesitate to fire back because
they have lost all hope.

The ceasefire between the army and the FLN was signed six
days ago. A peace agreement for the Arabs. A shame—worse
than a betrayal—for the ordinary Europeans living in Algiers.

Hidden behind the parapet of a terrace on the top of a
building, Sigma is watching French soldiers walk down the
streets of his quarter as if they owned it. A tank precedes them,
followed by three half-tracks. About twenty soldiers are
advancing on foot at the same speed as the armored vehicles,
scrutinizing the windows and rooftops, moving from the shelter of a doorway to that of a palm or plane tree.

This military violence is the sequel to a civil horror. Sigma
has to acknowledge it: madness has seized the city over the
past several weeks. The madness of the French of Algeria first
of all. As soon as the first rumors of negotiations began, terrible violence broke out. The fun-loving, easygoing neighborhood of Bab-El-Oued became the scene of unspeakable butch-
ery. Hordes of furious ordinary citizens turned the quarter into
a bloodbath. Indiscriminate attacks. Peaceful husbands and

loving fathers killed people. They killed other fathers, other husbands, and also women, old men, and sometimes even children. With their fists or their feet, with hammer blows or with knives. For the simple reason that they were Arabs. Their broken, bleeding bodies were left on the asphalt or in the gutters. One wouldn't dare leave the bodies of dogs that way.

As an OAS combatant, Sigma recognizes that he, too, has executed defenseless Arabs. He doesn't feel ashamed of it. It was only justice. And eye for an eye, a tooth for a tooth. The FLN has never bothered to make distinctions, killing both soldiers and civilians alike. But Sigma has acted on orders. Always.

He is a soldier in a clandestine but legitimate army. His acts were not blind. They responded to what he is convinced is a rigorous organization. If he has not always understood the reasons, he is certain that his superiors know why they had to kill. And Sigma killed cleanly. With determination, without excessive violence, and almost without hate.

That has nothing to do, in his opinion, with the savage acts of recent weeks.

After the ceasefire was announced, the OAS went mad in turn. General Salan, its leader, issued a communiqué decreeing that the French army should now be considered an occupying force, a foreign army, and that they had to fire on its soldiers.

Shoot to kill.

And French soldiers died. Shot down by other Frenchmen.

On March 22, grenades rained down on the French army's first patrol. Eighteen men were killed. The next day, the crowd fired on the contingent's draftees. Seven boys, most of them Sigma's age, died.

The madness can't stop now. There's no longer any way out.

Sigma feels disgusted. Tears roll down his cheeks as he watches the soldiers advance. Tears that have little to do with the heady odor of gunpowder and the tear gas.

How did they all get to this point? What went wrong? The army didn't side with French Algeria. Why? Out of obedience to that aging clown in the Elysée Palace. And to whom does that former hero owe his current position as the leader of the nation? To them, to the French of Algeria who raised him to power, with joy and hope, in 1958.

Yes. Something went wrong. That's clear.

Sigma hears footsteps behind him and whips around. It's only a young woman neighbor who has come to join him on the terrace of their building. He wipes away his tears with his sleeve and goes back to watching the sad spectacle in the street. A delicate hand is laid on his shoulder. A gold-plated bracelet is on the wrist. The other hand points to his submachine gun resting on the parapet.

"So what is your gun for, then?" the young woman asks with astonishment.

"What would you like me to do with it, Françoise? Do you want me to fire a burst and have the army destroy our building in retaliation? I'm too alone, I can't stop anything."

"Where are your friends?"

"They've left the neighborhood."

"I thought it was completely surrounded?"

"They managed to get out just two days before it was sealed off. They were helped by a colonel who sympathizes with our cause and who waited until they left before carrying out his orders."

"And where are they now, those brave men, when the neighborhood needs them?"

"They're in Oran. Don't ask any more questions. It's secret."

They received their orders just as the quarter was being surrounded. Sigma refused to follow them. He couldn't imagine leaving his grandmother alone during these times of violence. Babelo accepted his refusal. That was lucky. Especially since he didn't like the assignment. They were supposed to hold up a branch of the Bank of Algeria. The clandestine army needed money to continue its madness.

Sigma and Françoise look up. Two helicopters with grenade launchers have taken off from a nearby base and are approaching Bab-El-Oued. When they arrive over the neighborhood, they are met with bursts of machine-gun fire from the roof of a nearby building. The helicopters immediately return the fire. A terrace explodes and the machine guns fall silent. Perhaps forever.

Behind Sigma and Françoise, there are hysterical cries. They jump up. The young woman's mother rushes at them like a fury, with her housecoat thrown over her shoulders and old curlers in her faded hair. She slaps Françoise on both her cheeks.

"You're crazy," she screams. "You're going to get yourself killed by these barbarians."

As she passes by him, she gives Sigma a look of hatred. She'd like to have slapped him, too. Henriette Servant's grandson, she's known him since he was a child. But he's a man now and he's got a gun.

## Algiers, March 28, 1962

"You shouldn't go out, Grandma."

"I don't have a choice. We don't have anything left to eat."

"Well then, I'm going with you."

Henriette Servant strokes her grandson's hair, which has been cut short.

"You know very well that you can't do that. The army allows only women and old men to go out on the streets of Algiers."

She turns off the sewing machine and puts on her wool overcoat. Then she gets her shopping trolley out of the entry closet.

"Wait, at least let me help you."

Jean Servant picks up the trolley and starts down the stairs. Four floors lower, he puts it down in the building's little lobby. He opens the door. Henriette kisses him on the cheek before going outside.

Jean goes back up the stairs two by two. From the window of their apartment, he watches his grandmother. He sees her waiting in front of a barbed-wire barrier. A military patrol has set up a checkpoint. A soldier examines pedestrians' identity papers while an officer scans the roofs and terraces with the help of binoculars. The rest of the group keep their hands on their weapons, ready to fire at the slightest alert.

Jean feels a shiver run down his spine.

After she has waited for a few minutes, it's Henriette's turn. The soldier studies her papers. His eyes move from her face to the identity card and then from the card to her face. He nods, hands the documents back to her, and without a word signals to her that she can move to the other side of the barrier. Jean watches the slender, weary figure walk up the street and then disappear after having passed in front of a wall covered with a big splotch of white paint. That is where yesterday the three magic letters "OAS" were still displayed. Jean is in a good position to know: he's the one who painted them there a few months earlier. His first act on behalf of the OAS.

**Algiers, March 30, 1962**

The army has finally lifted the blockade of Bab-El-Oued. For five days it has surrounded the quarter, searched hundreds of apartments, seized tons of weapons, and destroyed the residents' last hopes.

Jean Servant has met his companions in arms in front of a building pocked by the impact of bullets. Back from Oran, Babelo, Omega, and Bizerte have had to wait, hidden by an accomplice in a house in the suburbs of Algiers. The leader of the commando proves to be considerate with his young fighter:

"So, Sigma, it wasn't too hard? Did your grandma hold up all right?"

"She's clearly been affected. For her, everything is lost; she wants to go to France. She says a distant cousin has agreed to put us up temporarily somewhere near Bordeaux."

"Don't let her do something that stupid. It's still secret, but our next instructions from the organization will be categorical: Every French person who tries to leave the country will have to be executed."

Sigma sighs. After having killed Arabs and fired on French soldiers, the OAS is getting ready to execute civilians in its own camp.

"It's total war," Babelo tells him. "Those who leave will be considered deserters."

Sigma prefers to change the subject.

"What about you? Did things go as you hoped in Oran?"

Babelo's face lights up. Omega and Bizerte also smile.

"If you're talking about the holdup, it was a piece of cake, yes!" Babelo said, stroking his pencil mustache. "It was as if we'd stopped by to pick up the cashbox from an agency that belonged to us. When we went into the bank, the employees spontaneously handed over the money to us. They were all supporters of our cause."

Bizerte had a greedy look on his face.

"There was more than two billion old francs, can you imagine?

"And obviously you turned all that over to the proper authorities?"

"Not yet," Babelo said, grimacing. "We have to put it into Degueldre's own hands. For a sum like that, it would be better to wait until the situation calms down a bit. But don't worry, for the time being the dough is in a safe place."

Omega gives Sigma a friendly slap on the back.

"I hope you'll be with us the next time."

"The next time?"

"War is expensive," Babelo explains. "Our needs are increasing. With the ceasefire, the French army has chosen its camp: it's for the *fellaghas* and against us. We've got to equip ourselves more seriously."

As if to prove his point, three T-6 airplanes fly over the city at low altitude, making the windows and people's hearts tremble.

# CHAPTER 33

Gilles Sebag had already thrown his jacket over his shoulders when Julie and Joan burst into the office. They were returning all excited from their mission to South Catalonia. They'd scoured the car rental agencies in Girona and then in Figueres. It was in the latter city that they'd found the "Holy Grail."

"Once again, Madame Irma has won," Joan joked, adopting the nickname that Molina had kindly given his partner.

"Your intuition turned out to be right, in fact," Julie confirmed. "The killer and the reckless driver are one and the same person. There is now no possible doubt. Ten days before he rented a SEAT in Girona and turned it in the next day in Montpellier, Manuel Gonzales Esteban reserved a white Clio in another agency in Figueres. On exactly the day of Martinez's murder and the accident that killed your daughter's friend."

Joan continued:

"The guy at the rental agency described an old man with a squarish face, a full head of white hair, dark, thick eyebrows, a big mouth, and a determined chin. His description is much more precise that the one given by Mercader, your witness from Moulin-à-Vent. Tomorrow the Mossos will have a real Identikit picture made of him."

Sebag savored the moment. He took several long, voluptuous breaths and felt the warm blood flowing through his dilated veins. He thought of Séverine and was sorry that he'd announced the news to her too soon. If he'd kept the information to himself, he could have returned home as a triumphal hero.

Then he thought about Estève Cardona. He was going to be able to tell the news all at once to his colleague in the Accidents unit. Slap it right in his face. A wicked smile immediately flickered on his lips.

Joan pulled him out of his sweet reveries:

"Jacques is waiting for us at the Carlit to celebrate. Are you coming with us?"

Sebag didn't hide his surprise and disapproval.

"It's a little early to celebrate anything. The murderer is still on the loose, I remind you."

"That's what I told Jacques," Julie broke in. "He admitted that there was still work to do but said that was no reason not to celebrate. I think he's one of those people who never miss an opportunity to have a drink."

"That's right, you've got him pegged," Sebag chuckled. "O.K., then, go ahead, I'll join you in a few minutes, I've still got a couple of things to do here."

Llach already had his hand on the doorknob but he stopped and turned around toward Gilles.

"By the way, did you talk to Lloret? My cousin in the Mossos wasn't able to reach him."

"He finally called me back a few minutes ago, yes. I was planning to tell you about it at the Carlit."

"Tell me right now, I'm impatient."

"Not an easy guy to get along with . . . "

Sebag summed up the delicate conversation he'd had with the infamous Babelo.

"I'm convinced that he didn't tell me everything," he added after he'd finished. "When I told him that Martinez and Roman had been killed with a Beretta 34, I sensed that he was startled. That gun reminded him of something, I'm sure of it. But he refused to say anything about it."

"We'd better meet with him tomorrow," Julie suggested. "We can't leave it at a simple phone call."

"He'll refuse, that's clear."

"We have to protect him, too," she insisted.

"I didn't even have time to talk about that with him. The conversation was cut short. He hung up very fast. Right after I mentioned the Beretta."

"My cousin told me that he'd have a surveillance car park in front of Lloret's house in Cadaqués tonight," Llach said, "and that tomorrow officers would be assigned to follow him everywhere."

"He's not going to like that," Sebag commented.

"Otherwise he's going to die!" Llach replied, irritated.

"Somehow I wonder if that's not just what he wants . . . I have the impression that he'd prefer to settle this all by himself."

First, Sebag called Jean-Pierre Mercier to be sure that nothing bad had happened to him.

"I've just looked in my mailbox and I didn't find any new threats," the treasurer of the *Pied-Noir* Circle told him. "I didn't notice any suspicious people in the neighborhood, either, but I have to admit that I haven't gone out much today. My brother was able to get free; he's arriving tonight on the 9:22 train."

Sebag told him what they had learned during the afternoon regarding the anonymous letter.

"There were no fingerprints on the letter or the envelope, that is, nothing that would allow us to find the people who wrote it. As I promised, patrols in the neighborhood have been increased. But be careful anyway."

Then he called Pascal Lucas. It was time to tell the van driver the news. A shout almost burst his eardrum.

"Wahooo! I told you that car existed, goddammit! You were right to believe me. You're brilliant, Inspector! A champ, a real ace."

Lucas went on and on in the same vein. Sebag felt it necessary to curb his enthusiasm.

"You're welcome, Monsieur Lucas, but I remind you that although your responsibility for the accident will probably be reduced, one fact remains unchanged; Mathieu is dead and won't be coming back!"

The van driver's jubilation stuck in his throat.

"Excuse me, Inspector," he said. "I'm sorry."

"Even if it is now proved that a car forced you to swerve, you're still the one who hit the scooter, Monsieur Lucas. And you were driving under the influence of alcohol. If you hadn't been drinking, you probably could have avoided it."

"I . . . uh . . . You're right."

"Goodbye, Monsieur."

He hung up without giving Lucas time to continue his excuses. Then he called Josette Vidal to give her the telephone number of the real estate agency in Cadaqués.

"I think you can take your time clearing out the apartment. The owner is not in a hurry."

"All the same, I'm going to move out Bernard's things and the furniture as soon as I can. Thanks for your help, Monsieur Sebag."

After he put down the receiver, Gilles contemplated the photos on his desk. They were all at least three years old; he had to replace them. Léo and Séverine had changed, grown a little, and matured a lot. Claire hadn't changed at all—at most, a few wrinkles at the corners of her eyes were slightly more pronounced. What was no longer the same now was his relationship to her, his doubts . . .

He felt dark thoughts starting to invade him. He didn't struggle against the rising tide.

In the photos, Claire seemed to be smiling for him alone. That was true at the time. Now their intimate connection seemed to have evaporated and this loss was as painful to him as infidelity itself. Behind his back, Claire might have exchanged sweet words with another man, she might have met him for secret rendezvous. Behind his back, she had perhaps told her girlfriends, Pascale and Véronique, about her affair. They might have laughed about it together. How had she presented this adventure? As a folly that could endanger their marriage or as a nice interlude that had awakened her from a long sleep?

Jealousy gnawed at his stomach. Being excluded from all these secrets made him feel sick. His hands closed into fists. He felt he could become violent, he was usually too calm and too levelheaded. He thought about Cardona and the pleasure he'd felt in taking him by the neck.

But jealousy wasn't a pleasant feeling, and these days it was no longer regarded favorably. A husband who was a cuckold was already ridiculous; if he was jealous as well he became laughable. It used to be that in French courts of law, jealousy and drunkenness were considered attenuating circumstances for all sorts of crimes and misdemeanors. Today, they had both become aggravating factors.

A sign of the times. Adultery had ceased to be a mortal sin.

Could one still swear eternal fidelity when the length of that eternity never ceased to grow? In a century, individuals' life expectancy had doubled. That of couples had potentially tripled, even quadrupled. Did fidelity still make sense? Did it have synonyms other than frustration, boredom, and sacrifice? He had found statistics that said that in the United States 70 percent of people admitted having been unfaithful at least once in their lifetimes. What if one day he himself . . .

Every time the tempest of his feelings buffeted him, he clung to that idea as if it were a life buoy. Claire's infidelity gave him back his freedom. He could also allow himself, without feeling any pangs of conscience, a little sensual adventure, a romantic interlude. He thought of the female faces that were part of his everyday life. Elsa Moulin, Julie Sadet, Martine the woman cop at the reception desk. Jeanne, the boss's secretary . . . Ah, Jeanne and her enticing clothes, Jeanne and her provocative double entendres. A smile flickered on his lips, but he immediately repressed it. No point in thinking about that. Every skirt chaser at police headquarters had tried and failed. So, Jeanne? In your dreams.

And then, the idea of deceiving Claire didn't attract him. Lying, inventing stories, going to some seedy hotel at noon for a quick fuck . . . He didn't like that sort of thing, didn't want to do it. He felt too tired for that.

He knew that lassitude's name but refused to utter it.

If only he'd been able to talk about it with someone. A friend? He didn't have any, and then in any case he would never have talked about such intimate matters with a friend. A priest or a psychologist? Impossible: he distrusted the former's ready-made solutions as much as the latter's absence of response. He'd never believed in those two religions.

Morality couldn't be of much help to him, either. There were no longer any norms in that domain, Good and Evil didn't exist anymore. Today, it was up to each individual to set his own rules, to work things out on his own with his conscience, his temptations, and his feelings. Claire had found her path; Gilles didn't find it reprehensible and would have so much liked to simply come to terms with it. His concern was that his reason dictated a path that his gut rejected. Whatever he thought, whatever he told himself, jealousy was still crouching in his belly, ready to attack him whenever his vigilance lapsed. He'd thought himself a free, thoughtful man, but in reality he was no more than the plaything of the obscure forces that inhabited him.

His weakness also undermined him.

He suddenly gave himself a slap that surprised him. Letting his ruminations have free rein didn't help him in any way. He had to get a grip on himself, otherwise . . . Otherwise he felt he might send everything flying. Claire, the children, his job . . . Yes, that state of mind had a name. He didn't want to hear about it.

He tried to breathe calmly. To stop thinking about all that, especially not to think at all. His wife loved him and he loved her, his children were growing up without major problems, they were all in good health, he had a job. He took a breath. There were worse things in life. He took another breath. He had to resume the normal course of his existence. Beginning with his investigation. There was still one thing he could do that would put his mind on another track.

He concentrated on Cardona's mocking face. He had an account to settle with him. He was still breathing. Deeply. But above all, no violence. He'd won his wager with that imbecile. He had to control his nerves.

Afterward, he'd join his colleagues at the Carlit. He'd sit down with them and drink an aperitif. Then he'd quickly drink another one.

He brusquely put the photos in the drawer of his desk and stood up.

Sebag gave three sharp knocks on the door.

"Come in," Cardona's voice ordered.

He entered his colleague's smoky office and couldn't help coughing.

"Excuse me," Cardona said, crushing out his cigarette in a plastic cup in which a small amount of cold coffee was stagnating.

Cardona got up, opened the window, and then came back and held out his hand. Surprised, Sebag shook it without saying a word.

"You've come at the right time, I was just about to go see you. Sit down, please."

Gilles was disconcerted by this sudden friendliness. He took a chair and cautiously sat down on it.

"I've got something new," Cardona declared.

"I do, too."

Cardona repressed an annoyed grimace.

"You go first, if you want."

"No, no, please go ahead."

Cardona didn't have to be asked twice:

"O.K., fine."

He ran his hand through his greasy hair and swept it back. He took a deep breath. Apparently what he had to say wasn't easy.

"I've thought a great deal since our . . . " Unconsciously, he put his hand on his neck. "Since our conversation the other day. I re-read my file with fresh eyes and noticed . . . let's say . . . a few . . . things that weren't fully explored."

He leaned on the edge of his desk, picked up the cup and twirled the cigarette butt around in the remaining coffee.

"So I decided to resume the investigation and I went back to the neighborhood."

He put down the cup and finally looked at Sebag. He smiled, embarrassed.

"I went there several times, hell, I spent hours there. Damn, it wasn't easy!"

He stopped, seeming to be waiting for encouragement. Sebag gave him no sign. Confronted by his colleague's friendliness and embarrassment, all his aggressiveness had disappeared. But for all that he wasn't going to make the task easy for him. Cardona cleared his throat before going on:

"I finally found a witness. Finally! Just one, despite all my efforts. A single witness, but that's enough. He's a young man of eighteen who was waiting for his girlfriend in front of her apartment building."

Cardona paused again.

"The kid saw the car—the Clio, I mean—he saw it run the stop sign. You . . . you were right. There was in fact another driver who caused the accident."

"I never insisted that there was another car," Sebag said. "I just said that we had to look for it. I looked, and I found evidence that suggested that it existed. Evidence you refused to consider."

Cardona nodded gravely. He realized that he'd been wrong.

"Tomorrow I'll go talk with the van driver and I'll rewrite my report."

"Just between us, I'd advise you to rewrite it this afternoon."

"Really? Why?"

Sebag explained how they had managed to prove that the Clio existed.

"So, that way the reckless driver would be a murderer, and a little old man into the bargain . . . How is that possible?"

Sebag shrugged. He wasn't going to tell Cardona right now all about the case that been occupying him for almost two weeks. Cardona understood and stood up.

"I'll rewrite my report immediately, then. My wife will complain, she's waiting for me, but that's how it is! When you have to work, you have to work, right?"

He forced himself to laugh and then cleared his throat again.

"Otherwise . . . uh . . . you haven't said anything to Castello about our little . . . quarrel?"

"He doesn't know anything about it, no."

"So he'll never know . . . I mean, it's as if I'd found the Clio all by myself!"

"As if we'd each worked independently and arrived at the same conclusion, yes."

"Super!"

He began to rock from one foot to the other.

"I think that . . . I should thank you somehow."

"Is it so hard as that?"

Cardona put his hand on his neck again. Consciously, this time.

"A little, yeah. There's no love lost between us. And then . . . it's never easy to admit your mistakes."

"And do you admit them?"

"Well . . . yeah."

"Bravo! I find that very admirable on your part. You surprise me."

Cardona's face lit up. His mouth opened wide, revealing tobacco-stained teeth.

"Is that true?"

"Affirmative."

Cardona huffed.

"It's true that I'm don't usually do that kind of thing. When I was a kid, my father always told me: 'Never make excuses, son, it's a mark of weakness.'"

"My father told me that, too, but I've grown up since then. I've understood that above all it's a proof of stupidity!"

Sebag was wandering idly around his house. His return had not been in any way triumphal. Since Séverine had complete confidence in him, she didn't need a confirmation to know that he'd been right. Now she was with her mother, watching her favorite cop show, which was full of heroes almost as good as her father. Léo was spending the evening as usual, holed up in his room in front of his computer.

An ordinary evening for an ordinary family. A happy family, no doubt. On the table in the entry hall, Gilles found a packet of cigarettes that had already been opened. He put on a jacket and went outside

Sheltered from the wind, he lit a cigarette. He rarely smoked and had opened this packet two weeks earlier. At the time of Mathieu's funeral. He felt a need for tobacco only on important occasions. Great joys or great sorrows. And also during periods of boredom, moments of ill humor, or anxiety.

This evening, there was a bit of all of those.

The aperitif he'd shared with his colleagues had not allowed him to escape his preoccupations. When he'd entered the bar, Molina was proposing a toast to Ménard, "who is bored stiff in Marseille instead of taking advantage of the break he's being given." Then the discussion had moved on to the *Pieds-Noirs* who were "never satisfied" with their situation. Llach and Molina hadn't foregone making further allusions to the fortunes of certain repatriates. Sebag had tried to start a separate discussion with Julie about her reasons for coming to Perpignan, but failed because his two pals were talking too loud and the young woman cop didn't seem inclined to talk about personal matters.

He crossed the driveway and started walking through the deserted streets of Saint-Estève. A little exercise would do him good. He hadn't run often enough lately. In the autumn, it got dark early and his workdays had turned out to be too long. Usually, he managed to get away at noon, but with this investigation that had not been possible. He missed running. He felt it in his body and in his head.

He needed to air himself out. He just had to avoid letting the great tide of dark thoughts sweep over him again.

He'd stayed at the Carlit for only a quarter of an hour. He'd tried to turn the conversation to the investigation but hadn't succeeded. For his colleagues, the day was over. He hadn't persisted so as not to appear to be a spoilsport.

The metallic and irritating buzz of a little scooter took him by surprise in his cogitations. He heard it coming before he saw it. At night, that wasn't acceptable. When the scooter neared him, Sebag saw that the kid on it, not content just to ride without his lights on, had also pushed his helmet to the back of his head, with the chin strap on his forehead instead of his chin. That was the latest fashion among kids. Ultracool. Sebag had already warned Léo that if he caught him doing that even once, he'd immediately sell the scooter.

He took a furious last drag on his cigarette and then threw the butt in the gutter. He was trying to decide whether to light another one or start out for home when his cell phone rang. A fortunate diversion. It was Ménard.

"Am I bothering you?" the inspector asked politely from his exile.

"Not at all. Have you got something new?"

"Nothing special. I was calling mainly just to talk."

"Are you bored in your little hotel room?"

"Kind of, yes."

"Any news from home?"

"Not much. My wife is at the movies with a girlfriend and my son is with one of his pals."

Sebag thought about the inappropriate comments that Molina might have made in his place. Look out for the tide.

"It's depressing here in the evening," Ménard went on. "I've never liked hotels: they give me the blues."

"What does your historian say?" Gilles asked to get Ménard to think about something else.

"Not much. Michel Sonate and I tried to run down other *barbouzes*. But we didn't find any interesting leads."

"And there was no Manuel Esteban among them?"

"Obviously. Otherwise I'd have called you. But Sonate also put me in contact with a journalist who has done a lot of work on the former participants in the Algerian war, both the *barbouzes* and the members of the OAS. Some of them got together again in Argentina during the dictatorship of the 1970s."

In turn, Sebag told him about his day and the latest developments in the investigation.

"Interesting," Ménard commented. "We're moving ahead slowly, but we're moving ahead."

"Nothing new about Maurice Garcin?"

"No. His sons are getting more and more worried."

There was a silence. They'd said what they had to say. But Ménard didn't feel like hanging up yet.

"Apart from that, thanks to my historian, I've been learning more about the last years of the Algerian War. It's fascinating. My father fought in that war, but he never talked to me about it."

Gilles recalled that his father had also had to leave at the age of twenty to do his military service in La Mitidja.[15] He'd never said anything about that, either. Besides, Gilles had never really talked with his father. He remembered mainly their quarrels.

"The last months of French Algeria were really tragic," Ménard went on. "There were countless deaths in both camps. Today, it would be unimaginable. Nobody controlled anything anymore, with gunfire and explosions everywhere. Genuine anarchy! I wouldn't have wanted to be a cop over there at that time. Not to mention the fact that crime also literally exploded. All kinds of crime. Including bank robberies. It's true that the OAS needed money."

Gilles wasn't very interested in the history lesson, and he was beginning to feel the coolness of the autumn evening. He'd long since turned around and was now in front of the door to his house.

"Money has always been at the heart of war," he said, to give the impression that he'd been following.

"Whatever the period or conflict, there are always certain constants."

Sebag saw the curtain on the picture window pushed aside.

---

[15] A large plain in the interior of Algeria.

Claire's worried face appeared. He reassured her with a brief smile and then concluded his conversation with Ménard.

"O.K., François, it's not that I'm bored but I was outside and I'm freezing. I'm in a hurry to warm up by getting into bed with my wife."

"Lucky bastard . . . "

Sebag went inside and plugged his telephone into the charger.

"Work . . . " he explained to Claire, feeling that he was only half lying.

She came up to him.

"Oh, but you've been smoking?" she said, surprised. "Has this investigation worried you that much? Are you sure it's only work?"

Claire's blue-green eyes looked deeply into his. Once again, she was throwing him a line. But once again he withdrew when faced with the obstacle. He didn't want to think about that.

"Of course . . . "

When he was a child, Gilles had fallen off his bike and broken his wrist. When they examined him, the doctors had divided into two camps, those who wanted to operate on him right away to insert a pin and those who said that they should first try to repair the wrist with a simple cast, and that they could always think about operating later on if that didn't work. The cast had been enough. With his wife, he was determined not to operate unless there was no other choice.

"Hello! Are you still there?" Claire cried, waving her hand in front of his eyes.

Gilles came back:

"Excuse me. Really, this case . . . We're on the home stretch, we can't mess up. We already have two dead men on our hands and I'm afraid we're soon going to have a third."

Claire decided to talk shop.

"And there's nothing you can do to prevent that?"

Sebag smiled. Without knowing it, with one sentence Claire had swept away all his personal annoyances. Now he was going to think only about work. Work, all the work and nothing but the work. He knew that there would no longer be any room for sleep that night. How could he think about sleeping when a third crime was probably being prepared on the other side of the border?

# CHAPTER 34

T he road had one curve after another. Sebag didn't like driving at night, and the descent into Cadaqués seemed to him interminable. At the same time that he was following attentively the narrow strip of asphalt, he was looking at the orange and yellow lights of the village down below. They made the silhouettes of the roofs and antennas stand out against the dark mass of the sea and served as beacons on his route.

Sebag slowed down as he entered the village. The bell of the church of Santa Maria tolled twelve sinister strokes. He drove through streets as deserted as those of Saint-Estève. At midnight during the off-season, Cadaqués once again became the isolated village it used to be. The statue of Salvador Dalí greeted him on the main square just in front of the beach. One of the Catalan painter's hands was in the pocket of his suit, the other pointed down with the index finger, as if to say to him: "Yes, it's here. You're in the right place." Sebag obeyed and found a parking place nearby.

A semblance of activity remained on the square, which was protected by an immense parasol pine. A group of drunken young people were carrying on a lively discussion. It was probably about the latest match between Barça[16] and Real, because soccer is now the only sport that people are still really passion-

---

[16] The Barcelona professional soccer team.

ate about. Sebag knew that the second *clásico* of the season—the summit match between Real de Madrid and Barça—had taken place that evening. The score had been announced on the radio, but he didn't remember what it was. He recalled only having received the information as he was crossing the border. He'd said to himself that he was leaving the country of rugby and entering that of soccer. Sport remained an immaterial border between the Catalans of the north and those of the south.

Sebag walked over to a map of the village painted on a wall. He used the flame of his lighter to illuminate it, and easily located himself. He had only to follow the street that ran along the beach. Before putting away his lighter, he lit another cigarette. He had a bit of trouble because of the cold, damp breeze blowing off the sea.

*What the hell am I doing here?*, he wondered, pulling up the collar of his raincoat as he walked along. At this hour of the night, he could have been nice and warm in bed, next to his wife's delicious body. But he'd preferred to give up cozy comfort to walk all alone through the streets of a foreign town. Here, he was nothing, he couldn't do anything. He'd brought along his gun, even though it was completely illegal to do that. He hoped he wouldn't run into the local police on night patrol.

He was soon approaching Georges Lloret's home. A police car was already parked in front of the property. He kept his distance, looking at the light that still burned in a large picture window on the upper floor. Maybe Lloret suffered from insomnia as well. From the immense terrace the view over the village, the bay, and the sea must be magnificent. Sebag thought again about his discussion with Llach and Molina. Yes, some *Pieds-Noirs* had done very well in their exile, but who could blame them for that?

The light soon went out, and it seemed to Sebag that he felt the cold more. He shivered. It looked like it was going to be a long night. He told himself that his presence was useless, but that since he'd come this far, he might as well stay. He spotted some parking places in a side street that ran alongside Lloret's house and decided to go get his car. It would be more comfortable to wait inside it. And less conspicuous. He didn't want to be noticed by a possible murderer, and even less by his South Catalonia colleagues.

So he spent a large part of the night in the driver's seat, alternating between periods of dozing and others of incredible lucidity. He reviewed both his family life and his professional life and realized that everything wasn't necessarily as bad as he sometimes thought it was. In the end, the vagaries of life were as important as you made them. A little will and determination sufficed to sweep away all his problems. That seemed absolutely clear. But he felt just as intensely that in a few hours, it would no longer seem so clear.

Around 4 A.M., he had a sudden and brief fright. He was half asleep when he saw a bent-over figure moving toward the Lloret residence. The figure passed under a streetlight and became an old man leaning on a cane. Sebag reached into the glove compartment and took out his gun. The old man passed the property without even looking at it. He was dragging along behind him a skinny little dog, a kind of anorexic dachshund, as old and lame as his master. Sebag put his gun away.

Around 5 A.M. he saw that nothing was going to happen that night, and decided to go home. He had a hard day ahead of him. He drove up the winding road that led to the pass. On the way, thoughts, images, and words collided in his tired brain. The luxury of the property, Lloret's enigmatic answers on the telephone, Molina's and Llach's criticisms, Ménard's history lesson . . . All that mixed, tangled, collided in his head, he was no longer in control of anything. He let the collisions go on. A regular chain reaction. When he crossed the pass above Cadaqués and started the steep descent toward

Figueres, the explosion occurred. Then a calm. As sudden as the explosion.

He'd seen the light. A simple glimmer at this point, but one that might suffice to guide him toward the solution.

He got home an hour and a half later, bringing fresh bread and croissants with him. Sévérine and Léo received him as if he were the Messiah. Claire greeted him more circumspectly, worried by the mixture of exhaustion and exaltation that she saw on his face. She gave him a long kiss, pressing herself against him sensuously. Claire knew her husband, she knew better than he did that he was finally approaching the goal.

# CHAPTER 35

**Algiers, May 22, 1962**

Sigma no longer understands anything. Unless perhaps that the French have lost Algeria. It's too late, there's nothing left to do.

Two months since the ceasefire was signed, and the war continues. The OAS no longer has any leaders. Lieutenant Degueldre? Arrested on April 7 and taken back to France that same evening. General Salan? Arrested two weeks later, and also immediately taken to the other side of the Mediterranean. The OAS continues to run around like a chicken with its head cut off. Everyday it kills more. Seven Arab housekeepers killed with a bullet to the back of the neck the same day in the center of Algiers. Sixty-two people killed at the port on May 2 when a car stuffed with dynamite, bolts, and scrap iron exploded. Men, women, and even children melted into a terrible mush of flesh and blood.

The European neighborhoods are emptying a little more every day. The French are rushing to get on ships and planes. They are "returning" to France, that country many of them have never known and that has just betrayed them. Despite the OAS's repeated prohibitions, whole families are fleeing. The organization is striking them every time it can. The OAS is no longer an organization of combatants but a band of desperados whose objective is to leave behind them a scorched earth and as many corpses as possible.

Sigma signed up for the battle for the honor of French Algeria, not for this nameless, endless horror.

And yet, he, too, continues to kill.

He gets out of the Dauphine, following Babelo and Bizerte. Omega remains at the wheel, ready to take off. The three men move toward the entrance to the branch of the Bank of Algeria.

Sigma doesn't want to desert. He doesn't want to run away from the fighting. He feels bound to his group, to his companions, to his last friends in this land of Algeria. But he has nonetheless secretly prepared everything to put his grandmother out of harm's way. A ticket on a ship is waiting, hidden between two books in the cabinet in the living room of their apartment. Or rather two tickets, because Henriette would never have agreed to leave the country alone.

The two sentinels guarding the bank lay down their arms when they see the commando coming into the building. One of them even gives them a military salute. Sigma, holding a submachine gun, remains in position near the door while Babelo and Bizerte approach the teller's window. Three customers, including a woman, are waiting in line. They move aside without saying a word.

The teller has already opened the safe built into the wall behind his seat. He grabs a large canvas bag and starts filling it with one bundle of bills after another. The operation takes no more than a minute. The employee closes the safe and passes the bag, which has the bank's logo on it, over the counter. Sigma sees his superior put down his gun near the counter before plunging his hand into the bag. He pulls out a bunch of bills that he casually throws down.

"That's for the trouble."

Then he picks up his weapon and turns away, followed by Bizerte. Just as all three of them are about to leave, the sound of glass breaking makes them jump.

On their right, three armchairs grouped around a small coffee table form a lounge where the employees of the bank sometimes receive customers. On the table, there is an intact goblet, and alongside it, shards of glass. Two naked feet, dirty and tanned, stick out from behind an armchair.

"Come out of there!" Babelo shouts.

The two feet start trembling but don't move. Babelo fires a bullet that shatters the second goblet.

"I said, come out of there."

The terrified face of an elderly Arab timidly appears behind the chair.

"Stand up," Babelo orders.

The man, resigned, obeys and begins mumbling a prayer. He knows what's coming. Sigma does, too, and goes out of the bank. He hasn't taken three steps before a shot rings out. Soon followed by a second one. More muted. A *coup de grâce* fired point-blank.

The three militants get back into the Dauphine. The leader sits alongside the driver, Bizerte and Sigma in the backseat. An odor of gunpowder fills the car. Omega calmly starts the engine. Babelo puts both hands on the bag that he's set between his legs.

"Too easy . . . John Ford wouldn't make good westerns with bank robberies like that one."

# CHAPTER 36

He woke up with mixed feelings of torment and joy, impatience and profound weariness. The day before he'd listened to the evening news on the local radio station and learned that he was responsible for the death of a fourteen-year-old kid.

Damned old avenger. Because of him, the war had another innocent victim.

Damned panic, too.

He hardly recalled what had happened after his "conversation" with Omega. He'd left the apartment to go back to his car and it was in the stairway that he'd felt the fear coming. He'd even almost fallen down a couple of times. He was no longer used to death. He'd reached his car as quickly as his arthritis allowed. He'd stupidly made the tires squeal when he drove off. Then he remembered having run a stop sign and forced a van to swerve. He didn't remember anything else. According to the radio, when the driver of the van swerved he hit the scooter. And the kid on it.

Damned bum luck.

Damned old avenger.

He ran the razor over his rough cheeks. The whiskers had lost their vigor as he grew older. They no longer grew as fast, as thick, or as dark, but he still shaved every morning. Precisely because their hirsute, disorderly appearance immediately gave his old face a neglected look.

He dressed painfully, trying to think about what remained

for him to do. His mission had to take precedence over his scruples. The boy's death would be even more sordid if he didn't accomplish the task he'd set himself.

However, he was having trouble recovering the meaning of this mission. He forced himself to think about those long-ago atrocities. The bodies in the streets. The smell of gunpowder and human flesh that was masked by the iodine fragrance of the sea. All that had to have a meaning.

Damned war. Damned hatred.

Damned asshole.

Damned OAS.


Sebag stared at the pavement of the autoroute. Llach was driving a hundred and sixty kilometers an hour. He passed two trucks—one Lithuanian and one Bulgarian; the latter, in violation of the most elementary safety rules, was tailgating the former.

When he'd arrived at headquarters around 9 A.M., Sebag had run into Llach. Joan was nervously pacing up and down the corridor, his cell phone glued to his right ear. He was talking in Catalan in a worried and tense voice. He'd signaled to Gilles to wait beside him.

"That was my cousin in the Mossos," he explained after hanging up. "Lloret gave the patrol that was keeping an eye on him the slip. He parked his car in the underground parking garage of his real estate agency in Rosas, but instead of going into the agency, he went out through a door that gave onto another street where a taxi was waiting for him. Our colleagues couldn't do anything. By the time they got back to their car in the parking garage, it was too late. They have the taxi driver's number, and they're trying to reach the company he works for."

"I suppose they asked the agency's employees if they knew where their boss was likely to go?"

"Apparently no one knows."

"Or they don't want to say anything."

"According to my cousin, they're sincere. He explained to them that Lloret was in grave danger and that they themselves were risking big problems if they hid anything. Lloret's secretary gave them her boss's appointment book, but the page for today had been torn out. All she remembers is that Lloret had an appointment with a major Argentine customer. In Girona or Figueres, she doesn't quite remember."

Llach slowed down as he approached the Boulou toll plaza, the last stop before the Spanish border.

"My cousin is waiting for us at the La Jonquera toll plaza. The patrols in Figueres and Girona are on alert; they've got the taxi's number. All we can do now is cross our fingers."

"If you don't mind, I'm going to do it for both of us. At the speed you're driving, I'd prefer you to use both your hands in the usual way."

### Algiers, June 12, 1962

"Jean . . . I smell trouble."

Standing behind the bar, Charles, the owner of the bistro, is watching the action in the street. Jean Servant goes over to the window. About thirty gendarmes are taking up a position behind parked cars.

He turns his head and sees that the end of the Rue Michelet is blocked by tanks.

"Do you think it's for me?"

Charles shrugs his broad, former wrestler's shoulders. Apart from a sleeping drunk, Jean is the only customer in the bistro. Out on the street, a bullhorn is conveying orders to them.

"In the name of the high commissioner, we ask all customers of this café to come out holding their identity papers in their hands and keeping their hands high."

Jean moves away from the window but continues to watch

the street from a distance. All the gendarmes have aimed their rifles toward the bar, their fingers on the trigger. Even if Le Populo has long been known to be a lair of OAS activists, this is not an ordinary papers check. The gendarmes don't act at random. They have precise information. They're looking for someone. Something. Sigma. Money. Weapons.

"Do you have your papers, Charles?"

The owner opens a drawer at the other end of the bar. He takes out an old, tattered ID card and shows it to Jean.

"Good. You'd better leave, then."

Charles comes around the bar and stops in front of the drunk sleeping off his anisette. He points to him.

"What about him?"

"Do you know him?"

"Not really. He's some poor devil who moved into the neighborhood a few months ago. When he's drunk, he tells everybody his story. He was a colonist in the interior. One day he found his house burned down. His wife and his children died inside it. Burned to a crisp by the FLN."

"Well, leave him alone then. They won't do anything to him."

Jean has other plans for this unfortunate fortuitous companion, but he can't say what they are. Not even to Charles.

The old man has left his hotel in La Jonquera without regrets. Now he's driving through the suburbs of Girona. As before each operation, he feels calm. He used to remain calm afterwards, too. Now he's old. He has less control over what follows, his stomach that cramps and his hands that tremble. He feels terrible when he thinks about the kid on the scooter.

Once his old accounts are settled, he'll have to pay this new debt.

He has no trouble finding a parking place in a shopping area in Girona. He parks his rental car. Again, he has chosen a small, common model. A white Fiat Uno. As a precaution, he has dropped his Spanish name. Even if the French police investigation doesn't seem to be advancing very fast, he prefers to be careful. He made his appointment with Babelo under his Argentine name. Juan Antonio Guzman. He likes this name. And not only because he's used to it. He finds it chic.

His rheumatism makes getting his stiff carcass out of the car a torture. He has the feeling that the illness has gotten worse since his return to the Old World. A day will come when just breathing will make him wince with pain.

He takes the bridge over the Onyar, the river that runs along the edge of the old quarter of Girona. The ancient buildings are huddled along its bank. Reassured by the lofty, protective presence of the Santa-Maria cathedral, their pastel-colored façades are bathed in the autumnal sun, shamelessly contemplating their reflections in the clear water of the river. The laundry hanging on the half-open windows reminds him of certain mornings in Bab-El-Oued.

After crossing the town of Boulou on the Tech River, the A9 autoroute climbs the slopes of the Albères range toward the Le Perthus pass. Llach is still driving at the same speed. Speedometer steady at a hundred and sixty kilometers an hour. Sebag uncrosses his fingers and dials Gérard Mercier's number. He has to act quickly. In a few minutes his call will pass through the Spanish telephone system, which will cost him extra. He dispenses with the usual polite chitchat.

"You didn't tell me everything about the Babelo commando's actions during the last weeks of the Algerian War."

" . . . "

"In addition to attacks on Arabs and operations against the *barbouzes*, they committed a few holdups."

"It didn't occur to me that that might be important. All the clandestine armies resorted to that kind of thing to get the money necessary to continue the struggle. It was pretty common."

"It was also common, I assume, that some uncontrolled groups started showing a little too much zeal in that area?"

"What do you mean?"

"That kind of operation sometimes leads to a career . . . "

"I still don't see."

"Yes, you do."

After a long hesitation, Mercier finally replies:

"That's possible. During those last weeks, they wouldn't have been the only ones who were quietly preparing for their . . . new lives, let's say."

The puzzle that Sebag is trying to fit together is still far from complete but the main pieces are beginning to fall into place.

The owner of Le Populo comes over to Jean Servant.

"You do know that there's a back door that opens onto the alley?"

"Yes, I know."

"The gendarmes are probably waiting for you at each end of the alley, but not necessarily behind the door. Or in front of the service entrance to the building next door . . . If you slip out on one side and in on the other, they won't see you."

"The problem is that they must know my name and my address, and they're probably already at my apartment."

Charles shrugs his broad shoulders. Then he holds out his hand.

"I wish you luck, my friend."

"Thanks. Can you do me one last favor?"

"Gladly."

He points to the drunk, who is still asleep.

"Don't tell them that there are still two of us in here."

"O.K."

Llach lowers his speed to below a hundred kilometers an hour to cross the border post at Le Perthus. Last year, you still had to drive through very slowly and show your papers to the customs officials. But the European Commission made it clear that it considered that kind of border crossing outdated. Within a year, the police huts and customs posts were shut down. As a result, traffic moves much more smoothly, especially in the summer.

"Do you think we'll get there in time?" Joan asks.

"Get where in time?"

That's really the question . . .

He contemplates the buildings of medieval Girona. He's ahead of time and is taking the opportunity to enjoy the sun that is warming the bones of his old back. He has an appointment on the other side of the bridge, in the Barri Vell, the old quarter, which has now become the main attraction of Girona. Babelo must have made some fabulous deals there, he says to himself.

It was not easy to get this appointment. He had to pass himself off as a rich Argentine who wanted to retire in the land of his Spanish ancestors. He even presented a false family tree going back to the eighteenth century. Thanks to a few accomplices in his adopted country, he added to his file a very impressive bank statement. Babelo couldn't resist the opportunity to make a large profit.

After all, it's only fair.

The owner of Le Populo shakes Sigma's hand again and then goes out of the bar, his hands in the air. The three gendarmes immediately point their weapons at him and take him behind the shelter of the armored vehicles. Their leader takes his papers to examine them.

Jean draws the gun he's stuck under his belt. He's had it on him ever since he joined the OAS. He even sleeps with it. It's his mistress. He cocks the Beretta and aims it at a gendarme only half hidden behind a Chevrolet. He fires and hits his target.

Intense gunfire immediately responds, but he is already lying on the floor. The windows explode, and the big mirror behind the bar does, too. The drunk opens one eye, snorts, and then goes back to sleep. Jean crawls to the back room. There he picks up the backpack he brought the day before in preparation for an operation planned for that afternoon. He hefts it and laughs. A good five pounds of dynamite; that will do the trick.

Sheet metal rectangles, billboards, and trucks—that's all you see of La Jonquera when you drive past it on the autoroute. Llach stops at the toll plaza. He pays, asks for a receipt, and then parks the car on the little lot located just beyond the empty police huts. A blue and white vehicle belonging to the *Mossos d'Esquadra* is waiting for them. A policeman in uniform is leaning on it.

"That's Jordi, my cousin," Llach says.

The two French inspectors get out and greet their colleague. Llach gives him a hug, Sebag shakes his hand.

We have the address for the meeting," Llach's cousin tells them, signaling them to get into their car. He sits in the back.

"You can follow our car, Joan. We're going to Girona."

The cousin has spoken in Catalan. Short sentences and simple words, Sebag has understood. The Mossos' car turns on its siren and gets on the autoroute. Llach stays right behind it.

Jordi continues his explanations, but this time Joan is forced to translate:

"The Girona police found the taxi parked in front of a bar. The driver was inside drinking coffee. Lloret had given him a hundred Euros not to pick up his phone for at least an hour. But he didn't hesitate to give them the address where he left Lloret. It's in the old quarter, a palatial house that's for sale. It will take us half an hour to get there, but a Girona patrol is on its way and will get there before we do."

Then Sebag presents his own conclusions. In his view, the robberies allowed the Babelo commando to build up a considerable pile of loot and that is what made it possible for Lloret, Roman, and Martinez to make their investments after they left Algeria. Lloret became a very rich developer and Roman a prosperous auto salesman. Only Martinez had not succeeded in turning his nest egg to good account.

"Do you really think this vengeance is just a matter of money?" Llach asks skeptically.

"That's not really what I mean, no."

Sebag hesitates to reveal more. He has pushed his reasoning further and the hypothesis he's worked out seems persuasive to him. But for the moment it's not based on anything tangible. What he's convinced of is that the most ferocious and tenacious hatreds always arise within one's own family. In one's own camp.

The explosion has made every wall in the area around the bar tremble. Sent flying by the force of the blast, one of the café's tables has landed on the windshield of a car behind which a cluster of gendarmes is hiding. They remain prudently in its shelter until the smoke dissipates.

Then the lieutenant commanding the group stands up. In the street, frightened faces appear at apartment windows whose glass has been blown out. Every time he meets someone's eyes, the lieutenant sees the face immediately disappear behind the walls. A rapid reflex. Like those hairy insects that roll up in a ball as soon as you touch them. Millipedes, he seems to recall. The term often came up in the crossword puzzles his father used to like to do.

The lieutenant signals to his troops that they should come out from behind their makeshift shelter. He assigns two men to move toward the café. Glass fragments crackle under their thick, tough soles. Le Populo is no more than a pile of iron and wood, from which a few wisps of smoke emerge here and there. The two men advance very slowly, their guns pointed toward the unknown. The lieutenant gives another sign and two more men start to follow them at a distance of three meters.

They are crossing the city of Figueres and its barriers of buildings when Gilles's cell phone vibrates in his hand. Ménard's name is displayed on the screen. He hesitates. The conversation is likely to be long and expensive. Too bad!

"I've got something new," Ménard says, excitedly. "The journalist I was talking to you about last night has just called me back: now I know who Manuel Esteban is . . . "

Gilles doesn't tell him that he thinks he knows, too. He's not sure of anything. So why throw cold water on his colleague?

"I'm listening."

"Manuel Esteban is a former OAS activist who fled Algeria during the final battles. He took refuge in Spain, but remained there only a few months. Then, along with other members of the OAS, he left for Argentina. He reappears in the 1960s. He has a new identity, and under the name of Juan Antonio Guzman, he is supposed to have been a member of the famous Death Squads, the nebulous, clandestine groups responsible for murdering dozens of left-wing opponents. But do you know the best thing about this Esteban-Guzman?"

This time Sebag can't resist revealing to Ménard the name that is haunting him. After a few seconds of silence, his colleague said, an aggravated voice:

"One sometimes wonders what use it is to work with you . . . "

The old man has gotten a little lost in the streets of medieval

Girona. He has had to ask directions twice, and this time he's
late. He doesn't like that. Fortunately, he finally finds Ferran el
Catòlic Street. The house he's supposed to want to buy doesn't
flaunt ostentatious luxury on its street side. However, the
façade of stones polished by time and wind conceals—he
knows, because Georges has sent him numerous photos—a
regular little palace. Ten rooms, each with a marble fireplace,
are arranged around a patio carpeted with grass and flowers.
He approaches the massive wooden door and rings the bell.
He smiles at the cold eye of a surveillance camera. Even
though he doesn't hear a chime behind the thick walls, he
doesn't have to wait long. The metallic click of a latch resounds
joyfully in his ear. Then he recognizes a voice coming from
another age, another time, another life:

"I'm here: come in, it's open."

As if he needed to support himself on something, the old
man rests a sclerotic elbow on the lens of the camera. He takes
advantage of this to use his other hand to draw the old pistol
he took with him when he left Algeria. His only souvenir of his
country.

Banging, screeching, belching, the café seems to be groan-
ing with surprise and pain. It's bleeding. The soldiers advance
cautiously. The smoke is still thick. It clouds their vision,
deforming lines already twisted by the explosion.

A young gendarme stumbles over two soft legs lying on the
ground. He crouches, puts his hand on a shoe and, in the persistent fog, moves his fingers carefully up the fabric of the
pants. He follows the tibia, recognizes first the knee, then the
thigh, then . . . nothing. His hand sinks into a red, gelatinous
mass. He abruptly stands up and turns aside to vomit. A fellow
gendarme calls out in a trembling voice:

"Lieutenant . . . "

The officer is already behind him.

"Is that him?"

"Hard to say."

Despite their efforts, the gendarmes find no other part of the corpse. The body has been pulverized. The liquid dripping from the ceiling is a mixture of water from a broken pipe and sticky blood. A quick examination shows that the victim was wearing a belt full of dynamite. Behind the bar, the gendarmes find a backpack. It contains identity papers in the name of Jean Servant, born in Algiers in 1942. The investigation goes no further.

A few weeks later, the last French soldier will leave independent Algeria.

Georges Lloret is waiting in the middle of the patio, sitting on the edge of a little stone fountain.

He smiles.

He knows.

Jean advances slowly and looks at the man facing him. Wrinkles have appeared on his face but haven't altered its harmony. His mane of white, swept-back hair bares a rectangular forehead creased by furrows. His long, slender nose connects two eyes, sparkling with cunning and satisfaction, to his mouth, which is still greedy.

"Hello, Sigma," Lloret says.

"Hello, Babelo."

"I'm surprised to see that you're alive."

"You surprised me a lot, too."

"I suspected I would."

After Ménard's call, Sebag tells Joan everything, and then Joan translates it for his cousin. Then no one speaks for a moment. His jaw set and his hands gripping the steering wheel, Joan stares at the road and the back of the car in front of him. For their part, Sebag and Jordi try not to think of anything.

They know that they'll arrive too late. The only thing they can still hope for is to receive a call informing them that the patrol of the Mossos of Girona has succeeded in preventing another murder. But the damned telephone refuses to ring. The cousin looks at his cell phone every ten seconds, but no call comes through, even though he has good reception.

Lloret's smile grows wider, making two dimples appear on his crumpled cheeks.

"It's been a long time . . . When did you finally understand?"

Jean does not reply. He doesn't want to tell him. He has no desire to talk here and now about his Gabriella. About how his granddaughter patiently taught him about computers and how one day he'd had the idea of Googling the names of his former associates. How he had discovered their current affluence and how, little by little, doubt had crept into him. A doubt that had ended up disturbing the tranquility of his old age.

"I understood that you betrayed me, and worse than that, you betrayed our cause."

Lloret's mouth tenses.

"We fought for French Algeria with passion and sincerity. Just as you did. No less. We just realized sooner than you did that it was all over and tried to prepare for our lives afterward. We gave the money from the first robberies to the Organization. And then we started keeping some of it. And then more and more."

"Without telling me.

Lloret sniggers.

"And if we had?"

Jean's dark eyes plunge deep into his former boss's Mediterranean blue ones.

"I'd have killed you," he acknowledges.

"You see: we had no choice."

"You didn't have to finger me to the gendarmes."

"Maybe . . . "

Lloret seems to reflect for a few seconds. As if fifty years afterward he's still weighing the pros and cons.

"I knew that despite the anarchy that was raging in Algiers, the army was after us and that it was getting dangerously close. We weren't ready yet to go back to France. We needed a little more time. We put the gendarmes on your trail and that was enough. I always had the feeling—from the moment I met you—that you had a taste for martyrdom. I gave you an opportunity to sacrifice yourself for French Algeria."

Lloret sniggers again.

"I thought you'd taken advantage of that opportunity. It was a great explosion. A death worthy of a hero. Too bad . . . "

"Too bad for you: I've come here to kill you."

"As if I didn't know that!"

Lloret slowly gets to his feet. Despite his eighty years, he holds himself very erect. His hand moves his jacket aside and caresses the gun that he's stuck under his belt.

Jean's eyes light up. He smiles.

"I see you still like westerns."

"Still."

"There aren't many of those these days."

"That's true. But so many were made during the years of our youth. I watch one every Friday night. I have a special room in the house, a home cinema with Dolby stereo sound. It's great."

Jean moves his jacket aside as well. His Beretta is ready.

The three policemen jump when cousin Jordi's telephone rings. Despite the Mossos officer's quick response, Sebag has time to recognize the notes of a melody by Lluis Llach, whose name sounds like Joan's and who is the greatest living singer of South Catalonia.

Gilles doesn't understand anything Jordi says, but the tone is unequivocal: the cousin is angry, and makes a disgusted gesture as he ends the call. With gritted teeth, he utters two curt sentences to Joan, who hastens to translate them.

"That was a call from the patrol asking him for the address again: the guys wrote it down wrong and they can't find the place."

Sebag takes a deep breath before speaking:

"Tell him that we find it somehow reassuring to know that there are idiots on their force, too. As for the rest, fuck . . . *Insha'Allah*!"

Jean wiggles the fingers of his deformed hand to loosen them up. He's afraid he can't make them obey fast enough.

"You do know that John Wayne died a long time ago?" he asks.

"I know. Gary Cooper, too. And James Stewart . . . "

"Gregory Peck."

"Randolph Scott."

"Alan Ladd."

"Kirk Douglas."

"Richard Widmark."

Jean hesitates.

"Dana Andrews."

"He's better known for detective films."

"Anthony Quinn."

"Karl Malden."

This time, Jean comes up empty. Lloret continues on alone. He's the one who's a specialist.

"Robert Taylor, Audie Murphy, Robert Ryan, Rory Calhoun, Robert Mitchum . . . "

"Clint Eastwood. He's still alive."

Lloret grimaces.

"I never liked spaghetti westerns."

Jean senses that Georges' hand is tensing. Then he sees it reach for the gun. He tries to react. His fingers send violent electrical discharges through his body as he grasps the Beretta. At the same moment, he feels another pain in his body. Stronger, more gut-wrenching.

# CHAPTER 37

They finally left the autoroute, but they still had a couple of kilometers to go before reaching the center of Girona. The two cars moved swiftly ahead despite the density of the traffic. With its siren still blaring, the first vehicle cleared the way and the cars in front of it moved aside like the waters of the Red Sea before the Jews led by Moses.

Jordi received another call, and the three policemen jumped even more than the first time. Without taking his eyes off the road, Llach was listening attentively and from time to time slipped Sebag an explanatory sentence or two.

"He's got the patrol on the line. They're there."

"The Mossos have found traces of blood in the entry hall of the house."

"There's a body in the patio."

"They arrived too late."

"It's the body of an old man."

For the first time since he'd begun following the Mossos' blue and white car, Llach shifted down into third gear: he had to cross an intersection and the light was red. Once he'd passed the obstacle, Joan resumed his litany:

"They say the old man is dead; he's not breathing."

"He was hit by two bullets, one in the belly, the other in the heart."

"A doctor will soon arrive to certify the death."

Sebag got impatient.

"Who's dead? They didn't find his ID?"

Jordi had heard the question. He shook his head and continued his conversation for a few more seconds. After ending the call, he said a few angry sentences to Joan, who translated:

"He asked the officers who are there not to touch anything. If they can no longer do anything for the victim, he doesn't want them to contaminate the crime scene."

Sebag turned his head toward the Mossos officer. Putting his finger to his forehead, he gave him an imaginary salute to indicate that he was in agreement with that way of proceeding. He added a brief "*Molt be*"[17] just for good measure.

Jordi thanked him with a wink.

The two cars finally arrived on the scene. Parking behind another police car and an ambulance, they completely blocked the narrow street. Cousin Jordi didn't seem worried about that.

An officer in uniform greeted them. He first showed them the traces of blood in the entry and the hall before taking them to the patio. The victim's body was lying on the soft green grass. His head lay at an odd angle because when he fell he'd hit the nape of his neck on the last step of the fountain. Through the opening over the patio, a ray of sun was whitening the old, parchmentlike face. Sebag thought of a poem by Rimbaud about a pale young soldier lying dead in the grass. But unlike the young soldier, the old man hadn't died peacefully in this green nook: he'd tried to fight to survive.

Llach went up to Sebag and pointed to the gun that Georges Lloret still held in his hand.

"I can't believe it. You'd think they were playing out the gunfight at the O.K. Corral . . . Two old men settling an old quarrel the cowboy way . . . We've seen everything now."

Sebag stepped back, saw a bloodstain three meters from the body, then spotted a bullet hole in a corner of the wall. He had

---

[17] "Very good."

to face the facts: the two old men had fought a genuine duel here.

"Lloret held all the cards. He knew who was after him and why. He didn't want either our protection or our intervention. He must have thought it was up to him to settle this."

"And he died as a result," Llach said.

"That was the risk. A risk he was willing to take. May his soul rest in peace. No matter how black it was."

After giving instructions to his team, Jordi came back to join them. According to an already well-established ritual, he spoke to Joan, who translated.

"He's going to issue a search bulletin throughout Catalonia in the names of Jean Servant, Manuel Esteban, and Juan Antonio Guzman. Hoping that our man doesn't have a fourth identity in reserve. The bulletin will also be transmitted to the Guardia Civil. An hour from now, every police agency in Spain will have been informed."

"Perfect. Now we just have to do the same in France. I'm going to call Castello immediately. "

Sebag talked for a few minutes with the superintendent, who did not conceal his disappointment. To be sure, his team had largely solved the puzzle, but it hadn't been able to prevent the third murder.

"We're in check. If we don't want to be checkmated, we've got to intercept this Servant. Let's hope he'll return to France . . . Otherwise, we won't have a chance to redeem ourselves."

Sebag tried to protest but his boss hung up without giving him the opportunity. He had a deep sense of unfairness. Of course, they hadn't succeeded in arresting Servant before he killed again. But whose fault was that? They'd been able to identify the third target when he was still alive and they'd tried to protect him. But how can you stop a man who wants to go alone toward his tragic fate?

Sebag and Llach left in order to let their colleagues in the

Mossos work. They went to have a coffee on the terrace of a nearby bar. The sun was shining brightly and there wasn't a breath of wind. Even though he'd been living in Catalonia for eight years, Sebag still marveled at the mildness of the climate: he had a hard time realizing that it was autumn. He closed his eyes the better to let himself be caressed by the sun.

And on top of that, the coffee was delicious.

Between one horror and the next, life occasionally provided some sumptuous moments.

Llach tried to bring him quickly back to reality.

"So, the killer is Sigma, their former accomplice! And from the outset we've been looking for the murderer among their former adversaries. We were on entirely the wrong track. Or rather: he really fooled us, that little old man. By writing OAS on the scene of his crimes, he made us think that he was giving us the motive. And we walked straight into the trap: We looked in the camp of the enemies of French Algeria. Bravo, Grandpa! Well played . . . "

Sebag limited himself to nodding his head. There were still many unanswered questions in this case.

"I'm not sure I've really understood this Sigma's motives," Joan went on. "Was it just about money? Nobody kills someone for money fifty years later!"

"You're right, money is only secondary here. Betrayal has to be behind it. Sigma must have thought his former buddies had betrayed their cause. Maybe he even suspected them of having betrayed him as well."

"Even if he did . . . Half a century afterward?"

"There are probably other factors that we don't know about. The only way to know exactly what Sigma's motives were is to arrest him."

"Do you think he's going to go back to France?"

"He's attained his objectives: now his goal is to return to Argentina, where he must have a family. Flights are more numerous and easier from Spain than from France, but what will he think it's smartest to do? I don't have the slightest idea?"

"He could go by ship."

"Do you think there are still transatlantic passenger connections?"

"Ocean liners, I don't know, but there are definitely freighters. And freighters sometimes take passengers on board."

"Secretly?"

"No, no. Some commercial ships have cabins and do it officially."

"That's interesting. Because I suppose surveillance is far less strict than in airports these days."

"Obviously."

"That's a line of investigation we mustn't neglect. You should talk to your cousin about it. Especially since if he's planning to take a ship, then there's hardly any doubt: He'll be leaving from Spain or Portugal."

After they finished their coffee, the two policemen took a little walk through old Girona. The cathedral, the old Jewish quarter, the iron bridge the Eiffel Company built over the Onyar in 1877 . . . Llach agreed to serve as a guide for Sebag's benefit. Then the two returned and sat down on the terrace of the bar and ordered another coffee. Jordi soon joined them. He showed them a sheet of paper. Sebag grabbed it. It was the page torn out of Lloret's appointment book. It had been crumpled up.

"He found it in the victim's pocket," Llach explained.

At the top of the page, Lloret had written in the 10:15 appointment in Girona. The name "Guzman" was scribbled in blue ink right next to it. Then, with a different pen—one with red ink—he'd later written another name. "Sigma." Followed by a question mark.

As Sebag was looking at the page from the appointment

book, the Mossos officer was reporting the initial results of his team's investigation.

"As we suspected, the two grandpas were facing each other when they fired. Hard to say who was the faster. Each hit the other, but Sigma was more precise. He hit Lloret in the abdomen and apparently finished him off with another bullet to the heart. The autopsy should confirm that chronology."

"Sigma was wounded, wasn't he?"

"Yes, but they say the bullet went right through him, because they found it embedded in a door. Given the angle of fire, he was probably hit in the shoulder."

"He must be in pretty bad shape."

"Definitely."

"He's no longer a young man."

"We should be able to find him easily."

"We or the Mossos."

"Yeah. Or else the Guardia. But I wouldn't count on his being alive when he's found."

"He's capable of going to die somewhere where we'll never find him," Sebag said anxiously.

"Do you think?"

"It wouldn't surprise me."

"Always the optimist, aren't you?"

Cousin Jordi was following their rapid exchanges, moving his head back and forth like a spectator at Wimbledon. He looked happy when their conversation paused, and he gave them a friendly smile. Gilles smiled back. Then he stood up and held out his hand:

"*Molt gracias.*"

Night was falling on Perpignan, putting an end to a day that had been much too long. Cars were moving at a snail's pace down the Avenue de Grande-Bretagne, which was congested by Friday night traffic. His forehead pressed against a windowpane in his office, Sebag sighed. For him, there wouldn't be any weekend with his family. He was going to have to be content with a few moments gleaned here and there. Saturday morning, for instance. Sévérine had asked him to take her to the cemetery in Passa. She wanted to put fresh flowers on Mathieu's grave. Her friend had been buried two weeks before, and she'd been told that all the flowers set out on the day of the funeral had since been overturned by the rain and wind. She wanted to do this for Mathieu's parents, who had fled their sorrow abroad. Gilles had promised. They would be there when the cemetery opened. Then he'd take her home before going to work.

Unless, of course, there was something new in the investigation on Jean Servant, alias Juan Antonio Guzman, alias Manuel Esteban, alias Sigma. The old fellow was giving them a very hard time. He was a tough nut to crack. A methodical man who had been able to organize his crimes masterfully. But there'd been nothing Machiavellian about his planning, and luck had given him a helluva helping hand.

Sebag had been thinking about the question most of the afternoon. He was now persuaded that by writing "OAS" next to the corpses, Sigma had never intended to lead the investigators astray. He had simply wanted to sign his crimes. To claim them in the name of that organization. The OAS had disappeared long ago, but Sigma had never succeeded in really leaving it behind. He had remained married to it.

For better and for worse.

Sebag's eyes followed a car that parked in the lot in front of police headquarters. Raynaud and Moreno got out of it. With the same movement, they opened the two rear doors to get their old gray raincoats. The color of sadness. Pensive and bored, the two cops then moved toward the building. They climbed the steps and disappeared from view.

So far as he knew, the two lieutenants were still investigat-

ing the destruction of the monument in the Haut-Vernet cemetery. The recent developments in his criminal investigation had
made him completely forget that side of the case. Was it
resolved with the identification of Sigma?

He shook his head vigorously. More than ever, he was convinced that this vandalism could not have been committed by
the murderer. Why would Sigma destroy a monument to the
memory of his heroes? It was inconceivable. The presence of
that white hair near the monument had a quite different cause.
All they had to do was arrest Servant and ask him about it. All
they had to do . . .

Thus he remained convinced that their initial intuition had
been the right one: Other people had taken the opportunity to
get people riled up and increase tensions in the city. The same
reasoning held for the attack on Guy Albouker and the threats
against Jean-Pierre Mercier. Who was behind these acts? The
question might never be answered. That wouldn't be satisfying
but they'd have to put up with it. When the murders were
cleared up, calm would probably return and the people who
perpetrated these acts would probably go back to their usual
lives.

The door opened behind him. He turned around.

"Hi, François. Happy to be back?"

As soon as he'd learned that Maurice Garcin was no longer
a suspect, Ménard had taken the first train for Perpignan.

"You bet!" he confirmed. "I couldn't imagine spending the
weekend up there."

"It's a beautiful city, though."

"Maybe."

Ménard didn't seem inclined to discuss Marseille's tourist
attractions.

"So?" he asked soberly.

"Nothing for the moment. No news of Sigma. We don't
even know if we should be looking for him in France or in

Spain. Everybody is still mobilized: you can forget about that weekend with your family."

"I'll be home in the evening, that will still be better than in Marseille. You know, he's a strange fellow, this Sigma!"

Their telephone conversation that morning had been limited to the strict minimum. Ménard took out of his pocket the sheets of paper on which he'd taken notes. Sebag watched him searching through them; there must have been at least a dozen pages, covered on both sides with his delicate and orderly writing.

"I see that you've got a lot to tell me."

"I hope so. If you tell me that you already know everything about Sigma, well, I'm just going to resign on the spot."

"Don't worry, I don't know anything. Except that he's still alive, and that he's enjoying a particularly active killer's retirement. Go ahead, tell me everything."

Ménard parked a buttock on one corner of Molina's desk.

"In the 1980s, Marie-Dominique Renard, a journalist for a news magazine, began an investigation into the military dictatorship in Argentina. I don't know if you remember General Videla, it was the time when the Argentine soccer team won the World Cup . . . "

"If you're going to try to awaken my memories of international politics by using sports reference points, I'm going to call a halt right here."

"O.K., excuse me. Anyway, the military dictatorship in Argentina lasted from 1976 to 1983. Close parenthesis. Marie-Dominique Renard rapidly discovered that many former OAS activists who had initially taken refuge in Spain had fled to Argentina in the course of the 1960s. The dictatorship had not yet been established but military men were already playing an important role in politics. The governments of the time even gave them land under false names. That's practically a tradition over there; the country had already welcomed with open arms

Frenchmen who had been collaborators during the Second World War. The journalist even claims that these extreme right-wing militants served as . . . Wait, I'm going to find the exact term . . . as . . . as . . . "

He ran his index finger over his notes, stopping at the bottom of a page.

" . . . as an 'ideological matrix in which Argentine state terrorism was rooted.'"

"Excuse me?"

"Yes, I know, the formula is a little convoluted. You have to know that when people talk about state terrorism, they're referring in fact to the death squads that murdered left-wing opponents and that had protection at the highest levels of the state and the army."

He turned the page over, the rest being on the back.

"The two most famous French activists who became Argentines were Jean Gardes—he'd been a colonel in the French army and a specialist in psychological warfare, was later responsible for recruitment within the OAS, and was sentenced to death in absentia in 1961—and General Paul Gardy, one of the Organization's last leaders. It was in digging around in the latter's entourage that the journalist came across Juan Antonio Guzman. She has traced his various identities back to Sigma."

"Does she have any idea how he managed to make people think he was dead?"

"She hasn't really tried to find out; that wasn't important for her investigation. But she thinks that it must not have been that difficult: there was so much confusion during the last weeks of the French presence there."

"What role did Sigma play in Argentina?"

"At first, he gravitated around this General Gardy. He owned land in La Pampa, around Pigüé, a village that was founded by French settlers in the eighteenth century and has always had a large number of residents who came from France.

Then Sigma sold his land and moved to Buenos Aires. He got married there and started a family. But that didn't mean that he'd changed his ways. According to Marie-Dominique Renard, he belonged to the Argentine Anti-Communist Alliance, one of the main death squads. Since the end of the dictatorship, he hasn't attracted any attention. He retired and lived on his investments."

"Until he got back into the game for a reason that remains unknown to us."

"He must have wanted to settle one more account before he died."

"Let's assume that for the time being."

Sebag shivered. He'd been leaning against the window, which had cooled off as night came on.

"By the way . . . Do you have any news about Maurice Garcin?"

"No. He's still missing, he's simply disappeared. Our colleagues in Marseille have decided to start searching for him tomorrow morning if he doesn't turn up in the meantime."

"I think it's about time, now."

Two sharp raps made his office door vibrate. Llach's head appeared.

"Ah, you're still there. Super."

He came in and closed the door after him.

"My cousin has just called me: I've got something new."

"They've arrested Sigma?" Sebag asked, feeling to his great surprise a combination of hope and concern.

"If they'd arrested him, I would have told you right away. I wouldn't have said, 'I've got something new.'"

"That's true. So what's new?"

Llach took Molina's chair and Sebag sat in his own to listen to him.

"The Mossos have found a car rental agency in La Jonquera that provided Sigma—or rather Juan Antonio Guzman, since that's the name he used—with a white Fiat Uno. The car was rented last night and has not yet been turned in. And for good reason! Thanks to the license plate, our colleagues found the car still parked on a street in Girona. It already had a parking citation. The ticket left on the dashboard was valid until only 11 o'clock this morning."

"So he's still in Girona?" Ménard asked.

Llach dismissed that possibility with a wave of his hand.

"The Mossos questioned the town's taxi drivers. One of them remembered having picked up a little old man in Girona's Barri Vell who spoke Spanish with a strong South American accent. He took him to the train station. The trail ends there. We don't know which train he might have taken. It was almost 11 A.M. when he arrived at the station, and three trains left during the following hour, for Barcelona, Madrid, and Paris . . . via Perpignan, obviously."

"There may be a chance that he's on this side of the border, then," Sebag said hopefully.

"It's possible," Llach confirmed. "But if he's in France, he could have gotten off in Montpellier or Nimes, or continued on to Paris. So far as we know, he has nothing more to do here."

"That's true," Sebag sighed. "But we have to act as though he'd stopped here. He no longer has a car, he'll need to rent a new one. We have to contact all the rental agencies again."

Ménard looked at his watch:

"In ten minutes, it will be 7 o'clock; it's too late to do anything this evening."

Sebag tapped his fingers on the top of his desk.

"We should have thought of that earlier and given his description to all the rental agencies in the department."

"Easy to say after the fact."

"I should have thought of it."

"In any case, Gilles, there's no chance that Sigma is in Perpignan."

"Who knows what that old madman has in his head."

"If we were sure that he was here, we'd send patrols to all the hotels in the region; he has to sleep somewhere."

"That's an idea."

"Are you kidding? Ask Castello, you'll see what he'll tell you. They're not going to mobilize all the police and gendarmerie teams in Pyrénées-Orientales on a Friday night when the suspect could very well be hundreds of kilometers from here. In Paris, Barcelona, or Madrid."

Sebag had to admit that Ménard was right. There was so little chance that Sigma was in the area! He suddenly realized that Llach had listened to their discussion without saying a word. He guessed why:

"Have you got other information, Joan?"

Llach smiled.

"In fact, I do. The Mossos traced Sigma to La Jonquera and they found the hotel where he's been staying for the past two weeks. He checked out early this morning. He'd presented himself as an Argentine tourist."

"A tourist in La Jonquera?"

"They must not be very frequent, but that was apparently enough for the hotel manager. According to him, Sigma really looked like a harmless little old man."

"We've certainly encountered enough 'harmless little old men' in this case," Ménard pointed out.

Llach and Sebag granted him a smile that was friendly but not without a certain condescension. Humor wasn't their colleague's strong point. Sebag suddenly felt immensely tired. His short, uncomfortable night was coming back to him. He sat up on his chair. His back was hurting. The inspectors looked at each other but no one said any more. A silence full of discouragement gradually filled the room. Gilles closed his eyes for a moment.

# CHAPTER 38

Dim streetlights were throwing an orange-colored light on the dirty façades and the damaged asphalt. Closed metal shutters covered with tags completed the street's sordid look. Jean Servant grimaced with pain as he stepped off the curb. He put his right hand on his shoulder to support it. For once, his pain had nothing to do with his arthritis.

He was walking even more slowly than usual. Despite his caution, he unintentionally kicked a beer can that had been left in the gutter. The can rolled across the street and stopped when it hit the heel of a young Arab, who suddenly stood up, looking for the person who had committed the offense. Jean's right hand slipped from his shoulder to his belt. Under his overcoat, he still had the Beretta read for use. But the young man, seeing that it was only an old man with white hair, transformed his aggressive scowl into a pleasant smile.

Jean went on his way.

He found this part of Perpignan particularly dirty and wretched. Even the suburbs of Buenos Aires seemed to him better maintained. Was France slowly being transformed into a third-world country? He recalled that some people used to say that the loss of Algeria would mean the loss of France's grandeur. He'd never really believed that at the time. Or more precisely, he didn't give a damn about it. Unlike his hero Lieutenant Degueldre, Sigma had not engaged in the battle out of patriotic passion but in the single, mad hope of spending his whole life in the country of his childhood. Political commitment came later. And even then . . . Had he really ever had real political convictions? All his life he'd acted more on the basis of affinity and loyalty than on that of dogmas or certainties. His friends in Argentina had often needed his help. He'd given it to them freely.

And he'd never hesitated to kill.

Death was part of his nature and his education. Of his childhood and youth. The Second World War had killed his parents, the conflict in Algeria had killed his illusions. Today, young people grew up in the comfort of living rooms and a haze of marijuana smoke; he'd grown up on the street amid the bitter fragrance of gunpowder. Today, no one could still understand the violence that survived in him. Moreover, his daughter had never accepted it. She'd stopped speaking to him when she'd discovered the details of his past. In Algeria and then in Argentina.

Fortunately his daughter had learned about his turpitudes only long after Gabriella's birth. Bonds of intimacy and love had had time to be woven between the grandfather and his granddaughter, and Consuela hadn't dared break them.

Gabriella . . . Would he see her angelic smile again someday? Would he enjoy again the pleasure of hearing her honeyed voice and her pure, crystalline laughter? Without this fierce desire to see his granddaughter again, he would never have tried to escape after Lloret's death. Exhausted by the hunt, wounded by his old accomplice, he would have sat down in that delightful patio and calmly waited for the police to come. Or he would have killed himself. Maybe, yes, he might have had the courage to do that. Babelo had told him that he had all the marks of a martyr. Perhaps he hadn't been completely wrong?

He grimaced again.

The cool night air made his wound hurt again. The bullet

had passed through his shoulder just below the collarbone. Nothing serious. He'd found what he needed to clean and bandage it in a pharmacy in Girona, and knew that he no longer had anything to fear. In a few days, he would be healed. But it was painful, and he was less and less able to endure pain.

He felt old and tired.

He was weary.

He looked up at the plaque attached next to a kebab vendor's sign. Rue Lucia. He was no longer very far from his hotel. Soon, he would disinfect his wound again and change his bandage. Then he'd take his pills and go to bed, dreaming about Gabriella.

He hoped he would be able to leave France the next day. He'd reserved a seat on the train to Genoa, via Marseille and Nice. Only the French and Spanish police must be looking for him. In Italy, everything would be easier.

He had to get to the train station in Narbonne by late morning.

But first he had to complete a final mission. Or rather he had to pay a debt. That was the reason why he had come back, contrary to all prudence, to spend a night in Perpignan. He was aware of the risks, but he'd never compromised when it came to honor. Whatever might be said about his crimes and misdeeds, it also was in the name of that value that he had lived, and it was in the name of that old-fashioned and quaint notion that he had come to carry out the last three murders in his life.

So the next morning he would get into his new rental car and set out for a small village in the Catalan outback. He would put a ridiculous gift on a stone. A gift that was valuable precisely because of the risk he was running.

CHAPTER 39

Sebag was walking quickly down the main street in the North African quarter in central Perpignan. It was now completely dark and cold as well. He pulled up the collar of his jacket. In the evenings, the only activity on Rue Lucia consisted of a few young North Africans standing around talking.

He'd dozed off for a few minutes in his office, and that little nap had revitalized him. After Ménard and Llach left, he'd felt the need to go outside. Not getting any exercise was beginning to weigh on him more and more. In every sense of the term. When he'd stood on the scale that morning, he'd been annoyed to see that he'd gained almost five pounds since summer. He certainly didn't want to develop a paunch. For him, that would be the sign that he was giving in to age.

On the way out of headquarters, he'd let Claire know that he wouldn't be home before 8 P.M. And then he set out to walk through Perpignan.

As he strode along, he'd passed a dozen hotels and hadn't been able to resist going in to ask whether a room had been reserved in the name of Guzman, Esteban, Servant, or even Sigma. He was well aware, however, that there was no chance of that. Especially since in France, it had been a long time since hotels were required to ask their guests to show an ID card. People could easily give their names as Michel Dupont, Jean Moulin, Charles de Gaulle, or Jean-Luc Godard.

He noticed the sign for another hotel, but this time he didn't go in.

He left Rue Lucia and started up a side street that led toward the gypsy quarter. He had to edge along the wall of a building to get past a car that was parked right in the middle of the narrow street. Here, parking places were rare and residents paid little attention to the regulations. They left their cars wherever they could. Wherever they wanted.

Sebag liked to stroll through these old neighborhoods. Sedentary Gypsies had taken up residence in Perpignan's historic center, making it one of the last downtown areas in France where the poor still lived. Everywhere else, they'd been forced to move to the outlying areas. Sebag liked the atmosphere in this quarter.

He came into the Place du Puig, the neighborhood's nerve center. Men dressed in black from head to foot went on talking without paying any attention to him. He passed in front of a group that was huddled around a guitar player. A young man let out a long, guttural wail and the others started clapping their hands. For these Gypsies, the day was just starting.

After the Place du Puig, Sebag turned off to the left and walked back down toward the city's more respectable commercial center. In a quarter of an hour he'd be back to his car, and in less than half an hour he'd be home with his family. With his children and his wife. His . . . faithful? unfaithful? . . . wife.

He was tired of these unresolved questions that were accumulating in his mind and weighing on his stride. And on his life, too . . . Where had Jean Servant gone? Who had wrecked that damned monument? Who had attacked Guy Albouker and threatened Jean-Pierre Mercier?

And who was that bastard who might have slept with his wife?

A stupid idea crossed his mind, an idea worthy of the teenager he hadn't been for at least twenty-five years. He swore under his breath: "If I don't solve this case, Claire and I are going to have it out, face to face."

Then he spat on the ground to seal that ridiculous promise. He preferred to laugh stupidly than to weep sadly.

# CHAPTER 40

Sebag and his daughter got to the cemetery in Passa shortly before 10:30. She was holding a big bouquet of roses and he was carrying a pail of water in which he'd thrown a large sponge.

In front of the gate to the cemetery, Séverine had stopped and smiled at her father.

"I'm not sure I've really thanked you for finding the person who was really responsible for the accident," she told him. "So thanks, Papa."

She stood on tiptoe and gave him a kiss on his forehead. He would have liked to take her in his arms but the pail was in his way.

"I'm not sure I deserve congratulations. The guy is still on the loose."

"But you're going to arrest him, I'm sure of that."

He didn't know what to reply and limited himself to putting his free hand on her shoulder.

"Shall we go? It isn't too hard for you to come back here to Mathieu's grave?"

"I'll be O.K. And then, you're with me. Thanks for that, too."

They pushed the heavy gate open and went in. Before leaving the house, Sebag had called headquarters. Llach was on duty but there was nothing new. Not on the French side, and not on the Spanish side, either: Cousin Jordi hadn't called. To keep busy, Joan had gone back to the list of the car rental agencies he'd contacted three days earlier with Julie Sadet. He was planning to call them again, one by one.

"It's either that or do nothing at all . . . And then, you never know!"

Mathieu's grave was separated from the entrance only by a short row of vaults. After that of the Vila family, they turned left. Sévérine froze, speechless, in front of a shiny marble tomb surrounded by a garland of red and yellow flowers. The name "Mathieu Farre" was engraved on it in gilt letters.

"I don't understand . . . "

Sebag's eyes jumped from his daughter to the carefully maintained tomb and back to his daughter. Sévérine seemed embarrassed by her bouquet.

"Friends of Mathieu's parents, the Vidals, called me yesterday. They told me that the tomb was covered with mud and that there were no longer any flowers. I . . . I don't understand."

"Somebody else must have come first."

"Who?"

"Mathieu had other friends, didn't he?"

"But when did they come? The Vidals called me late yesterday afternoon. The cemetery had just closed, and since they couldn't come this weekend, they asked me to take care of it."

"And if I correctly read the plaque at the entrance, the cemetery has been open for only half an hour . . . "

As he talked, Sebag was making a rapid calculation. Half an hour was not very much time to clean up and arrange all these flowers. If someone had come this morning, they should at least have seen him in front of the cemetery. He knelt down near Mathieu's grave. A white thread caught his eye. He picked it up and had a closer look at it. It was a hair. In a flash, he saw in his mind's eye Elsa Moulin, his colleague on the forensic team, standing in the rain with her yellow rain parka and her red boots. She was putting a white hair in a plastic bag. They were in a different cemetery.

"It's not possible."

"What isn't possible, Papa?"

Sebag did not reply and started to examine the tomb and its surroundings. He soon found a red stain on the gray gravel. He touched it with his index finger. It was wet. He rubbed his finger with his thumb. It was sticky. He held his finger to his nose and sniffed it.

"Blood."

At the same moment, he heard the cemetery gate squeak.

"Damn . . . "

He put his hand on Séverine's arm and whispered an order to her:

"Above all, don't move."

Then he started running toward the gate.

To avoid being noticed, he'd parked his rented VW Golf a hundred meters from the cemetery. Jean would have liked to run, but after such a long time his legs had forgotten how to do that.

In any case, it was bad luck.

He'd just finished decorating the tomb when he'd heard footsteps on the other side of the cemetery wall. Then he'd overheard the conversation between the father and his daughter. There was no doubt about it: the guy was a cop! He'd hidden behind a vault and kept an eye on the two intruders. He'd seen them coming closer. No, really, what bad luck!

Another fifty meters to reach the car.

His legs hurt terribly and his wound did, too. He'd felt it opening up when he got behind the wheel. A little more at every turn. Then it had bled while he was cleaning the tomb of that poor boy. Soon it would stain his raincoat.

He heard a sound behind him and turned around.

The policeman had just come out of the cemetery and had spotted him. Jean put his right hand on the Beretta stuck into his pants.

"Excuse me, Monsieur . . . "

Sebag had reached the gate in no time. Now he saw him. The infamous Sigma. A broad, muscular figure shrunken by age was hurrying with difficulty toward a red car parked at the curb.

"Excuse me, I'd like to talk to you."

He saw the old man stop and turn around to face him. He saw the dark eyes. He saw the big, gnarled hand moving toward the belt. He glimpsed the pistol, which was raised toward him like a snake preparing to strike. He saw its dark, gaping mouth ready to spit out death.

He didn't have a weapon on him. He never carried one.

He stopped.

His blood froze in his veins when he noticed the sound of footsteps behind him. He couldn't keep his head from turning partway around. His gut cramped when he saw Séverine. She had disobeyed him. She was there, without any protection other than her father's body.

He put himself squarely in the line of fire.


It was bad luck, really.

Servant had taken a risk, he was aware of that, but he'd never imagined he would have such rotten luck. Being taken by surprise by the cop assigned to the investigation. An unarmed cop who'd come there with his daughter! At least if there had been several of them and they'd taken out their revolvers, he would have fired the way people cast dice.

And then *Insha'Allah*.

The wound to his left shoulder was shooting jolts of pain through his body. He gritted his teeth and thought very hard about his little Gabriella. He mustn't flinch, not now, if he wanted to hold her in his arms again someday. He shouted, in his firmest tone:

"On the ground, that's an order."

He saw the policeman turn to his daughter and speak to her. The girl lay down on the ground and put her hands on her head. The policeman seemed to be about to do the same. He went down on his knees.

Sigma's hand relaxed on the gun.

His knees on the ground, Sebag told himself that he wouldn't go any lower. No question of lying flat on the ground. Not here. Not like that. He tried to control his breathing. Keeping breathing meant keeping calm.

"Nothing's going to happen, Séverine, don't be afraid. And above all, stay flat."

Sebag said to himself that Servant had taken a hell of a risk coming to put flowers on Mathieu's grave. The old man was a ruthless, methodical killer, but he still had a conscience. Moreover, Sebag had seen his relief when he began to obey him.

He raised one knee and then put his foot on the ground, watching Sigma's reactions. Despite the thirty meters that separated them, he could discern a little trembling at the corners of Sigma's mouth. This sign of perplexity encouraged him. He put his other foot on the ground and stood up very slowly as he continued to speak to Séverine.

"Keep down, honey, don't move."

What is that idiot doing? Sigma's hand tightened again on the Beretta, sending an electric shock to the old man's brain.

Why has he stood up?

He watched uneasily as the man took off his jacket and let it fall to the ground. Thus he could be sure that the policeman wasn't armed.

"I told you to lie on the ground."

Sigma cursed himself inwardly. His voice had lost its assurance and betrayed his agitation. The policeman took one step forward and then another.

"Don't try to be a hero, don't force me to shoot you."

Sigma bit his tongue. He was talking too much. A man who was determined to kill didn't waste his breath. Too bad! His big finger deformed by arthritis caressed the trigger. The cop took another step in his direction. Sigma shook his head and fired.

"Papa!"

Sévérine had screamed before she raised her head. She saw the smoke come out of the barrel of the gun. Her father was still standing. She heard his astonishingly calm voice.

"Don't move, Sévérine, please."

The sound of the shot had shattered the calm of the morning. Despite his painful eardrums, Sebag had heard, just after the discharge, the dull sound of the bullet crashing into the pavement. Bits of the asphalt had spattered on his shoes.

He took another step.

"I've already killed cops," Sigma threatened, taking a step backward toward his car.

"I know."

Sebag moved forward again. He remained lucid and knew he was staking his life on a gamble. He himself thought it was idiotic. He thought he'd be better off letting the old man get away, he couldn't go far. As an experienced cop, he'd already memorized Sigma's license number and every feature of his face. His description would be precise. The old man had no chance of escaping.

But there was Sévérine. The title of a film came back to him. *My Father, the Hero.* A third-rate film with Gérard Depardieu, he seemed to recall.

"I've killed many people, often in cold blood."

Sebag looked straight into Sigma's eyes:

"You're trying to convince yourself."

The second shot made him jump again. He let the echo of the detonation subside and then took another step forward.

He couldn't let the old man doubt his determination. Sebag was now no more than five meters from Sigma. In this poker game, he held the crucial cards.

"You've never killed someone in front of a child."

Sigma remembered the tears in the eyes of the little Arab, back then, in the streets of Algiers. One day in November, 1961. He'd just completed his first mission, he was part of the Babelo commando, they'd killed a dozen Arab workers—enemies!—and he was proud.

"You're wrong, my boy, you're wrong," he replied firmly.

Nonetheless, he felt a veil pass in front of his eyes. The pride had not lasted long. The love of his native Algeria and the fierce desire to continue to live as a free man had not been enough to transform a massacre into an act of bravery. He'd never considered that kind of action legitimate, and had always preferred operations against the cops or the *barbouzes*. Babelo had sensed his reservations. Very soon, he'd begun to distrust the young fanatic. But Sigma hadn't understood that until these past few weeks.

The little Arab's eyes had come back to haunt his sleepless nights, sometimes fusing in nightmares with those of Gabriella. Dark eyes shining with terror and incomprehension. He'd glimpsed the same flicker in the eyes of the cop's daughter. He shivered.

"You're wrong," he repeated mechanically.

Sebag understood that Sigma was telling the truth, but didn't allow that to fluster him. He'd seen the shiver, and thought he'd deciphered its meaning. His life now depended on the correctness of his interpretations.

"Then you won't do it again," he said.

Another step forward, the left foot, then another, the right foot. His life also depended on his resoluteness.

"Not in front of my daughter."

Sebag was now only two meters away. If the old man fired

now, at point-blank range, he wouldn't survive. He slowly reached for the gun and took a last step. Sigma waited a few more seconds, but Sebag knew that he'd won. The old man wouldn't fire now.

Sigma nodded solemnly. It was over. He'd never see Gabriella again. Farewell, my granddaughter. His life would end in a gloomy French prison. He gave the policeman an admiring look and handed him the gun.

"I could have done worse."

Sebag seized the Beretta. He put on the safety and slipped it into the waist of his pants. Then he heard the light footsteps of someone running up behind him. He turned around and Séverine threw herself into his arms. He hugged her hard.

"You're crazy, Papa, you're crazy. I was so scared for you . . . "

He ran one hand through her long, silky hair. He was proud of them. Of her, and especially of this old Sigma. Of himself, too, a little. His feelings became confused and he ended up wondering if courage could be anything but victorious reck-lessness.

A cell phone rang somewhere far away. His cell phone. Sebag saw Séverine pick up his jacket. When he took his phone out of one of the pockets, it had stopped ringing. There was a message from Llach. Without taking the time to listen to it, he called his colleague back.

"We've got him!" Llach exclaimed triumphantly. "Guzman rented a car near the train station in Perpignan yesterday. This time he chose a more conspicuous model, a red Golf, probably in order to throw us off the track. I've sent the license number of all our teams and to the gendarmes. Have you got anything new?"

"5704 TM 66."

Llach remained silent for several long seconds. Gilles imag-ined him with his phone in his hand, mouth gaping.

"You can call off the searches," he continued, after giving his colleague the details of Sigma's arrest.

"I think I'm not the first one to tell you this, but it's really discouraging to work with you," Llach said. "Really!"

"I came across him by chance. A lucky break, that's all. Will you send a car? We'll wait."

Putting away his cell phone, he found the open package of cigarettes. He took one and offered another to Sigma.

"The last cigarette of the doomed," the old man said, accepting it.

Then they both smoked in silence.

# CHAPTER 41

G illes was impatiently pacing up and down the corridors of the hospital in Perpignan. Sigma had lost con-
sciousness during the car trip and Sebag had decided
that they first had to take him to the emergency room for tests.
He'd left Séverine at the entrance to the hospital and Claire
had come to pick her up and take her home.

The initial medical reports were reassuring. Sigma's wound
to the shoulder would soon no longer be a danger. Even though
it was very infected, antibiotics would soon clear that up. But
the doctor, who had thought the wounded man showed signs
of severe stress, wanted to carry out a complete cardiac examination. Sebag was awaiting its result before questioning his
prisoner. Castello had joined him, and did not hide his satisfaction.

"I have to admit that I no longer thought we'd catch him.
That was an incredible stroke of luck we had!"

He added to avoid seeming disparaging:

"A stroke of luck that you were able to use. Anyone but you
would probably not have noticed the white hair and the blood-
stains. And wouldn't have acted so quickly. One minute more
and that joker would have escaped us again."

"He was going to be caught, anyway," Sebag replied colle-
gially. "Llach was on his trail, and wouldn't have let him get
away."

"By the way . . . "

Sebag sensed that the superintendent was going to

reproach him for the risks he'd taken to arrest Sigma. But Castello didn't finish his sentence. He must have decided that this wasn't the right moment for that, and preferred to change the subject.

"By the way, I talked to our colleagues in Marseille before I came. They've located Maurice Garcin."

"A police patrol found him this morning in an abandoned area of an industrial zone north of Marseille: completely dehydrated, but he should recover. A real miracle . . . he'd walked off from the retirement home in his pajamas."

"He really does have Alzheimer's."

"There's no doubt about that."

A man in his fifties wearing a white coat came toward them with a bouncy step. He was almost running.

"Dr. Prévost. I'm the one who's treating your prisoner. He's fine. You can go talk with him now. Just don't tire him out too much. We've put him in a room on the second floor, at the end of the corridor. It's a room with bars on the windows. I don't recall the number, but you can't miss it: two of your men are guarding the door."

"That's procedure," the superintendent said apologetically, "We're going to put him into police custody."

"You should be able to transfer him tomorrow to the infirmary at the penitentiary."

He gave them a brief, summary handshake and hurried off. Sebag had already met him. The guy never stopped and at his bouncing pace must cover as many kilometers a week in the corridors of the hospital as Sebag ran on the paths of Roussillon.

The superintendent and his lieutenant had no difficulty finding Sigma's room. They greeted the guards and went in. The old man was dozing in his immaculate white sheets. His relaxed face seemed to have lost its wrinkles. All that remained were two deep furrows that ran upward from his nose, dividing his forehead. Sebag realized that Jean Servant was only seventy, after all. Seventy? The beginning of old age. He made a rapid calculation. His own father would be that old two years from now. He remembered a man who held himself proudly erect, who had a tanned face and a splendid head of hair. Very different from this little, stunted old man. In his mind's eye, he saw again Sigma's shrunken figure and his laborious race to get away from the cemetery. He looked down at the swollen hands resting on the white sheet and understood that disease had accelerated time. For Jean Servant as for Maurice Garcin.

The window of the room was rattled by a gust of wind. The north wind had come up in the course of the morning. A radiant sun was flooding the hospital's parking lot with light, but visitors were pulling up their collars to protect themselves against the gale. The temperature hadn't changed but it felt much colder than the thermometer said it was. Meteorologists call it the "windchill factor." Once again, Sebag contemplated the hands that looked like vinestocks and said to himself that arthritis had made Servant look much older than his birth certificate said he was.

The vinestocks moved. Jean Servant emerged from his half-sleep. He stared at Sebag with his dark eyes. The lieutenant did the introductions.

"My name is Gilles Sebag and I'm a lieutenant at the Perpignan police headquarters. This is my superior, Superintendent Castello."

Servant merely looked at them and said nothing. Sebag took a chair and moved it closer to the bed. He got out his notebook.

"So you are Jean Servant, born in Algiers in 1942 . . . "

He paused. Sigma was still looking at him.

"We have only the year of your birth. Could you tell me the day and month, please?"

Despite the routine nature of the question, this was an

important moment. Sebag and Castello held their breaths. What attitude was Servant going to adopt? The old man temporized but did not seem hesitant.

"I was born on June 9," he replied in a soft, composed voice.

Gilles wrote the information down as if it were the key to the case. It was only an appetizer; he didn't want to rush things. Above all, it was essential to establish a good climate.

"And you died a few days after your twentieth birthday, on June 12, 1962, in an explosion at a bar in Algiers?"

Sigma's mouth opened wide, uncovering two rows of well-aligned teeth. With a gleam of pride in his dark eyes, he confirmed what Sebag had said.

"It was a great fireworks show. My last 14th of July."[18]

"What about the body that was found in the café?"

"Some poor slob, a drunkard."

"Did you kill him?"

"He was already dead. The FLN had already killed him."

Sebag wrote down his answers before going on:

"Later you appear under the name of Manuel Esteban, a Spanish citizen, and then you become Juan Antonio Guzman, a resident of Argentina. Is that correct as well?"

"Yes."

"Can you tell us how you obtained these false identities?"

"Yes, I can tell you."

The reply borrowed from Pierre Dac[19] made Sigma's smile grow still broader.

"I'm listening, Monsieur Servant," Sebag said patiently.

"The papers in the name of Esteban I got during my first

---

[18] The French national holiday.
[19] A French humorist and actor (1893–1975) who was also a prominent member of the French Resistance during World War II.

weeks with the OAS. We all had double identities. We had numerous friends within the French government, it was easy. The papers in the name of Guzman were given me after my arrival in Buenos Aires. The Argentines have always been very hospitable to the French."

"Yes, I learned that recently."

Sebag turned a page in his notebook.

"Now that your identity has been established, I inform you that you are officially placed in police custody. We plan to question you regarding the murders of Bernard Martinez, André Roman, and Georges Lloret . . . "

"I protest, Inspector," Servant interrupted, a malicious gleam in his eye. "In Lloret's case, I am going to claim legitimate self-defense. He fired first." He put his swollen hand on his wounded shoulder.

"He was faster but he didn't aim well enough. What do you expect, Inspector, even John Wayne had bad eyesight at the end of his life."

A silent laugh shook Sigma's old carcass under the bedsheets. This interrogation was amusing him enormously.

"Please, Monsieur Servant," Castello broke in, pretending to be indignant. "This is no laughing matter. We're talking about the death of three persons . . . "

"Traitors. They deserved to die! They got a long reprieve, that's already good enough. You mustn't include them in your statistics for the year, they should be put down to the account of the events in Algeria. Several hundred thousand dead: three more won't make any difference!"

Sebag took the opportunity to put the interrogation back on track.

"In what way were Roman, Martinez, and Lloret traitors?"

Servant looked hard at him for a few seconds. He suspected that the policeman already knew part of the truth. Should he tell him everything? He decided he should and started in.

He spoke only to Sebag. He never looked at Castello; the superintendent no longer existed for him. He plunged himself back into the last weeks of the war, he told about the OAS, its commitment, its battles, the ones he was proud of and the ones that had left a bitter taste in his mouth. He explained that the first robberies were a way of financing the organization, while the motivations for the later ones were murkier. Then he came to June 12, 1962, the day that the army surrounded the Le Populo cafe in the wee hours of the morning.

"I'd always known that someone denounced me to the authorities, but I never imagined that it was my own friends. Even if I had reservations about some of our operations, I never questioned the necessity of our combat, and I would have given my life to protect my companions in arms. They betrayed me, but they also betrayed the cause, and that is above all why they had to be punished. It's a matter of principle."

"Fifty years later, that's no longer meaningful," Castello objected.

Servant glanced furtively at the superintendent, but replied to the inspector.

"I've known about that betrayal for only the last six months."

"How did you learn about it?" Sebag asked.

"The internet is amazing, isn't it?" He raised his deformed hands and contemplated them for a moment.

"However, it's not easy to use a keyboard with mitts like these, but I had someone to help me. My granddaughter Gabriella . . . "

He fell silent. The old killer's eyes misted over.

"When my wife died, I suddenly had a desire to look into my past," he went on. "Strange, isn't it? I thought I'd closed the door on all that when I moved to Latin America. I felt as though I had two successive lives: one Algerian, one Argentine, the second having erased the first. But after my wife died, everything got mixed up. It was as if Maria's death had closed the parenthesis of this second life, and Algeria had come back on me. Pitilessly. I began reading lots of books on the subject, works by historians and autobiographical accounts, and I remembered so many things that I thought I'd forgotten forever . . . In fact, I hadn't lost anything; it had all remained inside me, but was completely buried."

Servant tried to reach a carafe of water on the table next to his bed but the effort gave him acute pain. Sebag poured him a glass and handed it to him. Servant took a long drink and kept the glass in his hand.

"The hatreds and passions were also intact. I had some hard nights arguing with old phantoms. It could all have stopped there, but as I already told you, my granddaughter showed me how to use the internet. I made contacts, participated in *Pied-Noir* forums, and especially amused myself by looking up people's names. And I found interesting information about what had happened to my old pals. I found out that Lloret and Roman had gotten rich by investing money as soon as they got back from Algeria, and I saw that Martinez, even if he was less lucky, had also had a considerable nest egg when he arrived in Roussillon. Obviously, from that I deduced that they must have kept for themselves part—and probably even a large part—of the money we had obtained during the robberies. That already made me angry, and then, one thing leading to another, I understood that it was probably they who had denounced me to the cops. I was in their way. I'd never have let them leave Algeria with all that cash in their valises. The valise or the coffin, we were told at the time . . . They left Algeria with valises full of money. I have returned from the past to bring them the coffin they deserved."

He ran the tip of his tongue over his dry lips.

"So many *Pieds-Noirs* needed money; I would have forced

them to hand out all that dough. Besides, I believe I remember that on several occasions I'd already mentioned that idea."

He stopped to drink another sip of water. The sun was beating on the window. The little hospital room was beginning to feel like a sauna.

"I repeat my question," Castello said. "Do these murders really have any meaning fifty years afterward?"

Servant replied looking at Sebag.

"Honor has always had a meaning for me. It's not a question of how long it has been."

"I've learned to distrust grandiloquent formulas," Gilles replied. "In politics and in the police."

Servant's eyes grew darker and the timbre of his voice grew duller.

"Then let's forget the big words. My father joined the Free French Forces in 1943 and was killed in Cyrenaica the following year. My mother died in 1947 when she was hit by a truck on a street in Algiers. It was my grandmother who brought me up. We lived in a little two-room apartment in Bab-El-Oued. She was a seamstress and worked every day until her eyes burned so that I would lack for nothing. After the explosion at Le Populo, I had to leave Algeria in a hurry and I wasn't able to take care of her. I didn't even say goodbye to her. I left her a ticket for the ship to Marseille but she never left. She was one of a few hundred French of Algeria who disappeared after the cease-fire. I never found out what happened to her. Killed by the Arabs, probably. Or else she died of sorrow and was buried in the potter's field."

Sebag filled Servant's plastic glass with water. He would have liked to drink some, too.

"You're right: It's not only a matter of honor," Servant went on. "Because of those three bastards, I wasn't able to protect my grandmother. I blame them especially for that."

Sebag hesitated before this murderous grandfather talking

about his own grandmother with tears in his voice: did he find him moving or simply ridiculous? He replied in order not to have to make up his mind:

"How could you be certain that your old friends betrayed you? That was only a supposition . . . "

"My doubts were sufficiently strong to make me decide to cross the Atlantic. I wanted to know exactly what happened. It's no accident that I looked up Martinez first. I knew that he was the weak link in the trio: he confessed it all. I'd let him think I wouldn't kill him if he told me everything."

"Your sense of honor, no doubt," Castello broke in. He'd made up his mind: he didn't find this bloodthirsty old man moving.

"I didn't promise him anything," Servant retorted, "he was the one who wanted to believe it. I didn't disabuse him."

"Sure, that must be it."

"They were three assholes who didn't deserve my pity."

"Because you're capable of pity?"

Sebag turned around toward his boss and frowned. There was no point in irritating the old man. They were cops, not judges. Their job was to clarify the case and if that required their being indulgent with the murderer, they had to do it. Castello seemed to get the message. He stepped back, leaned against the wall, and kept quiet. Sebag resumed the conversation.

"So you wanted to avenge your grandmother, is that it?"

Servant gave him a skeptical look.

"My grandmother, to be sure, but all the others, too. There were too many deaths in that war. Too many French, too many Arabs, too many children and old men. French Algeria was a magnificent country that was well worth dying for. But only for it. In the end, it was hatred that won out, and that was why people went on killing. It was probably inevitable. Fate—*mektoub*, as the Arabs say. But killing for money, that was truly ignoble. For me, it's a war crime, a crime against humanity. I thought international justice didn't have a statute of limitations on that kind of monstrosity . . . "

"That's a very personal conception," Gilles said.

"No doubt. It's mine."

"It wasn't for you to judge and inflict the punishment."

"Yes it was. Without realizing it, I helped those bastards betray our cause. I found no other way to repair that mistake."

Then Sebag had him talk about the three murders, one after the other. Servant gave precise answers to all the inspector's questions. Then it was time to mention the destruction of the monument to the OAS.

"I read about that act of vandalism in the newspaper," Servant said, "but I had nothing to do with it."

Sebag felt Superintendent Castello quiver alongside him.

"We found one of your hairs on the site," Sebag said. "The DNA analysis leaves no doubt."

Servant shrugged.

"That's possible. I did in fact go there to pay my respects." He wiped his damp forehead with the sleeve of his hospital gown. It was steadily getting warmer in the room.

"I also went to the Wall of the Disappeared. It's magnificent. I found there the name of my grandmother, can you imagine that? I'd thought everyone had forgotten her . . . Would it astonish you to learn that I was moved to tears?"

Sebag stopped taking notes and lifted his pen.

"You categorically deny any act of vandalism against the so-called 'OAS monument'?"

"Why would I have damaged it?" Servant said with astonishment. "I was so happy to learn that our dead could finally have their own monuments in France. It was about time, wasn't it? For me, it was a great occasion to see it."

"What day was that?"

Servant thought for a few seconds.

"Last week. I'd say Tuesday. Yes, that's right, Tuesday."

The monument had been destroyed during the night between Wednesday and Thursday. Sebag thought it was strange that the hair had remained there for days among the pebbles but he didn't see why Servant would lie about it. As he had supposed long before the murderer had been identified, the act of vandalism didn't fit with the murders. Any more than the attacks on *Pieds-Noirs*. Sebag nonetheless asked all the questions he had to ask.

"Do you know Guy Albouker?"

Servant searched his memory before responding.

"No, I don't think so. Who is he?"

"What about Jean-Pierre Mercier?"

"Never heard of him, either. Am I supposed to have killed them, too?"

Sebag smiled and explained the other case that preoccupied him.

"Sorry, Inspector," Servant replied. "You'll have to find someone else to be responsible for all that. I didn't have anything to do with it. You have enough evidence, I think, to put me behind bars for the rest of my life, don't you? No point in piling on."

Servant closed his eyes. Suddenly, he seemed very tired. Sebag glanced at his boss. Since Castello had no further questions, Gilles closed his notebook, making the cover slam rather hard. Servant reopened his eyes.

"Are you done?" the old man asked.

"I think so, yes."

"Have I been sufficiently cooperative?"

The question surprised the lieutenant.

"Yes, that's fine."

"Then can I perhaps ask a favor of you?"

"Go ahead . . . "

"I've got a granddaughter in Argentina. Her name is

Gabriella. She's an angel. Anyway . . . she's my angel. Could you ask her mother to tell her that I died?"

"Excuse me?"

"I think it's better to let her believe that her grandfather died, in a traffic accident, for example, than that I'm going to spend the rest of my life in prison for a triple murder. Her mother will agree with me. In any case, I've been dead to her for a long time. Consuela hasn't spoken to me since she discovered everything I did. In Algeria, of course, but also in the death squads in Argentina, and all that nonsense."

Before promising, Sebag glanced at his boss out of the corner of his eye. He wrote down the telephone number in Argentina that Servant gave him. He would have liked to continue the conversation to find out a little more about this strange murderer, but his job was done. The prosecutor would soon take over, and then an examining magistrate. In a year or two, a court would try Sigma. There was in fact very little chance that the grandfather would ever see his granddaughter again. A strange family, he said to himself, in which the strongest bonds skipped a generation each time.

Jean Servant shook Sebag's hand with his big, swollen paw. He warmly thanked the lieutenant and then closed his eyes. He seemed exhausted. And at peace as well.

CHAPTER 42

I'd like to go running with you this morning."

Claire's proposal took him by surprise. His wife had always hated jogging. Her fitness classes at a gym had been amply sufficient for her.

"Of course, you'll have to agree to slow down by at least half."

Gilles searched her blue-green eyes for a twinkle of mockery. It was Sunday, eight in the morning, and they were in lingering in bed, still waking up. It could only be a joke. But no matter how much he scrutinized her eyes, he couldn't see anything. He had to accept the obvious: Claire was serious.

"I find I'm getting out of breath too easily. When I have to climb two flights of stairs at school, I'm tired when I get to my classroom. Age . . . "

Gilles ran his finger over the little wrinkles that bordered her eyes. In a few weeks, Claire would turn forty.

"I'd be delighted to run with you," he said.

"I'm not sure you'll think that for long."

After jogging five hundred meters, Claire was in fact already huffing and puffing. But Gilles had foreseen this and had led her to the edge of the Lake of Saint-Estève.

"You walk the next lap and catch your breath, O.K.?"

"And what will you be doing in the meantime?"

"Let's say I'll do three or four laps."

In fact, Gilles had time to run the path along the edge of the lake five times, Claire having taken advantage of her rest lap to do a few stretching exercises. They continued that way for an hour: Gilles jogged with Claire on one lap, then did five alone, without forgetting to slap his wife on the butt every time he passed her by.

It was a beautiful autumn day, without wind or clouds. The sun, already high in the sky, warmed the joggers' naked arms and legs.

On the way back, they walked along silently. Sebag was reflecting. Part of the case remained unsolved. Who had vandalized the OAS monument? Who had attacked Guy Albouker and Jean-Pierre Mercier? Were the same persons behind both these acts? He wasn't sure he would ever find the answers to those questions. He and his colleagues hadn't even the beginning of a lead. Just a hypothesis, the same as at the outset, which had returned stronger than ever after Servant's denials: a few morons had tried to take advantage of the murders to sow panic in the *Pied-Noir* community. And they had acted amazingly fast, hardly three days after the discovery of the first crime. Now that the murders had been solved, these individuals would not be heard from again and they would never be identified. He had to be content with this return to calm.

Sebag stopped walking. He untied his right running shoe and removed it to take out a pebble that was bothering him. The pebble rolled into the gutter and disappeared from sight. If only one could cope with all life's cares that way . . .

They resumed their walk. Claire took his hand and then put her head on his shoulder. Gilles smiled. He thought again of the silly teenage promise he'd made himself two days earlier, an oath that went something like "If I fail in this case, I'll talk to Claire." Confronted by this semi-success, what should he do? He sighed. He'd never emerge from that dilemma. Maybe someday he should try flipping a coin.

"Are you thinking about your work?"

His sigh had not escaped Claire.

"A little. I'd like to find an answer to all the questions I'm asking myself and I don't know how to go about it."

"Can I help?"

Gilles stopped to look at his wife, but he couldn't decipher the tender smile that was crinkling her blue-green eyes. Had she understood his double entendre?

He limited himself to saying, "Thanks, that's nice of you."

They shivered at the same time. Their bodies had cooled off since their run.

"Shall we start running again?" Gilles suggested.

"If that's the only way to avoid catching cold . . . "

They trotted down the service roads that ran alongside the broad avenues in Saint-Estève. Ten minutes later, they were entering their house. Séverine was reading on the living room sofa and Léo was finishing his breakfast. Claire said she was exhausted.

"My legs are so numb I can't tell if they're still there," she complained as she took off her running shoes.

"Well, I can tell that your feet are still there," Gilles said, pinching his nose.

He had a shoe thrown at his head as a reply.

Sunday was passed in a pleasant and restful ambiance.

Gilles grilled pork chops on the barbecue and prepared fennel to go with them. The whole family ate on the terrace, probably for the last time that year. Unfortunately, the winter cover had already been put on the swimming pool, which no longer cast bluish reflections on the surrounding trees. As they ate their dessert, the Sebags unanimously adopted Claire's proposal. After having a quick coffee, they would all go together to the North Perpignan Cineplex. Claire and Séverine chose Pedro Almodóvar's latest film, while Gilles went with his son to see a famous and aging American actor confront a series of terrible catastrophes. When the words "The End" appeared on the screen, the star had just saved the world for the umpteenth time, but one observation was ineluctable: he hadn't been able to do anything to save his career.

In the late afternoon, Claire and Gilles sat down together on the living room sofa. They surfed the satellite channels and finally chose a news commentary show. A report on the situation in the Near East had caught their attention. Gilles had never understood the quarrels in that troubled region. This was a chance to learn something about them.

Despite his good intentions, Gilles was repeatedly distracted by thoughts about his work. He lost the thread of the report. That part of the globe was definitely going to remain a mystery to him. Nevertheless a few sentences suddenly grabbed his attention.

The journalist was interviewing some Israeli extremists, guys who were ready to set the whole region afire and who not only rejected any kind of peace treaty but even seemed to have a deathly fear that one might be signed. "Peace means the assimilation and disappearance of our people," these fellows said. "Although war kills Jews every year, peace would be the end of all of us." According to them, Israel, in a peaceful Near East, would be in danger of nothing less than the loss of its soul and its identity. So that Jews might remain proud of their religion and their values, they had to live forever in a hostile environment, like that they had known during two thousand years in diaspora. If over all those years, the Jewish community had not aroused animosity and sometimes hatred among the surrounding peoples, it would have been assimilated and would now have completely disappeared. The same trap was awaiting Israelis today. The trap of peace combined with that of globalization. The Jews could survive only in the context of eternal war. "That is the burden of the chosen people," these cranks maintained.

These notions elicited a strange resonance in Sebag's mind, but he didn't understand why.

After the documentary, Claire and Gilles watched the local news. France 3 simply reported Servant's arrest, and the rest of the Sunday broadcast resembled the Dukan diet: sports, sports, and more sports, a protein-rich menu without any gustatory interest. Claire suggested that they'd be better off watching Michel Drucker's talk show. Gilles switched to France 2 and got up to make the evening meal. He put soup on to heat and washed a head of lettuce.

Gilles went to bed early and quickly fell asleep. He was still behind on his sleep.

But in the middle of the night, disturbing thoughts started interfering with his recuperation. He got up and poured himself a glass of water in the kitchen. He drank it slowly, standing in front of the picture window that looked out onto their terrace. The shadows of the palm fronds were silently dancing on the tarp covering the swimming pool.

All of a sudden, he understood.

# CHAPTER 43

D o you really think that he can still tell us something important about the attack?"

Jacques Molina didn't conceal his skepticism. He saw no point in calling in a victim early on a Monday morning. Especially a victim who had already been questioned several times.

"He told us everything, that fellow."

Molina was annoyed by his colleague's silence.

"Do you think he knows his attackers and isn't telling us their names?"

Hiding behind the local newspaper, Sebag was reading the whole page devoted to the arrest of Jean Servant and the solving of the triple murder case. Each time, Jacques's questions made him lose track of the article. Molina got up to have a look at his concentrating face.

"Oh, when you're like that, it's because you've got something brewing," he said. "A hypnosis session, is that it? Do you think a hypnotic trance is going to help the guy give us information that his subconscious is repressing?"

He crushed his empty paper cup and threw it in the wastebasket. Then he tried a different tactic to cheer up his colleague.

"Do you know what they call the process of curing sexual problems through hypnosis?"

Sebag gave Molina a vacant look. Jacques, smiling, was undeterred.

"A trance-sexual!"

Sebag, defeated, granted him a vague smile.

"Well, finally!" Jacques exclaimed with relief. "It takes a lot of work to get a sign of life out of you on a Monday morning."

"Don't tell me that to produce that kind of joke you had to make a great effort."

"You should know . . . "

The telephone on Sebag's desk rang. He picked up the receiver.

"Hello? Who? Have him come up, please."

Sebag hung up and turned to Molina.

"I'm going to need your help."

"At your service."

Sebag quickly explained to Molina what he wanted him to do. "Understood?"

"I understand what I'm supposed to do, but I don't know why. You weren't real clear about the reasons."

"Naturally, I didn't say what they were."

"Oh, that's why . . . And were you planning to tell me?"

"Not really."

Two knocks on the door of their office allowed Sebag to evade Molina's questions.

"Come in!"

The ruddy, puffy face of Sergeant Ripoll appeared in the doorway.

"You're expecting someone, it seems?"

"Absolutely."

"He's here."

The sergeant stepped aside to let Guy Albouker come in. The president of the *Pied-Noir* Circle shook Sebag's and Molina's hands one after the other. The bags under his eyes had grown so large that they looked like a second pair of cheeks. Sebag pointed to a chair and Albouker sat down, pressing his hand to his stomach.

"Is the wound still painful?" Sebag asked.

"A little, yes."

"Not sleeping well at night?"

"No, every time I turn over it wakes me up."

"The wound should have begun healing over a week ago."

"According to the doctor, the wound is healing properly, but it's still painful."

Molina got up and went over to put his hands on Albouker's shoulders in a familiar way.

"I was once shot in the side, and it was just like that. Even though during the day the pain seemed to be decreasing, it seemed to me that it came back during the night and was just as strong as ever."

"That's more or less how it is, yes."

Sebag gave him a friendly smile.

"And all the worries caused by this whole business haven't helped, right?"

"No, they really haven't."

Guy Albouker's voice had become increasingly monotone, mechanical. The president of the *Pied-Noir* Circle was well aware that he hadn't been asked to come to police headquarters to talk about his health; he was waiting to find out the real reason.

"I wanted to talk to you about our case and its successful conclusion," Sebag reassured him.

"I read about it in the newspaper, you needn't have taken the trouble."

Molina moved away toward the door. Before going out he winked at his partner. Sebag was still smiling at Albouker.

"I wanted to keep you up-to-date. You treated us so well during this investigation . . . That couscous, my word . . . My wife and I will remember that for a long time."

"You're welcome. We'd be glad to have you again . . . "

Sebag thanked him and then told him about Jean Servant's

confession. He elaborated on the newspaper article and provided a few explanations regarding the perpetrator's life, but gave no additional detail regarding the essence of the case. The press had not mentioned the matter of the white hair, and Sebag was careful not to do so, either. When he had finished his account, he stood up and started pacing up and down the office as Albouker watched him with a worried look.

"Our problem, as you have probably already understood, is that Servant absolutely denies any implication in the vandalism, the threats made against your treasurer, and, of course, the attack on you."

Guy Albouker cleared his throat.

"I was attacked by two young men wearing hoods, I never mentioned an old man. And on the basis of what I now know about the motives for the murders, I don't see how this attack could be connected with them. It's clear that these people were trying to take advantage of this case to sow panic and confusion . . . "

Sebag sat down in front of him.

"That's exactly what we think!"

"I know: you told me so."

"The problem is: who? Who could have wanted to sow panic?"

Guy Albouker crossed his legs.

"The *Pieds-Noirs* have no lack of enemies."

"Enemies?" Sebag said, astonished. "I recognize that colonization and the Algerian War remain sensitive topics in our own time, but the term 'enemies' seems a little strong."

"Every one of our initiatives and our commemorations provokes counterdemonstrations."

"At most about fifty left-wing militants—always the same ones—who are very worked up, I grant you, but entirely harmless."

"Every camp has its fanatics."

"Certainly."

Sebag pretended to scribble a few words on a piece of paper. Albouker uncrossed his legs and then crossed them the other way. He put his hand on his knee.

"We can't exclude the possibility that the young men who attacked me come from left-wing milieus, but are rather . . . uh . . . well . . . "

"Yes?"

"I don't like casting aspersions on people like that, I . . . Above all, I wouldn't want to appear racist . . . But I might have been attacked by young Algerians. Fanatics, as I said."

"Hmm, hmm."

Sebag made an exaggeratedly skeptical face.

"It seems to me that young Algerians don't give a damn about that time. They were born thirty years after independence. Everything that still seems so important to you is prehistoric for them!"

"For Algerian youth in general, that's true, but as I was saying, it takes only a few fanatics."

"Hmm."

Sebag deliberately made a pause. He gave Albouker a friendly glance and smiled at him distractedly. He drew out this moment as if he were reflecting on what they would talk about next. He knew what he had to do, but considered it useful to let things ripen before putting his cards on the table. He had a phony trump card up his sleeve that he had to turn into a winner.

He took a deep breath, opened a drawer, and took out a plastic bag that he threw on the desk. Albouker couldn't help moving closer to look at it. Sebag said nothing.

"What is it?" the president of the Circle finally asked.

"A hair."

"I see that."

"A white hair."

Albouker ran his index finger and thumb over his fleshy lips. Then his fingers pushed down the corners of his mouth, unconsciously making him look disillusioned.

"I don't understand."

"We found this white hair in the Haut-Vernet cemetery. At the foot of the vandalized monument. Contrary to what we'd thought, it does not belong to Jean Servant. But we have every reason to think that it belongs to the person who destroyed the monument.

Guy Albouker uncrossed his legs and put both feet on the floor.

"So it wouldn't be young people . . . "

"So it seems."

"That gives you a larger number of potential suspects . . . "

Sebag deliberately did not take the cue. Looking straight into his interlocutor's eyes, he dropped the little bomb he'd prepared.

"So far as I'm concerned, I see mainly one suspect."

Albouker's black eyebrows shot up over his eyes.

"Now I don't understand you at all."

"I have to say that I had trouble understanding you, too."

"Excuse me?"

Albouker furtively ran his finger over the narrow space between his mouth and his nose, on which a drop of sweat had formed.

"Can you explain, Lieutenant Sebag?"

The inspector put his left elbow on the desk and rested his chin on his upright arm.

"You understood me, Monsieur Albouker. I think you are the person who destroyed the OAS monument. I think you faked the attack on yourself, and put a threatening letter in your treasurer's mailbox."

Albouker leaped out of his chair, holding his stomach with both hands.

"What's wrong with you, are you crazy? You think I stabbed myself in the stomach? You're taking me for a madman."

"Sit down, please," Sebag replied calmly. "No one's crazy. Neither you nor I."

Albouker was stamping his feet. He had removed one of his hands from his stomach and was waving it in the air.

"Listen, I have no desire to listen to your wild imaginings. I thought we had sufficient esteem for one another, and here you are speaking to me as if I were a criminal . . . "

"Calm down, Monsieur Albouker. I'm well aware that the criminal in this case is Jean Servant. You've committed only a few misdemeanors."

"I've heard enough, I have no further business here."

Albouker turned on his heel and headed for the door.

"I won't say goodbye to you, Lieutenant Sebag."

"I won't say goodbye to you either, Monsieur Albouker, because you're not going to leave. Not immediately, at least."

The president of the Circle turned around and faced Sebag.

"Are you going to stop me?"

"The sergeant who brought you here is waiting on the other side of the door. He has instructions not to let you leave this room.

Albouker took two steps toward the desk. He'd gone pale.

"Am I to understand that I am in police custody?"

"Not yet."

"Then you don't have the right to hold me . . . "

"Monsieur Albouker, you're going to sit down willingly and listen to me." He put his hand on the receiver of his telephone. "Otherwise I'm going to call the prosecutor and ask his authorization to put you in police custody."

"You're crazy, you don't have anything on me."

Sebag smiled. The clumsy formulation sounded like the beginning of a confession.

"I recognize that for the moment I don't have much. That's why I'd prefer to wait to put you in police custody. But I should have something new any second now, so if you'll oblige me . . . "

Albouker consented to sit down.

"What is this information you are about to receive?"

"And then, as decent people, we ought to be able to dispense with this rather onerous procedure. Put you in police custody? Frankly, if I can avoid . . . "

A profound silence followed. Albouker did not dare reformulate the question that was on the tip of his tongue and that the inspector had just evaded. Everything in his attitude confirmed Sebag's suspicions. The president of the Circle had pretended to be indignant whereas he should have responded only with amused surprise. He'd agreed to sit down again instead of playing out the trial of strength all the way to the end. And above all, for the last few seconds a damp, stale air had filled the room. Sebag recognized the smell of fear.

He knew he'd scored a hit.

But he still had to play a subtle game because his file was empty. Desperately empty. He had only presumptions and no proof. He turned his chair around to face his computer and began to write up a report.

"Last name, first name, age, and occupation?"

Albouker looked at him feverishly for a few seconds before replying. Instead of writing down what he said, Sebag was writing a quick e-mail that Molina was waiting to receive on his iPhone. He sent the message and continued his questions.

"What were you doing in the wee hours of last Wednesday night?"

"That's a long time ago . . . I was probably sleeping."

"Can your wife confirm that?"

"I suppose."

"Does she have a good memory?"

"In general, yes."

"So she'll remember very well the night you were sleepless last week?"

" . . . "

"You don't recall that? She talked to us about it during that lovely couscous dinner at the Circle's offices . . . According to her, it was Martinez's murder that had upset you."

"I remember that now. It's true that I sometimes have trouble sleeping."

"She told us that you went out that night . . . "

"That's possible . . . I do that occasionally when I can't sleep at all."

"As you did last Wednesday night?"

"I don't remember for sure."

"Why aren't you asking me why I'm so interested in that night?"

Albouker looked at him. The bags under his eyes were trembling.

"Don't take me for a fool. I suppose that's the night the OAS monument was destroyed."

"That's exactly right."

"Even if I did go out that night, that doesn't suffice to make me a suspect."

"I completely agree with you. If there were only that, I wouldn't have bothered you. But that plus . . . plus the rest, is disturbing. Fortunately, I have other evidence."

"Why would I have done that? It's ridiculous!"

The door to the office opened and Molina came in. Perfect timing, Sebag said to himself, up to this point everything is going as planned. Next to the plastic bag containing the white hair found near the monument, Jacques tossed another bag that also contained a white hair. Sebag picked them and up compared them. One of the hairs was grayish white, the other bluish white. But at a certain distance, the illusion was perfect.

He held them for a few seconds before putting them in a drawer. Then he turned to Molina.

"Well?"

"The analysis is conclusive. They're the same."

Sebag sat back in his chair and affected an air of satisfaction. He slammed both hands down on the desk.

"So there we are! Now I have what I need to call the prosecutor."

Albouker fidgeted on his chair.

"Can . . . can you explain?"

"With pleasure."

Sebag rapidly took the hairs out of the two plastic bags, one by one.

"When my colleague put his hand on your shoulder a little while ago, he picked up one of your hairs. He has just had our lab run a DNA analysis on it. And as you've just heard, that analysis is conclusive."

"What does 'conclusive' mean?"

"That it's the same DNA!"

"I thought DNA tests took longer than that."

Sebag noticed that Molina had started. Their eyes met. They were both thinking the same thing. If he'd been innocent, Albouker should have first been astonished and then protested and screamed that that wasn't possible, that he'd not been in the Haut-Vernet cemetery recently, that the hair couldn't be his. Instead, he'd asked that question about the supposed length of time required for DNA analysis.

"In fact, the rapidity of a DNA test depends chiefly on the priority it is given. And then I also have to acknowledge that here we have carried out a quick analysis which is not 100 percent reliable. But what is its reliability, Jacques? 91 percent? 92?"

Surprised, Molina didn't know what to say. But he recovered and played his role.

"For this precise analysis, our experts told me 92.3 percent."

"92.3 percent," Sebag repeated. "At that level, can we still talk about a genuine doubt, Monsieur Albouker?"

The president of the *Pied-Noir* Circle did not reply. His chin was trembling and his forehead was shining with sweat. All the wrinkles on his face, normally cheerful, had sagged. He looked ten years older. Sebag decided the time had come to conclude.

"There are only a few ways this can go, Monsieur Albouker. If you tell us everything now, and then I send you to the prosecutor for indictment, in that case, you'll be released this afternoon. But if you persist in denying your responsibility, we begin with police custody and after that, I warn you, you're in the system. You'll be put in a cell to give you time to reflect, and we'll proceed to make more refined analyses. We'll have two days for more intensive and certainly less pleasant interrogations. Moreover, I'll be replaced by colleagues who won't be as well disposed toward you as I am. In short, all that to end up at the same conclusion forty-eight hours later: an indictment for destroying funeral monuments, making threats, and a false claim of having been attacked. But in that case, you will not only be indicted but put into detention. At least for a few days. But I prefer to warn you: in general, the first days are the hardest . . ."

Sebag had gone all out, and watched Albouker's face complete its collapse. He'd become livid. His upper lip was jerking uncontrollably.

"But . . . really . . . why would I have done that? It makes no sense."

Sebag seized the opportunity he'd been given. However, he didn't think it would be useful to mention the television report on the Israeli extremists. He'd already had occasion to note that when he tried to explain the origin of his intuitions, he confused people more than he enlightened them.

"I began to have doubts last night, and I spent part of the night tracing the sequence of events and our various conversations. I didn't sleep very much, I have to tell you. And it was when I said to myself that my night was spoiled that I recalled your wife's reflections on your bouts of insomnia. That gave me the first serious lead. The rest came later. First, your passion for your culture and your roots. According to Jean-Pierre Mercier, those are the only things that can make you really intransigent."

Albouker tried to laugh but it rang false.

"If that kind of evidence is enough for you, you've got hundreds of thousands of suspects in our community."

"Ah, your community . . . You cherish it, don't you? And you have one great worry: that it might fall apart and that the repatriates might one day no longer feel themselves to be *Pieds-Noirs*. Above all, you don't want it to be assimilated into French society. On that Sunday you said that if your wounds were healed, not only your Algeria would disappear, but you yourselves would disappear as a community. That's your obsession, isn't it? So what to do? That, too, you told me, at our very first meeting. I reread my notes last night and I found it."

He opened his blue notebook, flipped through it, and stopped at a dog-eared page.

"I wrote it down verbatim. You told me that two things still bound the *Pied-Noir* community together, and I'm going to quote what you said. The first is 'the love of our lost country.' In that respect, no problem, it's clear, it's explicit, it's the goal of your association. The second—and here I'm quoting you again—is 'the incomprehension and even hostility of other French people.'"

He abruptly closed his notebook.

"There, your main concern is that after fifty years that hostility has nonetheless greatly decreased. So you wanted to make everybody think it was still very much alive."

Albouker stopped moving. He seemed even to have stopped breathing.

"So you organized these marks of hostility yourself: you destroyed the monument, you stabbed yourself—bravo, that takes courage—and you put a threatening letter in your friend Mercier's mailbox. You went to see him at his home, didn't you, the day after he'd discovered that letter?"

Albouker didn't answer. His Saint-Bernard head was nodding mechanically like those of the plastic dogs people put in the rear windows of their cars. He was staring vaguely at his feet without seeing them. The world around him had ceased to exist. It was no more than a formless mass of sounds and colors.

Sebag reflected. Albouker was ready but he still had to get him to spit out the truth. For the moment, the file contained only suppositions and a phony analysis; without a confession, it would remain empty. Sebag signaled to Molina to go get a glass of water at the fountain in the corridor. Twenty seconds later, Jacques put his hand on Albouker's shoulder and set a plastic glass in front of him.

"Drink, Monsieur Albouker," Sebag said. "It will do you good."

The president of the Circle raised his head. His dazzled eyes blinked. For him, light suddenly returned to the room. He took the glass, brought it to his trembling lips, and emptied it without taking a breath first. His eyes recovered a little life.

"You have to tell me everything now, Monsieur Albouker. You'll see, you'll feel better afterward."

The haggard man shook his head as if to resettle his mind. He gave Sebag a sad and stunned look.

"What can I tell you that you don't already know?"

His hand still on Albouker's shoulder, Molina massaged it a little.

"You know everything, you're very smart," the president of

the Circle told him. "Too smart for me, in any case. It's as if you'd put a microphone in my brain."

Sebag looked at Molina, then at his computer. Jacques understood and sat down in front of his monitor. His hands hovering over the keyboard, he was ready.

"I have the impression that you decided to act very quickly," Gilles began in a soft, calm voice.

"Yes, right after your first visit . . . I was already thinking about it very seriously."

He licked his dry lips.

"My friends' initial reactions convinced me. When they were told about your questions regarding the OAS, they screamed that it was provocation and persecution, and even talked about injustice. I said to myself that all it would take was a little push from fate . . . "

"Do you think your community is eroding that much?"

Albouker ran his hand over his thighs, then raised his head and looked Sebag in the eyes for the first time.

"There are only old people in our association, you could see that yourself at our lunch. Why do you think I was elected president? Because I'm the youngest, that's all! But over the past couple of days a dozen new members have joined, including three who are under fifty years old. My idea wasn't all that stupid . . . "

He shrugged.

"And then, after all, I didn't harm anyone. Except for myself!"

Sebag did not agree, but gave him a sympathetic smile.

"Why did you begin with the monument?"

Albouker lowered his eyes again.

"Can it really be said that I 'began' with the monument? In fact, I didn't plan anything, and I didn't foresee what would come next. The monument is an important symbol for us, but it's very controversial. Destroying it would necessarily make our people angry without eliciting others' compassion. And then it was an easy target. The Haut-Vernet cemetery is not guarded and the perimeter wall is not very high. I've never been athletic, but it wasn't difficult to climb over."

Sebag glanced over at Molina. He was waiting until Jacques had finished typing before continuing with Albouker.

"How did you decide to pull the crazy trick of stabbing yourself?"

Albouker sat up straight. Of that act, he seemed prouder.

"I'm not sure I understand that myself. A psychiatrist would say that I wanted to punish myself. There's probably some truth in that, I had to pay a personal price. And then who else? I wasn't going to stab Jean-Pierre, after all!"

Sebag let a shiver run down his spine.

"I have a hard time imagining sticking a knife into my own belly . . . "

"It often happens, you know, that people held in prison cut off one of their own fingers to attract the attention of the judicial system or the media. And they do it with whatever tools they can find. I bought a good quality, well-sharpened knife and carefully disinfected it. Then for half an hour I held an ice pack to the place I was going to stab. I don't know if I really succeeded in reducing the pain."

"Did it hurt?"

"It was excruciating. I've always been a softie."

"You must be joking! I'd like to be a softie like you," Molina chimed in.

Albouker couldn't repress a nervous laugh that ended in sobs. Long sobs punctuated by grimaces. He had to hold his stomach with both hands to control the pain. Sebag took advantage of this sudden decrease in tension.

"On the other hand, I'm sure that you enjoyed writing the threatening letters."

"Of course," Albouker said, still sobbing. "As a teacher of French, it was a first to deliberately make spelling errors."

"And sending one to your treasurer, that was amusing too?"

"Absolutely! I'd love to have seen his face when he opened it. Mercier has always annoyed me. He's belonged to the association for more than twenty years and would have liked to be president. But our members elected me, not him! I think he's never forgiven me for that." He abruptly stopped.

"Obviously, it's not very hard to guess who the next president will be. Because now I'm going to have to resign."

Sebag would have liked to ask other questions, but he decided that Albouker was ready to sign a confession. Relieved to have gotten it all off his chest, the future former president of the Circle had not yet realized that he'd been duped. He mustn't be given an opportunity to retract what he'd said. Sebag gestured to Molina to tell him to start printing the report. Jacques typed a few more words on his keyboard before the printer started spitting out two double-sided pages. He caught them as they came out and handed them to Sebag with a congratulatory wink.

Gilles put the report on the interview in front of Albouker and slipped a pen into his hand.

"You can reread it if you want."

"What's the point?"

"Then sign at the bottom of each sheet, please."

Albouker did as he was told and Sebag could hardly repress a sigh of relief. He picked up the report and gave it to Molina. Jacques immediately left the room, leaving Sebag alone with Albouker.

"Am I going to go to prison?"

"No, I don't think so. My colleague went to show the document to our superintendent, who will then transmit it to the prosecutor. You are going to wait here at police headquarters until the prosecutor can receive you for the indictment. But I'd be surprised if he decided to put you in detention. You've been very cooperative."

This remark seemed to reassure Albouker. The French teacher was proud to be seen as a good pupil.

"The only criminal in this case is behind bars," Sebag went on. "So far as you're concerned, you harmed chiefly yourself. And I'm not talking about your wound in the stomach."

"I've hurt my wife as well. The poor thing, when she finds out that . . . "

"That aspect of the case does not concern the police or the courts. It will be for you to tell her about it."

"I don't know how I'm going to do that."

It was no longer prison that Guy Albouker feared now.

"What would you advise?"

"Oof," Sebag groaned, suddenly getting up. "I'm not the best marriage counselor."

This sudden reaction amused Albouker.

"But you and Claire are a very harmonious couple. The adjective may seem strange to you but it's the one my wife and I both spontaneously used."

"Thank you," Sebag replied evasively. "I also sensed a great deal of affection and closeness between you and your wife. She loves you, she'll understand. And she'll forgive you."

Albouker ran his fingers through his white hair.

"You're right. After all, for her it's not as serious as if I'd cheated on her with another woman."

"Since you say so . . . "

Sergeant Ripoll opened the door of the office.

"Lieutenant Molina told me that there's someone here who's to be put in a cell."

The unfortunate expression alarmed Albouker.

"A cell?"

"Don't worry," Sebag said, glaring at Ripoll reproachfully. "It's only while you wait to be called before the prosecutor. If it were up to me, I'd have you wait here and we'd just chat for a while, but you can see that that's not possible."

He added with a friendly smile:

"It's police headquarters, after all, not a tea room."

He held out his hand to ask him to get up. Albouker rose, shook himself, and smoothed out his wrinkled coat.

"All right. Maybe we'll see each other again?"

"Definitely not in the context of the investigation, my role is over. But somewhere else, another day, why not?"

Albouker warmly shook his hand.

"I'm going to say something that is undoubtedly stupid, but what the hell: I wouldn't have wanted to be unmasked by anyone other than you, not for anything in the world."

Sebag chuckled briefly and put his hand on Albouker's arm. Then he let him follow Ripoll. The office door closed on a puzzled lieutenant. Albouker's last remark made him pensive, because it was largely the same as the one Jean Servant had made to him the day before. This wasn't the first case in his career that had ended with mutual esteem between him and the men he'd succeeded in arresting.

Sebag would have been more comfortable feeling less empathy. But delinquents and even criminals turned out to be more human in life than in films or television series. True psychopaths, child-killers and perpetrators of crimes against humanity were rare. Sebag wondered if he'd ever taken an undivided pleasure in sending someone to rot in prison. He made a quick review of his career. Yes, that had in fact happened two or three times . . . Fortunately!

He went over to the window of his office and leaned his forehead against the glass. He looked down on the activity in the Rue de Grande-Bretagne without seeing it. A sweet melancholy was gradually taking hold of him. As it did at the end of each investigation. His own form of postpartum blues. It wasn't getting any easier, either. On the contrary. He thought of something Victor Hugo wrote: "Melancholy is the happiness of being sad." That note was just right, in perfect harmony with what he felt.

Inevitably, that state of mind led him back to Claire.

He imagined his wife sitting in his office as Albouker had been a few seconds earlier, Claire confessing, Claire admitting that she'd had a lover, Claire telling him with a somber smile blurring her shining eyes: "I wouldn't want to have been unmasked by anyone other than you, not for anything in the world."

He banged his head several times against the glass.

He'd been able to cleverly lead Albouker to confess, but he had no illusions: the president of the Circle was eager to do it. To confess his sins. Claire might also want to do that. If he asked her the question, she would immediately confess. How often had she given him a cue he'd refused to take?

In the office next door he heard Molina's triumphant voice announcing "their" success to their colleagues. He recognized Llach's and Ménard's exclamations, Lambert's surprise. Julie Sadet was probably with them but said nothing. Or didn't say it loud enough. In the bits and pieces he overheard, he perceived a few familiar and conventional expressions. They were talking about having an aperitif at the Carlit, to celebrate their success. His colleagues would soon be bursting into his office. They would joyfully clap him on the back, congratulate him, tease him in a nice way.

He'd have to smile and rejoice in how things had turned out. After the first glass, it would be easier.

A heavy melancholy was numbing his body and his mind. For each investigation, how many lives were broken, how many bodies lay in the cemetery, and how many souls were locked up behind four damp walls in a prison? And how many wounded hearts were there among the survivors? Josette Vidal, Mathilde Roman, Marie Albouker . . . and little Gabriella. And no doubt others he didn't know.

Voices were now resounding in the corridor. Only a few seconds left to get rid of these blues and this immense weariness.

He had to get a grip on himself. Quickly.

He thought again about Claire and the idiotic promise he'd made himself. He'd completely solved the puzzle. He didn't have to fulfill his oath. But he felt no relief.

Then he made himself another promise. A date, a deadline. In a few weeks, by the end of the year . . .

He still gave himself that extension.

If by that time he still hadn't recovered a taste for living together, the sense of carelessness and the pleasure of loving, he would speak. He'd ask Claire the questions and he'd have the answers. He would take the risk of opening the Pandora's box of admissions and regrets. The worst misfortunes wouldn't necessarily emerge from it. You can't always control your destiny, and therefore there's no point in trying to anticipate everything. He had to act in accord with his heart and his temperament. And his abilities.

If he couldn't endure his torments, he'd lance the boil that was spoiling his life.

And then?

Then . . . *Insha'Allah*!

## About the Author

Philippe Georget was born in Épinay-sur-Seine in 1962. He works as a TV news anchorman for France-3. A passionate traveler, in 2001 he traveled the entire length of the Mediterranean shoreline with his wife and their three children in an RV. He lives in Perpignan. *Summertime, All the Cats Are Bored*, his debut novel, won the SNCF Crime Fiction Prize and the City of Lens First Crime Novel Prize